About the Authors

Cathy Williams is a great believer in the power of perseverance as she had never written anything before her writing career. From the starting point of zero, she has now fulfilled her ambition to pursue this most enjoyable of careers. She would encourage any would-be writer to have faith and go for it! She derives inspiration from the tropical island of Trinidad and from the peaceful countryside of middle England. Cathy lives in Warwickshire with her family.

Sheryl Lister has enjoyed reading and writing for as long as she can remember. When she's not reading, writing, or playing chauffeur, Sheryl can be found on a date with her husband or in the kitchen creating appetizers and bite-sized desserts. She holds a B.S. in Occupational Therapy and post-professional M.S. in Occupational Therapy from San Jose State University. She resides in California and is a wife, mother of three, and works as a paediatric occupational therapist.

Clare Connelly was raised in small-town Australia among a family of avid readers. She spent much of her childhood up a tree, Mills & Boon book in hand. She is married to her own real-life hero in a bungalow near the sea with their two children. She is frequently found staring into space – a sure-fire sign she is in the world of her characters. Writing for Mills & Boon is a long-held dream. Clare can be contacted via clareconnelly.com or on her Facebook page.

European Escapes

July 2023
Madrid

February 2024
Prague

August 2023
Sicily

March 2024
Athens

September 2023
Sweden

April 2024
London

January 2024
Paris

May 2024
Berlin

European Escapes:
Madrid

CATHY WILLIAMS

SHERYL LISTER

CLARE CONNELLY

MILLS & BOON

First Published in Great Britain 2023
by Mills & Boon, an imprint of HarperCollins*Publishers* Ltd,
1 London Bridge Street, London, SE1 9GF

www.harpercollins.co.uk

HarperCollins*Publishers*
Macken House, 39/40 Mayor Street Upper,
Dublin 1, D01 C9W8, Ireland

European Escapes: Madrid © 2023 Harlequin Enterprises ULC.

The Forbidden Cabrera Brother © 2020 Cathy Williams
Designed by Love © 2019 Sheryl Lister
Spaniard's Baby of Revenge © 2019 Clare Connelly

ISBN: 978-0-263-31947-7

This book is produced from independently certified FSC™ paper
to ensure responsible forest management.

For more information visit: www.harpercollins.co.uk/green

Printed and Bound in the UK using 100% Renewable Electricity
at CPI Group (UK) Ltd, Croydon, CR0 4YY

THE FORBIDDEN
CABRERA BROTHER

CATHY WILLIAMS

CHAPTER ONE

SOMETHING, DANTE THOUGHT as he nursed his whisky and stared out at the floodlit manicured gardens that comprised the grounds of his Spanish estate, wasn't making sense.

Behind him he could hear the muffled sound of voices and laughter—all those people, from dignitaries to old family friends, who had gathered to welcome Alejandro, his older brother by four years, and his fiancée.

It was a star-studded event, even though it had been arranged at fairly short notice. Such was the long arm of the Cabrera family's influence that an invitation from them—especially, Dante recognised, one that would be hosted at his own sprawling mansion—pretty much guaranteed attendance.

Intricate lanterns twinkled up the long winding private avenue that led to his house. Behind him, on a warm summer night, the bank of French doors at the back of his house had been flung open wide to a vision of exactly what extreme wealth could get. The serving staff on high alert for empty glasses, the blaze of yet more lanterns adorning the strategically placed trees and illuminating the still splendour of his infinity pool, the massive ice sculpture of a couple, which his mother had insisted on having. And, of course, the very elegant, barely noticeable and extremely expensive trio of violinists providing subtle background music. Here, in this setting, the women in their high-designer elegance and the men, formally dressed, were birds of paradise at home in a setting with which they were largely familiar.

His parents, naturally, were bristling with excitement at meeting a woman who, as far as they were concerned, was roughly five years overdue. Tradition was tradition and, as the eldest in the family and now in his mid-thirties, Alejandro should have been duly wed and well on the way to producing an heir or two to the throne.

The vast fortunes tied up with the Cabrera name needed to be kept in the family and Roberto and Isabella Cabrera had been making noises about grandchildren for some time now. How else could the family lineage remain intact if both their sons decided that playing the field was a far better option than settling down to the rigours of domestic life?

Dante was as keen as his parents were for Alejandro to get married and have kids because if he didn't, then it wouldn't be long before their parents began looking to Dante to do his duty in that area and he most certainly wasn't up for that.

So when Alejandro had phoned three weeks ago with the happy tidings that he was engaged, it had been champagne all round, a suitably lavish engagement party hastily arranged and expectations running high.

One small snag, though, was the fiancée.

Where the hell was she?

Shouldn't the loving couple have arrived together? Holding hands and staring into each other's eyes with undisguised adoration? It wasn't as though they had been dating for years and had had time to settle into the comfortable routine of taking one another for granted. Oh, no, the fiancée had been produced like a white rabbit from a magician's hat, so young love should still be fresh enough for the woman to have accompanied Alejandro to the opulent engagement party happening inside.

Except, she hadn't and—Dante glanced at his watch before swallowing the remainder of the whisky—it was a mere two hours before the elaborate buffet was set out and the speeches began. Half an acre of lawn had been meticulously roped off so that tables could be laid out with no small detail spared, from the linen cloths to the magnificent arrangements of red roses, as befitting a couple in love. The seating was casual because it was a party, and yet it still managed to feel incredibly formal in its opulence.

He wondered whether the mysterious bride-to-be would deign to make an appearance in time or whether his brother would have to mumble his apologies while the guests tucked into finest prepared rib of roast suckling pig in the absence of his fiancée. Certainly, Alejandro was strangely phlegmatic about the woman's appalling lack of manners. Maybe he had become a little too accustomed to the behaviour of a high-maintenance woman who felt that drama was some kind of selling point. Dante wryly thought that he had encountered a few of those himself.

He was about to turn away and head back into the sitting room, where champagne and canapés would be in full flow, when something caught his eye. In the twilight gloom, he glimpsed movement up the winding tree-lined private avenue that led to the courtyard in front of the house.

Standing still, he squinted and there it was again, a movement barely glimpsed between the trees.

He dumped his glass on the broad concrete ledge, straightened up and headed down the sweeping arc of stone steps that descended gracefully towards the open courtyard and then out towards the drive.

Caitlin could barely see. Up ahead, the lawns and a mansion of unseemly proportions were illuminated by the sort of floodlit extravaganza that could be seen from space. Here, as she half ran up the tree-lined avenue leading to the house, the path dipped in and out of the shadows. Any minute now and her already nightmarish trip would be compounded by an even more nightmarish ending, which would involve her tripping over something, breaking her ankle and having to be carried ignominiously into the house on a makeshift stretcher.

Everything had gone wrong, starting with her mother sobbing down the end of the phone just as she was supposed to be leaving for the airport, and ending with the taxi, booked by Alejandro to fetch her from the airport and deliver her to her own engagement party, for heaven's sake, getting a flat tyre just when she didn't need it.

Now, three hours late, she'd decided that creeping into the house and at least having the option of getting ready somewhere private was far the more sensible choice, rather than the screech of a taxi alerting everyone to her lateness.

She shuddered at the thought of all those assembled guests piling out of the front door to witness her dishevelled appearance. In his understated way, Alejandro had warned her that it was going to be *something of a bash*—which, in Alejandro-speak, meant that there would be ten thousand people there, all waiting for her arrival.

As luck would have it, Alejandro was, as always, nowhere near his mobile phone and her quiet entry through a side door somewhere was disappearing with each reluctant step forward. She'd tried calling him a dozen times and every single time it had gone to voice-mail and she was fed up of leaving increasingly despairing messages.

They were supposed to be in love! In the real world, he would be hanging on the end of the line, worried sick about where she was!

Caitlin thought of him and couldn't help but smile because that was just Alejandro. He would have dumped his phone on a random table somewhere and would have to be reminded that she still hadn't arrived, which was something of a big deal because the engagement party his parents had arranged had been for both of them.

Not for the first time, she felt a twinge of intense discomfort at this story they had concocted. Back in London, it had seemed almost inevitable because it had satisfied so many disparate concerns, but here...

She stopped in her tracks to catch her breath and gazed at the mansion towering ahead of her, ablaze with lights. The courtyard was massive, as big as a football field, and it was crammed with high-end cars of every description. They were parked at haphazard angles but, when she squinted, she could make out two men in uniform and she guessed that they would be in charge of parking so that any of the luxury cars could be moved at the snap of a finger. She shivered with apprehension.

This was reality now. They weren't in London any longer. They weren't sharing their sob stories over a bottle of wine. A plan had been made and she had temporarily turned a blind eye to the fact that plans made in one country appeared completely different when viewed in another.

Posing as Alejandro's fiancée had been the answer to both their problems and, in London, that solution had seemed a logical conclusion.

But here…

With the sounds of summer insects around her and the grandeur of a sprawling house reminding her that this was where a simple game was always going to lead…

Her heart raced and she half looked over her shoulder with an instinctive urge to run away.

About to speed-dial Alejandro for the umpteenth time, she was only aware of a man stepping out of the shadows when he was practically on top of her and she didn't stop to think before taking action. It had been drummed into her by her parents the minute she decided to leave Ireland for the streets of London that it didn't pay to trust anyone. London, they had intoned worriedly, was a dangerous place. Accordingly, Caitlin had learned the basics of self-defence and now those ten lessons at the local town hall once a week coalesced into a blood-curdling shriek as she swung her holdall at the looming figure, striking a direct hit against his shoulder.

She had been aiming for his head, but the man was tall, way taller than her five foot three. She snapped her hands into action and eyed him narrowly for a few seconds as she debated which manoeuvre to take.

If only she were taller! Leaner! Stronger! Instead,

she was short, round and it was dawning on her at speed that she probably wasn't going to land any significant punches because this stranger was built like a house.

She grasped her holdall tightly and took the next most sensible option, which was flight.

She didn't get far. One minute, she was half running and panting with her eyes pinned to the mansion in the distance. The next minute, a vice-like grip was holding her back, at which point she spun round and kicked.

'What the…?' Dante demanded, holding her at arm's length as she struggled and tried to sling punches at him.

'Get *off* me!'

'Stop trying to kick me!'

'Stop trying to attack *me*! You have no idea who you're dealing with! I… I'm an expert in martial arts!'

Dante released her. He was temporarily stunned into silence. He couldn't quite make her out because it was dark, but he could see enough to realise that the pint-sized spitfire rubbing her arm was about as expert in martial arts as he was in ballet dancing.

'I don't know who you are,' Caitlin gritted, backing away just in case he decided to lunge at her, 'but if you don't clear off, I'm going to make sure that the police are contacted as soon as I get to…' she nodded brusquely at the house, which should have been a lot closer considering how far she'd walked but still seemed a hundred miles away '…that house you can see up there.'

'You're going up there? Why?'

'That's none of your business.' She spun round and began walking as fast as she could towards her destination. If the guy lurking in the grounds was up to no good, then he had obviously realised that she didn't make a good candidate to be robbed. One glance at her dress code would have given the game away. Long flowered skirt, sensible shoes, her favourite flowing blouse over which, because it was cool even though it was summer, she was prudently wearing a cardigan... not a diamond in sight.

She clasped her holdall ever tighter, because you never knew... She didn't want to look at him, even though her skin tingled because he had fallen into step alongside her. She had no intention of making eye contact.

'It might be.' Dante had always had the knack of making people stop dead in their tracks without raising his voice and, on cue, she stopped.

'What are you talking about?'

'Engagement party? Alejandro? Name ring bells?' He folded his arms and stood perfectly, watchfully still.

Caitlin turned to the stranger. They had progressed out of the shadowy overhang of trees, into more light, and she could make him out far more clearly and suddenly her mouth went dry and her nervous system seemed to temporarily forget what it was meant to do.

He had stepped back and she saw he was dressed for—yes, an engagement party. Black trousers, white shirt with the top couple of buttons undone as though he couldn't be bothered with a formal dress code, no tie. He'd shoved his hands in his pockets, dragging down the trousers ever so slightly, and that seemed to emphasise the perfection of his muscular frame.

Her breathing went from fast to slow and back to fast in record time. She blinked, confused at a reaction that was so out of keeping with the person she knew herself to be.

When she met his eyes, she had to try to ignore the impact of a perfectly chiselled face. The man oozed sex appeal. He was also ever so slightly familiar, but she knew that she would remember him if she'd ever met him, or even laid eyes on him. He was not a man anyone could meet and forget.

'You're here for the engagement party, as well.' She finally found her voice and then, because she was irritated with herself for being thrown by him, she belatedly added, 'In which case why are you lurking in the grounds and jumping out at perfect strangers?'

She began walking, once more, in the direction of the house. Time was of the essence at this point and she couldn't waste any more of it chatting to someone who made the hairs on the back of her neck stand on end.

But this time her awareness of him, once again falling into step alongside her, was acute. She could feel the rasp of her breathing, and the shadow he cast as the winding tree-lined avenue became ever more brightly lit sent shivers racing up and down her spine.

Only when she was standing to the side, with the massive edifice of the house in front of her, did she stop to take stock, at which point she tried Alejandro's number once again. She felt sick and out of her depth. She'd always known that Alejandro came from a wealthy background, but to be thrust into the very vortex of it, as she was now, made her stomach clench.

The cars that filled the vast courtyard gleamed with the patina of priceless machinery. Up close, the house, brightly lit, was beyond impressive and the distant thrum of noise was a sick reminder that the part she had undertaken to play was not going to be an easy one.

Predictably, Alejandro failed to respond.

'Problems?'

'Why are you still here?' Her voice was laced with agitation.

'I thought I'd personally escort you to the premises,' Dante said.

'Don't you believe that I'm a legitimate guest?'

At that, Dante inspected her with leisurely thoroughness, his dark eyes roving from the tips of her toes, along her body and finally coming to rest on her scarlet face.

She had gone into attack mode from the second he had surprised her and she was still in it. If she was a guest, then she was a highly unlikely guest.

'Are you? Because you don't seem to be dressed for the part.'

At that, Caitlin reddened even more. Her parents had always made a point of telling her that she was beautiful, inside and out, but parents were notoriously partisan and she had always been sensitive about her looks. She'd stopped longing to be five inches taller and fifteen pounds lighter, a leggy brunette free from the curse of freckles and hair the most skilled hairdresser would have found impossible to tame, but right now…

With this impossibly sexy and perfect guy lounging in front of her and staring with just the hint of a condescending smile on his face…

'I have clothes in here,' she said coldly, indicating her holdall with a curt nod. 'And in case you're in any doubt that I actually *have* been invited to this engagement party, I should tell you that I happen to be the… er… Alejandro's fiancée.' It wasn't a declaration that rolled easily off the tongue. Downright lies seldom did.

Dante said nothing. He was too stunned to speak.

'I'm running a bit late…ah…anyway…'

'Alejandro's fiancée?' He found his voice. He was seldom thrown, but this time he was.

'There's no need to sound so incredulous.' There was, actually, every need. Not even she, with her imagination going full pelt, found it easy to believe that she could possibly be Alejandro's fiancée. They came from such different worlds. Whatever his back story and however close they had become over time, he was Spanish nobility and it was there in the way he held himself and his casual disregard for money. He could do as he pleased, even if he was funny and caring and considerate, which always left you with the illusion that he couldn't buy the world, which he could. Somehow, you always expected the super rich to run roughshod over people and Alejandro completely disproved that theory. That, of course, was one of the reasons why she absolutely adored him.

They were also so different to look at. She was pale, with freckles and green eyes and copper-coloured hair. He was swarthy and dark-haired. They were both short, though, and plump and she felt wonderfully comfortable with him.

'Miss Walsh?'

'Caitlin. Look, I can't hang around here chatting to you. I have to…' She squinted at the imposing edifice of the house and tried to work out a possible side entrance through which she could sneak, although heaven only knew what she would do if and when she did enter the house if Alejandro was still missing in action. Fumble her way to the downstairs loo so that she could change into her finery? Hope that she didn't trip over anyone in the process?

So poorly conceived all of this, a plan born on the spur of the moment without much thought being given to the technical detail. It was just as well that once this engagement party was over and done with, they would both return to London where life would carry on as normal.

She pulled her long, tumbling hair over her shoulder and fiddled with it while she tried to work out various house-entry options.

'You were saying...' Dante prompted.

Caitlin looked at Dante and shivered again. The guy had the strangest effect on her. Since when had she ever gone for the brooding Alpha-male type? She'd learned long ago to steer clear of those sorts.

Besides, men this good-looking were always far too fond of themselves for her liking. And as a postscript, she belatedly thought, she was engaged. Or at least, for all intents and purposes she was engaged. Which amounted to the same thing.

'As you mentioned,' she conceded, 'I'm not exactly dressed the part and I can't get hold of Alejandro. He's terrible when it comes to his mobile phone. It never seems to be on him.'

'I'm surprised he isn't scouring the four corners in search of his errant bride-to-be,' Dante murmured.

'What do you mean?'

'Shouldn't he be out looking for you? If you haven't been able to get hold of him to warn him of your late arrival?'

'Oh, right. Yes. I see where you're going with that,' Caitlin mumbled. 'He... We are quite relaxed with one another when it comes to stuff like that.'

'What a novel approach to a serious relationship.'

'I need to change into my glad rags.' Something about the man's tone of voice triggered a wave of unfocused apprehension in her. 'And you never introduced yourself. You are…?'

She paused and stilled him with her hand. Her eyes met his questioningly.

For a couple of seconds, Dante's cool, rational mind seemed to shut down, then he drew back and returned her wide-eyed gaze narrowly.

'Do you know the layout of the house?' He smoothly changed the conversation, while at the same time politely removing her hand and hustling her between the cars and past the uniformed valets standing to attention outside.

Was this his brother's fiancée? Dante couldn't quite believe it, but then how was he to know what sort of woman his brother liked? He had never met any of Alejandro's girlfriends. Different countries, awkward schedules, fleeting meetings over snatched drinks in random bars. He and his brother had long mastered the art of saying absolutely nothing of any genuine importance to one another.

That said, Dante had always assumed that his brother would go for the same kind of women he did, refined thoroughbreds who moved in the same social circles as they did. When Dante thought about those women, he felt a certain amount of boredom, but the one thing he knew about them, and it was very important, was the fact that they were all independently wealthy. Largely they came from families who, if not in the same category as his, were in a similar ballpark. No gold-diggers and, from bitter experience, he knew that gold-diggers were a breed best avoided.

A memory pushed its way to the surface. He'd lost his heart once, at the tender age of nineteen, to a woman ten years older who had played him so well that he had ended up handing over wads of cash to her. A small fortune. He'd fallen for a tale of a broken marriage and a violent ex and a vulnerable toddler. She had been poor but still touchingly hopeful in the face of personal tragedies, desperate for a new start yet tentative about accepting anything from him, which had made him insist on giving her even more, and of course so breathtakingly beautiful that common sense had been quickly abandoned to a raging libido hooked on the thrill of the unknown. It had been wildly exciting after his tame diet of beautiful, predictable young socialites and privately educated heiresses. When he reflected on what might have been had he not caught her in bed with the father of her child, no less, he was filled with shame at his own stupidity, but every mistake taught a valuable lesson and he had never again strayed from what he knew. Rich, beautiful, well bred. Known territory. If they were self-absorbed and sometimes shallow, then that was a price he was willing to pay.

Caitlin Walsh was not known territory…and while *he* might have the nous to know how to handle any woman who wasn't known territory, did his brother?

A broken heart, Dante figured, was no bad thing. It made you stronger. But his brother was engaged, and once rings had been exchanged a broken heart wouldn't be the only thing to deal with. The family fortune had to be protected and Dante had no intention of letting that out of his sight.

If Alejandro was taken in by Caitlin Walsh, then

Dante saw no reason why he couldn't do a bit of probing of his own, for no other reason than to make sure
Alejandro wasn't about to make the biggest mistake
of his life.

Wasn't that what brotherly love was all about?

'I've never been to the house before,' Caitlin responded tartly, 'so it would be impossible for me to
know the layout. I had hoped that Alejandro…'

'It's his engagement party. He's probably busy entertaining the troops. You're in luck, though. I happen
to know the place very well. You might say that I know
it like the back of my hand.'

Caitlin stopped and stared at him with undisguised
relief. 'Would you mind…? I need to change and I would
rather not…' She made a vague gesture to encompass
her state of dress. 'I should have got here ages ago…but
with one thing and another… If you know the house, I
would really appreciate it if you could maybe…'

'Sneak you in so that you can change into your finery?' Dante stood back and looked at her from the towering height of his six feet two inches. The holdall was
quite small for finery. 'Why would I do that when I've
been accused of attacking you?'

'You surprised me. Naturally I reacted accordingly.'
Caitlin's voice was stiff.

'You could have caused me permanent damage,'
Dante inserted smoothly, 'what with you being an expert in martial arts.' Silence greeted this remark. He
could see that she was itching to launch a few verbal
missiles. His antennae were still on red alert, but the
woman was in a league of her own, and what had promised to be something of a tedious social occasion was
looking up. When you were someone who could always

call the shots, a little bit of *different* went a long way. He was beginning to enjoy this little bit of different...

'Fortunately,' he carried on magnanimously, 'I am not a man to bear a grudge and I would be delighted to secrete you away somewhere private where you can freshen up.'

'I don't know how to thank you,' Caitlin said, in a voice that was far from oozing gratitude.

Dante said nothing but, just for a second, something weird and strong raced through him, heating his blood and tightening his groin. He spun round on his heels and began heading towards the side of the house, away from the brightly lit entrance.

'You'll have to be quick,' he said, slowing briefly so that she could catch up with him. 'The party's in full swing. The longer you take, the more dramatic the reception is going to be.' He glanced at her. The braid was not quite enough to keep her fiery hair in order and wisps floated around her cheeks. She was flushed and breathing fast. His eyes dropped to breasts that were more than a handful. Small-statured and large-breasted.

Infuriated by the sudden lapse of self-control, he stiffened. If the woman was up to no good then he intended to find out before the situation became financially messy, but she was engaged to his brother and he wasn't going to forget that. Forbidden thoughts would be culled before they could start interfering with what had to be done, and in very little time because if she had angled for a profitable engagement then she wasn't going to hang around waiting for the wedding ring to seal the deal.

He took her to one of the many spare bedrooms. Each and every one was permanently prepared to a high state of readiness although it was rare for guests to stay overnight. Dante loathed that sort of thing and, indeed, the only time the vast mansion saw an influx of people was when he happened to be away and it was lent out to friends or family members. He valued his privacy far too much.

'Make yourself at home,' he drawled as she stood still and looked all around her. 'I'll wait outside for you. You won't know how to find your way down to where the action is.'

As she was busy appreciating a level of luxury she had never seen in her life before, it was a few seconds before Caitlin responded, then she eyed her holdall.

'I'm sure I'll manage,' she said dubiously.

'I'll wait.'

'Why?'

Dante felt a twinge of guilt. He needed to get a feel for her, work out if his suspicions were well founded, and time wasn't going to be on his side. His intentions could not exactly be called noble and something fleeting in her eyes, an expression of helpless, vulnerable apprehension, made him flush darkly.

'Call it good manners,' he said brusquely.

'Okay.' She hesitated, then smiled tentatively. 'I might need a bit of moral support. I'm not accustomed to…events like this… When Alejandro and I…' She reddened.

'When you and Alejandro…?'

'I knew there was going to be a party,' she said hurriedly, 'but I had no idea that it would be on this scale.'

'Alejandro comes from an extremely high-ranking family,' Dante murmured, his keen eyes taking in everything, missing nothing. 'With more notice, it would have been even bigger. As it stands, two hundred is reasonably well contained.'

'I… The cars parked outside…' She sighed. 'I'm not sure I've brought the right clothes…'

Dante thought of the women milling around downstairs, dressed to kill and dripping in diamonds. He noted her anxious expression and reminded himself that the most efficient gold-digger would always be the one the least obvious. His lips thinned because he knew that better than most.

'I'm sure you'll…fit in just fine…'

'You haven't seen my outfit.' Caitlin grinned and met his veiled gaze with a roll of her eyes. 'Once you have, feel free to change your mind. I just didn't think…'

'You just didn't think…?'

'That it would be quite like this, like I said,' she told him honestly. 'I never thought that the place would be so…lavish.'

'Yet you knew that your fiancé came from a wealthy family…'

'Yes, of course, but… It doesn't matter. I'm here now so there's not much I can do about… What you can't change you might as well accept, and I definitely can't change the outfit I brought over with me. Anyway… I'm going to get ready so if you don't mind? I won't be long.'

He gave it forty minutes at the very least. Longer if something had to be done about her hair. She was so unexpected and novel an entity that he literally couldn't imagine what the transformation would be like and it annoyed him that he couldn't resist letting his imagination break its leash and run away. He responded to that by lounging against the wall, flipping open his phone and scrolling through work emails.

He was settling in for the long haul when the bedroom door was pulled open and out she breezed, all of a fluster.

He pushed himself from the wall and slowly moved to stand directly in front of her.

'That was quick.'

She looked...amazing. Gone was the fashion-disaster outfit she had been wearing. In its place was a figure-hugging jade-green dress that lovingly emphasised each and every delectable curve of her small but insanely feminine body.

The sight of it made Dante stiffen as he acknowledged, once again, just how inappropriate his reaction was.

'I forgot the diamonds at home.' There was a nervous edge to her voice and she fiddled with the thin gold chain around her neck, a sixteenth birthday present from her parents.

'I doubt anyone will notice the oversight,' Dante murmured. She was playing with a thin necklace round her neck and his dark eyes zeroed in on her slender fingers and then on the shadowy cleft between her breasts. He gritted his teeth and quickly looked away.

'It's kind of you to say so.' She fell into step with him, taking it slowly because the heels were stupidly high and falling was a distinct possibility.

'I doubt anyone has ever called me *kind*. How did you and Alejandro meet?' Dante realised that he had asked very few basic questions about the relationship that had materialised out of thin air. 'We were all...a little surprised by the speed of the relationship...'

Dante barely noticed the endless miles of corridor along which they were walking, although he was keenly aware of her wide-eyed awe. Telling but hardly surprising if there was an agenda to the fifteen-second relationship, he thought wryly. To one side, ornate wrought-iron railings offered a view of acres of marble on the ground floor and white walls on which were hung huge statement pieces of abstract art. An enormous crystal chandelier, as delicate as a waterfall, dominated the vaulted ceiling, dropping five metres down to the central hallway, which was manned by several uniformed men and which they had successfully avoided.

'We go back a way,' Caitlin said vaguely.

'He's never mentioned having a serious girlfriend in the past.'

'We were…er…friends…before…' Slanted green eyes collided with dark, coolly thoughtful ones. 'You still haven't told me who you are. I guess you must know Alejandro and his brother really well considering you're so familiar with this house. It's pretty amazing, isn't it?'

'Admittedly,' Dante murmured, completely ignoring her question, 'he hasn't let on much about anyone there in London.'

The noise was increasing in volume and then they exited into the massive hall manned by the uniformed guards, who half bowed but were clearly trained to remain in the background. The paintings here were more traditional, less abstract and more impressionistic.

Caitlin was drawn like a magnet towards one of them and inspected it minutely, lost for a few moments in the exquisite mix of colours and recognising the somewhat obscure artist behind it. It was the artwork of a connoisseur.

'It's a lovely piece.' She turned to Dante, her eyes gleaming with appreciation.

'You know about art?' Dante raised both eyebrows questioningly.

'Why shouldn't I?' Caitlin stood back. 'I'm a photographer but I studied art at college. I probably know a lot more than Alejandro's brother, even though he owns this house. I'll bet he hasn't got a clue who this artist is.'

'Why would you say that?' Dante asked silkily.

'He's a businessman,' she said with a shrug. 'I gather making money is his number one priority. I'd say that if that's the case, then he's probably commissioned someone to bulk-buy a fortune's worth of valuable artwork that will do its job and appreciate over the years and make him yet more money.'

'That's quite a statement,' Dante murmured. 'You must have gleaned that impression from somewhere… Is that what his brother has told you?'

'Of course not!' She cleared her throat. 'Alejandro never has a judgemental word to say about anyone. Not that I'm being judgemental…just expressing an opinion…'

'But surely you would be partisan, considering you're his besotted better half?' Dante was outraged that a woman who had catapulted herself into the centre of their family, for reasons that were open to a lot of question, should dare insult him in his own house. Actually, should dare insult him, full stop.

'Sorry?' Caitlin blinked then blushed. 'Yes. No. I mean, *yes*, of *course* that's what I am, but no, I'm not at all partisan. I don't know why I'm telling you all this. I still don't even know who you are!'

'Oh, haven't I introduced myself?' He gave a mocking half-bow and then fixed her with his amazing eyes. 'My oversight. I am Dante Cabrera, Alejandro's brother.'

CHAPTER TWO

'WHY DIDN'T YOU pick up your phone?' was the first thing Caitlin demanded when she had finally managed to corner Alejandro, who had already been tipsy by the time she'd located him.

When she and Alejandro had discussed this charade, and it had been a discussion that had not happened on the spur of the moment or even overnight, she had not foreseen the very real stumbling blocks she might encounter.

She knew that she only had herself to blame. An optimist by nature, someone who had been brought up to see the silver lining behind every cloud, she had spent months lost in the unfamiliar world of uncertainty and hopelessness. Misfortune had rained down on her from the very moment she'd found out about her parents' horrendous financial problems, and from that point on things had only seemed to get worse. Her parents had always been her biggest fans and the very backbone of her life, there for her through thick and thin, always in her corner. They had instilled positivity in her and a belief that things could only get better whenever she'd been a little low. She'd relied on them, and to see her father tearful and broken…to have faced the repercussions as they had unravelled over the past few months…

She had had to step up to the plate in a way she had never had to before. She had had to go into caretaker mode. It had been debilitating, especially as she had been working in London and commuting as often as she could back to Ireland, spending money she could ill afford because every penny she earned now had to be earmarked for the gaping hole the financial catastrophe had left in her parents' lives.

Alejandro's suggestion had, at first, fallen on barren ground. The thought of any deliberate deception had been anathema to Caitlin. Every moral code instilled from birth had risen up against the thought of lying, but he had persisted. He had his very pressing reasons, in many ways as urgent as hers, and he had persuaded her that she would be doing him a favour, that in return he, with his limitless millions, would be honoured to return that favour. As a friend, he had insisted, it would be an insult to him for her to turn him away in her moment of desperate need. If friends couldn't help one another when help was most needed, then what was the point?

He had said all the right things at the very time when she had been absolutely dazed at the speed with which disaster after disaster had been battering her naturally upbeat nature.

From the minute she had accepted Alejandro's offer, a weight had been lifted and the sun had tentatively begun to peek out from behind the bank of raging dark clouds.

She had been able to see a way forward. The silver lining had been slowly restored and that, she realised now, had been her undoing, because she had contrived to overlook the fact that what had started as a straightforward solution might throw up unexpected obstacles.

She hadn't banked on the brother.

She'd been apprehensive about meeting his parents but nowhere in that scenario had she given a second thought to Dante, even though there had been sufficient mention of him over the time she had known Alejandro to have joined the dots and worked out that he was ruthless. With a light at the end of the tunnel, she had allowed her optimism to take over and that had been a mistake.

When Dante had disclosed his identity, her brain had done a rapid overview of the conversation they had had from the moment she had attacked him on the walk up to the house and she had realised that she would have to be careful around him.

He had laid bait for her to take and if she didn't watch out, he would…do *what*? Caitlin didn't know, because what on earth could the man do in the space of twenty-four hours, after which she would be gone? But that didn't prevent a shiver of apprehension from feathering along her spine at the nebulous thought that she should be on her guard.

She determined to avoid him for the remainder of the party, which, as she glanced now at her watch, still had a long way to go. And where on earth was her wandering fiancé? He had become close friends with the champagne and, between trying to keep an eye on him and also on Dante, she had had a hellish hour and a half.

His charming parents had almost been welcome relief. They were over the moon that their eldest was finally settling down. She had been so distracted by the tug of war inside her at having to avoid Dante, while watching out for an increasingly inebriated Alejandro, that she had only paid scant attention to their polite but searching questions about what she did and whether she would continue doing what she did once she was married. She had tried to appear focused as she had listened to their gentle but insistent hints about the grandchildren they hoped would be forthcoming sooner rather than later while her brain had conjured up alarming scenarios of what a suspicious Dante might do should he decide to make mischief. Or worse.

She had barely had the chance to feel awkward even though she knew, on some level, that she really didn't belong with this glamorous, pampered crowd. So many of them, swarming in confident groups. So many beautiful women and expensive men, barely glancing at the waiting staff as they did the rounds with champagne and canapés. To the right, there was the glorious sight of tables laid out for outdoor dining. It should have looked casual and homely but it looked, instead, madly opulent. There was something strangely intimidating about tables formally dressed under the stars, manned by formally attired waiting staff, like a Michelin-starred restaurant in a five-star hotel, suddenly exposed to the elements.

She would have been a lot less nervous had she not been agonisingly conscious of Dante, a tall, brooding presence, glimpsed just enough for her to know that he was keeping an eye on her.

And it wasn't just the fact that he was an unknown threat that made her jumpy...

She also remembered the way her body had reacted to him, nerves all over the place and pulses racing a mile a minute. She hadn't known who he was and her response had been instinctive and physical and shocking.

Things felt as though they were getting beyond her control. She'd barely managed to exchange two words with Alejandro, just sufficient to scramble through what had happened en route to the big event.

Now, as everyone made their way through a huge archway of flowers and lanterns into the magical outdoor eating area, Caitlin felt that she had to vent some of her panic and frustration on her so-called erstwhile fiancé, before he tipped over the edge from too much champagne.

Thanks to his absent-mindedness when it came to his phone, and his preoccupation with hurrying along the occasion by drinking as much and as fast as he could, she had ended up in a place she had not banked on and she just wasn't equipped to deal with it. Subterfuge wasn't in her genetic code and she was terrified of blurting something out to Dante, who struck her as the sort who wouldn't release the bone once he had got it between his pearly white teeth. Which he had.

His watchful, speculative dark eyes brought to mind a shark in search of prey.

When she looked at Alejandro she realised that he was miserable, and she prayed that she was the only one to spot his unhappiness underneath the broad smiles and perspiring bonhomie.

Alejandro was not being Alejandro and he was clearly a lot more uncomfortable with the situation than she was. She cornered him.

'This is a nightmare.' Alejandro was busy relieving the waiter of another flute of champagne as he leant into her. 'And I'm sorry about the phone, Linny. No idea where I left it. Still haven't found it. It's probably buried under a cushion somewhere. There was a lot of sitting around earlier today. Talking. God, this is a nightmare. And I can't believe your bad luck running into Dante on your way to the house.'

'Slow down on the drinking!' was Caitlin's anxious response to that.

'I can't. It's the only thing that's propping me up.'

'Oh, Alex.' She sighed and rubbed his arm sympathetically. 'You need to be honest with your family.'

'I will. Just not yet. Once Dante finds a woman and settles down, then the pressure will be off me and then…' His voice drifted off. It was a conversation they had had before. 'Are you going to be all right?'

'What do you mean?'

'People can sit where they please but close friends and family members are at the top table. Wedding style. Look at where you're sitting.' He'd been propelling her along on unsteady legs and now he nodded to the one and only table with a seating plan. It occupied an exalted position on a makeshift podium that was adorned with striking flowers in urns of various sizes.

'Why have they stuck me next to your brother?' Caitlin was appalled and panic bloomed inside her. She had optimistically thought that she might have seen off Dante for the remainder of the evening. She had planned on vanishing with Alejandro at a respectable hour, when the guests started drifting off. A flight had been booked. He had assured her that his parents wouldn't bat an eye because they were used to work commitment cutting short all kinds of family gatherings, usually courtesy of Dante.

Still reeling from the prospect of sitting next to Dante, she raised her eyes to spot him heading in her direction. His gait was leisurely, his body language was relaxed but he was a man on a mission. She shivered.

The shark looked in the mood for a meal and she quailed at the thought of being the tasty morsel. She was barely aware of Alejandro. She was too busy telling herself that the evening would be over soon enough.

'I suppose,' she surfaced to hear Alejandro muttering gloomily, 'the intention is for you to get to know the nearest and dearest. Don't worry, Uncle Alfredo to your right is okay and Dante has Luisa next to him on the other side.'

'Luisa?' She was riveted at the sight of Dante weaving his way through the crowd, so graceful, so dangerously, darkly beautiful. He was compelling. She felt a little sick and wished all over again that she had stuck to her guns but, when she thought about her parents and the mess they were in, she could see why she had done what she had.

'Not here yet. She enjoys making an entrance. My hopes are high for Dante and Luisa to do what everyone expects they'll eventually do.'

'What's that?' she asked vaguely.

'Tie the knot. They dated a year or so ago and broke up but everyone thinks it's just a matter of time before it all kicks off again. Anyway, I have to go, Caitlin. You'll have my moral support from across the table. Feel for me. As the guest of honour, I will have both parents on either side so it's going to be an evening of the Spanish Inquisition. I just can't cope.'

'You'll have to,' Caitlin said sternly.

There was a bewildering array of wine glasses in front of them and she only hoped that his nerves wouldn't propel him to have them all filled so that he could duly empty them. He wasn't a drinker. Frankly, she was surprised that he was still standing.

When she shifted her attention away from him, it was to find that Dante was settling into the chair next to her and she shivered and began a hurried conversation in broken Spanish with Uncle Alfredo, as he wanted to be called, who was very happy to carry the conversation.

The night air was balmy and the sky was velvet black, dotted with stars. It was a perfect setting and were this a real engagement party, it would have been heavenly. She thought back to that distant time when it had looked as though marriage might have been hers for the taking and felt a rush of sadness. It had ended and it had been for the best, but sitting here, in this wonderful, magical setting, she could almost airbrush away the expensively dressed people and imagine what it might be like to be celebrating a true engagement to a guy she loved, under the stars, with the gentle sound of violins harmonising with the chirping of invisible summer insects.

'We meet again...'

Caitlin blinked and landed back on Planet Earth with a resentful bump. 'You should have told me who you were,' she said stiffly, bypassing small talk, which seemed irrelevant now, considering they were already acquainted.

'Is that why you've spent the evening avoiding me? Because you were embarrassed?'

'I wasn't avoiding you.' While there was a buffet service for the guests, this select table benefited from an array of assiduous waiters whose duty was to make sure they were fed and watered without having to exert themselves at all.

It was over-the-top luxury that Caitlin could have done without. No opportunity to take her time hovering in front of tables groaning with food. No opportunity to duck Dante's dark, fascinating, menacing presence.

There wasn't even Luisa there to distract. Whoever she was. Caitlin had paid scant attention at the time, but there was an empty chair next to him so the woman was obviously going to be a no-show.

'I, naturally, would have told you who I was but you gifted me a unique opportunity to get to know the real you. The real Caitlin Walsh, mystery fiancée.'

'There's nothing mysterious about me.' Her heart was racing and her mouth was dry.

'Which, in itself, is something of an enigma. I've watched your interaction with Alejandro and, yes, I can see that you two are close. He seeks you out with his eyes when you're not around.'

'Like I said,' Caitlin said, sotto voce, picking at an arrangement of appetisers on a plate that had found its way in front of her and pointedly making sure not to look at Dante, 'we've been friends for ages.'

'Yes, the friend bit,' Dante intoned smoothly, his low murmur matching hers, 'is evident. It's the other bit I'm not seeing.'

'I have no idea what you're talking about.'

'Where's the touchy-feely, loved-up, starry-eyed, can't-stand-a-metre-apart-from-one-another couple?' His voice oozed concerned curiosity and Caitlin gritted her teeth together and wished he would just disappear.

'We're not those people.' She shifted back as a waiter bowed to remove her plate. There seemed to be an army of them, moving as one, making sure that everything went to plan. 'We don't believe in public displays of affection. Not everyone does.' Refusing to be threatened, Caitlin peered past him to the empty seat on his left.

'And speaking of which, where's the guest who's supposed to be sitting next to you? Luisa, I believe? That's what Alejandro told me. He said that you two are practically engaged?'

Dante's lips thinned and he turned so that he was looking directly at her. 'Is that so?' he said in a sibilant murmur that would have served as a warning shot to anyone else.

'Yes...' Caitlin tilted her head to one side, considering his rhetorical question as though it were deserving of an answer '...but, of course, he may have got it all wrong. He said something about you two being an item in the past and everyone assuming that it's going to end in marriage even though you're on a break?' She couldn't help herself. She'd never thought that she could take pleasure in watching someone squirm, but for the first time since their paths had crossed Dante wasn't calling the shots and she liked it.

'This conversation is going nowhere,' he growled, under his breath.

'Lots of people go on breaks,' Caitlin murmured wickedly. 'Sometimes, taking a step back from someone can make you realise how important they are in your life. We don't know one another at all, so I hope you'll forgive me for saying what's on my mind.' She didn't give him time to do any such thing. The last thing she intended to do was stop saying what was on her mind. 'Marriage and tying the knot can be scary. Are you scared, Dante? I would say that you should let go of all those apprehensions and show Luisa how much you really care about her.' She wondered what this mystery woman was like. Beautiful, captivating...

she would have to be if she'd managed to get to a guy like Dante Cabrera.

'I don't believe I'm hearing this. No one—*no one*— has ever dared address me in this way!'

'In that case, please accept my apologies,' Caitlin said without a hint of apology in her voice. 'But you feel free to ask me whatever you want to so why shouldn't I return the favour?' Their eyes collided and she felt such a rush of weird *sensation* race through her body, like the surge of an electric charge, that she blinked in utter confusion and for a few seconds couldn't say anything at all.

Then the moment was lost because there was a sudden lull in the din of people talking and all heads, as one, swung round to the arch where a leggy brunette was poised theatrically, her beautiful face a picture of exaggerated remorse. The glow of the lanterns and the backdrop of light from the house did her a lot of favours. She was aiming for drama and she was delivering it in bucketloads. Her lips twitched with amusement, inviting everyone at the honoured top table to get in on the joke with her. Caitlin could only admire the spectacle.

Then Luisa was stalking towards them, tossing her hair as a waiter scurried to hold out a chair, then it was all about Dante.

Caitlin thought she might be gaping. Up close, the woman was even more stunning than she had appeared at a distance. Perfect features in a perfectly oval face. Her hair was waist length, curling down a narrow back and, although she was olive toned—just a shade lighter than the guy sitting next to her—she had the most incredible bright blue eyes.

Caitlin politely turned away as more food continued

to arrive, but she could hear breathless murmurs coming from the woman in question and not much from Dante.

Caitlin's head was whirling. She suddenly felt self-conscious. A little ridiculous in her newly acquired fancy dress and her silly high heels, pretending to be someone she wasn't.

She was back to feeling like that girl who had been ditched by the boy everyone in the village had assumed she'd end up with. Ditched for a five-foot-ten beauty from Latvia. All the insecurities Caitlin had felt then assaulted her now in a full-frontal attack, a reminder that this silly party wasn't real, that there was no engagement, that love and marriage were not things on the cards for her, and no amount of optimism and silver linings could camouflage that fact. This charade was a pragmatic solution to a problem that had been tearing her apart.

She wasn't a beauty queen like Luisa. She was the girl next door and she was ashamed of those taboo stirrings she had felt with Dante, that slow uncurling of something sexual that had blindsided her. Had she completely lost her mind? Had two glasses of champagne gone to her head?

She surfaced to find that the business of eating was beginning in earnest. The alcohol was flowing. The courses were coming thick and fast, each one a testament to what a talented chef could produce.

'I never remembered Alejandro drinking quite so much,' a deep, velvety voice to her left murmured.

Caitlin had glazed over at Alfredo's long-winded monologue about a game of golf he had played three weeks previously. She snapped to attention in a hurry at the sound of Dante's deep, dulcet tone.

She looked narrowly at Alejandro, who was flushed, before turning sideways to Dante.

'He…he…'

Dante's dark eyebrows winged upwards in a question.

'He's thoroughly enjoying his own engagement party?' Dante queried helpfully before she could think of something to say. 'If I didn't know better, I'd almost think that he was a man trying to drown his sorrows.'

'Thankfully—' Caitlin stabbed a piece of succulent chicken breast '—you don't know better.' Her skin tingled. Something about his voice, his accent, barely there and stupidly sexy.

'Mind you,' Dante mused thoughtfully, 'he's stuck between our parents. They will be asking him all sorts of probing questions he probably doesn't know how to answer.'

'Such as what?'

'Oh, the usual. Timelines…venues…food preferences for the wedding meal…'

Caitlin remained silent. Yes, she'd been plied with a couple of those questions herself but poor Alejandro would be squirming like a fish on a hook, trying to fend off *probing questions*.

'Poor Alejandro,' Caitlin murmured softly, without thought. Too late, she realised that that was the last thing she should have said because those questioning eyebrows now conveyed less mild curiosity and more scorching interest.

'That's an odd response. Why do you say that?'

'Because…'

'Because…?' Dante prompted silkily. 'I'm all ears.'

He had moved closer to her so that his shoulder was almost but not quite brushing hers and she could smell the warmth of his breath and whatever woody cologne he was wearing. Out of the corner of her eye, she could see that Luisa had turned the full, glowing wattage of her undivided attention to the elderly man sitting next to her. There was lots of noise, people talking, laughing, getting merrier by the second as the alcohol continued to flow, served by the army of solicitous waiters. The lanterns swayed in the breeze, picking up the glitter of expensive jewellery, adding a layer of mystery to the wildly glamorous gathering.

Amidst all this, the low murmur of his voice in her ear somehow seemed to wrap them in a bubble of their own.

'We haven't talked about…er…concrete plans for anything.' She tentatively tested the waters to see whether this evasive response would have the desired effect of shutting him up. The dress was beginning to feel uncomfortable, or maybe it only felt uncomfortable because she was beginning to perspire with a sense of rising panic.

Across the table, Alejandro was not helping matters. He was tugging at his collar and guzzling champagne as though his life depended on it. She would have to corner him, somehow, and steer him back on the straight and narrow, but she had no idea how she was going to do that because there was still a long way to go with the wonderful never-ending meal and then, presumably, speeches.

'I confess I'm surprised.'

'Why?'

'I always thought that once rings were on fingers, the first thing a woman wanted to do was pin her man down to a time and a place.'

'Has that been your experience?'

'I've never been engaged. I'm surmising.'

'I guess you and Luisa...must have discussed things of that nature?'

'It won't work.'

'What won't work?'

'Trying to get me off-piste with this conversation. Don't you want to set up house as soon as you can? Alejandro is no longer a boy in his twenties. I'm sure he's keen to set the date so that he can start producing heirs to the throne.'

Caitlin contained a shudder of horror.

'It may not have occurred to you,' Caitlin said stiffly, 'that in this day and age a woman might actually want to further her career before she starts having a family. I'm only twenty-five.'

'No, if I'm being honest.'

'No *what*?'

'No, it hasn't occurred to me.'

'I love what I do.' She slanted her eyes sideways and instantly looked away because the lazy intensity in his gaze unsettled her. 'I left Ireland to make my way in London and I managed to land a very enjoyable job freelancing at a magazine. Every day is different and I have a lot of opportunities to go somewhere with my career. I may not want to sacrifice all of that to have kids when I'm still young.'

'Photographer for a magazine...' He let that musing statement hang tantalisingly in the air between them for a few seconds. 'Very interesting. Tell me, how did you and my brother meet? There's quite a chasm between the world of business and the world of entertainment and I'm racking my brains but I'm pretty sure publication isn't part of the family holdings.'

Caitlin had a moment of sheer panic. What, exactly,

had Alejandro told everyone? She had been vague when questioned but the man sitting next to her wasn't going to let her get away with vague.

'No one spends all their time working,' she said faintly. 'Everyone has hobbies and Alejandro discovered that he enjoyed photography. It's…relaxing…'

'A straight answer, Caitlin. Is that asking too much? How did you meet?'

'He dropped by.' She took a deep breath. 'I happened to be renting space in a workshop. I still do, as it happens. He dropped by and we got chatting.'

'Why would he drop by a workshop?'

'You should ask him.'

'But you're sitting next to me,' he responded smoothly, 'and so I'm asking *you*.'

'He dropped by—' Caitlin glanced across to Alejandro, who was now looking the worse for wear '—and we just happened to click.'

'But you didn't start going out with one another. That happened later…'

'That's right.'

'Why is that? Was it not love at first sight? Maybe he was involved with someone else at the time? Or maybe you were?'

His low voice was a persistent murmur in her ear.

'Why are you asking all these questions?' she breathed. 'I get it that you're curious about our relationship, but, honestly, isn't it enough that I'm here? Your parents haven't pried into our…our relationship…'

'My parents are already in love with the idea that their eldest son is going to be tying the knot. They have grandchildren on their mind. They see what they want to see, but my vision is slightly less rose-tinted. Alejandro might be older than me but he's gullible in places I'm not. Gullible enough to fall hook, line and sinker in love with a woman who might not be…let's just say, right for him. So my curiosity? Natural. Your reticence on the subject of love and marriage, not to mention your reluctance to go into detail? Less natural.'

She was thinking hard. Thinking about how to address those suspicions. Loathing the man for putting her on the back foot, for not accepting what she had to say, for not being satisfied with polite small talk.

She was still thinking, still sweating with discomfort when it happened.

The crash was deafening. For a few seconds, she just couldn't seem to focus on what exactly had happened because everything seemed to have slowed down. Then she realised, in a flash, that Alejandro had fallen. He had begun standing up, but he'd had so much to drink that his legs had refused to co-operate. He'd fallen, dropped backwards like a stone, catapulting the chair behind him and crashing to the ground.

She sprang to her feet. Everyone had sprung to their feet. Then it was all a blur. She raced over to where Alejandro lay sprawled in an unnatural position on the ground, with one arm flung behind his head and his leg twisted underneath him. He was perfectly still and as she shoved her way to his side Caitlin desperately wondered whether he was breathing at all. Tears had sprung to her eyes and she was whimpering when someone pulled her back.

She felt the hardness of muscle against her back and then Dante was whispering urgently into her ear.

'Don't panic. He's alive and there's a doctor here. Take it easy.'

The voice that had filled her with discomfort and hostility only moments earlier now soothed her, but she barely had time to question the phenomenon because amidst the chaos someone was pushing forward and taking charge, ordering people to stand back while simultaneously reaching for his phone and jabbing at it as he bent towards Alejandro.

Caitlin couldn't bear to watch. She spun round and buried her head against Dante. He could have been anyone. She just couldn't look at her friend lying there on the ground. There was a roaring in her ears, which she wanted desperately to block out.

She wasn't quite sure what happened next. She knew that people were being ushered inside. So was she. Her feet were moving, propelling her towards a sitting room where she was settled on a sofa, a quiet place which was good, left on her own, time to gather herself. What had just happened replayed in her head in slow motion.

It was dark in the sitting room, with only one of the lamps on a side table on, but that suited her. Her thoughts were going crazy in her head and just when she was about to go out because she couldn't sit on her own any longer, the door was pushed open and she saw Dante outlined, a shadowy silhouette filling the frame.

'You need to sit down, Caitlin.' His voice was low and serious as he moved towards her.

She fell back against the sofa, too scared to say a word. He'd moved from the shadows into the pool of light from the lamp and his expression was as serious as his voice.

'What's happened, Dante?' she whispered.

'Sit and I'll tell you. Good news and bad...'

CHAPTER THREE

SHE WAS SHAKING like a leaf and she barely noticed the glass of brandy Dante had brought in with him. He'd been thinking ahead, she dimly registered, predicting her reaction and knowing that she would need a stiff swig of something to deal with whatever he had to say.

If the gravity of his expression wasn't enough, the very fact that he had come equipped with brandy said it all.

He'd sat her down on the sofa and he sat next to her and waited until she had fortified herself by duly sipping some of the fiery alcohol, even though she didn't feel she needed it.

'Just tell me,' she whispered.

'There was a doctor there. An eminent surgeon, as it happens. A relative on my father's side. Of course, he couldn't do a complete test but it would seem that Alejandro fell at an awkward angle. If I could draw a parallel, it's a bit like someone collapsing to the ground because the chair they'd planned on sitting on has been yanked out from under them.'

'An awkward angle...'

'He didn't fall far, but what's certain is that he's broken several small but significant bones in his ankle.'.

Caitlin looked at him and blinked. Her thoughts were lagging behind but a few broken bones didn't seem like the end of the world and she said as much, breathing a sigh of relief and closing her eyes.

'Not so fast,' Dante said, and he held her gaze when she opened her eyes to stare at him.

A person could drown in those eyes, she thought distractedly. She hadn't noticed how deep and dark they were before, because she'd been arguing with him, resentful and defensive at his suspicions, which had made her question all over again the wisdom of embarking on the charade. They weren't arguing now, and something shifted and filtered through her defences. Now, as their eyes locked, she could see that his were the deepest shade of bitter chocolate and fringed with thick, sooty lashes that any woman would give her right arm for.

He was a good-looking guy and she was up close and in a state of shock. It was understandable that those first impressions, that whisper of sexual attraction, felt stronger now. 'You said he just broke a few bones...'

'Preliminary findings show that he struck his head on the marble flooring at an awkward angle. He's concussed at the moment and we won't know more until more detailed examinations are made at the hospital, but Roberto seems to think that Alejandro could slide into a temporary coma.'

'A *coma*?' Tears gathered. 'But he just had a little fall...'

'It's not a certainty so there's no need to start getting upset.'

'Of course I'm going to be upset! I should be there with him.' She stood up while Dante remained seated, his long legs stretched out and lightly crossed at the ankles.

Why wasn't he responding? How could he look so cool and collected at a time like this?

'I need to get to that hospital,' she repeated, with mounting urgency. 'You need to take me *right now.*'

'You're in shock and you're better off here. Rushing to the hospital isn't going to achieve anything. Right now, and for the next few hours, if not days, Alejandro will be out of it, undergoing a battery of tests. Trust me, I will be the first to know of any developments.'

Caitlin hesitated, soothed by his assertiveness. She realised that it had been a long time since someone else had taken charge and it felt good. 'I feel so helpless. He must be terrified.'

'Caitlin, he's in the equivalent of a deep sleep. He'll be as peaceful as a newborn.'

All that stress, she thought, riven with guilt. Yes, he'd fallen, but was a part of him retreating from the awkward situation he had obviously found difficult to cope with? Had his brain decided to conveniently shut down just for the moment?

There were so many cases of people forgetting traumatic events, relegating them behind closed doors in their head because they just couldn't cope with the memories.

Had Alejandro done the equivalent?

And yet, she thought feverishly, they had both been so cavalier about this arrangement.

Alejandro was gay. This was a revelation that had seeped out over a period of months and Caitlin had been more surprised at his shame at the admission than the admission itself. After all, in this day and age, who thought twice about someone being gay?

But she didn't understand, he'd said matter-of-factly. His background, generation upon generation of accumulated wealth, was mired in tradition, his elevated birthright an albatross around his neck.

He was the older and expected to marry and produce. It would kill his parents if they found out about his sexual persuasion. Nothing Caitlin had said over the months could assuage his anxiety but it was only when he told her that his parents were becoming increasingly vocal on the subject of his love life that she began to see just how much it was affecting his state of mind.

He'd begun playing truant from work. He'd stopped caring about whether his increasing absences were noted or not. If only his brother would get married, he'd told her. That would let him off the hook. He'd be able to remain free for longer, at least until he sorted out what he would do in the future. But Dante, he had said, just wasn't playing ball.

And his parents wanted to know what was going on. Why had they not been introduced to any girlfriends? They had someone in mind for him, a lovely girl, daughter of one of their friends. They were insistent on a meeting.

And from there, Alejandro and Caitlin's plan had been born.

He'd been desperate and so...had she.

She wasn't going to think of her own circumstances. This was about Alejandro and the fact that he was in hospital and she couldn't help but blame herself because she hadn't seen just how stressed he'd been at the whole mess and at lying to all his friends and family.

'Where are—what's happened to everyone?'

'Gone.'

'Gone?'

'Shuffled out in an orderly line. My parents went to the hospital but they've heeded the consultant's advice and returned to their place.'

'What is the prognosis?'

She'd been borderline hysterical but now her brain had re-engaged and she was a lot calmer. Dante's sense of calm was mesmerising and infectious.

'Excellent.'

'Would you lie to me?'

'Of course I would.' He smiled, and just for a second she understood how power, charm and incredible physical perfection could be an intoxicating mix.

Her heart picked up a beat and she suddenly felt hot and bothered.

'But,' he continued, still smiling, 'in this instance I'm not. Yes, there are broken bones, and it'll be a while before those completely heal, and, yes, he's been concussed, but all his vital signs are good and if he's out of it just at the moment, Roberto, the consultant who was here, has assured us that a full recovery is to be expected.'

'But you said that he's in a coma.'

'He's out of it at the moment, yes. Perhaps *coma* might be something of a dramatic term.'

'So how long do you think…does the consultant think…?'

'Can't put a timeline on it. Could be a day, could be a week. Doubtful that it'll be longer. All the signs are good.'

'That's such a relief.'

'It's a disappointing end to what should have been one of the best nights of your life,' Dante murmured, briefly lowering his eyes.

'Yes, it's a shame,' she returned politely as her mind hived off in other directions.

'You don't sound too distraught.'

'Of course I'm distraught.'

'You were certainly upset when he toppled over.' Dante was getting that feeling again, that vague, shadowy feeling that something didn't quite add up but he couldn't put his finger on *what exactly*. It was frustrating. In Dante's world, everything added up. There were no loose ends because he always made sure that there weren't any. He never asked himself whether he was missing out on the adventures that spontaneity could bring.

When he glanced back over his shoulder to the kid who had allowed himself to be carried away on the spontaneous adventure of straying out of his comfort zone with an older woman from a different background, it was like looking at a stranger. The stupid thing was that he knew that what he had felt at the time, and what had propelled him into throwing himself into his ill-advised affair, had had nothing to do with love. Infatuation, yes, and lust, most definitely, but that had been it. Everything else had stemmed from a defiant act of rebellion against a life that had been preordained from birth. Someone had to take the reins of the family empire and he had known, even then, that it probably wasn't going to be Alejandro.

How had he known that? Dante could only assume it was because his parents had begun, automatically, to turn to *him* for his opinions on the stock markets, on trends, on modernisation, *on the way forward*. Bound within the confines of this life, he had broken free in an act of rebellion that had cost him dearly and not just in terms of the money he had recklessly flung at the woman. His pride had been injured and he had glimpsed a vision of weakness inside him that had required eradication. He had shut down his emotions and ruthlessly taken control of every aspect of his life.

Vague, shadowy feelings didn't sit well with him. Neither did the way his body refused to obey his head when he looked at the pocket-sized redhead, who had no business getting under his skin the way she did. Her intentions were open to question and getting to the bottom of what she was up to with his brother was a straightforward matter. He would then respond accordingly.

So the jostle of unwelcome responses inside him that had nothing to do with the business of finding out what she was up to was an unwelcome reminder of a weakness he'd thought he had put to bed. It got on his nerves.

She wasn't lying when she said that she had, indeed, been distraught when his brother had hit the ground. She just didn't seem overly upset at the fact that he had hit the ground at their engagement party, thereby ensuring a premature and unwelcome conclusion.

Now that he thought about it, he couldn't remember her flashing the diamond ring at all. What excited bride-to-be didn't flash her engagement ring at her own engagement party?

He glanced at her finger. She was absently fiddling with the ring, slipping it off and on her finger, twisting it round and round. It was startlingly modest in its proportions.

Unwittingly, he looked at her, felt that tightening in his groin again.

'I knew he'd been overdoing it with the drink.' Caitlin spoke her thoughts aloud, eyes sliding away from Dante's over-the-top masculine presence. Her conscience still plagued her. This had been a terrible idea, an awful plan and she should have argued more against it, but she'd allowed necessity to override common sense, and now thinking about poor Alejandro, lying unconscious on some sanitised hospital bed in an impersonal, clinical hospital room, filled her with remorse.

'I should have done something about that. He's not used to drinking a lot. He's quite abstemious normally.'

'Yes, that's a curious one, isn't it?'

Caitlin looked at him. 'What are you talking about?'

'I did recall that my brother doesn't tend to hit the bottle hard. I just wondered why, of all nights, he should decide to sample every drink that went past him on a tray...'

He wasn't going to let up. That was the thought that ran through her head. There had been a lull in the attack amidst the chaos of Alejandro being rushed to hospital, and during that lull she had glimpsed another Dante Cabrera, but normal proceedings had resumed and he *just wasn't going to let up.*

The man was like a dog with a bone, and not just *any dog.* Nothing she could turn her back on and ignore. This dog with a bone wasn't a loveable poodle. He was a pit bull and he wanted to sink teeth into her until he prised every little secret out.

She had no intention of letting him do any such thing but her blood ran cold as she felt him circling her.

'Who doesn't feel nervous on an occasion like that?'

she responded smoothly. '*I* was a bag of nerves. As you know.'

'You *were* concerned about your outfit,' Dante agreed. 'But, moving on from the troublesome subject of my brother's alcohol intake and his hospitalisation, the question is what happens from here?' He vaulted upright and paced towards the window, his movements as elegant and as stealthy as a jungle cat. He stared out for a few moments, then turned to look at her. 'Like I said, Alejandro probably won't come round for a day or two, but even when he does there's the business of those broken bones. He's going to be off his feet for some weeks, I would imagine…'

'He's going to go stir-crazy.'

'We can agree on that,' Dante said ruefully. 'Not that anything can be done to change that situation. On the upside, he'll be able to keep on top of work. Much of what needs to be done can be done via email and conference call. Thank God we live in a connected world.'

'He'll be thrilled to hear that,' Caitlin said sarcastically, without thinking, and then she flushed as Dante looked at her through narrowed eyes.

'You think he should refrain from working while he recuperates?'

'I think…' She shot Dante an accusatory look from under her lashes because she was now in the awkward position of having to explain what she had meant.

Didn't he know *anything* about his own brother? How was it possible for there to be such vast gaps between them? She'd never had siblings. When she was young, she'd *yearned* for one. It was heartbreaking, really, to witness a relationship that was so fractured.

'Yes?'

'I think...' she toed the middle ground '...he might appreciate a bit of peace from...er...the world of business...'

'What are you trying to tell me?'

He sounded genuinely perplexed and Caitlin sighed and decided to take a risk. A *tiny* risk. Wasn't it a starting point for these brothers to know a bit about one another? Alejandro, one day, would find the courage to explain who he was to his family and, when that day came, it would be so much smoother if Dante at least knew how his brother felt about working for the company.

'I'm not sure Alejandro is as...*besotted* with working for the company as you are...'

'Besotted?' Dante stared at her with rampant incredulity at yet another intrusion into areas of his life no one dared to explore.

'I know Alejandro tries to be as diligent as possible...' For Alejandro that actually meant working the minimum number of hours as efficiently as possible so that he could spend the remainder of his time exploring all those creative interests that he was more intrigued by.

Dante scowled and raked his fingers through his dark hair. 'I realise,' he conceded grittily, 'that he, perhaps, doesn't have the same drive as I have when it comes to running the company. Why do you think I've succeeded in diverging from the family business to build my own computer-software research companies? Because I've had nothing better to do? No, Alejandro doesn't have the same drive, but I've had no complaints from any of the directors...'

Personally, Caitlin was sure that that was because Alejandro was loved by everyone he met. He could put in an hour a day and she knew that everyone would be loath to report him. The fact was that he did his job perfectly well, if he was to be believed. He just didn't enjoy it and he spent as little time as possible there.

'No…well…it's just…' She breathed in deeply and decided, like a diver staring down at a very tiny pool of water miles below, to take the plunge. 'It's not that he doesn't have the same drive as you do. It's just that his heart has never really been in finance and business.'

Fulminating silence greeted this remark.

'He's really a creative soul,' she ploughed on while Dante watched her without saying a word, his face wiped of expression. 'That's why we get along so well. He's very interested in all aspects of photography. He loves exhibitions. He's even thinking about dabbling in a bit of sculpture or maybe even going for a course in woodwork…'

'Sculpture? *Woodwork?*'

'So you see he won't mind not being connected to the outside world while he recuperates.'

'Why would Alejandro not enjoy the work he does?' Dante demanded. 'He's never had the responsibility for any decision-making. I run everything. The buck stops with me. He has always had the easy ride of keeping the customers happy. What's not to like?' He flushed darkly. There was an admission there somewhere and he refused to shine a light on it. For once, the forbidding wall of privacy he had constructed around him revealed foundations that weren't as solid as he had thought.

He wanted to lock the discomforting thought away, but a series of connections were happening in his head that made him wonder whether the distance between him and Alejandro didn't hark back to that gradual alignment of responsibilities. Had there been something inside him that had resented the fact that he, although younger, had been the one to assume the reins of leadership without asking for it? Had that resentment spilled over, gradually, into the relationship he had with Alejandro?

The clear green eyes searching his lean, rigid face made his jaw harden in proud rejection of any sign of weakness.

'Maybe you judge him the way you would judge yourself,' Caitlin suggested quietly. 'Maybe because *you* enjoy being a workaholic, he must also enjoy being a workaholic because you share the same genetic code. But that's not how it works.'

'No one *enjoys* being a workaholic,' Dante responded coolly.

'I've offended you. I'm really sorry.'

'Offended me?' Dante scowled. 'Don't flatter yourself, *querida*.'

Caitlin flushed as she recognised a kick in the teeth when it was delivered.

'You asked for my opinion,' she returned shortly. 'And I gave it to you. Forget I ever said anything. You said something about Alejandro being in hospital for some time to come. Is there any chance that he could be transferred to a hospital in London?'

'If my brother was miserable in his job, he should have said something to me. As for being besotted with work… This vast family estate won't run itself because I'd rather have fun lazing around and going on holiday.' Dante was annoyed that he couldn't give it up.

'That's not what Alejandro is about!'

'Duty demands that the business falls to the sons. As

it stands, I have my own concerns that occupy much of my time. The family business is now just part of something bigger for me, even though our father no longer busies himself directly in its running. However, it is up to the pair of us to take up where he has left off. Would Alejandro rather abandon his obligations so that he can pursue a life of fun and enjoyment?'

'Your own concerns?' Caitlin had latched onto his phrase…*duty demands*. It gave her a very clear idea of why Alejandro was so loath to be open about his sexuality.

'My parents built their company on import and export. I have single-handedly brought it into the twenty-first century and it has become a gold mine, but it is overshadowed by my own computer-software empire.'

'So you work hard. But you volunteered for that, didn't you? You weren't content to just run the family business. You wanted your own, I guess because you enjoy that kind of ruthless, cut-throat lifestyle. Alejandro just isn't built along the same lines. And the reason he hasn't said anything…' she sighed but it was too late to start wondering whether she'd got in over her head with this conversation '…is because of this whole duty and tradition thing. He knows he has to join the family business whether he likes it or not but…'

'He's never uttered a word of complaint to me,' Dante said roughly. 'I could…work this out differently… I have been thinking of taking my computer business into a different area—the leisure industry always has room for improvement.' He frowned, padded across to a chair and sat down, stretching his legs out to the side. 'The wheels are in motion for me to take over a couple of boutique hotels in South America. There would certainly be scope for some creative advertising.'

'He would absolutely *adore* that.'

'This is something my brother should have brought to my attention. It's ridiculous that I have only found this out via a third party.'

'Maybe he was scared of disappointing,' she murmured. 'Haven't *you* ever been scared of disappointing?'

'Disappointing who?'

'I don't know. Your parents…your girlfriend…'

'To answer your question, no.'

Such self-assurance, Caitlin thought with a fascinated shiver. Little wonder Alejandro, so full of insecurities and doubts, had never thought to confide in his much more confident younger brother.

What must it be like to go out with a guy like Dante Cabrera? Personally, she had never been drawn to tough Alpha-male types but something feminine quivered inside her just for a moment at the thought of being with someone so absolutely in command. He was born to take charge and she remembered how that had made her feel when she had been frantic with worry earlier on. *Safe.*

Yet, he was willing to make concessions because, whatever his relationship with his brother, however distant they were from one another and however wildly different their personalities, he cared enough to try to see things from Alejandro's point of view.

He wasn't just a man of action. He was a listener. The problem was that Alejandro had never tried talking and Dante did not invite confidences.

'We were talking about the fact that Alejandro will be in hospital for a while,' Dante picked up the conversation from where they had left off before they'd gone down various byroads, 'and I couldn't help but notice that you travelled over here light.'

Caitlin looked at him with puzzlement because she wasn't sure where he was going with this.

'You're going to need clothes, so we have to decide how we're going to play this.'

'What are you talking about?'

'Well, you won't be returning to London for a while. Presumably your company will allow you suitable time off?'

'Time off?' Caitlin parroted.

'Alejandro is here and he won't be going anywhere any time soon.' He paused, giving her ample opportunity to see where he was heading with this.

How could she abandon her fiancé after the first night when he was lying in hospital, unconscious?

She blanched.

'I… I hadn't actually banked on spending much time over here…' *Or any at all, for that matter.* 'I don't know what the company policy is on…on time off for…for…'

'Compassionate leave? That does exist in your company, doesn't it?'

'Of course, but you know… I'm a freelance photographer… Yes, I'm employed by them, but I get called on to do various shoots and I'm paid accordingly…'

'That hardly sounds a satisfactory situation.'

'I'm working my way up. It's not something that happens overnight…'

'So…what…? They're going to quibble over giving you time off because the guy you plan on marrying is lying unconscious on a hospital bed in Spain? What kind of crackpot organisation are we talking about here?'

'It's a very reputable company!'

'Good, then that's all sorted. You'll have to call them first thing in the morning.'

'Yes, but...' She'd been standing on fairly solid ground but now a roller coaster had whipped past, scooped her up and she was in mid-air and travelling at speed.

'I'm not getting what the problem is here, Caitlin. Either you want to be with Alejandro or you don't. Which is it?'

'Of course, I would love to be around to make sure that he's going to be okay!'

Dante frowned. 'Good. Then let's not put unnecessary obstacles in the way. Back, though, to what I was saying earlier. You seem to have travelled over here with next to nothing. You'll need clothes. Do you want me to arrange to have some of yours brought over for you?'

'That won't be necessary,' Caitlin muttered. The walls had well and truly closed in and there was no point trying to reconfigure the space. 'I expect if you point me in the direction of the nearest town, I'll be able to buy one or two things.'

Dante shrugged. 'I'd look at a fortnight here.'

'*A fortnight...?*' She tried not to sound appalled.

'And naturally, you will have to stay here.'

'Here?'

'Where else?' He raised his eyebrows and held her dismayed gaze. 'Unless you'd rather stay with my parents? They're not very handy for the hospital, but I'm sure they would not object to putting you up for however long you think you'll need to stay...'

'What? No!'

'Didn't think so. Not many brides-to-be would leap

at the chance of staying with their in-laws, especially when they've only known their in-laws for a matter of a few hours.'

'I wouldn't want to impose,' Caitlin objected faintly, and Dante took his time looking round the huge sitting room with its high ceilings and sprawling bay windows. His dark eyes were cool and amused when they finally rested on her face.

'I wouldn't worry about it. I don't think we'll be bumping into one another because I live in a shoebox. Fact is, I doubt my brother would appreciate me turning you away at the door, given the circumstances.'

Caitlin, in her head, begged to differ. Alejandro would understand completely if she headed for the airport, clutching her bag. They were friends, after all, and certainly not the couple Dante assumed they were.

That said, if she ended up staying in Spain, he would also have sympathised with her perfectly reasonable desire to hit the nearest B & B because sharing space with Dante would be like sharing space with a hungry tiger on the prowl.

Realistically, though, was there any way that she could turn down the man's offer? He was already casting his net of suspicion far and wide.

'If it makes you feel any better, I'm rarely around. Naturally the staff will be here so you won't have to worry about anything at all. I know you'll be worried sick about Alejandro…but, rest assured, he is in the best hands, which I'm sure you know because you're certainly handling the shock better than I would have expected.'

He had vaulted to his feet and was heading for the door. She followed.

'What did you expect?' They were back in the body of the house and it was quiet. The army of staff who had scurried with their trays of champagne and caviar had had another role to fill and had removed all evidence of the party, so that now it was as though it had never been. A dream. Except...*not*.

'Well...' He spun round so suddenly that she almost crashed into him. She hastily stepped back and their eyes collided, startled green meeting cool, speculating midnight black. 'Call me stupid, but I thought there might be some hysteria involved.'

'Hysteria?'

'Naturally, you were clearly upset and shaken, but... let's just say I admire your self-control...'

'I'm not that type.' Caitlin licked her lips nervously.

'So it would appear,' Dante murmured lazily. 'I like that. And yet that seems to contradict the firecracker who attacked me outside the house.'

Caitlin flushed. How on earth was she going to manage spending a few *hours* here, never mind a few days?

He was so different from Alejandro. She wished her so-called erstwhile fiancé had told her a bit more about his forbidding younger brother. She might have, at least, come prepared. As things stood...

'No matter,' Dante said smoothly, spinning back on his heels and striding towards the curving staircase, one of two that dissected the mansion, 'we all have our different ways of dealing with distressing situations.'

'Where are we going?'

'Your rooms. Your bag will follow.'

He paused, pushed open a door and stood back so that she could precede him into a self-contained apartment that was the last word in luxury, from the thick velvet drapes to the rich Persian rug that partially covered the highly polished wooden floor. Through interlinking doors, she could see a sitting room.

'Thank you.' Gratitude didn't seem quite the emotion she was feeling. 'Please don't feel that you have to look out for me *at all*. I'll be more than capable of making my way to the hospital and into the town while I'm here. I'll call work in the morning and find out what sort of leave I'll be allowed...' His silence was oppressive.

'No need to thank me.' He lowered his lashes, shielding his expression, then looked at her. 'And banish all thoughts of making your way anywhere. I'll have a car waiting to take you to the hospital tomorrow and also to the town so that you can stock up on clothes.'

'Of course.' How on earth was she going to afford a new wardrobe? How was any of this making any sense at all? Why, why, why had they jumped head first into water without first finding out how deep it was?

'In the meantime...' he strolled towards the door and lounged against the door frame for a few seconds, looking at her with a veiled expression '...try and relax. Have a soak. By the time you're out of the bath, your clothes will be here. And when it comes to shopping? Buy a swimsuit. There's a superb infinity pool. I think you'll like it.' He straightened. 'When you're not agonising about Alejandro, kick back a little. You'll be waited on hand and foot. You may find that you won't be able to resist thinking of it as an unexpected little holiday...'

CHAPTER FOUR

HOLIDAY? *HOLIDAY? WAS the man mad?*

Caitlin peered out of the sitting-room window and wondered which of the cars parked outside might be the one designated to take her into the city. Would she be summoned by someone? One of the members of staff? There was no helpful chap in a uniform poised by an open car door to offer her any clues and she wasn't quite sure what she should do.

She'd had a restless night as the consequences of what had transpired began to take shape in her head.

A week here. At the very least. Work, at any rate, had been sympathetic but she was new to the job and freelance so she didn't know just how long the sympathy would last.

Her parents had been puzzled.

'Spain? Why are you in Spain, darling? You never mentioned going on holiday…'

No, of course she hadn't! This fleeting visit was supposed to last a handful of hours, after which she would have been able to see a clear way forward with all the problems that had disastrously landed on her lap without warning.

Instead, here she was, peering out of a window and wondering what more disasters lay in wait.

Lost in her thoughts, she was unaware of footsteps behind her until she heard Dante's voice.

'Have you been waiting long? After last night's adventures, I thought you might want a lie-in.'

Caitlin spun round to see him lounging in the doorway. She'd expected an empty house. Dante had more or less reassured her that if she stayed under his roof, there would be almost no chance of them bumping into one another. The house was as vast as a castle and she had assumed that he would be out of it anyway, back working, but now she wondered how she could have been so naïve. Whatever brief periods of respite there had been since Alejandro's accident, Dante was still determined to piece her together and dig deep to find out what was going on.

She had to be on guard, but as she looked at him she knew that she would have to fight her own physical responses to him, which threatened to undermine her resolve at every turn. She couldn't work out how someone who made her hackles rise and threatened her peace of mind could have the sort of effect on her that he did. Was it because she just hadn't been interested in any guy since Jimmy? Or was it because she had always assumed that if she ever looked twice at another man, he would be in her league, someone reliable and grounded, someone *who made sense*.

There was no chance that she had caught him on his way out because he wasn't dressed for work. He was in a pair of black jeans and a black polo-necked shirt with a distinctive red logo on the pocket. He looked darkly, sexily *dangerous* and her nervous system went into immediate overdrive.

'I thought you would be at work,' she said, already

on edge. 'I…er…wasn't sure what to do about transport into town.'

'You're looking at your transport.' Dante straightened and glanced at his watch.

'What are you talking about?'

'I've decided that it would be inappropriate to abandon you in your time of need. You don't know this part of the world, I'm guessing, and you're going to need someone to show you around while you're here.'

'Show me around?' Caitlin couldn't think of anything she needed less than Dante playing tour guide for the next few days. 'Why? Don't you have more important things to do?'

'What could be more important than making sure that my brother's beloved fiancée isn't left alone and floundering in a strange city? Come on. We can hit the hospital first, and then I will take you to the shopping district where you can buy sufficient clothes to tide you over.'

Caitlin quailed at the prospect of spending money she didn't have on things she didn't need.

Dante wasn't hanging around, waiting for any further protestations from her. He was already heading out of the sitting room and towards the imposing front door, barely leaving time for Caitlin to trip along behind him, clutching her knapsack.

The clean-up job on the house had been spectacular. As she was progressed along at fast speed, she could only guess that an army of helpers had been hard at it, wiping away all evidence of the elaborate party that had come to such a premature end.

It was not yet nine thirty and already it was hot outside.

Dante ignored all four cars parked in the massive courtyard and instead headed to the side of the house, beeping open a low-slung, steel-grey sports car that hadn't been visible from the sitting-room window.

He held open the passenger door for her.

Caitlin dropped into a plush leather bucket seat that made her feel as though she was inches away from making uncomfortable physical contact with the ground. Peering over the sleek walnut dashboard was a challenge because of her lack of height.

Dante, on the other hand, as he slid into the driver's seat and donned a pair of dark sunglasses, looked like a racing driver about to do a few winning laps around a circuit.

'Good news from the hospital,' he said as soon as the car revved to life. 'Alejandro is progressing well. He still hasn't regained consciousness, but all his vitals are good and those broken bones are the only damage he appears to have suffered. They can't work out how he lost consciousness and can only think that he must have dropped to the ground in a peculiarly awkward manner.'

'That's great,' Caitlin said with genuine warmth. 'Do we…er…have any idea how long he will be…out of it?'

'Absolutely none, but the signs are good for a speedy recovery on that front. I'm assuming you've contacted your people at work and been granted whatever time off you need?'

'I've phoned and told them that I will probably be here for about a week.' She braced herself for criticism.

Instead, Dante said smoothly, 'We'll head to the hospital first. You must be keen to see Alejandro.'

'Of course.' She noted the quick sideways glance Dante shot her but there was no way she could sound like a besotted lover, desperate to see her wounded fiancé.

Naturally, she was deeply concerned about what had happened and relieved that he had not had a more serious accident, given the wild abandon with which he had been drinking, but, much as she cared about Alejandro, he was, in the end, simply a very good friend and her pretence could only stretch so far. Not only would she have found it impossible to pretend to be loved up, but Alejandro would have had an even harder time of it.

It was just terrible luck that he happened to have a brother with eagle-sharp eyes and the prowling, suspicious nature of a trained sniffer dog.

'I guess your parents must be so relieved…'

'Naturally. They'll be visiting later today and, of course, they will want to see you, make sure you're okay, even though I've already told them that you couldn't be better. Given the circumstances.'

Caitlin gritted her teeth together at the implied judgement call in that throwaway remark but she remained silent, taking in the change of scenery as the grand and leafy outskirts of the city were left behind and the car began to nose its way into the main area of the very beautiful city.

She had never been to Madrid before, never been to Spain, if truth be told, and her artistic eye fully appreciated the beguiling mix of old and new, high tech and historic, sleek glass and pastel coloured.

'And you are okay, aren't you?'

Reluctantly she dragged her attention away from the passing scenery and focused on the aristocratic profile of the guy sitting next to her, one hand on the steering wheel, the other resting lightly on the intimidating gearbox.

So different from his brother, she thought a little helplessly. Chalk and cheese had more in common. She just had no idea how to deal with him or how to handle herself when she was around him.

Everything about him made her nervous, from his aggressive good looks to his cool, watchful self-assurance.

'Of course.' She cleared her throat. 'How far is the… hospital from here? Once I know the route, I would be happy to make my own way in to visit.'

'How would you propose to do that?'

'There must be some form of public transport close to your house?'

'Sadly not.' He shot her a sideways look that carried a hint of amusement. 'Of course, I could always arrange for my driver to take you but, like I said, I feel personally responsible for your well-being while you are here. We're twenty minutes away from the hospital, by the way.'

Caitlin was so tempted to protest, yet again, that he had no need to feel responsible for her in any way, shape or form, but why bother? The man was determined to take her under his wing and she hadn't been born yesterday. She knew that if she was under his wing, he would be able to keep a sharp eye on her and would be in a prime position to keep prodding away, poking into nooks and crannies, airing his suspicions and waiting for her to slip up.

How long would it take for that to happen? she wondered. How long before she slipped up?

Not long. She wasn't used to lying. Manoeuvring through the labyrinth she and Alejandro had innocently created was going to take the dexterity of a magician.

As they approached the hospital she finally allowed herself to think about the convoluted road she was now travelling down.

It had all seemed so straightforward not that long ago. She would pretend to be Alejandro's fiancée, thereby buying him time from his parents, who were pushing for a solid relationship from their eldest son and the inevitable production line of much-wanted grandchildren.

He would pay her, he'd said.

Caitlin had adamantly refused. Not only could she not see the reason for such drama, but the thought of being paid for it was ridiculous.

But then circumstances had changed in a heartbeat for her, and Alejandro, who had not abandoned his plan despite her initial refusal to co-operate, had found a way past her defences.

She had no interest in his money for herself because she didn't have a materialistic bone in her body, but when her parents had become involved, her love and loyalty to them had very quickly become the quicksand that had begun to drag her under.

'I don't believe it,' she had poured her heart out to Alejandro one evening, several months earlier. 'How could Dad have lost everything? There are news bulletins all the time about scammers, but he's gone and lost everything, Alejandro! His savings, his pension. Gone. *Pouf!* They have the house, of course, but how on earth are they going to afford to support themselves as they get older?'

'What about your mum?'

She'd known that Alejandro would be grappling with the concept of having nothing. The backdrop to his life was paved with gold and priceless gems. He, literally, would have no concept of just how agonising it would be for two pensioners to realise that their life savings had gone. But he had sympathised as she had talked to him about the situation, told him that, as the only child, it fell upon her shoulders to build up some kind of nest egg for them so that they wouldn't be terrified of growing old in poverty.

And even then, it had been awful but within the realms of possibility until her lovely, kind and gentle mother had had a heart attack and they had all been told by the consultant that stress could prove to be a fatal enemy.

The conversation that had been left behind, Alejandro's offer to pay her generously for helping him out, had begun to beckon.

When he'd raised the subject again, Caitlin's defences had been in a different place.

She had listened.

It still went against the grain. She still didn't get why he couldn't just come right out and tell the world that he was gay.

But she had listened.

Just a couple of days, he had told her with bright and breezy confidence. A small bit of acting, a make-believe relationship, enough to convince his parents that they were involved.

No dates would be set for anything and they would return to London, where they would resume their lives and he would be granted a reprieve.

Once his brother had married, he had assured her, everything would change and the pressure would be off. And of course, he had told her earnestly, he would tell them all the truth. It would be easier then.

And the money…

He had named a sum that had made her eyes water. All her parents' problems would go away. It would be like waving a wand. Caitlin had thought of her mother and the possible horrendous consequences of another heart attack brought on by ongoing stress… She'd thought of her father, who would never forgive himself for getting them into the mess that he had… She'd thought of two lives that would end in tatters…

And Alejandro's proposal had suddenly seemed like manna from heaven. She had swept past her hesitation and doubt and she had agreed.

Except, she was here now, and nothing was straightforward any more…

Not when Dante was in the driving seat, which he was. 'We're here.'

Caitlin surfaced and stared at the sprawling glass building facing her, abuzz with activity, its harsh, clinical contours softened by thoughtful planting of trees and shrubbery in strategic places.

Like royalty, Dante dumped the car right outside the building and it was efficiently collected by someone she could only assume was his driver, who had been forewarned to meet them there.

He strode into the white brightly lit corridors of the hospital and crowds parted. He glanced neither left nor right. He led the way with certainty and she tripped along in his wake, profoundly relieved that he knew just where he was going and what he was doing.

She spoke absolutely no Spanish and she couldn't think how difficult everything would have been had she come here on her own.

He spoke in rapid Spanish to a consultant who had been summoned, and then finally turned to her.

'I appreciate that you must find all of this very confusing.'

'I'm glad you're here,' Caitlin admitted with a smile. 'I have no idea how I would have coped. I would probably still be in a taxi trying to get the driver to understand where I needed to go.'

Dante shot her a sideways glance. 'I'm surprised you don't know any Spanish at all, given the fact that you're engaged to a Spaniard.'

For once, there wasn't that jagged edge of suspicion underlying his remark. He sounded genuinely curious as they began to walk along the corridor to the room previously indicated by the consultant.

'Alejandro did try,' she admitted. 'It only took him five seconds to realise that he wasn't going to get anywhere when it came to me picking up a second language.'

'Not interested?'

'Very interested but my brain just doesn't seem equipped to handle it.' She laughed.

Dante's dark eyes slid over to her. That laugh…as infectious as her smile. Unconsciously he glanced down at her sexy, round curves, the softness of her fair skin, the vibrant colours of her copper hair, which she had tied back into something resembling an untidy bun. She smelled faintly of flowers and sunshine. There was something intensely appealing about her lack of artifice and that appealing *something* dragged on his senses, made him hyperaware of her in ways he knew he shouldn't be. He knew the dangers of *different*. He knew what shame and wounded pride tasted like and he knew that the road that led there started with irrational temptation. It had that one and only time. It was a road he was never going to walk down again. On so many levels, the woman standing here was wrong and yet...

When he thought of the sort of woman he was destined for, a woman like Luisa, other thoughts pushed their way through, discomforting, uncontrollable thoughts that had no place in his life. Of course, he would never go there. He was supremely confident when it came to his ironclad willpower, but the mere fact that he couldn't stop his mind from wandering rankled.

'Somewhere along the line, I think my parents gave up on me being academic and so, in my head, I just ended up assuming that I couldn't do anything that wasn't creative. Hence my love of art and photography.'

'You should learn.'

'Why?'

'It might come in useful,' Dante interposed drily. 'Considering the circumstances.'

Caitlin laughed again. 'Oh, Alejandro and I won't be...' She went scarlet and came to a grinding stop.

'Won't be *what*?' Dante encouraged softly, his ears pricking up.

'Nothing,' Caitlin muttered. How could she have let all her defences drop with him? How had she managed to let that charm get under her skin and very nearly pull the rug from under her feet?

He was staring at her. She could feel the insistence of his eyes boring into her skin and she purposefully kept her head averted and, thankfully, they had landed up outside Alejandro's room so she had a very good excuse to ignore the guy towering next to her so that she could focus on her supposed fiancé, who was lying on the bed, for all the world looking as if he just happened to be in a deep sleep.

As peaceful as a baby, she thought, leaving her to deal with the fallout on her own.

'If it's okay, I'll go see him…on my own, if you don't mind.'

Dante didn't mind. He was still trying to work out what she had just said. It had slipped out and she had immediately regretted the oversight. He knew that and it wasn't just because she had gone a beetroot-red shade of intense discomfort, the intense discomfort of an adult who had very nearly broken the tidings to a gullible four-year-old that Santa wasn't real. He had *sensed* it, had sensed her horror at something that had very nearly been said.

What was it, though?

He was excellent when it came to reading people and reading, more importantly, what was between the lines. It was a talent he had ruthlessly exploited over the years, because it had always given him the upper hand when it came to the cut and thrust of dealmaking.

You never made it far by believing anything anybody said to you. He certainly never trusted anyone unless they had gone the distance to earn it. Few ever had.

Dante believed every word Caitlin had told him about her relationship with his brother, namely that they went back a way and had started out as great friends. He could see the *friend* bit clearly enough. It was what she *omitted* to say he found so intriguing, and that near slip-up she had narrowly escaped had compounded his suspicions.

She'd hurried into the room, closing the door behind her, and he watched through the pane of glass in the door as she pulled a chair closer to the bed and sat down, taking one of Alejandro's hands in hers for a quick pat and then leaning forward to talk.

There was no gentle caressing of the brow or tender kiss on the mouth, and after that perfunctory pat she had dropped his hand with shameless speed.

He would have given his right arm to have been a fly on the wall because, whatever she was saying, it didn't appear, reading her body language from behind, that she was soothing him with sweet nothings.

Dante spun round and was helping himself to some drinking water from a plastic cup when she approached to briskly thank him for delivering her.

'I can make my way to the shops from here,' she said firmly. 'We're in the centre of things. I won't need you to traipse behind me. If you want to visit with Alejandro, I can either meet you back here or else I'll grab a taxi to the house.'

'How did you find him?'

'He seems comfortable enough.' She sincerely hoped he'd heard every word she'd said when she'd told him in no uncertain terms that he'd been an idiot to have consumed his body weight in champagne and that she was really out of her depth having to cope with Dante, who watched her so closely that she felt uncomfortable every time she drew breath.

'Honestly, Alejandro,' she'd all but wailed, 'what on earth possessed us?' She wondered whether she had imagined the flicker of his eyes when she had said that. If he could hear her, then he was probably trying hard to blink in agreement.

'Wait here. I will come to the shops with you. You're about to tell me that there's no need but I wouldn't bother to waste my breath if I were you. You're new to Madrid and it's the very least I can do.' Under any other circumstances, Dante would have spent fifteen minutes with his brother and then continued on to his high-rise office in the city centre to pick up where he had left off on the work front, but the green-eyed, but-ter-wouldn't-melt-in-her-mouth redhead, trying not to look appalled, suddenly made all things work-related fade into the background.

'Fine.' Caitlin shrugged and took a seat outside the room and waited. For the first time, something loomed even more stomach-churning than the prospect of Dante lurking like a hangman's noose, and that was the thought of a shopping expedition she couldn't afford.

He wasn't long. Ten minutes at the most. Well, she thought, they barely had anything to say to one another when Alejandro was on top form, so lying unconscious on a hospital bed wasn't exactly going to be conducive to a lengthy visit.

'That was quick.' She'd aimed for sarcasm. She ended up with compassion because it was sad. Dante looked at her, his handsome face darkly rejecting the soft empathy in her voice and yet…as he raked his fingers through his hair and continued to stare, the atmosphere suddenly shifted. He wasn't retaliating, calling her to account, slamming the door in her face. He looked lost for words and, in that moment, intensely human and vulnerable.

'I'm sorry,' she said softly, reaching to rest her small hand on his arm.

'I don't do pity.'

'I'm still sorry. I always longed for a sibling but it wasn't to be. I'm sorry for both of you that, as brothers, you've drifted so far apart.'

'These things happen.'

'They do,' Caitlin agreed. Their eyes were locked and she had unconsciously stepped a bit closer towards him. 'But there's usually a reason behind it. I'm sad for you both because you seem to have just drifted into silence. It's crazy.'

'Not crazy,' Dante said roughly. 'In a busy life, things can sometimes drift. My fault. My brother's fault. Who knows? I agree…it's…not ideal.'

Caitlin smiled. 'Not how I would have described it…'

Dante smiled back. 'That's because you're emotional and I'm not.'

The silence that fell was brief, thrumming with something he couldn't put his finger on and broken when a woman said, from behind, 'Sorry, but am I breaking something up here?'

Dante spun round and Caitlin expelled a long breath and blinked at the leggy brunette staring at them with narrowed, assessing eyes.

'Luisa.' Dante pushed himself off the wall, his brain failing to instantly engage. It was sufficiently engaged, however, to bring home to him that Luisa was the last person he had any interest in seeing. She had been hard work at the aborted party the evening before, trying desperately to revive a relationship that was well and truly in the throes of rigor mortis. 'What are you doing here?'

Luisa pouted. 'I've come to see your brother, Dante. What else?' Her eyes were chips of diamond-hard ice as they briefly settled on Caitlin, who was fervently wishing that she could be anywhere but here. Deliberately eliminated from the conversation, she could only hover, acutely uncomfortable at being third wheel in whatever drama was unfolding between Dante and the other woman.

'I popped in to have a chat with your parents…' Luisa half turned, drawing Dante into a private huddle with her. 'They're so worried but I reassured them that Alejandro will be just fine.' She smiled broadly and lightly rested her hand on Dante's shoulder, making small stroking movements against the sleeve of his polo shirt. 'Maybe...' the smile was coquettish now and she had lowered her voice to a husky murmur '...you and I could go somewhere and grab a coffee? Maybe some lunch? That lovely little place we went to a few months ago would be perfect...'

'Did my mother happen to mention that I would be here?'

Luisa laughed nervously.

'No coffee, Luisa,' he said on an impatient sigh. 'No lunch. I'm heading into town. Caitlin needs clothes because she will be staying on. I am taking her shopping.' He glanced down at Caitlin and Caitlin saw a flash of venom cross Luisa's perfect face, gone in a heartbeat, replaced with a gentle smile of understanding.

'You're such a gentleman, Dante.' Luisa forced the smile in Caitlin's direction and flicked some non-existent fluff from her figure-hugging dress before shaking her hair and throwing back her shoulders. 'Of course, you must look out for your brother's fiancée, seeing that she has no one here at the moment and must be grief-stricken at what's happened. I'm sure I'll see you when things settle down.'

During this interchange, Caitlin hadn't said a word and she didn't as she and Dante both left the hospital and made their way into the bustling city.

CHAPTER FIVE

THERE WAS NO WAY to be polite and beat about the bush so Caitlin took the bull by the horns and said, bluntly, 'Is there some kind of market I could go to?'

She was discovering that going anywhere on foot was unacceptable to Dante. He had driven his sports car directly to the hospital, where it had been collected by his driver. She guessed it had been returned to the house, because no sooner were they out of the hospital and standing outside in baking heat than another car showed up, this time a black four-wheel drive with darkly tinted windows.

She was bundled into blissful cold and immediately turned to him to repeat her question.

'Why would you want to go to a market?' He frowned. 'Special dietary requirements? Tell me and I'll instruct a member of staff.'

'Not a food market, Dante. A flea market where I can buy clothes.'

'It's false economy buying cheap tat,' Dante returned smoothly. He spoke to his driver in rapid Spanish and she lapsed into fretful silence as they were driven to and deposited on a tree-lined avenue where elegant buildings with discreet pale awnings advertised a range of exclusive designer stores. Gucci rubbed shoulders with Louis Vuitton and Jimmy Choo, and some names she didn't recognise looked even more upmarket.

'Dante!' She turned to him with desperation as she was hustled out of the car to find herself on the pavement. 'I can't afford to shop in a place like this!'

'You're engaged to my brother.'

'What does that have to do with anything?' She literally had a vision of fifty-pound notes blowing away from her savings account.

'This is a ridiculous conversation. I can't believe my brother would not spend money on you.'

'I prefer to spend my own money buying my own clothes,' she retorted angrily. 'What sort of world do you live in, Dante? No, forget I said that! You enjoy throwing money at the women you go out with because it's easier than the other option!'

'You're crossing lines.' His jaw hardened. 'Be careful.'

'Or else what?' Caitlin rolled her eyes and placed her hand belligerently on her hips. 'Dante, it's easier to spend money than it is to spend quality time, isn't it?'

Dante flushed with outrage. 'More tête-à-têtes with my brother about me?'

'No! I'm just observant. I can see that Luisa is besotted with you but it's not returned—and, yes, Alejandro did say that you weren't keen on the notion of settling down.'

'Nor, presumably, is he, or he would have done it sooner.'

'It doesn't matter.' She sighed. 'I don't like accepting stuff from guys. It doesn't feel right. And I can't afford to buy anything in any of the shops on this fancy street.'

This was a first for Dante. The idea that a woman might resent having presents lavished on her puzzled him. What she viewed as some kind of insult to her feminism, he saw as an expression of appreciation.

'Caitlin, you're going to be here for at least a week. Who knows? Maybe longer. If you can't afford to spend money on yourself, then allow me. I do so on behalf of my brother. He can pay me back in due course, if it makes you feel easier. I hear what you're saying about not wanting to accept anything from anyone, but I feel that Alejandro would not want to think of you traipsing down to the local flea market. You're going to be entering a whole new dynamic when you marry my brother. Why not start adapting now? Besides, the flea market only opens on a Sunday.'

'Because people get engaged doesn't automatically mean they're going to get married,' Caitlin said vaguely. She realised that the deeper she dug her heels in, the odder it would seem to a guy like Dante, who lived in a completely different world from her. Alejandro shared that world. He would lavish gifts on whatever partner he ended up with.

She wasn't going to win this one.

'I suppose Alejandro—'

'Good.' He spun round on his heels and swept her along to a shopping experience she hadn't banked on.

This was how the other half lived. She'd seen it on a grand scale in his mansion. The priceless artwork, the acres of polished marble, the invisibility of his staff paid to make his life as fuss-free as possible.

For the next three hours, she experienced it first-hand when it was exclusively directed at her.

He had chairs brought for him so that he could sit,

his veiled expression revealing very little as clothes were fetched and carried. When money was no object, the attentiveness of the various boutique owners was ingratiating. They fawned and scurried and couldn't do enough.

And something deep inside Caitlin responded with a feminine enjoyment that was shameful because it just wasn't her.

Even before everything with her parents had fallen apart, plunging her into a financial nightmare, spending money on expensive clothes had never been her thing. Maybe it was her shape. In her head, expensive clothes were designed for a certain type of figure, one she didn't possess. Maybe it was the way she had been brought up. Her parents had always been sensible with money because they'd never had a great deal of it and it was an attitude that had been passed down to her.

Shopping with Dante Cabrera was not a sensible experience. The opposite. He snapped his fingers and people hastened to please. She was the beneficiary of his largesse and it was *thrilling*. She didn't want it to be, but it was.

Silk and soft cottons were laid for her inspection. The finest leather was brought out on show. She had had to resist the temptation to lovingly stroke some of the items of clothing.

'If you want an objective opinion,' Dante had drawled, standing next to her in that very first exclusive boutique, when the glamorous woman in charge had hurried off to find the right size for a dress Caitlin had guiltily admitted to really liking, 'then feel free.'

'No, thank you,' she had responded politely. But she had still *felt* his presence as he'd accompanied her on the shopping trip, had found her mind wandering back time and again to those dark, hooded eyes, his lean beauty, to the insane appeal of his lazy self-assurance.

His driver took bags of shopping to the car, patiently waiting wherever they happened to be.

It was exhausting and exhilarating at the same time and then, when it was over, when they were being ferried back to the house with half a store in the boot of the car, Dante murmured, softly, 'You should wear something you bought today to visit my parents. I accepted an invitation on your behalf. They're concerned about you...'

On a high from shopping, from breaking out of her comfort zone, temporarily freed from the unending stress of the past few months when every penny had had to be counted and allocated to a fund for her parents, Caitlin nodded. Yes. Why not? What was wrong with feeling like a living, breathing woman again? Just for an evening?

Dante's low-slung Ferrari glided through the iron gates, which opened silently at the press of a button.

It was mid-afternoon. He should still be at his glass high-rise in the Silicon Valley just outside the city centre.

Why was he here, driving up the tree-lined avenue towards his house?

Of course, he knew why. He hadn't been able to focus. He hadn't been able to focus for the past three days.

That shopping expedition...

Dante had been shopping with women before. He had always taken his laptop because, in between watching the inevitable parade of outfits, he had always been able to catch up on his emails as he'd positioned himself on a chair, in for the long haul.

He enjoyed lavishing presents on the women he went out with. Why not? He had more money than he knew what to do with. And women enjoyed being treated like queens.

Caitlin had not been one of them. Her remark about him throwing money at women because money was an easier sweetener to dish out than time and commitment had rankled. As far as he was concerned, it wasn't a case of one or the other. It was a case of him not being interested in commitment but enjoying being lavish. How were the two connected? He had refused to rise to the bait and had been outraged at yet another foray from the woman into his private life, which was and always would be out of bounds. She had accepted, finally, his offer to cover the cost of a new wardrobe, seeing that she was stuck in Spain, but he had then to persuade her that the purchase of cheap plastic shoes and disposable tat was out of the question.

What sort of man was Alejandro? he had privately questioned. Stingy? Surely not. He might not be on familiar terms with his brother, but stinginess didn't run in their family. So how was it that the woman he planned on marrying had to dip into her own pocket for essentials?

Dante knew that some might call him a dinosaur for thinking like that but he really didn't care. It was how he was, and he was shocked that his brother was not cut from the same cloth.

Accustomed as he was to the twirling of women as they tried on clothes, their insistence that he stay put so that he could give his opinion, Dante had been perversely fascinated by Caitlin's lack of interest in what he thought of her choices. Made sense, he knew, because it wasn't as though they were involved on any level, but he had still found himself dumping the laptop and watching what she went for even though there were no trying-on performances.

The three exclusive shops he took her to didn't offer anything he figured she would automatically make a beeline for. Nothing baggy. Nothing made from fabric better employed for curtains. Nothing designed for women who didn't want their bodies on show.

He'd found himself curiously keen to see the transformation and he had that very evening when he had stood there at the bottom of the stairs, glancing at his watch and waiting for her to emerge.

The dress she had worn to the ill-fated engagement party had revealed a figure she was at pains to hide. She had looked good but had clearly been ill at ease in it. The silk culottes and little matching silk vest she had worn to his parents' were much more her thing. She felt confident in them and that confidence spilled over into the way she moved, the way she carried herself, the way she walked. Did she imagine that, because they didn't cling to every inch of her, her figure was, somehow, less on display? If so, she was very mistaken. Knockout.

That was three days ago. The fierce pull of temptation had set alarm bells jangling in his head and he had dealt with the situation immediately. In between taking her daily to see Alejandro, he had cocooned himself away in his office at home and worked. He had told her that without the distractions that cropped up when he was accessible in his high-tech glass office, which was located some distance away from Madrid, in the equivalent of Silicon Valley, he could power-work and be at hand for any emergencies that might crop up at the hospital. They had met over dinner, prepared and left ready for reheating by one of his staff. They had made pleasant conversation about Alejandro, her job, the weather and various other bland topics. He had done his utmost to keep his eyes off her but, having told himself that she was out of bounds, he had been even more tempted to look.

He had noted the swing of her hips when she had carried her plate to the sink. He had been drawn to the fullness of her mouth every time she smiled. She had a tiny waist and that was apparent in the outfits she had bought—soft khaki shorts…a small denim skirt… a strappy dress with buttons down the front.

How could a man concentrate on work-related issues when the temptation of the forbidden had taken up residence in his head?

He had gone into his offices first thing that morning and had packed it in as soon as his meeting was over.

It was Friday. It was hot. He couldn't think straight. The constant interruptions had been getting on his nerves.

Made sense to return to his house and bury himself in his office as he had done previously. At least he wouldn't have to deal with his office door opening and shutting every three seconds.

So here he was. The simmering, dark excitement that seeped into his veins at the thought of seeing her was easy to dismiss as just the irrational pull of what was banned. The dangerous desire to hear her voice and indulge in those invigorating verbal sparring matches was a little more difficult to dismiss but Dante had every confidence in his capacity for self-control.

It was what made him the man he was today. No one ever rose to the top by allowing emotion to get the better of them and Dante, who had started with the sort of privileges most could only dream of, had risen to the very top, expanding his empire beyond belief, because of his ability to detach, his ability to suppress emotion in favour of cool-headed logic.

Cool-headed logic dictated that whatever temptations Caitlin posed, they were little more than titillating distraction in his high-powered but otherwise predictable life.

And anyway, he still wanted to find out what was going on with the woman, what the deal was between her and his brother, whether anything had to be severed before problems could arise.

So all in all...yes, it made complete sense to be returning home on a hot, sunny Friday afternoon...

From her bedroom window, Caitlin could appreciate the stretch of stunning manicured lawns, the clever array of trees that cast just the right amount of shade in just the right places. Facing towards the back of the house, she could almost delude herself into thinking that she was on holiday in some vastly expensive enclave for the super rich.

Dante was out of the house. She knew that because he had been leaving for work when she had descended that morning and had politely quizzed her about her plans for the day. His driver would be available, he had informed her, should she wish to go anywhere. He had already given her the guy's mobile number and she knew that, should she text Juan, a car would be ready and waiting to deliver her to any destination within seconds. When the wealthy snapped their fingers, people jumped to attention.

Were she on holiday, she now thought, stifling a sigh, then her head wouldn't be constantly buzzing with anxiety.

For the past few days, in between hospital visits and, on that one occasion, seeing Alejandro's parents for dinner, and generally trying to deal with Dante's unsettling presence, Caitlin had busied herself trying to sort out various stays of execution on loans she had discovered her parents had taken out, which they could no longer service. The deeper she dug into her parents' finances, and dig she did, the more rot she was discovering.

She communicated with her office but had already lost one job because she wasn't around to take it on. She felt their sympathy was not going to be limitless and her frustration was growing by the hour.

Dante had told her, on that very first evening, when Alejandro's fall had put paid to their carefully made plans, that when she wasn't worrying, she should see her stint out in Spain as a little holiday.

Caitlin had never heard anything quite so ludicrous but now, with the sun burning down on a vision of impeccable greenery outside the bedroom, in which she was trying vainly to concentrate on collating various archive photos for a project she had been working on for the past six weeks, she felt suddenly restless.

She had had eight months of unimaginable stress. She had functioned in her job, had tackled the problems thrown at her, had dealt with the horror of her mother's poor health in the wake of their financial woes, and she'd thought she was doing fine, all things considered.

But sitting here now, she felt that perhaps she wasn't. She felt weary, as weary as a hundred-year-old woman. Not only was she now anxious about Alejandro, but she feared she might lose her job if she stayed out here much longer and then where would that leave her? And her parents? She had worked out a repayment schedule for the loans with the intention of saving as much as she could to stockpile a little cash for them. What on earth would she do if she didn't have a pay cheque coming in? She certainly couldn't accept a penny from Alejandro, considering the outcome to what they had planned had crashed and burned.

Amongst the various items she had bought, there was also a swimsuit because, yes, she had seen the pool, and it had looked inviting and, besides, the swimsuit was the least wildly luxurious of all the items of clothing she had purchased. Two bits of stretchy black cloth.

Temptation beckoned. Dante wasn't around.

The house was vast and yet it still felt as though she saw too much of him when they were both in it. She tried to keep their conversation basic and polite whenever they crossed paths, but it seemed he had the knack of dragging confidences out of her because she always had to fight to stay true to the role she had taken on board, and not let her guard down.

When he fastened those dark, speculative eyes on her it was almost as though she were being slowly dragged into a vortex and she had to physically keep her distance from him just to hang on to some self-control.

Did he notice? She hoped not.

What mattered was that there would be no dark,

speculative eyes on her now. She had her window. Why not take advantage of it?

What else was she going to do? Think about all her problems and marvel that there was no way forward? Get depressed? Caitlin snapped shut her computer and headed for the chest of drawers to rifle through her meagre belongings for the bikini, which still had the tags on.

She changed quickly. She made her way down to an empty house. Everything that required doing had been done, and, in fairness to Dante, he was generous about letting his staff head home once their work was finished. It was Friday and the house was silent. Staff gone.

The unspoken rider to his generosity was that, should he discover any job half-done, then there would be all hell to pay. Caitlin assumed that that would be what he brought to the table in the work environment, as well. Total fairness. Big rewards for those who worked hard and deserved it but ruthless dispatch for those who failed to meet his standards.

She accessed the back garden through the kitchen door, which was spotless. There were always fresh flowers in a vase on the kitchen table and a balmy breeze lifted the muslin panels at the windows.

The scent of the flowers in the vase mingled with the smell of sunshine from outside and for a few moments the constant weight resting on her shoulders lifted, leaving her, for once, feeling like the young woman she was. Twenty-five, just, without a care in the world. The way it should be. Fresh in a job, going out with friends, with maybe a boyfriend in tow, and a future stretching out in front of her that promised everything even if, in the end, it fell short on delivery. Carefree. Happy.

Dante had told her that she should accept her en-

forced stay in Spain and enjoy it as a holiday rather
than an inconvenience. He had said that with barely
contained sarcasm as he had circled her like a shark
in a small tank, letting her know that he suspected her
motivations and would find her out in his own sweet
time. At the time, Caitlin could think of nothing more
unlikely than enjoying a second of her stay in Spain
under his roof, but it was so glorious outside and she
was so tired of being worn down and anxious.

The pool was wonderful, by far her favourite bit of
the estate. It was crystal clear, a flat blue infinity pool
flanked by decking that was slip proof but cleverly fashioned to look like glass. Around it, there was a verita-
ble plethora of shrubbery. Flowers in the brightest hues
of orange and yellow mingled with the deepest greens
of leaves and ferns, and strategically positioned trees
provided shelter from the sun, rather than umbrellas.
It was like a lake within a park.

Out here was tranquil in a way the inside of the house
never seemed to be. Even when there was no one to be
seen, she was always conscious of the fact that there
were housekeepers in the vicinity, cleaning and polish-
ing and preparing food and making sure that life was as
easy as possible for the master of the house.

Out here though...

Troublesome cares drained away as she basked in
the sun, slowly relaxing and letting the accumulation of
problems seep away. The water was wonderfully cool
and she swam lazily, up and down, up and down, getting into a rhythm.

Her eyes were half closed, her breathing even when
she surfaced at the deep end of the pool, blinked water
out of her eyes and realised that someone was stand-

ing directly above her, casting a long shadow over the crystal-clear water.

Dante.

His towering figure took shape as she blinked into the dazzling sun, shielding her eyes.

She clung to the side of the pool, heart suddenly hammering.

He was in swimming trunks and a tee shirt and barefoot and he looked spectacular.

Her mouth went dry and she couldn't think of anything to say, although, roaring through her head, was the single thought... *Shouldn't you be somewhere else?*

And if he was here...why wasn't he dressed in a suit and tie, on his way to a meeting somewhere? Why was he in swimming trunks?

'Thought I'd join you,' Dante answered the question she'd been asking herself. He looked at the pool, the calm perfect blue. He hadn't been in it for months. Longer. No time. But today, heading down the corridor to his bedroom to have a shower, he'd happened to glance through the long window on the landing and seen her. She'd been swimming, taking her time, her long hair streaming out behind her. He'd abandoned work early. The woman had put a spell on him and he knew that he had returned to the house because he'd wanted to see her.

He told himself that she was an enigma and that could only be a bad thing when it came to the situation between her and his brother. With Alejandro laid up in a hospital bed, Dante would have time to solve the riddle of what, exactly, was going on between the pair of them and take whatever steps were necessary. He could be decisive.

She was hiding *something*. Whatever happened to be going on between her and his brother, it wasn't a passionate and loving relationship between two people desperate to tie the knot.

So what was it? If Dante could excuse his preoccupation with her as the natural outcome of wanting to protect the Cabrera dynasty from a potential intruder, he would have. However, she failed to conform to the one-dimensional cardboard-cut-out image he would have liked.

She was witty, sharp and disrespectful. She should have been desperate to curry favour with him, to get him onside if her plan was to marry his brother and then set herself up in the enviable position of being able to lay claim to the family fortune. Her mission seemed to be the opposite. She was either ostensibly avoiding him or else openly arguing with him.

She fascinated him because she was so different from all the women he went out with and because he just couldn't work out what was going on with her.

So when he had glanced through that window and spotted her, he hadn't stopped to think. He'd headed straight to his bedroom, rummaged and found his swimming trunks, stuck on an old tee shirt, grabbed a towel and headed for the pool.

And here he was.

And there she was. Looking up at him, her face still wet, her hair dark from the water and fanning out around her like something from a pre-Raphaelite painting.

He hardened, felt that ache in his groin. He wondered whether coming down here had been the best of ideas. Maybe not.

'It's a hot day,' he muttered roughly, turning away to

strip off the tee shirt and then diving with fluid grace into the pool, only to surface and shake his head before raking his fingers through his wet hair.

Caitlin edged back in the water. 'I wouldn't normally have come in…but…'

'Don't apologise, Caitlin. I'm glad it's being used. It's maintained twice weekly and yet so seldom used that I can't imagine why I had it put in in the first place.'

She could feel her cheeks burning. She was very much aware of him barely clothed, his body so close to hers that she could reach out and touch him with no effort at all.

He was so beautiful.

Seeing him here, bare-chested, she realised that, somewhere deep in her subconscious, she had wondered what he might look like underneath his expensive gear.

He lived up to expectation. Broad-shouldered, narrow-hipped, his torso the right side of muscular. There was a strength to his physique that made her think that he could pick her up one-handed and not feel the strain.

Plus, he wasn't asking those questions, those vaguely pointed questions that always made her so uncomfortable and guarded and on the defensive.

He was being *nice*.

'Why did you, in that case?' she asked, looking at him briefly, eyes locking, before spinning away and swimming towards the shallow end of the pool because all of a sudden she had to escape the stranglehold of his presence.

He followed her. He covered the length of the pool in slow, lazy strokes and somehow ended up by her side without looking as though he'd expended any energy at all.

'I had the entire place renovated when I bought it years ago.' He picked up the conversation where he had left off, as though there had been no interruption. 'The architect and designer at the time both agreed that a swimming pool would be an asset.' He shrugged. 'It's very ornamental.'

'But as you say, if it's not used...'

'Maybe somewhere, at the back of my mind, I had high hopes of using it now and again.' He smiled ruefully and a tingle of heated awareness shot through her body, making her fidgety and uncomfortable.

'But then what happened?'

'Really want to know?'

Caitlin nodded. She was uncomfortable with the conversation because it felt strangely intimate, and yet she wasn't sure why she should feel uncomfortable because they weren't sharing secrets and he wasn't telling her anything he probably hadn't told lots of people who might have asked the same question she had. And yet...

'I never seemed to find the time. Alejandro went to London but here, in Madrid—this is the heartbeat of the company, and not just the family business, but all the other networks I have subsequently developed on my own. The heart never stops beating and I am in the centre of it. Finding time to use this pool became an empty wish.'

'You sound trapped,' Caitlin mused, looking at him with empathy before turning away to sit on the step. 'I always got the impression that there was nothing you enjoyed more than working.'

Dante lowered his eyes, his lush, sooty lashes brushing his high cheekbones. He seldom, if ever, had conversations like this with any woman but he was enjoying talking to her, enjoying her calm intelligence, her refusal to kowtow to him and, most of all, the fact that she wasn't flirting with him, doing her utmost to grab his attention by flaunting her assets.

She wouldn't be, though, would she? She was engaged to his brother. It was a reminder that was grudgingly acknowledged. She didn't act like someone who was engaged, but why did he constantly catch himself overlooking it? Was it a Freudian slip? Since when was he the sort of man who suffered from such weaknesses? After that one and only youthful error of judgement, from which lessons had been learnt, he had led a gilded life, where success after success had made him untouchable and given him an unshakeable confidence in his ability to control his destiny, so he was ill at ease with the fact that there were gaps in his armour he had never suspected.

'I'm far from trapped.' Was he, though? For one piercing second he envied the freedoms his brother enjoyed. He had an easy show to run, working in an office that was so well oiled he was barely needed at all, free to pursue just the sort of interests that had brought him into contact with the woman sitting next to Dante. He wondered whether there was a low-level, unconscious resentment that had fuelled the distance between himself and Alejandro.

Had he taken time to explore that possibility, was there a chance the chasm between them might have been bridged? And how was it that a stranger had been the one to propel him towards realisations he had barely acknowledged?

Caitlin shrugged and looked away. She was so intensely aware of him and the potency of his masculine appeal that she could scarcely keep her thoughts straight. She didn't trust herself to have the normal, inoffensive conversation the situation required.

Dante was finding her lack of interest in pursuing that tiny morsel of information thrown to her oddly annoying.

'And you?' he asked gruffly, shifting uncomfortably because he couldn't seem to look at the woman without his body misbehaving.

'What about me?' Caitlin raised her eyebrows with a slight frown.

'Do you feel trapped in the road you're going down? What's life like for you and my brother? What do you do together?'

Caitlin blushed. *What do good pals do*, she wanted to put to him, *except hang out together, listen to each other's woes, meet up as part of a group...?*

The charade stuck in her throat and for a few seconds she didn't say anything, but he was watching her, waiting for a response, and so she said, eventually, 'The usual.'

'The usual? What's that? Tell me?'

'What do *you* usually do with someone you're going out with?' Caitlin threw the question back at him, flustered.

'I wine them, I dine them, I shower them with whatever they want...'

'And then you dump them?' Caitlin was thinking of Luisa, the desperate yearning in her eyes when she had looked at him at the engagement party and the vicious jealousy when she had seen them together at the hospital, chatting. Was that how he handled all the women he dated?

Caitlin took a deep breath. The hot sun made her feel reckless and daring. The intimacy that was sending shivers up and down her spine was unfurling something dangerous inside her and suddenly she was fed up of tiptoeing around the danger. If the shark was going to attack, then why not weather the attack now?

'You're suspicious of me, aren't you? You think I'm after his money.'

'And if I am?'

'I don't know why you would be. What have I done to deserve your mistrust?'

If she cleared the air, then maybe he would back off. She didn't have to lie. She just had to be tactful. He couldn't very well call her a downright liar, could he? And if he was forced to tell her why he was suspicious, then she might be able to fudge her way through a few answers that might just satisfy him. She wouldn't be here for ever. A few days of peace was all she was after.

'I just can't picture the two of you together, as an item,' Dante murmured softly.

Caitlin thought of the leggy Luisa and she stiffened at the implied insult.

'I suppose you think I should be more like that ex-girlfriend of yours?' she said coldly. 'I suppose that, because that's the sort of woman you like dating, it's only to be expected that Alejandro should follow the same pattern? The last sort of woman he would ever go for would be someone like Luisa, even if, in *your* opinion, that would be the sort of woman you might be able to *picture* with him. As an item.'

Dante raised both eyebrows and there was a moment's silence.

'Are you insecure about the way you look?' he asked

lazily, and if Caitlin could have gone any redder, she would have.

'Of course not!' She whipped her head away and stared out at the marvellous vista, not really seeing any of it but instead conjuring up an unflattering picture of herself alongside Luisa. She thought of the woman her ex-boyfriend had fallen for and hated herself for returning to that unfortunate place, which she'd thought she had left behind. She thought of all those leggy beauties next to whom she knew she often came up short in the eyes of the opposite sex. Tears gathered in the corners of her eyes and she took a deep breath, refusing to give in to the weak temptation to feel sorry for herself.

'Because you shouldn't be.' The words left Dante's mouth, a silky murmur that was as dangerous as a dark incoming tide. 'The likes of Luisa Sofia Moore can't hold a candle to you.'

He raked his fingers through his hair. He'd broken eye contact but he was still alive to her warmth, the feel of her next to him.

'It's not just about how you look,' he breathed, reluctantly turning back to her, ensnared by the pure crystal green of her eyes. 'So why is he with you? That's what I find so puzzling. You're not background, Caitlin. You might not stalk into a room like Luisa, but you still know how to make your voice heard. Nobody has ever talked to me the way you have. So, you and my brother, Alejandro, who has never been known to say boo to a goose? No. I'm just not getting it.'

Caitlin didn't say anything and, into the silence, Dante continued roughly.

'Me,' he breathed, 'I'm the sort of man who could handle you. Not my brother.'

Those words hung in the air between them and then he leaned forward and so did she, without even realising it.

Her body moved of its own volition. A fractional movement. Her eyes closed drowsily and there was a buzzing in her ears as his mouth hit hers, hard and hungry and demanding. His fingers curled into her hair and she didn't want to, knew she shouldn't, but she returned that devouring kiss as though her life depended on it and then, just like that, he was pulling back.

She looked at him, horrified.

'If I had any questions,' Dante said in a flat, hard voice, 'trust me, they have now been answered.'

With which he vaulted out of the water, his bronzed muscular body glimmering with droplets that glistened in the glare of the sun, while she remained frozen in place, like a block of ice.

Watching and barely breathing as he walked away.

CHAPTER SIX

DANTE DIDN'T KNOW who repelled him more. Himself, for his lack of control that had propelled him into crossing lines that should never have been crossed, or her, for crossing those lines with him when she was engaged to his brother.

He didn't glance back as he strode away from the pool back towards the house.

All those questions that had been buzzing in his head ever since he had found out who she was now raged inside him, an angry swarm searching for answers.

Work.

He would bury himself in his work because that always did the trick. He hadn't made it to the house before he realised that no amount of work was going to do the trick this time. He didn't know what Caitlin was doing. He didn't want to know. His mouth still burned from where her cool lips had opened beneath his and so, much to his rage, did his body.

He'd never responded to any woman the way he'd responded to her.

Was it because she was off limits? Maybe there was some deeply buried need to take what belonged to his brother. Was that it? Dante didn't think so. He had never wanted anything Alejandro had possessed. In fact he had no idea what women his brother had dated in the past, but he was quite sure he would never have dreamt of lusting after any of them. It just wasn't in his nature. He'd never lusted after any man's woman in his life before. Hadn't come close. He was a red-blooded male with a healthy libido and he enjoyed the pleasure of sex but, even in that faraway place where mistakes had been made, he couldn't recall having experienced this fury of attraction that wiped out everything in its path.

What the hell was going on here?

He dressed fast, shrugging out of his swimming trunks, replacing them with jeans and the first tee shirt that came to hand, and then back out he went, to his car, which was parked at an angle in the courtyard.

Where the hell was she? He hated himself for even wondering.

He arrived at the hospital with no idea where he was going with this, but he had a driving need to confront his brother, which was ridiculous given the fact that Alejandro was dead to the world.

Dante had kissed her. She'd kissed him right back. No coercion on his part! She'd melted in his arms and he had enjoyed every second of it. He just had to think about the piercing sweetness of her mouth, the way her soft, small, luscious body had curved towards him, and he could feel the stirring of an erection. Her clear green eyes, as they had fastened on him with smouldering hunger, had woken a sleeping monster in him he hadn't known existed.

Dante was rarely confounded by anything or anyone, but he was confounded now.

The hospital was quiet as he made his way to his

brother's ward. They knew him at the desk so, when he nodded at the little cluster of nurses and medics chatting by the reception desk, they smiled and gave him the go-ahead to enter the room.

He was going to have to tell Alejandro what had happened. He was going to have to find answers to the questions rolling around in his head. He was going to have to try to find out what, exactly, was going on.

He had no idea how he was going to accomplish this because his brother wasn't going to be answering anything any time soon, but he had to get things off his chest.

Dante pushed open the door and let it swing on quiet hinges behind him, then he pulled one of the visitor chairs next to the bed and looked at his brother.

Now that everything had been stabilised, Alejandro could have been peacefully sleeping. His breathing was gentle and even.

'We need to talk,' Dante began.

He smiled at the incongruity of the statement, then the smile disappeared and he thought, out of the blue, when had he ever said that to his brother? When had he ever met up with him just so that they could talk? About everything and nothing? Without a sense of duty hanging over both their heads, aware only that, as brothers, meeting up now and again, however uncomfortable, was just something they should do?

'Something has happened, Alejandro...' He structured his thoughts. Caitlin's image popped into his head, and he gritted his teeth together because never had his body been so relentlessly disobedient. How was he going to break this to his brother? Was it even right to try? He couldn't be sure that Alejandro would hear a word he said and, even if he did, who knew whether he would remember any of the conversation?

Many of Dante's doubts stemmed from his interaction with Caitlin. He had listened and watched and everything inside him had questioned the relationship she was purporting to have with Alejandro. Her reaction to Dante earlier by the pool…that kiss…was just the icing on the cake.

She wasn't some besotted lover, starry-eyed over his brother, counting down until the wedding bells began ringing.

Nor did his brother seem to be head over heels, like a swooning hero in a fairy tale.

But what if he was wrong about Alejandro? It wasn't as though he knew how his brother thought. It wasn't as though they had the sort of bond that might allow him any insight into what went on in Alejandro's head and in his heart.

Was Dante willing to say what he had to say, to risk Alejandro taking everything in under that serene lack of consciousness and remember that the woman to whom he was engaged was not what she seemed?

Was Dante willing to break his brother's heart?

His jaw clenched. This sort of truth, he thought, was worth imparting. He wished to God someone had saved him months of pointless infatuation with a woman who had turned out to be as pure as mud, by setting him straight at the very outset.

Haltingly, expecting nothing in response, he began to explain.

Alejandro would sleep through it all. Dante was one hundred per cent certain on that point.

He was, however, wrong.

* * *

It took ages for Caitlin to get her act together because he had kissed her...no, they had *shared* that kiss...and everything inside her had gone into free fall.

She had felt his mouth on hers long after he'd disappeared back into the house and it was only when he'd gone that her brain had begun functioning and she'd remembered, with sickening horror, what he had flung at her when he'd walked off.

If he'd had any questions, then they'd been answered.

You didn't have to be a genius to get the drift. She'd kissed him and the sham of her relationship with Alejandro had been revealed. In a handful of seconds, she had done the one thing she'd been determined not to do. She'd given the game away. Nor could she now be honest. How could she? Alejandro's secret was his to reveal, so she would have to accept that Dante would now see her as the worst possible candidate for the role of his brother's fiancée.

She hurried back to her bedroom, fearful that she might bump into Dante somewhere in the house, but she didn't. Just in case, however, she dressed quickly, and called a taxi to take her to the hospital. While she waited for it to arrive, she remained locked in her bedroom.

She had no idea what was going to happen next, but, playing it out roughly in her head, it involved her going to see Alejandro, where she would just have to explain what had happened and tell him, whether he could hear her or not, that she had no option but to return to London.

She could always leave a text on his mobile phone and he would pick it up as soon as he came to, and, naturally, she would phone the hospital daily, but leaving was her only option when the alternative was to run slap bang into Dante at some unspecified time in the future.

She felt very bad about his parents, but what choice did she have?

On the spur of the moment, she wrote a note, which she left in her bedroom, to be given to his mother, apologising for her abrupt departure and blaming work demands.

She would have some appreciation of what that meant considering at least one of her sons had sold his soul to the workplace.

The minute she thought of Dante, her mind began shutting down and her heart picked up pace and she had to close her eyes and breathe deeply so as not to feel faint.

That kiss.

There had never been anything like it in her life before. Jimmy…solid, reliable, steady Jimmy had never made her heart beat fast. She had liked him and they had fumbled around a bit but neither had had the slightest urge to take things to the ultimate conclusion.

He'd lived with his dad and she'd been living with her parents and it was a small village where everyone knew everyone else. Renting a room in their one and only hotel would have been ridiculous.

They would look forward to really enjoying making love when they were married, they had vaguely told one another. Actually, she wasn't even sure they had discussed it at all, simply assumed that that would be how things worked out between them.

Afterwards, when he had dumped her for the improbable model, she had been realistic enough to conclude that he hadn't pushed for sex because, as much as he'd liked her, he hadn't been attracted to her. Not really.

She hadn't stopped to ask herself whether *she'd* been attracted to *him*.

She'd nursed her wounded feelings and escaped.

Now, Dante had kissed her and it had been a thunderbolt. *That* was what passion felt like. *That* was the sort of aching and yearning that would have been impossible to ignore. She felt as though she had been sleepwalking and now she was fully awake, for better or for worse.

The taxi driver took his time getting to the hospital. On the way, he insisted on having a long conversation with her in Spanish, even though her responses were limited to an array of vaguely interested expressions and non-committal murmuring.

In her head, she was working out how she might get a flight back to London. Bye-bye to yet more money she didn't have. She would just have to go to the airport with her bag in hand, get to a ticket desk and pay whatever it cost for the first flight out.

Funny thing, she mused, hurrying into the hospital and pausing for a few seconds to get her bearings because the place was just so huge and she couldn't seem to keep a mental tab on which lift she needed to take to get to his ward, Alejandro would have understood her dilemma.

They would have spent hours laughing and talking about the mess she'd got herself into.

She hit the ward and was heading towards the reception desk when she saw Dante.

His face was grim, drawn. Given half a chance, Caitlin would have fled in the opposite direction, but two things stopped her. The first was the sight of Dante striding towards her, a man on a mission, eyes firmly pinned on her hovering figure even though he was on his phone, talking urgently to someone at the other end.

The other was the fact that there was a commotion happening outside what seemed to be Alejandro's room, even though it was hard to be completely sure.

It was the latter that fired her forward and she reached Dante just as he shoved his phone back in his pocket.

'What's happening?' Caitlin breathed, trying to peer around his body but not getting very far. 'Is Alejandro okay? All those people… Is that his room or someone else's?' Her eyes were already filling up at the thought of her friend having some kind of unforeseen setback.

'My brother is awake.'

'What?'

'It is as if he's been having a nap and now he's up and ready to start the day.'

'That's…that's amazing. I have to go and see him, talk to him…' She took a step to the left and Dante reached out and blocked her from stepping forward with a hand on her arm.

Caitlin froze. Her mind emptied of everything. All she could feel was the burning touch of his fingers on bare skin.

'He's going to be wheeled off for a battery of tests,' Dante was saying, while she desperately tried to focus on something, *anything*, other than his hand on her arm. 'There's no point in you trying to get to him.'

'But—'

'I've just been on the phone to my mother and said exactly the same thing to her. As you can imagine, she is as keen to see Alejandro as you are.'

Caitlin finally looked directly at Dante and inwardly quailed because all too clearly she could remember the inappropriate kiss that had galvanised his appalled withdrawal and damning judgement.

Should she bury the memory and pretend that nothing had happened between them? Or bring it out into the open, get rid of the elephant in the room before it started wreaking havoc? Or did it matter anyway, considering she was planning on clearing off as soon as she got back to Dante's house?

The decision was taken out of her hands when Dante said, coolly and firmly, leading her away from Alejandro's room towards the double doors back out into the main body of the hospital, 'You and I need to have a little chat.'

'About what?' At that very moment, Caitlin decided that pretending nothing had happened was definitely going to be the best option. 'I really think I should stick around here for a bit…see what's happening with Alejandro before I go—'

'Before you go?' Dante pulled to an abrupt halt and stared down at her with a veiled expression.

'Work is beginning to get a little impatient, Dante. I honestly can't stay over here indefinitely. My parents are also… They're anxious about me…'

'You're a big girl,' Dante gritted. 'I'm sure your parents will understand why you've stayed on.'

Caitlin didn't say anything. She had spoken to her mother the evening before and had detected the stress in her voice with a sinking heart. Her parents were clinging to their composure by the skin of their teeth and, more than ever in their lives, relying on her to steady them in stormy times.

Soothing, long-distance conversations were just not the same as seeing them face to face, being able to have a cup of tea, to hold her mother's hand and assure her that everything was going to be just fine.

Her father was doing his best, but he had always been the easy-going one between the two of them and now that her mother was on the verge of cracking up, her father was fighting his own battle with low-level panic, paralysed by the fear that everything he had worked for, what little remained, would somehow be wiped out from under his feet, and plagued with guilt at the thought that he had been the one responsible for all their problems.

How much longer could she just hang around?

'Don't tell me what my parents can or cannot understand,' she said sharply. 'I'm overjoyed that Alejandro has regained consciousness. I had planned on leaving later today but now I'll see him when he's up to visitors and I will leave for London as soon as I do afterwards.'

Dante didn't say anything. He had no intention of having any kind of showdown inside a hospital, so he spun round on his heels, making sure to keep his fingers firmly locked round her arm, and began leading her quickly towards the exit, ignoring the bank of lifts in favour of the stairs.

His car, in the underground car park, was waiting for them and they made their way there in complete silence.

There would be enough to talk about in due course, he thought.

'Where are we going?'

'To a café I know in the Plaza Mayor.'

'But can't you just tell me what you need to tell me right here?' She knew what he was going to say. He was going to mention that wretched kiss. He was going to voice all the suspicions that had been playing around in his head ever since he had set eyes on her. As far as he was concerned, she had offered up conclusive proof that he had been right to have been suspicious. He was going to call her to account and she couldn't blame him.

But it surely wasn't going to be a long conversation!

Was it even going to be a conversation at all? Or a full-frontal attack, which she would deal with by being as unresponsive as possible?

Judging from the way she had been frogmarched to his car, she was going for the full-frontal attack.

But at least they would not be having it at his house. At least, in the public arena, she wouldn't feel quite so overwhelmed.

And the Plaza was just a wonderful place, a beautiful rolling arcade ringed with stunning sepia-and pastel-coloured buildings, a tribute to history and the stunning architecture of the period.

She might just be able to sideline his attack by absorbing her surroundings, a sort of displacement therapy.

The café was nestled in one of the sepia-coloured shops. From the outside, it looked as though it might be on the verge of collapse. Inside, it was a marvel of modernity, with a long steel counter behind which five chic young girls catered for the needs of the most discerning of coffee drinkers and pastry consumers.

'I had no idea my brother would come to when I went to see him,' Dante opened. 'I had to go because of what happened between us at the pool.'

Caitlin cringed. 'About that…' she said faintly. She couldn't look at him. She couldn't meet those arresting dark eyes that were pinned to her face. For the first time, she wondered whether he had kissed her because he had been caught up in the moment, just as she had been, or whether he had kissed her as some kind of test to find out whether she really was the adoring fiancée she claimed to be.

She felt sick. Her stomach churned. All her insecurities pointed her in the direction of that kiss being nothing more to him than a means to an end. Why else would a guy like Dante, a guy who could turn his back on a woman who looked like Luisa, look at *her*? Yes, he had said something about her being *sexy*, but of course he would say that to butter her up and lower her defences for the moment when he leaned into her for that kiss, testing the ground, feeling his way to the answers he had been seeking.

'Yes?' Dante enquired coolly. He sat back as his double espresso was put in front of him, the attractive waitress taking her time as she positioned the cup *just so*. His eyes remained fixed on Caitlin's face, keenly noting the delicate bloom of colour in her cheeks. A guilty conscience would do that to a woman, he thought tightly.

'I never meant for that to happen.'

'I'm sure you didn't,' he responded smoothly. 'Engaged to one brother but happy to get into an intimate clinch with the other? Not exactly an example of a woman with sterling moral principles, is it?'

Trapped by a secret that wasn't hers to share, Caitlin could only bow her head in silence.

She would accept the full force of his condemnation. She would be gone in a heartbeat and she would be able to put it all behind her, except she knew that that would be easier said than done. Idiot that she was, she actually *cared* about what he thought of her.

Somehow, she had been incapable of locking the man away in a convenient one-dimensional box. She'd tried, but he'd broken out of it and come right at her with all those complexities that had turned him into a living, breathing, fascinating guy who had fired her up in ways she would never have dreamt possible.

That was why she had kissed him. He stirred a crazy attraction inside her and she just hadn't been able to resist, but she knew how it looked on the outside. Kissing him had boxed her in as a two-timing woman who was happy to fool around behind her fiancé's back.

'You don't understand,' she said, without much hope of him paying a blind bit of notice to what she had to say. 'I know what it looks like, but I'm not that kind of person.'

'Thank you for telling me that. That answers all my questions.'

'There's no need to be sarcastic.'

'Then try coming at me with something a little better.'

'What do you want me to say?'

'What about the truth?'

'I'm telling you the truth. I'm not that kind of girl. I don't…' She looked away and fell silent because there was nowhere to go with an explanation.

'I told my brother about that kiss and you'll never guess his response.'

Caitlin was pretty sure she could.

'Actually, I had no idea my conversation would prove to be the thing that would rouse my brother from his deep and peaceful sleep, but it was. I started to talk to him…'

Dante paused and recalled the way he had felt, opening up to a sleeping Alejandro. For the first time he had felt something strong and bonding. It had been the one and only meaningful conversation he had ever had with Alejandro. The fact that Alejandro had been unconscious at the time had made it easy, had removed the inhibitions born over time.

Dante met her eyes and sucked in a sharp breath. So green, so crystal clear...so full of a disingenuous innocence that was way off mark. 'I started to talk to him and *bang*. He opened his eyes and was as with it as though he'd never been dead to the world at all. Funny thing, he didn't seem all that perturbed by what we did. I had expected some kind of forceful reaction, had braced myself for his disgust and loathing for my weakness. I didn't get any of that. Does that surprise you?'

Faced with that direct question, Caitlin frantically tried to compose an answer that would make sense. The truth was off the table. She stared down at her empty coffee cup and licked her lips nervously.

'He's...er...a very understanding kind of guy, as I'm sure you'd know if you'd ever taken the time to find out about him.'

Dante could only admire her attempt to divert him from her non-answer by launching a missile at him.

'Nice try but it won't work.'

'Maybe we don't have a conventional relationship.' Caitlin didn't bother to ask him what he'd just meant by that because she knew.

'What do you mean?' Like a shark sensing blood, Dante felt on the verge of a revelation. If his head had temporarily been elsewhere, he was now once again committed to the task at hand. He pushed his cup to one side and leaned forward, resting his forearms on the table.

'I know what you were trying to do when you kissed me,' she said, swerving round his question.

'Come again?'

'You wanted to see if I would respond. You pretended to be attracted to me, you said lots of stuff you didn't mean, because you knew that if I responded then you would have all your suspicions confirmed. You want to push me into a corner and paint me black, but leading me on? That's sly.'

'You think I'm *sly*?'

Caitlin looked at him in stony silence.

'You couldn't be further from the truth,' he gritted brusquely. 'I'm not a man who plays that kind of game.' This was getting off point and he dragged his runaway thoughts back to the matter at hand.

'You and Alejandro. You were telling me that what you had wasn't a conventional relationship. Explain.' He shifted in the seat and tried to focus. He wasn't going to let her derail the conversation by veering off at random tangents, but he couldn't help but admire the antics. She was a match for him and he liked that.

'We were both great friends.' She was going to have to tiptoe round all manner of minefields, but Dante wasn't going to let up. 'Things went from there.'

Dante waited. Nothing further seemed forthcoming. He was very happy to play the long game, but eventually, he said, 'You *drifted* into a relationship because you happened to be good friends?' He looked at her with rampant incredulity.

'Friendship is a very good basis for a relationship,' Caitlin said defensively.

'And you would have married him? He would have married you? I find that hard to believe. For starters, you're young. Why would you abandon the one thing most women seem to want? Love, passion and a belief in fairy stories about happy-ever-afters? Nor do I understand why my brother would do the same.' But Dante knew that *he* had no faith in the institution of marriage. Love and fairy stories? No way. His own experience had taught him that any permanent relationship should always have a solid basis in reality. He'd fallen for the wrong woman once upon a time and his guard was permanently up. Maybe Alejandro was fashioned from the same cloth. Maybe he, too, had had an unfortunate experience that had taught him that a marriage of convenience was the way forward. Who knew?

And his parents *had* been getting quite vocal on the subject of their eldest son settling down.

Maybe he'd decided to opt for the friend knowing that he wouldn't be troubled by a demanding or jealous woman who might end up wanting more than he was prepared to give.

That was certainly the lens through which he, Dante, viewed relationships...

He felt as though he was clutching at straws, but what else could explain his brother's nonchalant reaction to what had happened at the pool between himself and Caitlin?

But why would Caitlin have gone along?

'I had a terrible experience once upon a time,' Caitlin said softly, severing any further conclusions he might have been formulating on the subject of her and his brother. 'I was engaged to a guy. We'd known each other for ever, and in a small village like the one I grew up in that counts for something. Getting married was expected. Except no one—not me, not Jimmy, none of our family or friends—could foresee a five-foot-ten model swanning into his life and sweeping him off his feet.'

Reliving the moment, Caitlin realised that she felt next to nothing thinking about it now.

'He felt sorry for me. That was the toughest part. I suppose everyone did. I left for London and I put men behind me. I wasn't going to get involved with anyone ever again. Alejandro,' she tacked on truthfully, 'made sense.'

'Well, I hate to burst the bubble, but you might have to start rethinking that scenario,' Dante gritted. 'Alejandro's feathers weren't ruffled at the thought of me kissing you. Are you happy to settle for someone who doesn't really give a damn what you do and with whom?'

'I've talked enough,' Caitlin muttered, rising to her feet. She felt hemmed in and suffocated by Dante's oppressive presence and the sheer force of his personality. 'I'm going to see Alejandro...'

'No point.' Dante stood up, dumping money on the table, more than enough to cover the coffee they had ordered. 'Like I said, he's having a battery of tests. You won't be able to see him until tomorrow.'

'I'd planned on leaving this evening,' Caitlin reminded him, digging her heels in and refusing to be bullied.

'That's the thing about plans. They often have to change.'

For a moment, they stared at one another, and then Caitlin broke eye contact and began walking towards the door, only to stop because she was going to have to return to the house and with Dante, unless he decided to hang around in the city centre for no apparent reason.

'I'm very sorry about what happened at the pool,' she said in a stilted voice as they began leaving the city, heading out towards his house. *Clear the air*, she thought. He had and so should she. 'I think it's best if I pack my bags when I get back. Don't worry about me. I've got stuff to do. Tomorrow, I can easily take a taxi in to the hospital and then I can leave for the airport straight from the hospital. I don't know if I'll get a flight immediately but…but…' She ran out of steam and stared straight ahead at the scenery whipping past.

For a while, Dante didn't say anything.

He could sense her nerves. She had every right to be nervous. She also had every right to apologise about what had happened by the pool. He wasn't proud of himself, but he wasn't the one with a ring on his finger, even if the engagement was a complete sham from the sounds of it.

'I expect,' he said smoothly, 'that the touching engagement will now be a thing of the past? Our parents will be bitterly disappointed.'

Caitlin glanced at him.

This engagement was a charade but it was one that had suited both of them. So what happened next? It was something she would have to discuss with Alejandro. Did he still want to buy time? Dante might believe that theirs was just a convenient arrangement but many unions were based on less. She certainly wasn't going to commit to one thing or the other until she had spoken to Alejandro.

'Well?' Dante prompted sharply. They were nearing his house, all signs of habitation falling away to open land with the occasional manor to be glimpsed through imposing gates.

'I don't know what's going to happen.'

'You don't love my brother, Caitlin.'

'But I do.'

Dante killed the engine and swivelled so that he was staring at her with brooding intensity. Frustration soared through him. He'd thought he'd got what he wanted but had he? What did she mean by that?

'Love without passion is the recipe for an empty marriage. And then there's us…let's not forget about that…' His voice was lazy now and pensive.

'There's no *us*.'

'No,' he agreed, 'there isn't, but you went up in flames when I kissed you. Don't worry. It was a mistake to touch you but I won't be succumbing to the temptation again. It's not in my nature to pursue any woman who belongs to someone else.'

Caitlin laughed shortly. *'Belongs to someone else? What era are you living in, Dante? I don't belong to anyone.'*

'Oh, but you do. Friends or no friends, you're my brother's lover—'

'I'm not!'

Stunned silence greeted this. For a moment, Dante was lost for words. The idea that two people could be engaged without having consummated their relationship beggared belief.

'And on the subject of lies…' Did she think he was born yesterday? Was she hoping to airbrush away their little moment of intimacy by pretending that fidelity to Alejandro wasn't imperative because they weren't lovers?

'I'm not lying,' Caitlin whispered.

'Tell me my brother isn't a substitute for your ex-lover,' Dante said sharply. 'No man wants to bed a woman who's thinking of some love she had and lost.'

'You don't get it, Dante!'

'*What* don't I get?'

'I'm not some scarlet woman! I haven't slept with your brother and…and…'

'And?'

'And I don't have any ex-lovers tucked away in my head, demanding my attention and messing up my life! I don't have any *ex-lovers* at all!'

'I don't get what you're saying.'

'What do you *not* get?' Caitlin finally snapped. 'I don't have any ex-lovers because I'm still a virgin!'

CHAPTER SEVEN

CAITLIN DIDN'T KNOW who was more stunned by that admission, Dante or herself.

She didn't wait to find out either, pulling open the car door and leaping out, heading at speed towards the front door.

Dante, on the other hand, took his time getting out of the car, grasping the roof and swinging his long body out.

Virgin? *Virgin?* Could she possibly be lying about that? No. He had seen the mortified embarrassment wash over her face in a red tidal rush, and he had known that she'd been telling the truth.

But her confession left him more confused than he already was.

Why was she engaged to his brother? What was going on? But then, the cogs in his brain began to crank back into life and he knew that there could be only one conclusion.

Alejandro was very kind, one of the world's gentle souls. Growing up, he had been the one in the kitchen helping the housekeeper cook while Dante had been kicking a ball outside or climbing a tree. Later, when rugby and black-run skiing had replaced the ball kicking, Alejandro had remained in the kitchen, but this time enjoying the business of preparing food and eating it, happy to read and pursue isolated hobbies. Dante had never really been able to get it.

What he was getting now, though, was the reality that his brother had doubtless found himself in a pickle. Their parents had become increasingly anxious to see their eldest son settle down and produce a few heirs to the throne.

And into this scenario, cue stage door to the left, came Caitlin, wounded by heartbreak, disillusioned with the whole business of love, and yet still desirous of having a family.

Two and two had made four and although she and his brother weren't in love, they liked each other well enough to do a sensible deal.

Hence Alejandro's lack of reaction when he, Dante, had mentioned that kiss by the pool.

He truly didn't fancy Caitlin. That was something Dante simply couldn't understand because he had never in his life found any woman more alluring.

A virgin!

He looked at her for a second, pausing. She was standing by the front door, every part of her body trembling with the urge to escape as fast as she could after her admission.

She couldn't have been dressed in an outfit less appealing to Dante. Somewhere along the line, she'd bought two long flowered skirts that harked right back to some distant hippie era. She was wearing one of these now. The mesh of swirling colours would give anyone a headache were they to make the mistake of staring for too long. Twinned with this was a short-sleeved tee shirt that was neither loose nor tight.

And yet nothing could disguise the intense sensuality of her body. He clenched his jaw hard.

Okay, so maybe the situation was a little more blurred than he'd first thought. Maybe what was an engagement, given the weird circumstances, couldn't be called *a relationship* at all. Doubtless it was just a matter of time before she broke it off, because all that rot about love and friendship counted for nothing when the shimmer of passion hovered in the background like a steady haze, and he had shown her that shimmer of passion.

Would she easily be able to go back to the empty dryness of a situation in which affection was the sum total of what she felt?

She was glaring at him, her face tight with the strain of suppressing her emotions, her hair all over the place. She looked like a wild cat and he marvelled that Alejandro could ever have thought that such a fiery creature could submit to a non-relationship indefinitely.

Heartbreak or no heartbreak.

Dante strolled towards her. She didn't have a key or he was pretty sure she would have been firmly locked in her bedroom by now.

He slotted his key in the door, pushed it open and stood aside as she brushed past him.

'Caitlin.' His voice was rougher than he'd expected and he felt suddenly awkward.

'What?' She spun to look at him, her body taut and straight as an arrow, every nerve in her body still shimmering with heightened emotion. What had possessed her to share that most intimate of secrets with him? What?

'Join me in the kitchen for something to drink. Maybe eat. It's been quite a day.'

Caitlin opened her mouth to tell him that she would

rather not but then she thought, so she had let slip that detail about herself... What of it? She had simply tried to defend herself against the slur of being a two-timer without a conscience. What was wrong with that? And what was the big deal with being a virgin? Why should she be embarrassed? It was her body to give when she wanted, not when the world deemed it suitable. She would far rather live a life being choosy about the person she chose to share herself with than sleep with any and everyone just because...

Besides, on a more pedestrian note, she didn't want to spend the remainder of the day hiding away in her bedroom. Why give Dante the satisfaction of thinking that he had got to her?

She could either allow herself to be swept along on a fierce tide of helpless reaction or else try hard and fast to emulate his cool control.

She nodded and forced her reluctant legs to follow him into the kitchen.

Every gadget was high-end and polished to gleaming perfection, including the extraordinary coffee maker, which was a work of art in itself, but Dante bypassed that and headed for the fridge, which was concealed behind the banks of glossy grey cabinets.

It wasn't quite yet six but he offered her a drink, a glass of wine. Desperate to calm her nerves, Caitlin accepted with alacrity and finished glass number one at speed, instantly relaxing as the alcohol began coursing through her veins. It was easier to talk to Dante when she wasn't battling low-level panic and sickening awareness of his intense physicality. The wine lowered her defences and muted her nerves and, after a while, she knew that she was relaxing into normal conversation about Alejandro, now that he had regained conscious-ness, so she was unprepared when Dante suddenly sat forward, his dark eyes pinning her to the spot, his body angled forward so that she felt the heat he emanated.

'So talk to me. Tell me. I'm curious…' he said softly.

'Talk to you about what?' She had already finished two glasses of wine but as her eyes sought out the nearly empty bottle of Chablis, Dante relieved her of that easy route to Dutch courage by gently moving her glass out of reach.

'Why you've never slept with a guy.'

Instantly Caitlin stiffened. 'I should never have told you that.'

'But you did and I'm glad you did. The pieces are falling into place. So talk to me, Caitlin. Tell me why.'

'I already told you. I was hurt. I picked up the pieces and moved on.' She looked at him narrowly, alert for any show of mocking cynicism, but he was listening intently, his lean, beautiful face interested and non-judgemental, and she had a sudden fierce urge to con-fide. When she had left for London, she had locked away her past but now it was clamouring at the door, begging to be released. 'I just lost faith in relationships.' She paused. 'You wouldn't understand.'

'You might be surprised. I had a bad experience my-self once upon a time.' Dante was shocked by an ad-mission he had never shared with another living soul.

'Really?' Caitlin had never been more curious. 'Was it Luisa?'

That made Dante laugh, banking down his natu-ral unease with sharing anything of a personal nature with anyone.

'I was nineteen,' he mused, 'and she was…older.

With a child. I foolishly flung myself into something I thought had legs only to find out that she was not who she claimed to be. She was after my money and I had a lucky escape because I found out before I'd committed to something that would have ended up more than just a major headache. Nevertheless, I managed to squander a substantial amount of money in the process.'

Caitlin nodded, instantly understanding that, for a man as proud as he was, such a miscalculation would have been a source of bitter humiliation, even though he would never admit as much.

A low stirring began deep inside her. She felt hot and restless, her senses heightened in a way they never had been before in her life.

'But it wouldn't have occurred to me,' he continued, without breaking stride, 'to have given up on sex.'

'We're all different,' Caitlin said quietly.

'Know what I think?'

'I don't think I want to know what you think.' But she was frightened at just how much she really did.

'You know you do.' Dante tipped his finger under her chin so that she would focus on him and that simple gesture felt like something way more intimate, daringly intrusive even. Mesmerised, she could only stare at him. 'I think you're scared,' he said softly. 'I think my brother was the easy way out for you. Maybe you want a family and you can just about see your way to coupling with a man who couldn't possibly hurt you because you've handed nothing over to him, at least not the searing passion of real, complicated love. And perhaps my brother, who knows the weight of parental expectation, is prepared to buckle and accept what is on the table... Is that it?'

Caitlin said nothing. He had fumbled his way towards an explanation and, while he had hit the spot
with certain assumptions, he was way off target with
others, but then he was not to know the complexity of
the situation.

One thing she was realising, though, was there was
no way she could continue the pretence of an engagement to Alejandro, not to Dante or his family. He had
forced her to recognise that passion was there; she had
tasted it. The only problem was that the fruit she had
tasted was forbidden. Dante was not the man for her.

'Stop asking me to talk about this,' she whispered.

'Are you really going to go ahead with a farcical
engagement and a marriage that is going to eventually
end in tears, whatever your reasons for instigating it?'

Caitlin could look at him now and say, truthfully,
'No.' She sighed. 'Are you satisfied?'

'Are *you*?'

'I need to go up now. I... I'm tired. I just want to
have a long, hot bath and go to sleep.' She stood up
because if she remained sitting, remained in his orbit,
she knew that the urge to reach out and touch would be
too powerful. 'I'm going to talk to Alejandro tomorrow
and then...then... I'm going to head back to London...'

She talked to Alejandro. She'd thought that she might
bump into Dante the following morning, and after the
conversation they had shared she had been dreading
that, but when, at a little after nine, she stepped into
the taxi she had ordered to take her to the hospital, he
was nowhere to be seen.

She wasn't sure what to expect but Alejandro was
subdued, though very much with it and itching to leave

the hospital. He was going to recuperate at his parents' house, he told her. The bones would heal and he would be on crutches within a week. Mobile. They got past the formalities of two people circling what they both knew was going to be the main event.

'I know you must have feelings for him.' Alejandro was the first to cross the Rubicon. 'You forget how well I know you. You need to be careful. He has a terrible reputation when it comes to women.'

'I'm not about to get involved with him, Alejandro.'

'But you'd like to?'

'No.' She'd thought of the way her body went up in flames whenever Dante was near her. She thought of those taboo images that had flashed through her head at regular intervals, hot and sharp and leaving her weak.

They'd spoken, Alejandro had said awkwardly. Dante had talked to him, openly and honestly, thinking him to be out of it. He had talked about how much he regretted the passing of time when they had had so little to do with one another. Caitlin could see that the Alejandro who had emerged from his deep sleep was a different Alejandro.

The engagement was no more. He would, he told her, break it to his parents and hang the consequences. But he was still going to send her the money he'd agreed on, even though Caitlin was horrified and downright forbade it.

'I've already emailed my guy at the bank,' he warned her. 'A deal's a deal. Now, you go.' He smiled wryly. 'People are queuing to visit, including Luisa, for reasons best known to her. Can't remember her paying me a scrap of notice and I've known the woman since she was twelve.'

Something stirred in Caitlin. She remembered the

venom on the other woman's face when she had bumped into them on the hospital ward not long ago, and shivered. Why would Luisa still be hanging around? Not her business. She was an old family friend. Did those ever really go away?

'That fall,' Alejandro's parting words were, 'might just have saved my life, Caitlin.' His voice was pensive. 'You should do what you feel you have to do. Take it from me, when you have a scare it makes you realise that life is precious and you only get to live it once...'

Her mind was on so many things when, much later, she let herself back into the house, having remembered this time to take a spare key. Two were kept in a metal safe in the kitchen and she had had to sign it out.

Having not seen Dante before she left for the hospital, she had taken it for granted that he would be similarly absent when she later returned.

He wasn't. Just as she was about to enter her bedroom to pack her bags to leave, he appeared at the opposite end of the corridor. Coincidence or not? Was he intending to continue his interrogation? Hadn't they both said enough? She desperately wanted a surge of inner strength to accompany those bracing thoughts, but it failed to materialise as he strolled towards her.

'How was he?' Dante asked quietly. He was holding his laptop under his arm, on his way to the important business of catching up on work, she thought. And it was pure coincidence that they had collided in the wide corridor. She could tell because he was in a rush, stopping only because politeness dictated that he did. That was the feeling she was getting. Their intimate conversation of the evening before had been buried for him. Maybe he felt that too much had been shared.

'Good,' Caitlin returned. 'I think he's going to get bored of being in hospital very soon. Apparently the broken bones are healing nicely. He'll be hobbling about before you know it. He's going to go stay with your parents and then, I guess, in due course, he'll return to London.'

'A single man...' Dante looked at her as her eyes shifted from his. He'd had time to think overnight. He couldn't remember a time when he had ever had as open a conversation with anyone as he had had with her and that, he had concluded, wasn't a good thing. Telling her... about that incident in his past had felt like a weakness, but it was too late to retrieve confidences shared and he wasn't going to waste time beating himself up about it.

He'd also had time to think about what she had told him about herself, her startling confession that she had never slept with anyone. She had been neither ashamed nor proud of her virginity. It was as it was, her attitude had implied and, while he admired her for that, he was in no doubt that she wasn't nearly as casual about her relationship status as she claimed to be.

She was so...fiery...so full of personality...so *opinionated*. How could she really be the sort to accept the reality of a relationship that delivered on all fronts except the single one that mattered, which was passion?

She might kid herself that she had squashed any romantic streak she might have had because of some broken heart back in the day, but she hadn't, and Dante had firmly made up his mind that, temptation or not, and whether she was now a free woman or not, he wasn't going to go there. Wasn't even going to think about it. She lacked the experience to deal with a sex-with-no-strings-attached situation.

Yet the delicate flush in her cheeks, the nerves she was trying hard to conceal, the intensely feminine *smell* of her...were all beginning to wreak havoc with his high-minded, well-intentioned resolutions.

'I'm keeping you. I was just about to pack my bags.'

'Pack?' That felt like a punch to the gut. Wrong reaction on every front.

'I told you, I intend to head back to London and the sooner, the better.'

That single sentence clarified everything in Dante's mind. It was one thing to be sensible when temptation wasn't staring you in the face. It was quite another when...it was.

She would leave and he wouldn't be seeing her again. He would be left wondering *what if...?* whether he liked it or not. The woman had got under his skin, and if she walked away now she would remain under his skin for ever. A burr he would not easily be able to yank free. An annoying itch that he would regret not having tried to scratch.

'Don't.'

That single word hung suspended in the air between them. Caitlin marvelled that a single one-syllable word could have such a dramatic effect on her senses. Her heart sped up. Her mouth went dry. Her pulses began to race.

'Yet. Don't leave yet.'

'What do you mean?'

'You know exactly what I mean.'

She did.

'There's no *you and Alejandro* any more,' Dante breathed thickly. 'Once upon a time, there was a convenient charade. That's over. You're a free woman.'

'It wouldn't work.'

'What wouldn't? Are you telling me that when you look at me…you don't want to touch?'

His voice had sunk to a husky murmur that felt like feathers brushing against her skin. She shivered. So many things were going round in her head right now, but top of the list was—*I want you… I don't know why, or how I could feel so attracted to you, but I want you…*

'That's not the point,' she responded, angry at the telltale weakness in her voice.

'Why?' All his natural aggression and instinct to pursue what he wanted surged to the surface, wiping out every mental obstacle in its path.

'How could a relationship work between us? Your parents…your friends…your relatives…all those people who had gathered there for the engagement party… what would they think?'

'Why would they know?'

'I don't understand.'

'I'm not talking about a relationship, Caitlin,' he husked. 'This would be sex. Pure and simple. I want you and you want me and one and one makes two. I'm not interested in getting involved with anyone with a view to anything other than having some fun. Yes, you have to get back to London, but you don't have to get back *just yet*.'

Every shred of heartfelt romanticism in Caitlin rebelled against the unadorned brashness of his proposition. There was no attempt to wrap it up as anything other than what it was—two people having sex for a few days before they parted ways, a ripple in both their lives, gone before it had had time to become anything bigger.

Caitlin was an unintentional virgin. She hadn't been saving herself for the right guy to come along. She hadn't slept with Jimmy for reasons that had become blindingly clear after he had fallen for the model, and since then she had retreated into herself. No one, not a single guy, had broken through the wall she had erected around herself. She'd pretty much come to the conclusion that she was frigid.

Sure, she wanted kids and a family and one day, she had vaguely thought, a guy would come along and she would be attracted to him and things would fall into place. It was a thought that barely registered on her radar, because she was just so busy building a career and, lately, stressing out about her parents. When it *had* registered, she had assumed the guy who eventually showed up would tick all the usual boxes. Nice, thoughtful, good sense of humour, non-smoker.

And yet here was Dante, all dark and dangerous, and definitely *not* Mr Nice and Thoughtful… And she wanted him so much it made her feel weak.

'I'm gathering from the prolonged silence,' he said wryly, interrupting the frantic racing of her thoughts, 'that sex without a *relationship* label attached to it isn't something you would be prepared to sample.' He lowered his eyes and her heart raced even faster. 'Although you'd be shocked at just how much fun it would be…'

He straightened. Somewhere along the line, they had moved close to the wall and he had been lounging against it, a long, lean, powerful jungle cat prepared to have a bit of fun with the antelope.

Antelopes, Caitlin thought in confusion, never came off well in any encounter with powerful jungle cats.

He was strolling away when all of a sudden she was galvanised into action.

He wanted fun. He wasn't relationship material and he hadn't bothered to hide that fact.

What was so wrong if she wanted a bit of fun, as well? There hadn't been much of that around for the past few months. She was here and she was only going to be here for a matter of a few days if she decided to stay on. After that, she would return to the reality of life on the other side of the ocean, back to the stress and the worry.

'Dante!' Crunch moment. She took a deep breath and was suddenly filled with a wave of pure, fizzing excitement.

He'd stopped, turned round and was looking at her with lazy interest.

He hadn't expected her to stop him but now that she had, he was aware of a soaring sense of relief. He hadn't realised just how much it had meant for her to come to him, and not because he had kissed her or tried to seduce. He hadn't wanted her to be swept away in the moment. He'd wanted her to make a conscious decision in the cold light of day.

He looked at the sexy sashay of her rounded hips and banked down the fierce ache of an erection.

'Yes.' Caitlin cleared her throat and looked at him without flinching.

Dante didn't say anything for a couple of seconds, then he reached out and cupped the side of her face, his long fingers soft and tender, stroking the satin smoothness of her cheek.

When he kissed her, she finally discovered what it felt like for the earth to stop spinning.

CHAPTER EIGHT

THEY MADE IT to his bedroom, fingers entwined. He nudged the door, which was slightly ajar, with his foot and, instead of turning on the overhead light, he just wrapped his arms around her in the gathering darkness in the bedroom and held her close.

'Would you listen to me if I told you not to be nervous?'

It was the one thing guaranteed to calm her nerves and it did. She visibly relaxed and settled into the embrace, her head resting on his chest so that she could hear the faint beating of his heart.

She tentatively wrapped her arms around him, then slid them underneath the polo shirt and shivered at the feel of muscle and sinew under her fingers. Very gently, he mimicked what she was doing. Without making a big deal of it, he expertly unclasped her bra.

Caitlin gave a soft whimper as he curved his big hands under her breasts, stroking the crease beneath them and then, very slowly, working his way up until he was massaging both her breasts, and as he massaged them he rubbed the pads of his thumbs over her stiffened nipples.

'You have no idea how long I've wanted to do this,'

he murmured. 'I'm hard like steel for you. One touch and I don't know what the outcome will be. I might embarrass myself by not being able to hold back… If I make you nervous then, rest assured, you make me nervous, as well…' He wasn't kidding. The gentle, shyly faltering sweep of her hands along his body made him wonder whether he would be able to last long enough to actually get inside her.

'No, I don't,' Caitlin breathed. She was hopelessly drifting on a current of such pure, delicious sensation. Her nipples were tingling and, between her legs, her panties were wet. Her clothes felt like an impediment. It was as if, slowly but surely and without attempting to remove a single article of clothing, he was somehow managing to get her to a place where she wanted to rip them all off.

Dante laughed softly. He looked down at her upturned face and lowered his head to kiss her. It was a long, leisurely, lingering kiss, and he didn't stop touching her nipples, playing with them, teasing them so that she was squirming, her whole body hot and restless.

He made no attempt to touch her anywhere else. Just that kiss that went on for ever and the light, lazy caress of her breasts. It was driving her crazy.

She broke free and began tugging him towards the bed. She could hear her own breathing and then a low laugh from him.

'I'm taking my time,' he husked.

'You're driving me nuts,' Caitlin responded with staccato jerkiness, and he laughed again.

Through the window, the declining sun was casting long shadows into the bedroom. The open shutters turned the light into stripes. It was still very warm outside, but here in the bedroom it was beautifully cool. Thick walls, she assumed. A fortress of a mansion that could withstand the heat of summer and the cold of winter.

She was pulling him towards the bed and when she felt the side of the mattress against her knees, she sank down and then looked up at him. He was standing over her and, very, very slowly, he began to undress.

Nervous? No way could this man ever be nervous when it came to making love but, she thought, he'd been kind to have said so because he'd have known that she would have found it endearing and a little funny and it would have relaxed her even more.

Everything he was now doing spoke of self-assurance and complete confidence in himself.

Of course, she'd seen him in his swimming trunks, but it was different now because, this time, this was going somewhere. She was appreciating the broad, naked chest and the muscled width of his shoulders in an entirely different way.

He flung the polo shirt on the ground and then his hand hovered for a few seconds on the zipper of his trousers.

Caitlin's breath hitched in her throat.

'You're so perfect,' she breathed, and he burst out laughing.

'And you're so honest. I like that.' He stepped out of the trousers but kept the boxers on. 'You don't play games in bed. It's refreshing.'

She could see the bulge of his erection and it made her feel faint.

She was sitting on the side of the bed and he nudged her legs open so that he was standing between them.

'I want to see you.'

With a few words, her excitement was ratcheted up a few notches and she hooked her fingers under the baggy tee shirt and pulled it over her head, taking the bra with it at the same time.

Her instinct was to cover her nakedness with her hands, but Dante was far too expert a lover to allow her to hang on to her natural reserve and, with a few adept touches, she shed her nervous apprehension and began to relax.

Dante stared. He couldn't help himself. He'd seen some of the most beautiful women on the planet and yet this one…got to him in all sorts of places no one else ever had. That was a mystery to him, but then the circumstances were completely different from any he'd ever been in before and, beyond that, he had shared more of himself with her than with any other woman. Another mystery.

Her breasts were full, more than a handful and tipped with perfect pale brown discs, large and succulent and inviting.

He stifled a groan and reminded himself that he had to go slow. It was going to be a feat of willpower.

He lowered himself, boxers still in place, and knelt between her, urging her to sit up so that he could suckle her breasts one at a time.

Caitlin arched back, eyes shut, rocked to the very core. She curled her fingers into his dark hair. She needed to get rid of the rest of her clothes. When she'd walked towards him in the corridor, when she'd made that momentous decision to sleep with him, she'd braced herself for all the nerves she'd known would accompany her first time making love, but her nerves had disappeared, overridden by fierce, burning *need*. It cut through everything.

He pushed his hand under her skirt and skimmed her thighs. Her skin was satiny soft and smooth. He nudged his knuckles against her crotch and felt her dampness. For a second, he had to empty his head because the whole situation was far too erotic, from her soft moans to the pliancy of her sexy body. She was giving him the gift of her virginity and for a moment he was filled with doubt, then he wiped that clean from his head because they were both adults and choices had been made, eyes wide open.

And in a way, wasn't he doing her a favour? As time went on, her virginity would surely become an albatross round her neck, a prize to be given to Mr Right, except would there ever be a Mr Right? Did that person exist? Or would she end up trusting some guy like her ex, only to be let down? Wouldn't her heartache be a thousand times worse because she would have opened herself up to that person, expecting all the fairy stories peddled by the rest of the world? At least, with him, he wasn't selling her stories or making promises he couldn't keep. Theirs was a straightforward arrangement.

Dante pushed the skirt up and she wriggled so that it was ruched and gathered at her waist. It felt wildly decadent. He was still there, between her legs, and modesty slammed into her when he inserted his finger underneath the stretchy fabric of her underwear, but he gently eased her hand away.

He linked his fingers through hers and kept her hands still at her sides, then he nuzzled against the damp underwear, breathing in her musky smell. He tasted her through the silky barrier. He was going to go further, going to feel her wetness on his face, but not yet.

The need to be gentle, to take his time, to make sure she enjoyed this first experience felt crucially important. She never hesitated when it came to speaking her mind, and she'd had more to say on the subject of him and his lifestyle than anyone else in living memory, but, emotionally, he sensed a curious vulnerability and that vulnerability, now, was bringing out in him a protective streak he hadn't known he had.

He unclasped their hands and waited until he knew that she was ready, then he eased the underwear off and parted her legs.

No underwear now as a barrier and the honeyed sweetness between her thighs was a powerful aphrodisiac. Dante licked and sucked. Easily finding the throbbing nub of her clitoris, he began to tease it until she was writhing with mounting pleasure.

His own erection was a steady, pulsing ache in his groin. No problem. The second he entered her, he knew that he was going to come very quickly. For the moment, he would devote all his attention to getting her to that place where she was desperate for him to sink into her.

He continued to feast on her wetness until her cries became more demanding.

'Please… Dante…' Caitlin said brokenly. 'I'm going to… I won't be able to help myself…' She didn't want to come against his mouth. She wanted to feel the closeness of him inside her.

Never in her wildest dreams had she ever imagined that sex could be this good.

When he stood up, it left a cool void, and in the ever-darkening room she followed his progress to the dressing table, where he found his wallet and very quickly spun round, ripping off the tin-foil wrapping of a condom.

Protection. Of course. And in his wallet. A man who was not prepared to take chances.

She sat up and pulled down the skirt just as he did the same with his boxers. She gave a sharp intake of breath and a prosaic thought flitted through her head… *Will he fit inside me?*

He was impressively big. She watched as he walked slowly towards her. His eyes were pinned to hers but he was absent-mindedly holding himself with his hand. Watching as he stroked himself was an incredible turn-on.

Her eyelids fluttered. She shuffled into a horizontal position, barely able to keep any part of her body still, busily drinking in the truly beautiful sight of his nudity. Where she was milky white, he was so sexily bronzed, and when he joined her on the bed she could only marvel at the difference in colour between them.

He manoeuvred her so that they were facing one another and ran his hand along her side, enjoying the dip of her womanly waist and the flare of her hips.

It was incredibly intimate looking deep into his eyes from this close.

'Are you relaxed?'

'I wasn't to start with.'

Dante half nodded and smiled. He slipped his hand between her legs and cupped her. He didn't go any further than that. He just cupped her there and moved his hand until she wanted so much more, until she was quivering, her fingers digging into his shoulders and only then, when he had roused her to fever pitch, did he move over her and gently begin to insert himself.

He felt her nerves, the way she stiffened, and he began whispering into her ear, soothing her as he eased himself in.

She was so wonderfully tight, scared and nervous now but, oh, so eager for him.

Dante had to grit his teeth not to push hard and satisfy himself. Bit by bit he entered her, her wetness easing a path, her groans escalating in volume the deeper he was and when, at last, he had that final thrust, Caitlin was ready for him and her body responded with enthusiasm. He moved and she moved as well, their bodies in total harmony.

It felt so good. Unbelievably so. Dante came with an explosion that shocked him in its intensity.

Her own orgasm followed his. She arched up to him and cried out, all inhibitions gone in that moment.

Afterwards, it was like swimming back up to the surface having been underwater. Caitlin sighed and shifted so that they were belly to belly. Never had she felt closer to anyone and yet, even as she knew that, she also knew that that was an admission she should never make.

'That was the best,' she said with honesty. 'At least,' she added, even more honestly, 'for me. I don't suppose it was much of a deal for you.'

'Don't even think of saying something like that.' Dante kissed the side of her mouth and ran his fingers through her tangle of colourful hair.

Dante had become jaded over time. In business, he got what he wanted. He was single-minded, focused, ambitious and feared. Born into wealth, he had continued climbing up that ladder, unimpeded. The sense

of satisfaction he had felt when he had first started di-
versifying and doing his own thing, setting up his own
empire, had become a dull, background acceptance
of success. Winning deals, absorbing companies, the
thrill of being the first to spot the gold mine waiting
in the wings...the shine had worn off. Thinking about
his brother and his dislike of the job he had inherited,
his forays into other worlds that had nothing to do with
money but were adventures to be had and nothing more,
Dante felt a sharp pang of envy.

He was the younger but a lot more cynical.

And when it came to women...

Dante gazed at the woman lying next to him, warm
and drowsy post-sex.

He would tire of her. He always did. He wondered
whether his defence mechanisms against becoming too
involved with any woman were so finely honed that it
made it impossible for him to have anything approaching a normal relationship. No sooner had he slept with
a woman than his attention began to stray. It was something he had long accepted. It was why he found the
idea of marriage so inconceivable and why, if it ever
hovered at the back of his mind, it was in the shape of
something convenient, without the exhausting, futile
and complicated shenanigans associated with emotion.

'Penny for your thoughts,' Caitlin said lightly, her
clear green eyes not shying away from him.

She had her life to get on with. He had his. She would
find someone eventually and her belief in love would
be rekindled.

'You could stay awhile,' he murmured.

Caitlin looked at him seriously. 'I have a job to go
back to.'

'Jobs can wait.'

'That's fine for you to say. You're your own boss and you can afford to do what you want.'

But that invitation was so tempting, even though she could read the corollary... *Stay awhile because pretty soon I'll get fed up anyway...*

'Don't you want to...to do this all over again?'

She hesitated, and in that pause he smiled slowly.

'Because I really want to.'

'I have responsibilities.'

'I'm not talking about a long-term arrangement, Caitlin. I'm talking about a few days of uncomplicated fun before we go our separate ways.' He stroked her side and her eyelids fluttered. 'Your responsibilities will be waiting for you when you get back to London, I'm sure.'

They would, Caitlin thought. Her parents...the stress...the uncertainty...none of that would be going anywhere any time soon. Alejandro had told her that he had instructed his bank to deposit the promised money into her account. She had no intention of keeping any of it so she would be back to square one when she returned to London.

But was she really the sort of person who could enjoy a few days of guilt-free pleasure without consequences? She'd shrugged off the whole business of relationships but, looking back at it, she hadn't been tempted into any anyway, so shrugging them off hadn't been an issue.

But she and Dante had slept together.

Lust.

That was what it had all been about. Lust and maybe the allure of being in a different country, where grim day-to-day reality could be kept at a distance... It was as real as stardust.

He wanted days. She could do days. Lust faded. And what was wrong with snatching a little time out?

His parents wouldn't know. Alejandro would probably suspect but he would be amused. They would live in a little bubble for a week and then the bubble would burst and that would be that. No harm done.

'Okay.' She blushed. She reached out and did what he was doing to her: she stroked him, her fingers sliding over taut sinew and muscle, then lower to where his stirring erection left her in no doubt that what he felt for her was very, very genuine. 'You're right. Responsibilities can wait awhile...'

His parents wouldn't know. They would be spared the bewilderment of thinking that she had been engaged to one brother only to move on to the next. Without the complexities of the situation being explained, how could they think otherwise? They lived some distance away so it wouldn't be an issue. Somehow, Caitlin had managed to avoid another dinner invitation and she suspected that that was because they were too wrapped up with events to even think about entertaining their son's fiancée, however much they might have wanted to.

Dante, perhaps, had engineered things so that they could have time to themselves, in that very special bubble where the past and the future didn't exist, just a very physical and very exciting present.

'It's extraordinary,' he had told her the evening before, when they had lain together, their limbs entangled so that they were almost a single unit, 'but this is the best sex I've ever had.'

Caitlin had laughed and quelled the unexpected hurt she had felt. *The best sex...* Maybe there were women who would have seen that as a compliment. She could understand that. Dante was a man of experience, a man who could have any woman he wanted at the snap of an imperious finger, so doubtless when he'd said that, it had been said as a compliment.

But for Caitlin…since when had that ever been her dream? Since when had she ever thought that she would end up snatching time with a guy who wasn't interested in anything beyond a romp in the sack? Had she ever thought that she would be helplessly sucked into the sort of non-relationship she had been schooled to avoid at all costs?

And yet, those words had filled her with a guilty pleasure.

She had to keep reminding herself that none of that really mattered because she would soon be gone.

Alejandro would soon be leaving hospital. She had visited him first thing this morning and he had been upbeat. He had shrewdly asked her about Dante and she had not committed to any kind of answer, but he had gone ahead and warned her off him again anyway, as if she had needed that warning.

Right now, Dante would be on his way back from the hospital. He had gone to work—an urgent meeting, he'd said, but he would much rather have lazed in bed with her—and would be stopping on the way back to his house.

Caitlin had already been there for an extra three days. Mentally, she had dealt with extending her stay by a week. That gave her four more days to bask in their short-lived relationship. When she thought about boarding that plane back to London, her mind skittered away from the unpleasant feeling that that was the last thing she wanted to do and, she told herself sternly, that had nothing to do with the fact that she hated the thought of never seeing Dante again. It was simply because she was having a holiday from all her stress and who ever wanted a holiday to come to an end? No one.

Standing in the kitchen now, with a bottle of wine chilling in the fridge and a meal in the oven, prepared by one of the three members of staff permanently employed to make sure that no need of Dante's ever went untended, including the need to eat extremely fine food and drink extremely fine wine, Caitlin glanced down at her outfit.

She had forgone the usual uniform of loose skirt and loose top, which Dante referred to as her *hippie chick outfits*, and was wearing a pair of skinny jeans and a fitted top, which she had bought the day before. Huge extravagance and she had no idea why she had done that, except she'd been out with Dante and he had practically shoved her into the shop and then had declared the outfit an amazing fit when she had grudgingly paraded it for him. She'd been squirrelling every spare penny into an account for her parents and hadn't spent anything on herself for ages and suddenly, for no reason, she'd felt reckless.

Regrettable, considering her arrangement with Alejandro had bitten the dust, even though, up to this morning, he'd pressed her to take the money, which he didn't need and she desperately did, and not be silly. He'd refused to give her his bank details. She would sort that out as soon as he was out of hospital, she'd decided.

And she had to agree with Dante—the outfit suited her.

An uneasy thought surfaced. Was she, subconsciously, dressing to please him because she wanted to somehow persuade him into a relationship he had declared he didn't want? Did she want a week to stretch into a month? A year? Longer?

If that were the case, which she wasn't even going to give houseroom in her head, then she had obviously lost her mind.

She didn't hear him enter.

She'd been lost in her thoughts. Then she looked up and there he was and her heart skipped several beats.

He was so breathtakingly beautiful, so spectacular in every possible way, that she could only stare and blink for a few seconds, like a rabbit caught in the headlights. He was magnificent naked but no less so when he was kitted out in his handmade leather shoes and the designer suit that would have cost the earth.

He'd dumped his jacket somewhere along the way and unbuttoned the top three buttons of his white shirt, which was cuffed to the elbows. His trousers, pale grey and hand-tailored, were a beautiful fit and somehow managed to make him look businesslike yet crazily sexy. Quite an achievement, she thought faintly.

Eventually, their eyes met and she blinked.

'What's wrong?' How quickly she had become used to his eyes darkening when they rested on her, to the slow, unfurling smile that could make her toes curl and bring a surge of heated colour to her face.

Right now, as he remained standing by the kitchen door, his face was grave and that sent a chill of foreboding through her.

'We need to talk.' Dante didn't take his eyes off her as he walked directly to the fridge to pour them both a generous glass of Rioja.

'You think I might need a drink to cope with whatever you have to say?'

He'd moved to sit at the table and she followed suit, although adjacent to him with a chair between them. Close enough to lean into whatever conversation was about to take place but far enough for her to remove herself from the suffocating effect he had on her senses.

She tried to read what he was thinking but he was adept at concealing what he wanted hidden.

'It's about my brother.'

'But...' she half rose '... I was with him this morning and he was absolutely fine.'

Dante tilted his head to one side. 'He told me.'

'He told you...?'

'Caitlin...you should have said. No, scratch that... of course, you couldn't have broken the promise you made him but...' Dante rubbed his eyes wearily. 'I wish I had known.'

'Alejandro *told* you?' Shocked, Caitlin leaned towards Dante, her urgent green eyes colliding with his weary dark ones. He looked drained. More than that... he looked *saddened.*

She reached out and covered his hand with hers and breathed a sigh of relief when he curled his fingers into hers. He slumped back in the chair for a few seconds, eyes closed, then he opened his eyes and looked at her.

'We spent years growing more and more distant from one another. I had no idea how he felt about working for the company until you told me. I had no inkling that he was gay and the worst of it was that he felt so damned apprehensive about telling me. Yet he had every right to keep it to himself. When have I ever given Alejandro any indication that I was interested in his personal life? We were ships that crossed in the night, exchanging as little as possible of any significance.'

'That's sometimes how it goes,' Caitlin told him gently. 'But there is an opportunity now for things to change between you. He's your brother and you're so lucky to have a sibling.' She thought of the cares and troubles she was having to manage single-handedly. 'Alejandro is one of the kindest people I've ever met and I know he would be so happy, so thrilled and excited, to have you in his life. I mean, properly in his life.' She paused. 'Has he…er…broken this news to anyone else?'

'He's going to tell our parents later today. He's wary, he tells me, but it's something he said he should have done a long time ago. I think coming here under those false pretences, his fall…brought home to him the need to come out and be honest.'

'I'm really glad he has,' Caitlin admitted. 'You have no idea how hard I've tried to persuade him that living a lie wasn't a good idea.'

'You agreed to the charade,' Dante mused softly, 'because he was so desperate to do what he thought he needed to do, didn't you? He talked you into pretending to be his fiancée and you agreed because that's just the kind of person you are…'

Uncomfortable with this summary of events, Caitlin shuffled in the chair and wondered whether she should launch into the full account of the hare-brained scheme they had agreed upon.

She remained silent. What would be the point? The main thing was that all the hiding behind closed doors was over for Alejandro and a new chapter in his life was about to begin.

'Yes, I'm a saint,' she quipped. 'If you'll excuse me, I'll just vanish upstairs for a minute so that I can polish my halo.'

Dante burst out laughing. His eyes darkened with appreciation.

There was something *special* about her. The fact that she had stepped up to the plate and done something as dramatic as she had, for the sake of friendship, struck him as almost noble.

Would she have carried on with the pretence? And for how long? Yes, she had been hurt in the past, but would that hurt have propelled her into a permanent arrangement with Alejandro if events had not played out the way they had?

He also admired the fact that she could have told him. She could have broken that confidence, knowing that it would have put a completely different slant on things. She must have known, after that kiss they had shared at the pool, that his opinion of her would have been in the dirt when he'd walked away. But she hadn't followed him. She had remained true to the promise she had made his brother.

Self-serving she was not, and he really liked that.

And now...

Dante had truly thought that her novelty value would have worn off by now. Here they were, playing truant from reality like a couple of heady teenagers, and he had assumed that the sheer *difference* about her, the very thing he figured had got to him in the first place, would have worn thin by now.

Yet he saw her and he wanted her. He touched her and he had to stop himself from shaking. He heard that infectious laugh and he smiled.

And now everything had changed and a forbidden thought crept into his head like a thief in the dark.

What if they carried on for longer than the week prescribed? He wasn't looking for permanence and neither was she. He'd half feared that she might have begun to view what they had as more significant than he had told her it was destined to be, but there had been no hesitant forays into a future beyond the coming weekend. She had not hinted at wanting any more than what they had agreed upon. She had been as casual as him, living in the moment and enjoying it.

'I like your sense of humour,' Dante confessed, his thoughts still running unchecked. 'Women have always been way too eager to do what they think I might like. You're not like that…'

'You live in a different world, Dante.' But Caitlin was inordinately pleased by the compliment. 'I guess people suck up to you because of who you are and you've become accustomed to that. I don't live in that world and it's not how I've been brought up.' She smiled. 'We're all different.'

'And I like that. More than I thought I would.'

'What do you mean?'

'Things have changed with Alejandro's revelation. My parents, for better or worse, will find out that the engagement they had such high hopes for was all a pretence. Well intentioned, but still a pretence. Alejandro is terrified that they will pass judgement and he will be found wanting. I like to think that that is not going to be the case. At any rate…' he looked at her, his lean, handsome features decisive '…you will be able to face them for who you really are.'

'I won't be facing them, Dante,' Caitlin said with

alarm. 'I'm leaving in a few days. There's really no need for me to meet up with them again.'

Still accepting of her departure, Dante thought with appreciation. Not going beyond the brief. A first. He was accustomed to having his freedom threatened sooner or later by women who wanted more longevity than he was prepared to give.

He shrugged and smiled. 'You can go at the end of the week,' he concurred, 'or you can stay on. Better still, I can arrange to temporarily transfer to London, sort things out in my brother's absence...'

'You want to *carry on*?'

'For a while,' Dante said hurriedly.

He isn't bored yet, Caitlin thought. *But soon he will be.*

He wanted everything on his terms, but what about hers? She was in danger of forgetting them, and she couldn't afford to do that because every day something deep inside was being chipped away.

'I don't think so.' She didn't wait for temptation to start interfering with common sense. 'Let's have fun and then, at the end of the week, let's do what we agreed to do. Let's say goodbye.'

CHAPTER NINE

IT WASN'T DIFFICULT to find out where Caitlin lived. Far more difficult had been Dante's decision to travel to London and search her out, because it just wasn't in his nature to pursue anyone. Pursuit equated to weakness, but, after more than two weeks without her, Dante had managed to convince himself that the real weakness would be in staying put, in ignoring the perfectly reasonable desire to finish something that had not quite reached its natural conclusion. How could he live with himself if he remained where he was, pointlessly thinking about her and having nightly cold showers? Did that make any sense at all? If she turned him away, then so be it. He would shrug it off but at least he would have tried, and you couldn't do more than that. The not trying would have been the less courageous option.

As promised, she had remained in Spain for the remainder of the week, daily visiting Alejandro, who, having awakened from his deep sleep bright-eyed and bushy-tailed, had been frustrated at not being able to get out of hospital as fast as he had hoped, thanks to the small detail of broken bones that needed to rest awhile.

Part of his urgency to leave had been sheer relief at

having come out. He had told the world and the world had been a lot more forgiving than he had anticipated.

What his traditional and old-fashioned parents had made of the whole thing was a mystery to Dante. Outwardly, at least, they had been supportive and that had been the main thing.

And now that barriers had broken down between himself and his brother, they had begun the rocky but well-intentioned road of making amends for the silent relationship that had developed between them over the years.

Between building bridges with Alejandro, engaging with his parents and all those family members now on the receiving end of what would have been, at the very least, pretty startling revelations, and focusing on some major deals in the pipeline, he should have found Caitlin's easy disappearance from his life barely left a ripple in its wake.

It had been a source of constant frustration that he couldn't get her out of his head. He had been forced to conclude that it hadn't been just about the sex. He had enjoyed her company and he didn't much like that recognition, because it wasn't something he had factored into their short-lived relationship.

So here he was.

He could have asked Alejandro for her address, but he knew, instinctively, that his brother would have cautioned him against prolonging a relationship with someone he obviously cared about. Deep and meaningful conversations he and Alejandro might not have had, but that didn't mean that Alejandro was ignorant of Dante's womanising lifestyle choices. He wouldn't have understood that he and Caitlin were on the same page when it came to their relationship. She wasn't going to lose her head over him. She wasn't going to get hurt. Why else would she have found it so easy to walk away? There hadn't been so much as a hint that she'd been looking for more than what had been put on the table.

He'd asked his PA to get hold of her address and, lo and behold, it had taken under half an hour.

He hadn't known what to expect of her living arrangements and was shocked to discover himself standing, now, outside something that looked as though an act of kindness would have been to take a wrecking ball to it. But then, he acknowledged grimly, his background had not prepared him for the reality of living on the breadline.

It was a squat, rectangular block of flats, all connected by outside concrete walkways. Washing lines groaning under the weight of clothes only partially concealed chipping paint. Bikes were leaning in front of most of the flats. The lighting was poor and Dante concluded that that was probably a good thing, because in the unforgiving light of day the sight would probably be twice as depressing. He had never been anywhere like this in his life before and he was shocked and alarmed that she lived in a place like this.

Was she going to be in?

He'd taken a chance. It was after nine on a Wednesday evening. He was playing the odds.

He took the steps two at a time. There was a pervasive odour in the stairwell but he didn't dwell on that as he headed up to the third floor, then along the walkway, brushing past the washing, dodging the bikes and random kids' toys and finally banging on her front door because there was no bell.

And then, suddenly nervous, Dante stepped back and waited to see what would happen.

Caitlin heard the banging on the door and assumed it was Shirley three doors down. She had a good relationship with the much older woman. Too good, in some ways, because Shirley was a lonely seventy-something and, for her, Caitlin was the daughter she'd had but who now never visited.

Caitlin slipped on her bedroom slippers, pulled open the door and then stared.

The whole hit her before the detail. She knew it was Dante. Half lounging against the wall, hand poised to bang once again on the door. Yes, she registered that, then she absorbed, numbly, the detail. The faded black jeans, the grey polo shirt, the weathered bomber jacket because summer was morphing into autumn and the nights were getting cooler.

'What are you doing here?' she asked faintly, hovering by the door, so shocked that she could barely think straight.

She'd been thinking about him and he'd materialised like a genie from a lamp, as beautiful and as cruelly mesmerising as she'd remembered. She'd stayed those last few days and stuck fast to her insouciant *this-is-fun-but-it's-got-to-end* routine, but every second had been filled with the wrenching pain of knowing that she would never see him again, and since she'd returned to London the pain had not subsided. He'd filled her head every waking moment, obliterating everything, even the ongoing anxiety about her parents. And now, shockingly, here he was. They'd had a straightforward deal and she'd spent the past weeks reminding herself of that baldly unappetising fact, but now he was here and she felt the electric buzz of awareness zip through her body like a toxin.

Dante lowered his eyes, his long, dark lashes brushing his slanting cheekbones and shielding his expression.

The nerves had gone. She was standing in front of him and the nerves had been replaced by a racing excitement. She was in some loose, hanging-around, *who-cares-how-I-look?* clothes. Baggy jogging bottoms, baggy sweatshirt, weird fluffy slippers. Her hair was loose, a riot of vibrant curls spilling over her shoulders and down her narrow back.

He'd never seen anything quite so beautiful in his life before.

She'd asked him a question. What was it? His breathing had slowed and when he raised his eyes to meet hers, it was like being hit by a sledgehammer.

He said the one and only thing that came to mind.

'I've missed you.'

If it hadn't been for those three words…

Caitlin looked at the man sprawled in her bed with the stamp of lazy ownership embedded in the very core of his lean, elegant body. He was as addictive as the finest of Belgian chocolate and she couldn't peel her eyes away from his reflection in the mirror as she brushed her hair.

It was eight thirty. It was Sunday. They'd been talking about Alejandro and his rapid recovery. He had left the hospital a mere six weeks previously, but only now was he really fit to travel and he was packing up to return to London.

He was a changed man, light of heart and easy of spirit. Friends and family had been so supportive, he had repeatedly told Caitlin, in between preaching to her about the dangers of going out with his brother.

'Although,' he had mused only three days previously, 'he does seem to have changed. Very understanding about the whole work thing. I'm going to be heading up a team overseeing a new direction with the company. Boutique hotels. Three of them. Much more my thing than pretending to be interested in the financial side of things. He seems relaxed and I'm not the only one to have said that. He's been in touch with our parents several times since he went to London to take over, and off his own bat, which has always, it seems, been a rare occurrence. He's less stressed out. You've obviously removed a couple of his high-energy batteries when he wasn't looking.'

As a postscript, he had added, mischievously, 'At any rate, it's put Luisa fully in the picture. I had no idea she'd been that set on Dante.'

'Luisa's spending lots of time with your brother,' Caitlin said now, standing up and blushing because she recognised the brooding, sensual appreciation in his gaze as his eyes rested on her, naked and fresh from a shower.

'Poor Alejandro. The woman has always clung to our family like a limpet. Come to bed.'

'I know you said that that's because she has no family of her own.' Why was she worried about Luisa? Caitlin didn't know and her run-ins with her had been few, but she didn't trust the woman and her hands were tied when it came to saying anything to Alejandro because he never saw the bad in anyone. Besides, there was no way that she could set her sights on brother number two, bearing in mind that Alejandro had come clean about his sexuality! But the other woman's name had cropped up time and again, indicating a presence on the scene that felt vaguely threatening.

'Come to bed…' Dante repeated, and Caitlin smiled, their eyes still locking in the mirror on the wall.

Her breasts ached and her limbs felt languorous and there was a familiar ache between her thighs.

She'd never been so uninhibited. He did that to her. He'd shown up on her doorstep a month ago, had uttered those three words, and she'd been his. Her determination not to be swept away on a tide of pointless emotion had bitten the dust in record time.

He'd missed her. There had been a naked honesty in that statement of fact and it had echoed her own feelings. She had opened the door to him and even as she was doing so, she had been helplessly aware that the common sense that had driven her departure a fortnight previously was going to be ditched.

'I have things to do.'

'With me.'

'I have a deadline to finish a layout on that shoot I did last week…'

She was smiling, though, and not moving as he eased himself off the bed, splendid in all his proud, masculine, impressive and very turned-on glory.

He absently held himself as he strolled towards her, then he was standing behind her, so much taller and broader, his bronzed skin such a striking contrast to her own smooth, milky pallor. Two naked lovers, looking at one another in the mirror, eyes tangling. There was something wildly erotic about the way they were standing, her back pressed against his chest. He reached to cover her breast with one hand and she arched back, eyelids fluttering as he caressed it. Through half-closed eyes, she followed the motion of his fingers as they played with her pulsing nipple, teasing it, rubbing the stiffened peak. When he licked his finger and touched her again, she groaned and squirmed. He leant down to kiss her neck but he wouldn't let her turn around.

'I like you watching what I'm doing to you,' he murmured in a husky, shaky voice. 'Can you feel how hard I am for you right now?'

In response, Caitlin reached back to lightly touch him. She stroked the tip of his erection, a feathery caress, one she knew he liked. She felt him stiffen and smiled drowsily.

'You were saying something about work...' Dante breathed.

'I was...'

'Then I'd best not keep you and if we climb into bed, then you won't be getting much work done any time soon.'

Caitlin had to acknowledge that this was, indeed, very true. Dante never rushed things. When they lay in bed, he took his time. He touched her slowly, exploring every inch of her body until she was begging him for release. He was a man who could put his own desires on hold for as long as it took to satisfy hers. It showed a lack of selfishness when it came to making love and she had dimly registered, somewhere along the line, that underneath the sometimes ruthless and always sweepingly self-assured exterior was a guy who was, essentially, not driven at all by ego.

There was an overriding sense of fair play about him

that was admirable. Both Dante and Alejandro had so many admirable qualities, in fact, that it was shocking that their relationship had disintegrated so much over the years, and she knew that one of the really great things to have emerged from the situation had been the slow meeting of ways between them, a gradual journey discovering themselves as brothers and appreciating that the bond that had been lost could be rebuilt with effort and goodwill.

She looked at Dante in the mirror, the incline of his dark head as he nuzzled her neck, and she was filled with a wave of such tenderness that she was, momentarily, disoriented and terrified.

'We'll just have to be quick,' he was saying, his voice muffled because he was talking against her neck.

As he said that, he slipped his finger against the wet crease between her legs, and that momentary jolt of *awareness*, a feeling that something inside her was changing somehow, was lost as pure sensation took over.

She clutched his wrists with her hands, then they fell slack to her sides for a second, before she balled her hands into tight fists, straining against the rhythm of his finger as he stroked, delving deeper with each stroke, building up a tempo that left her breathless.

Their reflection in the mirror was unfocused because her eyes were half closed. She was dimly aware of their bodies pressed tightly together, her body at the forefront, partially concealing his. One big hand rested on her breast, the other was moving between her legs. Their eyes collided and she licked her lips in a gesture that was unconsciously erotic.

He'd said quick. She was going to oblige because she

could feel the rise of her orgasm, starting as a ripple then growing in intensity until it was taking over and she spasmed in a rush against his hand, crying out and arching back, her whole body stiffening as she came.

For a while, her mind was a complete blank, then gradually she came down from that peak and swivelled so that she was facing him. She touched his sides lightly, running her hands up and down and delighting in the feel of muscle and sinew. She stroked his inner thigh, then she knelt in front of him and teased him with her mouth and her tongue.

Dante curled his fingers into her hair.

She could turn him on like no one else on the planet, turn him on to the point where he lost the ability to think. He gave a guttural sound of satisfaction as she remorselessly pleasured him with her mouth and when he could hold out no longer, he came with a shudder that ripped through him, sending him rocking back on his feet.

And she still had work to do, she thought!

But he could do this to her, point her in a direction, knowing that she would follow because, with him, she was helpless.

Caitlin didn't get it because she had never been a helpless person. Even in the aftermath of her break-up with Jimmy, she had moved on, keeping herself to herself and picking up all the pieces without fuss. If London had overwhelmed her when she'd first arrived, then she had, likewise, taken it in her stride and faced down the unknown because what was the worst that could happen? She had her health.

But Dante…this man…

He made her feel helpless. She knew that she had

ended up doing what she had told herself she would never do, had ended up caving in to her emotions and that cowardice had made her vulnerable. Very vulnerable.

A world imagined without him was no world at all.

She had gone and done what she had been cautioned against. She had fallen in love with him and as she dithered and wondered what to do about it, the days went by, each one making her more dependent than the one before.

Meanwhile, loose ends piled up around her. She was saving hard, steadfastly ignoring Dante's insistence that she move in with him, move in to the vast penthouse apartment in Mayfair that he had used as a base in the past whenever he'd happened to be in London. That final step, she knew, would be a huge mistake. At least her little one-bedroom flat was hers and he had given up trying to persuade her out of it. His solution was to avoid it at all costs because the area made him feel uncomfortable and, gradually, Caitlin had grown accustomed to a life largely led in his rarefied part of the world.

The money Alejandro had transferred was still sitting in her account, untouched.

He refused to give her the details of his bank account so that she could transfer it back to him.

He'd told her that it had been thanks to her that he had finally moved forward with his life and was no longer trapped in a cage of his own making.

He owed everything to her, he had confided the last time she had telephoned him and brought it up.

She would give him back the cash, she decided, just as soon as he was back in London, which would be in five days' time.

Face to face, he would have to cave because she would just refuse to leave him alone until he did.

Looking back on everything, she understood why she had agreed to the arrangement and yet, somehow, when she thought of that cash, she was overwhelmed with a feeling of guilt and unease.

She knew that she was enjoying life with a desperation that could only end in tears, so when, the day before Alejandro was due to arrive back in London, she glanced up from the kitchen table where she was meticulously looking at a series of photos she had taken two days previously, to see Dante framed in the doorway to the kitchen, she was almost resigned to the axe about to fall.

It was there in his expression. She realised that she had become accustomed to him strolling in to greet her with a smile that was part pleasure, part desire. Without even consciously thinking about it, she had been lulled into a state of security that had always been fragile at the very best. God, she was in *his* kitchen, as comfortable as though it were her own! She had fallen into the trap of thinking that she could tame a tiger.

Even in the depths of passion he had never, not once, offered anything other than what had been put on the table from the very start. Impermanence. Passing enjoyment. Lust.

His expression was cool. He stared at her until she fidgeted, angry with him for his silence and with herself for the fear that was filling up inside her.

'Too good to be true,' he rasped stonily, 'is what comes to mind when I look at you.'

He clenched his jaw and for a moment he was catapulted back to Luisa, her unexpected knock on his office door less than an hour and a half ago. He hadn't welcomed her in. In fact, he had risen to his feet to escort her out but as he had moved impatiently towards her, she had extended her hand with a piece of paper grasped in her fingers.

'Before you throw me out—' she had halted him in his tracks '—you need to have a look at this.'

'You need to leave my office, Luisa.' But his eyes had already been drawn to the single piece of paper and he had snatched it because it had seemed the fastest way of getting rid of the woman. He had listened to Caitlin's intermittent noises about Luisa and had played them down, omitting to tell her that he had fended off an unpleasant phone call from the other woman shortly after he had arrived in London. Why open a can of worms? The minute Luisa had accosted him in his office, he had assumed that she was going to pursue her plea to think about their long family connection and the value of resurrecting their defunct relationship.

This time, he'd thought, he wasn't going to bother with politeness.

He had half looked at that damning sheet of paper and then had looked more carefully.

Now, standing in his kitchen, he could still feel the cold fury that had swept through him when he had registered what was written.

But before the fury…

The devastation of realising that, once again, he had been sucked into a relationship with a woman who had not been what she had seemed.

Worse, he had realised, with shock, that there was

something beyond devastation, beyond rage at his lack of judgement.

There had been the raw pain of knowing that what he'd felt for Caitlin had been far deeper than he could possibly have imagined, and on the back of that pain had come icy rage.

The self-discipline that was so much a part of his personality had masked all emotion as he had politely frozen Luisa out of the satisfaction of engineering the outcome she had anticipated, but his rage had not abated.

And now…standing here…

'Where did you get this?' Colour drained away from her face and her hand was shaking.

If ever there was a picture of guilt, he thought bitterly. What had he expected? Really? Some crazy explanation that might make sense?

Unfortunately, he knew exactly what he had expected. He had expected her to be different. When he looked back, he knew that he had thought her different from the very first moment he had clashed with her as she had skulked up the long avenue that led to his mansion. She had intrigued him, and she had continued to intrigue him, and when everything had come out in the wash about his brother he had done the unthinkable. He had dropped his guard and given her the benefit of the doubt.

For the first time in his life he had begun to play with the crazy notion of longevity.

He should have stuck to the brief and he was paying for straying from it now.

'Where?' she repeated. The beautiful lean lines of his face were unforgiving and she could understand

why. She had come to know this man in many little
ways, and for him to have proof positive that there had
been more to her relationship with Alejandro than an
altruistic desire to help him in his hour of need by pretending to be his fiancée would signal the death knell
to whatever he might have felt for her. Not love, no. But
affection, yes, and certainly desire.

The email to the bank was brief, simply giving Alejandro's private banker instructions to transfer a hefty
amount of money to her account.

'Does it matter?' Dante asked with glacial indifference.

Naturally it would have made zero difference if she
had tried to blag her way out of this, but he was still
enraged that she was making no effort to even try, and
angry with himself for caring one way or the other.

The game was up and she was showing her true colours. No more eager desire to please.

'I don't suppose it does,' Caitlin said in a low voice.
She couldn't meet his eyes. She couldn't bear the cold
accusation there, the *disappointment.*

'Is that all you have to say?' Dante gritted. '*"I don't
suppose it does"*? For the record, Luisa came by it and
very thoughtfully decided to hand it over.'

'Of course she did,' Caitlin said wearily.

'Luisa may be many things but her faults have always been out in the open. She happened to be helping
my brother pack his things and when he was out of the
room, she accidentally refreshed his computer when
she went to pick it up and curiosity got the better of
her when your name popped up on the heading along
with an account number. Quite a substantial sum of
money, I must say. A good day at the office, wouldn't

you agree?' He breathed in deeply and watched as colour suffused her. 'What were your plans for the money? Well-deserved spending spree? And did you decide that I might have been a more lucrative bet than my brother because if you managed to hook me, you might just have yourself a permanent passport to wealth instead of a one-off? Did you start as a fake fiancée only to imagine that you could become a real one but with the other heir to the throne?'

'How could you say that?' This time she *did* look at him, and with distress. 'Don't you know me at all?'

'It would seem not,' Dante grated harshly.

The truth was that he'd felt as though he *did* know her and even now, with the evidence of his own stupidity right in front of him, he *still* felt as if he did. It was an act of wilful self-delusion that enraged him further.

'Would you even make an effort to believe me if I told you that…' she sighed and blinked away a rush of miserable tears '…that it's not what you think, despite what it looks like?'

'It looks like you had a financial arrangement with my brother to cover your agreement to pose as his fiancée for the benefit of friends and family and to get our parents off his back on the business of marrying him off. How am I doing so far?'

Caitlin stared at him mutely.

'I'm gathering from your silence that I'm doing pretty good. Except you got here, and things didn't quite go according to plan. I should have paid a bit more attention to your striking lack of luggage when you arrived. I'm assuming the jaunt was supposed to be short-lived? A one-night charade then back to normal with a much-inflated bank account?'

'You're seeing it all in black and white…' But actually, every single word was spot-on and there was nothing she could do to defend herself. Her own sense of guilt would have stopped her anyway.

'No wonder you were so panicked at the thought of hanging around. Until, that is, you discovered that a little hanging around might work in your favour.'

'You know that's not true. You're making it out like I'm some sort of…of…*tramp*…some sort of…*sexual predator*…' She looked him squarely in the eye. 'You were my first, Dante.'

Dante had the grace to flush but then he aggressively told himself that that counted for very little when hard evidence of her mercenary nature was in front of him.

'Why are you still continuing with…' he waved his hand at the pile of photos spread across her side of the kitchen table '…*that*?' He vaulted forward, too restless to stay still any longer, and prowled the room before coming to stand in front of her, a towering and intimidating figure. 'And why are you still living in that dump? What was the money for, Caitlin? Debts?'

'Something like that.'

'What debts?' Dante didn't understand and he didn't like the feeling. 'Forget it,' he snapped, slashing the air with his hand in a gesture of conclusion. 'I'm going to go out for an hour. In that time, I want you to pack whatever things you might have here and leave. Put it this way, when I get back I don't want to find you still here.'

Dante was never going to listen to what she had to say, Caitlin realised. He had made his mind up. The only way he would ever have entertained hearing her out would have been if he had loved her, because if he had he would see what she saw, that it wasn't black and white but a thousand shades of grey, and he would have understood.

She was realising now what the fundamental difference between lust and love was.

Lust was essentially self-centred. It went so far when it came to seeing the bigger picture, to listening and forgiving, and no further.

Love was what bridged the gap, jumped over the chasm, having faith that you would reach the other side and being willing to take the risk.

She loved Dante and she knew that, had the shoe been on the other foot, she would have listened because she would have known, in her gut, that there was no way he could be the person circumstances were portraying him to be, that there would be another explanation, however things might look on the surface.

Well, there was no point hanging around and hoping for the impossible.

She nodded quietly. 'I'll be gone by the time you get back.'

CHAPTER TEN

IN THE EVENT it was two days before Dante returned to the penthouse apartment.

One hour? There was no way he intended to risk returning to find her still there, hunting around for the last of her things and, frankly, considering the fact that she had refused to move in with him, she had managed to find homes for a lot of her personal possessions. A couple of photography books here and there…spare bedroom slippers because she had to have something on her feet when she walked around…a selection of novels, all started and not one finished because she always lost interest somewhere between Chapter Three and Chapter Four…

He hadn't wanted to head back even after a day just in case she had forgotten something and had decided to return to collect it. He had forgotten to ask her to hand over the spare key he had insisted she have. She might have kept it. Who knew? She would leave it behind her in the apartment. He knew that without having to ask himself how.

So Dante had gone off grid for the first time in his life, dumping London altogether and heading to the coast for a couple of days to clear his head.

She was gone. She'd pulled the wool over his eyes and she was gone. End of story.

He would pick up where he had left off because the world was full of beautiful women and he knew, without a trace of vanity, that he could have any of them.

Including Luisa, should he so choose, but the very thought of her made his teeth grind together. Like the messenger carrying a poisonous communication, she had been sliced out of his life for good, whatever the long-standing family connections. What she had done had been done with the worst of self-serving motives. He would wait until she tried to get in touch, which she inevitably would, to tell her exactly what he thought, but right now he just couldn't be bothered.

He couldn't be bothered with anyone or anything. He escaped London thinking that he would escape Caitlin. It had been a remarkable failure on that front.

Dante spent the first night drinking way too much at the Michelin-starred restaurant in the hotel where he had booked for the two nights.

Then he spent the second night wondering what the hell he was going to do because things seemed as clear as mud.

But by the time he began the journey back to London, clarity was imposing itself.

Without the benefit of distractions, he could think, and in the confines of his Maserati, as he drove back to London, he finally began to see what had been lurking on the sidelines of his mind for so long now. Like wisps of smoke, warning him of a conflagration. He should have paid attention.

The warning bells should have started sounding the very second he'd decided to cross that ocean and meet her again. Then he had entered a comfort zone without even realising it. He had become accustomed to the way she laughed and looked at him, to the comfortable silences between them.

He hadn't been fazed by the sight of her toothbrush next to his or her photos spread across his kitchen table, as they had been when he had confronted her about that damned email.

Dante began joining all the dots on his way back to London and by the time he hit the crowded outskirts of the city, he was frantic to do what he should have done a long time ago. He had to be honest. He had to stop pretending that he was an island.

He had to move on from hard and fast notions that had dominated his life and kept his emotions under lock and key.

But first and foremost, he had to convince her to hear him out. He stopped at his apartment only to dump his bag and have a rushed shower.

All evidence of her had been carefully removed.

The place was immaculate, wiped clean of her presence. Not even the faintest of smells lingered. That flowery, clean smell that followed her wherever she went? Gone.

He knew the way to her apartment like the back of his hand, even though he had, very quickly, refused to go there, preferring the comfort of his penthouse.

At a little after midday, there were signs of life, with kids out and about in front of the block of flats, aimlessly cycling around. He headed up to hers, nodding a greeting to some elderly lady with whom Caitlin had developed a firm friendship.

'She's not there.'

Dante stopped dead in his tracks. 'I have a key. I'll wait.'

Shared keys…something else that should have set those bells ringing in his head. Since when had he ever come close to handing a key to his place over to any woman, far less having a key for hers?

'You'll be waiting a long time, son.'

'Why?' Panic gripped him, like a vice.

'She's gone to her parents'. Told me to keep an eye on her place because she might be a while.'

'Her parents'?' He realised that, despite his knowing so much about her, she had singularly failed to talk to him about her parents. She had told him about her ex, about where she had grown up, had passed occasional remarks about her childhood, but her parents…? No, she hadn't mentioned them and suddenly that failing felt significant. 'Would you happen to have their address?'

She did. She handed it over. There were a lot of questions, most of which Dante answered as honestly as he could and to the best of his ability, given that he was inept when it came to disclosing how he felt about anything with a complete stranger.

But he realised that he would, frankly, have done whatever it took to know how he could find the woman he had fallen hopelessly in love with.

He would climb a thousand mountains and walk a thousand miles, but on a more pressing level there was, he now realised, just one more thing he had to do first…

Caitlin heard the buzz of the doorbell. It was irritating, really, because this was the sixth night at her parents' house and the first evening she had had in on her own. The previous nights had been spent doing the rounds, as she had had to do the minute she'd appeared, unannounced, on her parents' doorstep.

It was a small village and people would have been offended if she hadn't immediately dropped by. Where her parents lived, being a recluse was practically a punishable offence, and it had been pretty reassuring visiting a couple of her parents' friends, knowing that they knew about the dire situation and were supportive.

The local vicar, another on the list of people she had seen and the first person who had shown up within hours of her arrival, was also fully in the know and very sympathetic.

They were all trying to keep spirits upbeat.

Everyone was rallying around.

Notwithstanding, that still left the matter of the finances that needed sorting out and this was her first evening in when she could really get down to seeing what was going on.

Her parents were out for the evening, dinner at friends'.

So the buzz of the doorbell, which she knew heralded another well-intentioned visitor, was...*irritating.*

She took her time getting to the door. She hoped that whoever was there might slink off, thinking that the house was empty.

But there was another buzz and so she pulled open the door and...

Déjà vu.

Hadn't she been here before? Staring at muscular legs encased in faded black jeans? At a body she had touched a million times? A face whose lines she knew from memory?

Hadn't this guy shown up, unannounced, on her doorstep once upon a time?

All those thoughts flashed through Caitlin's head in the seconds it took for her to register Dante's shocking appearance at the door.

'I know.' He tried a smile on for size. 'You're going to tell me that we've been down this road before.'

His voice was lazy and controlled but his heart wasn't. He was standing on the edge of a precipice, gazing down at a sheer drop and he wasn't sure whether there would be a safety net for when he took the plunge.

Rendered speechless, Caitlin could only gape.

'I went to your apartment.' Dante filled in the silence. He had to because he didn't want her to slam the door in his face. He could have inserted himself into the house, but that he didn't want to do because he was here with a begging bowl and he wasn't about to forget that. 'I met your neighbour. She told me where you were. She gave me your parents' address…so here I am.' He shuffled uncomfortably and flushed. Desperation bloomed. She wasn't saying a word and her expression told him nothing.

'Caitlin…'

'Stop right there!'

Why was he here? He had kicked her out of his life without giving her a chance to say her piece. He hadn't been interested then so…had he come bearing more tasty damning morsels? She didn't know and she didn't want to find out.

'You have *no right* to just show up at my parents' house! You should *never* have been given the address.'

'I've made mistakes…' He looked down, then raised his eyes to meet hers.

'Is that what you've come to tell me?'

'Please let me in.'

'I already did,' Caitlin said bitterly. 'I let you in and it was the biggest mistake I ever made.'

'Don't say that. I don't want to have this conversation out here, on the doorstep. I know your parents are probably in and… I am happy to talk to you with them present.'

'What?'

'What I have to say, I would be happy for them to hear.'

Caitlin hadn't been expecting that and she hesitated. If he was here about the wretched money, then she might as well get it over and done with. She pulled open the door with marked reluctance and stood back as he walked past her into the house.

He looked around and she saw what he did, but through his eyes. A small but tidy house. Her mother had always been house-proud, and her dad had never minded a bit of DIY, and the house reflected this. In her mind's eye, she saw his magnificent estate, the vast mansion shrouded in privacy, the acres of marble that told a tale of impossible riches, a penthouse with a priceless and exquisite Chagall painting hanging in the cloakroom, just the sort of casual afterthought only a billionaire could ever afford. Anger tasted like bile in her throat when she imagined him writing her off as a cheap, nasty gold-digger.

She walked towards the kitchen and was aware of him following in her wake.

'My parents are out at the moment,' she offered tersely, 'but they'll be back soon and I don't want you around when they get back. I don't want to have to explain…anything.'

'The last time I showed up unannounced,' Dante

said, declining the cup of coffee she offered although he knew he could do with a stiff drink in its place, 'I told you that I missed you.'

Caitlin blushed a furious red and waited in silence for him to get on with it. She'd been a sucker once and she wasn't about to repeat the exercise.

He was still standing but he sat down now and so did she, like two strangers facing one another in a board-room, not quite sure how the meeting was going to go. Her spine was rigid and her fingers were curled over her knees in a defensive, vice-like grip.

'When I saw that email,' Dante plunged right in, still very much conscious of the fact that he could be chucked out at any given moment and he wouldn't blame her, 'I… I felt like the bottom of my world had dropped out. I couldn't have been more shocked and I reacted in just the way I was programmed to react.' He held up one hand because he could see that she was on the point of interrupting and he just needed to carry on saying what he had to say, had to gather momentum and run. It was the only way he was going to be able to hurl himself off the edge of that damned precipice.

Caitlin was riveted. He shouldn't be here. She shouldn't be listening to him. But there was a gut-wrenching, despairing honesty about him that held her rapt.

'I'd been let down once and, after that, I built a wall around myself. There was no way that I was ever going to be let down again. Then I got that email and read it and realised that I'd done the unthinkable. I had dropped all my defences. It was the only thing that could account for the sickening feeling in the pit of my stomach, the feeling that my world had stopped turning.' He breathed in deeply and realised his heart was racing. 'You don't believe me?'

'You've never said anything like this before.'

'I didn't…know how.'

'I'm not drifting back into some sort of relationship with you because you still want me in your bed.'

'When I said that I missed you, I should have said the bits I miss most aren't the ones where you occupy my bed. Not that I don't miss those.'

'I don't know what you're trying to tell me.'

'I'm trying to tell you that I don't care. I don't care about whatever financial arrangement you had with my brother. I don't care whether you needed the money to cover a lifestyle of fast cars and gambling dens.'

Caitlin raised both eyebrows. She was still clutching her knees, but the white-knuckle ride was abating and something inside her was melting.

'You didn't even hear me out,' she said painfully. 'You just went ahead and assumed the worst.'

'I did and I will regret that for the rest of my life.'

'You searched me out once, Dante, because you felt that what we had should have carried on. I'm not that same person any longer.' She really wasn't, she thought. She was way too involved to risk having her heart broken all over again.

'I don't expect you to carry on with what we had,' Dante told her seriously. 'It wouldn't be what I wanted. I don't want a fling with you, *querida*. I want the rest of my life with you.'

Caitlin blinked and gaped.

'You're kidding…'

Dante reached into his pocket. The black box had been burning a hole there since he had entered her house. That thing he'd had to do, the final step he'd had to take.

The box sat in the palm of his hand, then he opened it, his dark eyes firmly pinned to her face, registering her tremulous disbelief, then the dawning smile that told him that everything was going to be just fine.

'Far from it. I'm deadly serious. I love you and I can't envisage a life without you in it. I want you to wear this ring and then I want you to wear my wedding ring next to it.'

Caitlin stared then she smiled and tentatively reached out to touch the ring with one finger. It was the most beautiful thing she had ever seen, a solitaire diamond glittering in its bed of white gold, and on the band were tiny diamonds, like perfect tiny stars paying homage to that single, glittering and much bigger one that nestled in the centre.

'Am I dreaming?' she murmured to herself. She raised her eyes, barely able to breathe.

'You're not dreaming.' He took a chance and slipped the ring onto her finger and then stared in silence because this was the biggest thing he had ever done in his life before. It literally rendered him speechless. He gently stroked her finger before continuing gravely, 'I had a few days away from everything after you left and I came to my senses. It took me a while. But how could I recognise the symptoms of something I'd never felt before?'

'You want to spend the rest of your life with me?' She couldn't stop staring at the ring, now on her finger, the perfect fit.

'Why do you think I told you that I would have this conversation in front of your parents? I want to marry you, Caitlin Walsh, so will you say yes?'

'Just try and stop me.' She breathed unsteadily, then went over to him and curled herself onto his lap, her arms flung round his neck, loving the tightness of his embrace.

'The money thing…' She pulled back and looked at him and sighed.

He reached to shush her but she held his finger in her hand and squeezed it.

Then she stood up and pulled a chair right up next to his so that her legs were pressed between his and she could rest her hands on his thighs. The gleaming diamond, so much a tangible statement of intent, so much *Dante*, who was a man of such intent, gave her the strength to come clean and broach the topic that had severed their relationship.

'Where to start? I knew that Alejandro was terrified about coming out. I think he felt that he had gone as far as he could resisting his parents' efforts to marry him off and, in his desperation, he came up with the idea of me posing as his fiancée, basically to bide time until…until you decided to settle down, which would take the heat off him. It was a crazy idea, really, and I didn't want to go along with it but I felt sorry for him. He said that it would be a business deal and I refused.'

She felt tears trying to leak out of the corners of her eyes as she thought back to the train of events that had led to her changing her mind.

'I kept refusing and then two things happened in very quick succession. My parents ran into some terrible financial debt. My dad had been scammed and he'd been keeping it quiet. I found out and basically… he'd been conned out of all his savings. I won't go into the details, but it was very clever. He was mortified.

His pension isn't huge, and those savings were going to be the foundation for their old age. Of course, I told them that I would help, but shortly after my mother had a heart attack. Stress induced, the doctor said.' She sighed. 'And there was Alejandro, with that plan still at the back of his mind. I caved in. I took him up on his offer. So you see, there were debts but not mine and not of my making.' She paused. 'Only thing was I hadn't banked on the guilt. I couldn't take the money in the end. Maybe if it had all stayed as a business arrangement, but then things happened and I got involved with you... The money is untouched and I intend to force it back to Alejandro as soon as he gets to London. He refuses to let me have his account details so I might just have to show up with a few sacks of coins and bills.' She smiled. 'I don't blame you for suspecting the worst.'

'You should blame me for everything,' Dante told her gravely. 'Most of all for being a fool and almost letting you go. Trust me, I intend to spend the rest of my life making you happy.' He leant forward and drew her towards him and kissed her.

It felt as if he was coming home. It was just where he wanted to be.

There was a lavish wedding in Spain. Tradition, Dante had told her wryly, was tradition and his parents were finally getting the wedding they had wanted for a while. Both sets of parents hit it off and there was so much parental involvement on both sides that Caitlin wasn't quite sure just how vital her contributions were.

But it all went off without a hitch. The dress was spectacular, as was the awesome cathedral. Her heart fluttered and her mouth ran dry the minute her eyes found Dante waiting for her with his brother to his right, the very proud ring bearer.

Then, a mere handful of days later, there was a far smaller do close to her parents' home, where family and friends celebrated the union over a home-cooked meal prepared by the caterer at the one and only hotel in the village.

The honeymoon was wonderful. Two weeks in the Maldives, where all those problems that had afflicted her once upon a time seemed very long ago.

But then, she was living a new life now, with the man she loved.

That very man was right at this moment pouring her a glass of wine while she relaxed on the sofa, a lovely vantage point from which she could appreciate him.

The honeymoon had come and gone. Reality of life with Dante was even sweeter than she could possibly have imagined.

'We need to sort out where we're going to live.' He handed her the glass and Caitlin dutifully rested it on the low coffee table next to her.

'Now that my brother is jet-setting in his new role, I think London will be my base. Naturally we can return to Madrid whenever we wish, but I feel that this would be more suitable for us, as a couple.'

Caitlin nodded and tried to imagine bringing up a family in a penthouse. Glass and toddlers were not a happy mix. Should she mention that now?

'And not here.' He grinned.

'Since when did you become a mind reader?'

'It's called being in love.'

She was wearing some comfy track pants and a

baggy top and when she shuffled along the sofa to snuggle against him, the warmth of her little body suffused him with the sort of deep contentment he had never envisaged for himself.

'Where were you thinking?' she asked, inclining her head so that their eyes met.

'To be decided. We can discuss where but I'm thinking within commuting distance from London but far out enough to be surrounded by some open land. And, of course, more in the direction of your parents.'

'That's a good idea,' Caitlin murmured, 'because we're going to need a bit of space and a bit of land and less sharp corners and glass surfaces.'

'We are?' Dante stilled, his sharp eyes noticing that the wine, her favourite brand, was untouched.

'I only found out this morning and I wanted to surprise you, my darling...'

'You've succeeded.' He angled her so that he could kiss her and kiss her he did. Then he looked at her and stroked her face with such tenderness that her heart expanded until it wanted to burst.

'A baby on the way.' He couldn't stop grinning. 'I love you, my darling. You make my life complete and a baby to come? It couldn't get any better...'

* * * * *

DESIGNED BY LOVE

SHERYL LISTER

For all of you who believe in love at first sight.

Chapter 1

"We miss you, Jeremy!"

Jeremy Hunter smiled at his family. They were huddled around his brother Cedric's iPad screen while Jeremy sat in his hotel room Sunday night. They were celebrating his cousin Alisha's three-month-old baby daughter's christening. "I miss you guys, too."

"How's Madrid?" his mother asked.

"So far, so good. The time difference is still giving me fits, but I slept a lot today." He had chosen to fly in two days early for the weeklong engineering conference that would start tomorrow.

"Don't forget to take a lot of pictures."

He chuckled. "I won't." His mother had only reminded him twenty times in the last week—in person, by phone and by text.

Cedric took the iPad back. "What day are you speaking?"

"Wednesday. I'm glad it's not tomorrow and that it's earlier in the week. It'll give me more time to relax, explore and not be worried about the presentation." He would be conducting a session on medical robotics.

"Hey, brother-in-law." Cedric's wife, Randi, waved into the screen. She sat next to Cedric and laid her head on his shoulder, and Cedric kissed her forehead.

Jeremy shook his head at his brother's expression. His diehard bachelor brother had fallen for the feisty fire investigator in less than three months, and Jeremy had lost a two-hundred-dollar bet because of it. "Hey, Randi. How are you feeling?"

She smiled and rubbed a hand over her belly. "Growing," she said with a laugh. "Eight weeks and four days to go, but who's counting?"

"I can't wait to be an uncle." He could hear the animated chatter in the background. His aunt, uncle and cousins from LA had made the trip to Sacramento, and Jeremy wished he was there. He laughed at the irony that in the past few years, along with his brother and three female cousins, all of his male cousins had married. Each of them had been adamant about keeping his bachelorhood intact, and each had met a special woman who'd made him change his perspective. Jeremy had always been the only one who believed in love and wanted to find Mrs. Right, and he'd told them he would know her on sight. He had endured years of teasing when they were younger, and yet he was the only one still single.

"Does that mean you'll be available for babysitting whenever we need you, Dr. Hunter?"

"Ced, with the way you hardly let Randi out of your sight, I'll be lucky to see my new niece or nephew before she or he is five."

Randi laughed. "You've got a point."

Cedric divided a glance between his brother and wife. "Isn't it past your bedtime, baby brother?"

Jeremy chuckled. "That worked when I was five, but I can do whatever I want now. You'll have to save that for your kids." He'd teased his brother about settling down before he got too old to have kids, but at age thirty-six, he had started to wonder the same thing concerning himself.

"I can't wait." He placed another quick kiss on Randi's lips. "Speaking of kids, you might want to hurry up and find that Mrs. Right you've always talked about, otherwise *you'll* be the one pushing a stroller in one hand and balancing a cane in the other."

"Whatever."

"Any prospects?"

"Not yet." The last woman Jeremy had dated complained that he didn't wine and dine her often enough. She had been upset when he'd suggested they have an evening in and acted almost offended by his offer to cook dinner. That had been right around Valentine's Day and Jeremy decided he needed a break. "It is almost midnight, though, and there are a couple of morning sessions I want to attend, so I need to call it a night."

"Okay. Email and let me know how your presentation went. If you can find someone, have them record it."

"Will do."

"I'm proud of you, Doc."

Smiling, he said, "Thanks." It meant everything to have his big brother's support. Initially, he had thought about going the same route as Cedric and working for their family's construction company, but, after being introduced to robotics, had changed direction. "Tell

Alisha I'll bring Kali's gift over when I get back." They spoke a few minutes longer, then ended the call.

Jeremy went to stand on the balcony and stared up at the dark sky. The daytime temperatures had reached eighty, but the nights dropped down into the fifties and reminded him of home. He stood there awhile, thinking about how fortunate he'd been in his career. He'd started his own medical robotics company three years ago after the notoriety he gained when he won an award for his contributions to robotics and automation. Since then, he'd secured a couple of grants and three contracts for building surgery robots. They'd afforded him the ability to hire three other engineers, along with his best friend and business manager, Christian Hill, and a receptionist. He did have some concerns about completing the latest contract, as one of his engineers had given notice last week. Jeremy had left Chris in charge of advertising and hiring for the position, and hoped there'd be some good news by the time Jeremy made it home next week.

His thoughts shifted to his presentation. He would spend a little time on it tomorrow, but he was as ready as he could be. He'd presented at a few smaller conferences, but not on the international stage. Recording the session would not only give his family an opportunity to see it, but also allow Jeremy to make adjustments. After a few more minutes, he went back inside and closed the door. He had already showered, so he set the alarm on his phone, turned off the lamp and slid beneath the covers.

Jeremy woke up Monday morning feeling refreshed. His body had finally adjusted to the time change. He ordered room service and, while eating, went over the conference schedule. This morning, he planned to attend workshops on soft robotics and autonomous robot design. The session that most excited him wouldn't be until Tuesday afternoon with a Dr. S. Edwards, who would discuss tactile sensors. It was of particular interest to him because he'd started a personal project to develop an artificial hand that closely mimicked human function.

On the way to his first session, he nodded greetings to a few people he'd met at other conferences. The long hall leading to the various meeting rooms had tables lined against either side of the walls with all manner of promotional brochures. Jeremy's steps slowed. A beautiful brown-skinned beauty sat in a chair next to an information table scribbling furiously on a notepad. She wore a pair of stylish rose-gold-rimmed glasses with some kind of bling bordering them and had a mass of curls sitting on top of her head. She lifted her head and their eyes connected briefly. He felt a jolt of awareness and his lips tilted in a smile. Her eyes widened and she looked away hastily before continuing to write. He noticed she wore the same badge identifying all the attendees but couldn't read her name from where he stood. Jeremy toyed with stopping to ask, but his session would be starting in five minutes and he still had to find the room. With any luck, their paths would cross later in the week. There were few women in the field of robotics and even fewer women of color, which aroused his curiosity further.

Jeremy found the room just as the speaker started and slid into a chair near the back. Fifteen minutes in, he could barely keep his eyes open. While the information presented was interesting, he couldn't say the same about the man talking. The monotone sound of the man's voice had several other people's eyes closing, as well. Jeremy sincerely hoped the rest of the day didn't go the same way. His mind drifted to the woman in the hall—beauty and brains, a lethal combination in his book, and he wouldn't mind getting to know her. As soon as he found her again.

"Excuse me, Miss. I seem to have gotten myself turned around. Can you tell me how to get to this room?"

Serita Edwards stared up at the man pointing to a room on the conference brochure and mentally counted to ten. He was the fourth person to ask her for directions in the past half hour. "I have no idea. I'm—"

He let out an impatient sigh. "What is it with you hotel staff?"

She lifted a brow. "*I beg your pardon.* I am not part of this hotel's staff. I paid my money just like you did to attend this conference, which is why I'm wearing the exact same badge as you."

The man had the decency to look embarrassed. "Oh, I just assumed since you were sitting here…"

Granted, she was sitting next to the information table, but not behind it. "There are two other people sitting on the other side of this table, yet you didn't ask one of them. Now, if you'll excuse me." Serita snatched up her belongings and with a parting glare stalked off down the hallway. She went to one of the cafés and ordered a cup of café con leche. She had never been a coffee drinker, but Caroline, a woman she'd met at a previous conference, urged her to try it yesterday when they'd had breakfast together. Serita had been immediately hooked. She would definitely be finding a good recipe for this once she returned home.

As she sipped the warm drink, she thought about all she needed to do when she returned to the States. As an adjunct professor, her appointment had been a temporary one and, after not having her contract renewed for the semester at the college where she taught in Nevada, she'd decided to move back home to Sacramento, California, at the end of October. That gave her a month to get her condo sold and all her belongings boxed up. Serita had already started sorting through everything and put the condo on the market, but finding a job topped her priority list. She'd been an adjunct professor for three years, but found she missed the excitement of working in the field. Glancing down at her watch, she realized she only had an hour before her session, and the butterflies began dancing in her belly. Her best friend, Gabriella Lewis, couldn't understand why Serita would be nervous, since she made a living talking in front of a class. In Serita's mind, talking to students was far less intimidating than speaking in a room full of peers, some who had much more experience and knowledge than she did. She was tempted to go over her notes again but resisted the urge. She knew the presentation by heart.

Serita closed her eyes and drew in a deep, calming breath. *You can do this*, she repeated to herself over and over. She relaxed, opened her eyes and met the amused stare of the gorgeous giant of a man she'd seen yesterday. Even though he stood behind a small group of people, his towering height gave her a clear view of his face. She wondered if there was some sports thing happening in the area because he certainly had the look and body of an athlete. She gave him an imperceptible nod and went back to her coffee. When she finished, she went up to her room for a moment to freshen up, then headed downstairs for her session.

Thankfully, her assigned room didn't have a session that hour, which gave her ample time to set up her materials and have the staff ensure the microphone worked. People started trickling in as she finished and Serita went back to the podium, clipped the microphone to her top and the battery on her pants waistband. She believed in starting on time and, at precisely two, began her presentation.

"What if we could create a tactile sensor that had the ability to measure touch and vibration, both in the air and under water?" She waited a moment and saw several people in the audience lean forward. She smiled inwardly, then continued her discussion of the uses and benefits of the device. She scanned the room and went still, promptly losing her train of thought for a brief moment. Sitting in the far corner of the room was Mr. Athletic. This time, unlike the previous times she'd seen him, she had a clear view of his badge. Shaking herself mentally, Serita refocused on her talk, grateful that she knew the information like the back of her hand. Two hours later, she ended with, "These sensors offer an alternative route to imitating the functions of human skin and are suitable for use with artificial skin applications, smart gloves for robotics, as well as surgery tools. They're cost-effective, and have a wide range of sensitivities and are able to operate wirelessly."

Afterward, Serita took as many questions as time allowed. Because there were no other sessions after hers, many people stayed around to ask more questions.

She collected business cards from those who wanted more information on the research and handed out the brochure she'd created. When the last person left, she gathered up the remaining materials and placed them in her tote bag.

"I don't know what impresses me more, beauty or your brains."

She whirled around at the sound of the deep, seductive voice. Mr. Athletic had a hip propped on the table a few feet away, his arms folded and a twinkle in his eye. He straightened and sauntered toward her with one of the sexiest walks she'd seen in a while.

"It's the brains, I'm thinking." He stuck out his hand. "I'm Jeremy Hunter."

"Serita Edwards, but then you already knew that." His large hand engulfed her small one.

Jeremy smiled and a dimple appeared in his right cheek. "That introduction was for the workshop, this one is personal. I really enjoyed your presentation."

"Thank you." Serita realized belatedly he hadn't let go of her hand and she gently pulled back. He towered over her five-foot-three-inch frame by a good foot or more and looked even better close up. He stared at her with such intensity that Serita felt her cheeks warm. To distract herself, she glanced around to make sure she had everything. "How long have you been in the field?"

"Sixteen years. And you?"

She tried to do a mental calculation. If he'd been in robotics that long, it would put him closer to forty and he didn't look anywhere near that age. "Just over eight years."

"Are you in a rush?"

"I… No." She really should have said she had evening plans, especially since she sensed his interest. She didn't do long-distance relationships—okay, she didn't do them at all right now—but couldn't resist the opportunity to talk shop for a few extra minutes.

"Great. Would you like to have dinner?"

"Dinner?"

He chuckled. "Yes, dinner. I thought we could continue our conversation over a good meal."

"Oh." Of course, he only wanted to discuss robotics. That seemed to be the story of her life. Either men only wanted to talk about work or thought she was too nerdy and wanted to change her.

"So what do you say? We can eat here, but I'd rather explore the city. Maybe we can check out Plaza de España. I'm sure we can find something in that area."

The Plaza de España had been one of the places Serita planned to visit and figured she'd be on her own, but it might be nice for them to go together. At least she'd have someone to take her picture, instead of trying to manage selfies that never turned out. "Actually, that's one of the spots on my bucket list. I'll accept your invitation."

Jeremy grinned, then checked his watch. "It's almost five now. What time would you like to leave?"

"The earlier we leave, the longer we can hang out. I can meet you near the registration desk in thirty minutes."

"Thirty minutes it is, Ms. Edwards."

"Please call me Serita."

"Only if you call me Jeremy." He angled his head thoughtfully. "Serita. I like that name." He paused. "It fits you."

She waited for him to say something else, but he continued smiling and gestured her forward. They made small talk on the way to the elevator and every time she answered him, she had to crane her neck. "How tall are you?"

"Six-four, why?"

"Because I feel like I need a ladder to see your face." Jeremy laughed.

"I think our conversations are going to have to be conducted while we're sitting. Otherwise, I'm going to need some serious therapy on my neck."

An elevator arrived as they approached and he stepped back to let her enter. He selected his floor and stared down at her. "I'd be happy to help you out." He lifted his hands and wiggled his fingers. "These babies right here can give you a massage you'll never forget." He tossed her a bold wink.

No way am I touching that comment. Serita didn't have to touch it. Her mind visualized his big hands massaging and stroking her body just fine. Warmth crept up her spine. She hit the button and clamped her jaws shut.

They got to her floor first and he held the door open. "I'll see you in a few minutes."

He was staring at her again in that penetrating way, as if he'd seen inside her mind and knew her thoughts. "Okay." She forced her feet to move and hurried down the hallway without looking back.

In her room, Serita changed into black jeans and a gray short-sleeved top. The temperatures had reached eighty that day, but she knew it would cool off in the evening, so she took down her black jacket and laid it over the back of the chair. She applied lip gloss, then stood in the bathroom trying to decide whether to leave her hair up or let it down. After a minute, she went with the latter. It had taken her a while to get her natural curls to behave, but she loved the style.

Since she still had some extra time, she powered up her laptop and checked her email to see if she'd gotten any responses from her job applications. Serita sighed. Not one had replied, as yet. Just as she closed the browser, her FaceTime popped up. She opened the application and smiled when she saw Gabriella calling.

"Hey, Serita. How did the session go?"

"It went well and I had a lot of questions at the end."

"I knew you'd be fine. I can't believe how worried you were." Gabriella rolled her eyes.

Serita had expressed her fears to her friend more than once. "This was presenting on an entirely different scale. I've seen people with far more experience tank in front of an audience, and I worked extra hard to make sure my name didn't get added to the list. Initially, I wasn't too happy about having my presentation on the second day, but now I'm kind of glad. I can relax and enjoy the rest of the week."

She smiled. "Be sure to take lots of pictures."

"I plan to."

"Any news on the job front?"

Serita blew out a long breath. "Not yet." She had hoped to find a job before her scheduled move back to Sacramento at the end of October. Although she missed her parents, she didn't want to have to move in with them.

"Well, I'm confident you'll find one soon. You know I've got you covered, girl. You can stay with me until something comes up."

She frowned. "What happened to Jodi?"

"Not paying her half of the rent on time for the past

three months is what happened," Gabriella said. She had allowed Jodi, another one of their college friends, to move into her two-bedroom condo six months ago, and lately the woman had one excuse after another as to why she never had her share of the cost.

"I thought she had a good job."

"She does, but her priorities tend to be on finding the latest and cutest outfit rather than her bills. So, I told her she had thirty days to find another place. That was two weeks ago. She keeps asking me about extending the deadline and, in the same breath, saying she needs more time to come up with the money. I'm *done*."

Serita didn't know what to say. Jodi had seemed so focused and together in college. Serita guessed she hadn't known her friend well at all. "Wow. I'm sorry." Gabby had always been a good friend, and people tended to take her kindness for granted until they found out Gabby didn't allow anyone to walk all over her.

"Me, too. Something told me it would be a bad idea to let her move in." Gabriella shook her head. "I should've listened. Anyway, it's just about dinnertime there. Are you going to try out one of those restaurants in the city?"

She gasped and glanced at the time. "Oh, shoot! I have to go. I'm supposed to be meeting Jeremy in five minutes."

Gabriella's eyes widened and a smile curved her lips. "*Jeremy?* I see you didn't waste any time. You go, girl."

She waved her friend off. "It's not like that. He attended my session and said he wanted to continue the conversation. It'll be just talking shop, nothing more." And it still bothered her for some reason.

"What does he look like?"

"About six-four, athletic build, bronze-like skin and fine with a capital *F*." An image of his smile floated through her mind, along with that sexy dimple. "I'll talk to you later in the week."

"Preferably tomorrow, so you can fill me in on *all* the juicy details of this date."

Serita chuckled. "I'll try." She ended the call, shut down the computer, and grabbed her jacket and purse. As she made her way to the lobby, she shook her head. It was just her luck to meet a sexy-as-sin man, and the most interesting thing she had to offer him was her expertise in robotics.

Chapter 2

Jeremy stood in the lobby waiting for Serita. The impulse to invite her to dinner had come out of nowhere. He hadn't been exactly forthcoming with her, however. Yes, he'd been captivated by the knowledge, but even more so by the woman. When he'd seen her in the hallway earlier, he had sensed something and wanted to know what it was. He straightened from the wall when he saw her exit the elevator. She scanned the area and, spotting him, hurried over.

"I'm so sorry I'm late. My friend called and I lost track of time," Serita said in a rush.

"Yeah, you're really late by like…" He glanced down at his watch. "A whole thirty seconds." He chuckled. "You're fine. Ready?"

She visibly relaxed. "Yes."

"Did you come up with any dinner suggestions?"

Serita stared up at him. "No. I had planned to Google some places, but didn't get a chance."

A group of people passed, forcing her to move closer to him. Whatever fragrance she was wearing played havoc on his senses. The mixture of sweet and sexy had him tempted to bury his face in her neck and trail kisses there. His gaze dropped to her gloss-slicked lips and he fantasized about tasting them. The urge to kiss her rose up so strong inside Jeremy it shocked him. "There are some restaurants within walking distance, so I'm sure we'll find something."

She nodded.

Jeremy gestured her forward and tried to understand why he felt so drawn to Serita. Outside, several other people seemed to have the same idea. They strolled leisurely down the street, stopping more than once to take in the sights.

"Have you been here before?"

He looked down at her. "No, it's my first time. What about you?"

"It's my first time, too."

"Then we should make each moment count." Their eyes held for a lengthy moment before she turned away and continued walking. The attraction between them seemed to be rising by the second. He knew they were both there for the conference, but outside of that, he wanted to spend as much time with her as possible. The tree-lined street had several storefront shops with second-story wrought-iron balconies. He wondered if the shop owners lived above their businesses.

"This is so nice." Serita pulled out her phone and snapped a couple of pictures. "Can you take one of me? I suck at selfies."

Laughing, he reached for her phone. "Sure." He got a number of shots with her in front of the different stores. She had the most beautiful smile, and Jeremy couldn't resist capturing it on his own phone before turning the camera toward the street. He held it up for a selfie, then bent close to Serita and took one of the two of them. He had no idea if he'd ever see her again and wanted a memory of their evening.

She peered at his phone. "Can I see?"

He showed her the photo.

"Mine never come out like that," she said with a pout. "They're either blurry, too close, or I cut off half my face."

Jeremy smiled inwardly. She had just given him his opening to spend more time together. "I tell you what— if you agree to be my tourist partner for the week, I'll teach you how to take selfies like a pro."

"I...um..." Serita folded her arms and studied him. "Exactly what does that entail?" she asked, still sounding a little unsure.

He shrugged. "Exploring the city and whatever else you want to do."

She didn't say anything at first. Finally she said, "Okay."

A grin spread across his face. Her agreeing to his proposal gave him a week to figure out whether the pull he felt was a pure case of lust or more. Jeremy needed to know if she was the woman he'd been waiting for. His Mrs. Right. He extended his arm. "Then let's get this party started."

She gave him a bright smile and hooked her arm in his. "Sounds like a plan."

They walked another few steps and came to a painted-brick-and-concrete storefront restaurant.

"What about here?"

He studied the menu mounted on the wall for a couple of minutes. "What do you think?"

"I think we have a winner."

Jeremy held the door open for her.

"Wow, it's a lot bigger than I thought."

The Dantxari had a cozy feel, wooden tables covered in red tablecloths with matching napkins, antique clocks and stained-glass windows. "I agree." They had a short wait before being led to one of the tables near the back. He went to pull out Serita's chair and she jumped. "Sorry, didn't mean to startle you. I just want to help you with your chair."

"Thank you."

Once she was seated, he rounded the table and took the chair across from her. "Does this mean you've never had a man pull a chair out for you?"

Serita picked up her menu. "I haven't."

He took quiet satisfaction in being the first. "No? Well, this week, you can expect your doors to be opened, your chair pulled out and me standing when you enter a room. Oh, and I'll be paying for dinner." Along with every other expense during their time together in Madrid.

She jerked her head up. "Wait. What? Why would you do all those things? And I was going to... You can't pay for my dinner."

He smiled inwardly at her flustered state. "To answer your first question, I'll do all those things because it's how I was raised to treat a woman. And second, why can't I pay for your dinner? I invited you."

"Because you can't. I mean, we aren't dating or seeing each other or anything. I just met you a couple of hours ago."

Jeremy laughed softly. She mentioned them not dating or seeing each other, but he wondered what she would say if he told her he wanted to do just that. "I realize this is the twenty-first century and some men choose not to maintain the chivalrous behavior of their fathers and grandfathers, but, again, that's not how I was raised. Whether we met two years ago or two hours ago won't change my perspective." She eyed him for a moment and he winked. He picked up his menu. "So, what looks good?"

Serita lowered her head. After a couple of minutes, she said, "I'm not sure."

A server came to the table and explained several of the dishes. They both decided on cod croquettes, white asparagus in butter sauce and beef steak for two. While waiting for their food, Jeremy got up and came around to her side of the table.

"What are you doing?"

"We're going to have your first selfie lesson?"

"Here?"

"Yes. I'm sure you want to show your family and friends the highlights of your trip. Restaurants top the list of photos."

She groaned. "Are you serious? I figured you'd just take one of me at the table and we'd start tomorrow or something."

He shook his head and smiled. "Come on, it's not hard."

She rolled her eyes and took out her phone. "I'd better come away with at least one good picture," she said, holding up one finger for emphasis. But she was smiling.

"I promise." He moved one of the chairs and sat next to her and explained the best angles to take the selfie.

Serita held the phone up and snapped one, looked at it and let out a sigh. "See, I knew it wasn't going to come out right. Every time I think I have it in the right spot, the camera moves when I push the button. Your hands are bigger than mine, so I need two hands."

"Actually, you can use the volume down button."

She stared. "Are you serious?"

"Yep. Try it."

She tried again. "Finally, a decent picture. All this time I could've been using that button, instead of trying to hold it in one hand and hit the button on the other." She shook her head. "It's still a little dark, but at least I didn't cut off any body parts this time." She smiled at him, then seemed to realize how close they were and backed away.

Once again, Jeremy had an overwhelming desire to kiss her. Instead, he went back to his seat. "That'll be lesson number two." The server returned with their food.

"This looks really good."

"It does. Great restaurant choice."

Serita snapped a picture of her plate, then turned the phone toward him. "Now, this one I can do."

He laughed and, after reciting a silent blessing, dug in. Jeremy found himself enjoying her more and more.

Serita sat across from her dining partner waiting for him to bring up the subject of robotics. They were almost finished eating and he had yet to ask one question. They'd talked about everything from the weather and jet lag to some of the sessions they had attended earlier. All except hers. She set down her fork. "I thought you wanted to talk to me about robotics."

Jeremy grinned sheepishly. "Actually, I just wanted to ask you out to dinner to get to know you. I wasn't sure you'd agree, so I said the first thing that came to mind. You aren't mad, are you?"

She stared. How could she be mad at a man who wanted to spend time with her for something other than work? "No. Truthfully, I'm a little flattered, and I probably would have said yes anyway."

A slow smile spread across his lips. "Good to know. So, next time, I'll just tell you up front that it's a date. But since you brought it up, how did you get into robotics?"

Next time? A date? He'd slid that first comment in so smoothly she almost missed it. "You think there's going to be a next time?"

"I most certainly do. Did you forget that you said you'd hang out with me this week in exchange for selfie lessons?"

Yeah, she'd forgotten that quickly. "Of course I remember." The smile on his face said he didn't believe her for a second. The heated intensity in his dark brown eyes said a whole lot more, and she resisted the urge to fan herself. She'd never had a man look at her the way Jeremy did and, although they'd just met, for a brief moment she fantasized about how it would feel to spend time with him past the week. A soft touch on her hand drew Serita out of her reverie.

"Hey, where did you go?"

"Oh, sorry. Just thinking about how we're going to manage the selfie lessons with the conference and all."

Serita applauded herself for being able to tell that lie with a straight face. She thought it time to change the subject. "You asked how I got into robotics. Initially, I'd planned to go to med school, but in tenth grade, my friend's father lost his arm in a factory accident, and I was fascinated by the prosthetic arm he had. Granted, they were nowhere near as functional as they are now, but I was intrigued nonetheless. I started researching and changed my direction. My high school had a pre-biomedical track and that helped. How about you?" Before he could answer, the server came back to clear their plates and take their dessert order. They both opted for the lemon sherbet with champagne and vodka.

Jeremy leaned back in his chair and continued the conversation. "I've always liked building things. My family owns a construction company and I figured I'd follow in my dad and older brother's footsteps, but I also enjoyed science. My parents sent me to one of those science camps when I was about eleven or twelve, and one of the options was robotics. I chose that one, since it included building a robot. It was the best time of my life, and by the time I left that camp I knew what I wanted to do with my life. Before I got to high school, I'd found the college I wanted to attend and did everything I could to make sure I got into that program."

The server returned with the desserts. After thanking her, Serita asked Jeremy, "Where did you go?"

"UC Davis for undergrad. I didn't want to be far away from my family in Sacramento, so I could easily drive to Davis and back daily. But I ended up at University of Michigan, Ann Arbor, for my doctorate."

Serita almost dropped her spoon. *Sacramento?* But since he'd been in the field so long, chances were that he still lived in Michigan. Even if he had moved back home, Sacramento was a big city. She doubted they'd run into each other. She tried to concentrate on the sweet, tart taste of the sherbet mixed with the crisp champagne.

"Where did you go to school?"

"University of Nevada at Reno."

"Is that where you live?"

"Yes." *For now.*

His smile widened. "That's only a couple of hours from Sac and an easy drive. We'll have to exchange contact information before the week is up. I'd like to keep in touch, so we can hang out together sometimes."

"Um…okay." He'd given her the perfect opening to mention her move back to their hometown, but she didn't want him to get any ideas. Professionally, it couldn't hurt to keep in contact, but that was as far as she wanted to go. She didn't have a good track record with men. While finishing dessert, the topics went from their respective careers to hobbies. She realized they had a lot in common.

"Do you want anything else?"

"No, thank you." She wanted to try to make him see reason about paying for her dinner but imagined it wouldn't do any good, so she kept her mouth closed.

Jeremy settled the bill, then came around to her side to help her up. "It's still pretty early and not quite dark yet. How about we walk off some of this food?"

"Sounds good." Their walk took them to the Plaza de España. The temperatures had dropped some and Serita shrugged into her jacket. She jumped slightly when she felt Jeremy's hands brush her nape as he helped her. The only other man she'd seen do these kinds of things was her father. "Thank you." With towers in the center and at either end, the semicircular brick building had a stunning architecture. Along the wall sat a number of alcoves with benches to represent each of Spain's provinces. In the front, a canal followed the curve of the building. She braced her hands on the railing. "This is amazing."

"And it's a good place for photos," he said with a wink.

She shook her head but couldn't stop the smile that peeked out. "You would say that."

His laughter rang out in the square. "Hey, I'm just trying to keep up my end of the agreement. I'm looking forward to the rest of the week."

"If you conduct all the lessons today, you won't have anything to do the rest of the week."

His hand came up and pushed a lock of hair off her face. "Oh, I'm sure I can come up with a few things."

The intimate gesture and the accompanying look made her pulse skip and nearly melted her in a heap. For a long moment, neither of them moved and she could feel her attraction rising. Serita reminded herself that she didn't do well in relationships and that she should put a halt to whatever seemed to be brewing between them. She took a step back. "I'm going to take a few shots of the building, then see if I can get a selfie without any help."

Jeremy gave her a soft smile. "I'll wait right here."

Serita nodded, her heart still racing. It took several seconds, but she finally tore away her gaze and went to take her pictures. Though the sun had started its descent, a fair number of people still remained. Many couples strolled hand-in-hand, cuddling on benches and stealing kisses near the water. It made for a romantic scene. On her way back, she saw Jeremy leaning with his forearms braced on the railing, his face turned slightly in her direction. In his short-sleeved pullover, the position put his muscled biceps on full display. With his good looks and toned body, he could have graced the cover of every model magazine. Instinctively, she held up her phone and hit the button. She wanted something to remember him by.

"Let's see what you've got," he said when she approached.

Smiling, she held out her phone, and he angled his head close to see.

"Look at you. You'll be a pro by tomorrow at this rate."

She glanced down at the photo of herself with the building behind her and smiled. "You think so?"

"I do."

"I have to admit it's the best one I've ever taken. I might have to blow it up, frame it and hang it on my wall, just in case I never get it right again." She faced him. "I had a great teacher."

"You think so?"

"Yep." The air between them shifted suddenly, and before she could blink Jeremy brushed his lips across hers in a soft, sweet kiss. They both gasped and Serita couldn't tell who was more shocked.

"I'm sorry. I—"

"It's okay," she added with a nervous chuckle,. "It's kind of hard not to get caught up with all this beauty." And she was definitely *caught up*.

"Are you ready to head back?"

"Don't you want to take some pictures?"

"I already did." As if it were the most natural thing, he reached down and entwined their fingers. He smiled at her once more and they headed back to the hotel in companionable silence.

Serita was glad for the reprieve because she needed to think. She wanted to blame the crazy feelings swirling around in her belly on the romantic surroundings, but she'd had the same ones earlier while standing in an empty conference room, so it had to be something else. *What is going on?* Okay, the man gave new meaning to good-looking, was a total gentleman and intelligent. And the kiss. It had only lasted a short moment, but even now the remnants of his warm, soft lips against hers lingered. With all of that, she would challenge any woman to remain unmoved.

When they arrived at the hotel, Jeremy walked Serita to her room. Standing outside the door, he said, "Thank you for your company this evening. I really enjoyed myself."

"So did I."

He seemed to be weighing his next words. "About the kiss…"

"You don't need to apologize again, Jeremy."

"I appreciate that, but since we agreed to spend time together this week, I don't want you to be uncomfortable around me." He stared at a spot above her head briefly, then back down at her. "I've never done anything like that before, and I can't explain why I did it tonight. There is something about you, Ms. Edwards, that has me acting out of character. I have the utmost respect for you, and I don't want you to think otherwise."

Serita remembered him talking about his upbringing and imagined it played a part in his thinking. She was admittedly flattered and, at the same time, wondered how she'd get him to do it again. "You're not the only one acting out of character, because I think I'd like you to kiss me again." She had never done something so bold in her life, and as the words tumbled out her heart rate kicked up once more.

He studied her. "Are you sure?"

Keeping her eyes on his, she said, "Positive."

"Then, we should step inside your room. We don't want to give anyone walking down the hallway a show."

Exactly what kind of show could a simple kiss cause? Surely it wouldn't be much more than what they'd shared at the plaza. Then again, she didn't want anyone from the conference to know her business, so he might be right. She used the keycard to open the door and was thankful that she'd left the room in reasonable order. Contrary to her daring request, as soon as the door closed, butterflies began doing a salsa in her belly. She placed her purse on the desk and turned to find him standing with his back against the door. He straightened and came to where she stood. He tilted her chin, bent and covered her mouth with his. The kiss went from sweet to hot in a millisecond. His tongue swirled slowly around hers and a soft moan escaped her. Without breaking the seal of their mouths, Jeremy turned. He sat on the bed, pulled her down onto his lap and deepened the kiss. His hand caressed her back, hip and thigh. She was completely unprepared for the whirlwind of sensations that gripped her, and she grabbed the back of his head to keep him in place. He left her mouth and trailed kisses along her jaw and throat. Serita's head fell back and her eyes closed. The way he touched and kissed her made her feel like... She didn't know how to describe it.

"Serita," he murmured between kisses. "We should—"

"Don't stop." She had no idea where the words had come from and she might be crazy, but she didn't want it to end. Any of it.

"If we don't stop now, we may end up taking this further than either of us anticipated."

"I'm counting on it."

His head came up sharply and he searched her face, as if wanting to be certain she meant what she had said.

"Yes, I'm sure. You said we could do whatever I wanted to do this week. Tonight, I want you." She would deal with the rest tomorrow.

Chapter 3

"I need you to know that I don't take this lightly, Serita." Jeremy had never been one to indulge in meaningless flings and preferred long-term relationships. Serita had drawn his attention from the first moment he had seen her and his attraction had risen steadily. And knowing she lived close enough to visit made him even more confident that their paths had crossed for a reason, the least being their love of robotics.

Serita stared up at him. "I thought this was just—"

He cut her off with a gentle kiss. "This is not *just* anything." He wanted to say more but held back. For now he would concentrate on giving them both pleasure. The rest could wait until he knew for sure what he was feeling. He slanted his mouth over hers once more, tasting, teasing. She met him stroke for stroke, making his arousal climb another notch. Jeremy took his time touching every part of her body, lingering on her toned thighs, the sweet curve of her hips and her round breasts.

"Jeremy," she whispered.

He loved hearing her soft sounds of pleasure and the way she called his name. "What, baby?"

"I need you inside me."

"I'll give you everything you need, everything you want, but I can't rush this." He kissed his way down the front of her body, pushed her shirt up and placed fleeting kisses around her smooth belly and up to the valley between her breasts. Jeremy slowly, methodically stripped away her clothes, leaving her clad in nothing but a black lace bra and matching bikini panties. With her hair spread all over the pillow, she made for an erotic picture and he felt himself growing harder. "Do you know how sexy you are?"

Serita laughed softly. "I don't think that's the case, but it's a nice thing to say." She reached up to take off her glasses.

Jeremy gently grasped her hand and placed a kiss in the center of her palm. "Leave them on."

"You want me to leave them on?" she asked, her brow knitted in confusion. "Why?"

"They make you look even sexier, and I can't tell you how much they turn me on. If it makes you feel better, next time I'll wear mine, too."

"Next time?"

"Mmm-hmm, but we can talk about that later. Right now, I want to kiss you again." He traced her lips with his tongue before reclaiming her mouth. Their tongues danced and curled around each other, and he groaned.

She grabbed the hem of his shirt, pulled it up and

over his head, then tossed it aside. Giving him a sultry smile, she skated her tongue across his chest.

He sucked in a sharp breath. After leaving the bed, he removed the rest of his clothes, dug in his wallet for a condom and donned it. He climbed back onto the bed and lowered his body on top of her hers, being careful not to place all his weight on her. His hand traveled down her left leg and back up her right to her center, where she was already wet. Her legs parted to give him access, and he used a finger to circle her clit. Her legs trembled and she opened wider. Jeremy slid one finger in, followed by another, moving them in a steady rhythm. She cried out and arched against his hand. A moment later, she screamed his name as she came. Jeremy withdrew his fingers, shifted his body and guided his erection inside her. Her tight walls tightened around him and he shuddered.

Serita moaned softly and wrapped her legs around his back.

"You feel so good."

"Mmm, so do you."

He smiled and started moving, teasing with short strokes, then long, deep ones. He rotated his hips and ground against her in slow insistent circles while lowering his head to take one dark nipple between his teeth. As he sucked gently, he kept up the languid pace and closed his eyes as the pleasure increased.

"Ohh..." Serita lifted her hips and gripped his shoulders.

Their breathing grew louder as Jeremy pumped faster and harder, rocking the bed. He crushed his mouth against hers and changed the rhythm again.

Serita wrenched her mouth away and screamed his name again as she convulsed all around him.

A heartbeat later, a raw expletive tore from his throat as the most intense orgasm he'd ever experienced shot through him with a force that stole his breath and left his entire body shaking. He held her tightly as they both trembled with the aftershocks. He held himself above her for several seconds before collapsing on the bed, rolling to his side and taking her with him. His heart still thumped erratically in his chest, and his breathing was harsh and uneven.

She stroked his cheek. "That was incredible."

"Yes, it was." He sensed something different, an emotional connection unlike anything he had ever felt with a woman. They shared another passionate kiss, then lay quietly in each other's arms. At length, Jeremy glanced over at the nightstand clock. It was just after ten. As much as he wanted to hold her all night, he had to make sure his presentation was perfect. "I need to go. I'm presenting tomorrow and I want to run through everything."

Serita lifted her head. "I didn't know you were one of the presenters. What time?"

"One."

"I'll be there."

"Thanks. Can you do me a favor and record it?"

"Sure. I'll get there a few minutes early so I can get a good seat in the front."

"I don't know about you sitting in the front. You're pretty distracting."

She smiled. "You're good for a girl's ego."

"Just speaking the truth." He captured her mouth in a long, drugging kiss. Reluctantly he rose from the bed and began to dress.

Serita pulled on a robe and followed him to the door. "Are you attending a session in the morning?"

"Yes, why?"

"I was hoping we could have breakfast."

"We could always do dinner in one of the hotel's restaurants."

"I'll go with that." Unable to resist, Jeremy leaned down to kiss her. His hand slid inside her robe and she clamped down on it.

"Your presentation comes first. I'll see you tomorrow."

Their eyes held. Never in his wildest dreams could he have imagined what it would be like to touch and kiss her the way he had, to make love to her hours after they'd met. And he couldn't wait to do it again.

Wednesday afternoon, Serita sat in front of the room recording Jeremy's presentation. She had to give it to him—the man was a gifted presenter and knew how to keep the room interested. He spoke with a relaxed demeanor and it made her suspect he did this kind of thing regularly. She had a hard time focusing on his words, however, because the sight of him reminded her of what they had shared last night. Serita didn't make a practice of sleeping with men she'd just met. The only ones lucky enough to get that far—and it usually didn't happen until weeks or even months into the relationship—were men she dated exclusively. She didn't know what had possessed her to break her rules for Jeremy and thought she might have some regrets later. At this point, though, her only regret was that the evening had ended so early.

Serita got so lost in her thoughts, staring at Jeremy,

that she instinctively lowered the phone. She jerked it back up and met his amused gaze. She hoped whoever he'd planned to let see the video wasn't his boss or someone tied to his job. She refocused her attention on the presentation.

"One of the biggest factors for using robots in surgery is minimizing invasive procedures. Previously, surgeons had to make large incisions to access a site, but, with these machines, patients can look forward to smaller incisions and scars, reduced risk of infection, shorter recovery times and, most importantly, less pain and discomfort. If you've ever had surgery, you'll be cheering."

Chuckles and nods of agreement greeted his statement. As he continued to discuss the advancements and growing popularity, Serita could only marvel at his knowledge. She could see him commanding a college classroom easily. When it ended, more than half the audience surrounded Jeremy, asking questions, telling him how much they enjoyed his session and shaking his hand. Serita sat off to the side and waited until everyone left.

"How did I do?" Jeremy asked.

"You were fabulous."

"Are you sure? I didn't think you were paying attention. I saw you drifting off into space the whole time," he teased.

Her mouth fell open. "I was not."

"What were you thinking about?"

She couldn't very well tell him that she'd been thinking about how it felt to have his hands touching her, his naked body against hers as he thrust deeply inside her.

"I wasn't thinking about anything except how knowledgeable you are on the subject of medical robotics. And what makes you think I wasn't paying attention? You weren't looking at me."

"Baby, I never lost sight of you. Even when I wasn't looking directly at you, I could still see you."

She didn't know what to say. How could he have been paying that much attention to her and still give a perfect talk? And he'd called her baby. The possessive way he'd said it almost made her think she *was* his baby. Not knowing how to answer, she changed the subject. "Here's your phone. I recorded the whole thing. Is this for your job?"

"No, my family. My brother wanted to see it, and I'm sure my mom will ask, so I'll have it when she does." He propped a hip on the table, stroked a finger down her cheek and brushed a soft kiss over her lips. "Thanks for coming. It was nice to have a familiar face in the audience...made it much easier."

Still reeling from the gesture, she managed to say, "You're welcome, but you didn't have anything to worry about. You're a natural and should think about teaching."

"Nah, I like being hands-on. I can't see myself standing behind a podium every day. It's only four. Do you want to get dinner now or wait until later? If we eat now, we'll have a little time to explore."

Serita stood. "Then I say we eat now." She waited for him to gather his belongings, then they dined in one of the hotel's restaurants. Because it was later in the day, they opted for another walk where she could practice taking selfies.

"You're getting better," Jeremy said, checking out the

last one." He handed the phone back. "I have a proposition for you."

"What is it?"

"How about we skip tomorrow's presentations and take the high-speed train ride to Seville? It's about two and a half hours."

She thought for a moment. She hadn't expected to meet someone like him and their time together would be over in a couple of days. "Let's do it." She wanted to store up as many memories as she could.

The next morning, they boarded the AVE train for the journey to Seville. Afterward he arranged for a taxi.

"Where are we going?" she asked a few minutes after the driver pulled off.

"I figured we could take a short city tour without having to walk." Jeremy pointed to a spot. "A horse-drawn carriage ride. What do you say?"

She had a lot of things to say and ask. Foremost in her mind was why he kept choosing all these romantic activities, as if they were a couple.

"Serita? If you'd rather do something else, that's fine."

"No, that's not it. I'd love to do the ride."

He paid the driver and helped her out of the car. "What is it?"

She tried to choose her words carefully. "The intimate dinners, a carriage ride, the kisses and the… you know…last night. All this stuff gives the impression that we're dating or something, and we both know that's not the case."

He smiled. "No, we aren't dating at this moment, but as I told you before, I want us to keep in contact. I like you and, hey, you never know what might happen in the future." He gathered her in his embrace. "How about we just enjoy this beautiful city and let the rest take care of itself."

Once again he'd slid in a comment that alluded to them seeing each other beyond the week. As much as she enjoyed his company, Serita's last couple of failed relationships had left her gun-shy, and she didn't know if she wanted to put herself through the hassle of getting her heart broken again. "Yes, let's just focus on now." Minutes later, she found out that Jeremy had actually made a reservation. The hour-long ride took them past several of Seville's city landmarks, including the Golden Tower built by moors to control navigation of the Guadalquivir River, a former tobacco factory from XVIII and the Plaza de Americana, a square inside a park containing two museums. During the tour, they enjoyed Spanish champagne, fruit and sweet treats.

Jeremy draped an arm around Serita's shoulder. "Serita, I want to thank you for agreeing to be my tourist partner this week. I don't think I would've enjoyed Madrid as much had we not met."

His serious expression had her heart thumping in her chest. "I'm having a good time, too, so thank you for asking." The tender kiss that followed sent a flurry of sensations flowing through her.

The corners of his mouth tilted in a slight smile and he pulled her closer.

For the remainder of the ride, Jeremy continued with subtle touches and caresses, each one drawing Serita further into his sensual aura. By the time they made it back to the hotel, her mind and body were in such turmoil it took only one kiss for her to go up in flames. She took his hand and pulled him into her room. The fiery kisses began again and Serita closed her eyes. If she wasn't careful, she could easily fall for him.

Chapter 4

Friday afternoon, Serita sat in her room thinking about Jeremy. She hadn't seen him today because they attended different sessions. She had made plans to have dinner tonight with Caroline when they'd had breakfast on Monday and now wished she could cancel. Tomorrow would be her last full day in Madrid, and she wanted to spend as much of her time left with Jeremy. She still hadn't told him about her potential move back to Sacramento. Things were good right now and they had both gotten caught up in the magic of being abroad, but she couldn't see it lasting. It never did.

Most of the men she'd dated had taken exception to her being somewhat of a nerd and suggested she get contacts and change her style. She had no intention of allowing a man to dictate how she should look or dress, as if her glasses, conservative dress style and love of science didn't make her an ideal candidate for romance. After one too many heartbreaks, she had decided to keep her focus where it belonged—on her career. She'd been fine doing that until now. Jeremy didn't seem to mind any of those things that defined her. In fact, he said they turned him on. The man had made love to her with her glasses on both times and told her how sexy they made her look. Her body heated up just thinking about all the ways he'd cherished her.

Serita glanced at the time. She still had half an hour before dinner, so she spent some time checking her emails and doing a job search. She clicked on one from Gabby and laughed. Her friend had sent a message in all caps letting Serita know that she was still waiting on information about the date with Jeremy. Because of the time difference, Serita hadn't had a chance to call, but she would tonight after dinner before hanging out later with Jeremy. She sent a quick email back to Gabby saying just that. The pediatric doctor's office where Gabby worked closed at noon on Fridays, which would give them time to talk before it got too late. Then she scanned the job-listing site and saw a couple of promising opportunities. Although one in a small company indicated there would be a thirty-day trial period before deciding on a candidate, she applied for it anyway— along with another one—knowing she had the skills to handle anything they threw her way. Not seeing any other jobs she liked, Serita shut down the laptop and left for dinner.

She saw Caroline waiting by the entrance of the restaurant.

"Hi, Serita. I already checked in, so it should only be a few minutes."

"Okay. Did you enjoy the conference?"

"I did. I learned so much and I'm kind of sad it's over. But I won't be leaving until Monday and can't wait to tour the city without having to worry about hurrying back. When are you flying out?" Before Serita could answer, the hostess showed them to their table.

Once they were seated, she picked up the conversation. "I'm leaving Sunday morning. That gives me one more day to see the sights."

Caroline's eyes lit up. "We should do one of the bus tours tomorrow."

"I already have plans, sorry."

"Oh, that's too bad." She smiled and waved. "I hope you don't mind, but I invited a couple of the guys I met at the afternoon session to join us."

Yeah, Serita did mind, especially when both men looked as if they'd come straight from the bar. But she nodded politely when Caroline made the introductions. The server came to take their drink orders and Serita ordered a glass of chardonnay.

"Forget the wine," one of the men said. "We need a bottle of your best champagne to celebrate the ending of another great conference."

"Ooh, that sounds fabulous," Caroline said.

Serita forced a smile. "No, thank you. You all are welcome to enjoy your champagne. I'll just stick with my wine." They proceeded to order a bottle of the most expensive sparking drink on the menu and she sincerely hoped they didn't expect her to chip in to pay for it.

After the server departed, the other man, whose name had escaped Serita, said, "I attended your session. It was really good. You seem to have a lot of knowledge for someone so young."

She wondered if he always handed out insults along with his compliments. "Thank you." She picked up her menu. *This dinner can't end soon enough.* Her dining companions launched into a discussion of the field and what they would like to see. Serita followed along but didn't comment. The server returned with drinks and took the food order. Once again, the trio ordered several appetizers and expensive entrées. When the appetizers came out, she declined, citing wanting to save her appetite. Over the course of dinner, they ordered more champagne and Serita shook her head. They laughed loudly at bad jokes, drawing stares from diners at nearby tables and, more than once, Serita was tempted to toss her napkin down and leave.

Caroline took a sip from her glass. "Ron, this is the best champagne. Great choice."

He toasted her with his glass and inclined his head.

"Serita and I were talking about taking a tour tomorrow. What do you guys say?"

"I'm in," Ron said. "What about you, Evan?"

"Definitely count me in."

Serita mentally counted to ten. She'd specifically told Caroline she had other plans. "You guys enjoy yourselves. As I told Caroline earlier, I won't be available." The chicken dish she had ordered was good, but her appetite had waned considerably. When it came time for dessert, she declined but had to endure until the bill came.

Evan picked up the bill. "Whoa. It's a good thing we're sharing the costs."

Serita had always been considered sweet and demure, but when they suggested splitting the bill four ways, her inner Cali girl made an appearance. "I beg your pardon. I will *not* be paying for any part of your meals or the multitude of drinks and appetizers you all ordered. I didn't even invite you," she added, glaring at Caroline. She looked up at the stunned server. "Please separate my portion of the bill."

The young man nodded and hurried away.

She sat there seething until he returned and placed the bill holder in front of her. She retrieved the money from her purse and included a tip. "Have a good evening." She rose from her chair and stalked out of the restaurant without a backward glance. Serita didn't stop walking until she got to the elevator. She jabbed the button and paced angrily. Of all the nerve! Did they really think she would contribute to the several-hundred-dollar cost of their meals? The elevator arrived and she moved aside to let the other people off before stepping inside and riding the car to her floor.

Inside her room, she took a couple of deep, calming breaths. Seeing that it was just after nine, she powered up her laptop and FaceTimed Gabby.

"Hey, girl. How's it going?"

"It was fine until dinner tonight." She related the incident. "They actually looked offended when I said I wasn't going in on the bill."

"It's a good thing it was you instead of me. I probably would've told girlfriend she could have dinner with those guys by herself and gotten my own table. People have a lot of gall." Gabby shook her head.

"I know. It takes a lot to get me upset, but I wanted to smack her. Then she told them we were hanging out tomorrow, when I had specifically said I had other plans."

"Plans that, no doubt, include the mysterious Jeremy."

"Yes."

"Obviously, you two hit it off, since I haven't gotten one call."

Serita didn't know how to explain how Jeremy made her feel. "He's incredible. Almost too good to be true. We've been exploring the city together and he won't let me pay for anything. On Thursday, he took me on a horse-drawn carriage ride, and it was the most romantic thing ever."

She released a dreamy sigh. "Aww, it sounds incredibly wonderful. How does he kiss?"

"Who said he's kissed me?"

Gabby gave her an incredulous look. "Girl, quit playing and answer the question."

"Like he created the art." A vision of his seductive kisses floated through her mind.

She laughed. "And memorable by the look on your face."

"Very. He makes me feel so… I don't know. Sexy, desirable."

"Sexy? Hold up. I know you didn't do the wild thing with a brother you just met." Serita's expression told all. "Okay, having dinner and exploring a city is one thing, but sleeping with him is something altogether different." She blew out a long breath. "Sis, what do you really know about this guy?"

Serita understood Gabby's point because she'd said the same thing to herself more than once. "He's intelligent, makes me laugh and treats me like a queen, despite just meeting me."

She nodded. "I can get with that. Maybe he has potential."

"And he lives in Sacramento."

Gabby's eyebrows shot up. "Seriously? That's fantastic—it'll make it easier for you guys to see each other."

"He doesn't know I'm moving back," Serita said guiltily.

"What? Why not? You just said the man was fabulous."

She scrubbed a hand across her forehead. "You know how my relationships end up."

Gabby waved a hand and wrinkled her nose. "Those guys were idiots. Jeremy sounds like he's the total opposite."

"He is." From what she'd seen so far, he impressed her as being a genuinely good guy, but she couldn't help but wonder what would happen once they returned to reality.

"Has he said anything about wanting you guys to keep seeing each other?"

"He's hinted around the possibility, but hasn't come right out and said it. He knows I live in Reno and seems to be willing to make that drive, so…" She shrugged.

"You should tell him about the move. Who knows? He might be able to give you some information about jobs in the area."

"True." Serita hadn't thought of that. "Maybe I'll ask him tonight."

Gabby grinned. "If you remember."

She lifted a brow. "Why wouldn't I remember?"

"If a man kisses like you say he does, I doubt you'll be able to remember anything, including your name."

Her friend had a point. Not only did Jeremy kiss like he'd invented it, he made love the same way. Yeah, she was in trouble. Big trouble.

Jeremy sat in his room, eating dinner and working on the design for a prosthetic hand that would closely imitate natural function. He wanted it to have a more natural feel and look, which was why he'd been so excited about Serita's presentation. This was a personal project of his and he wondered briefly if she would consider working with him on it. He sat back in the chair. She elicited a spark in him he hadn't felt in a long time, if ever. He still hadn't asked her about them continuing what they'd begun, but he had one more day to do it. He hoped she would be receptive. Just thinking about her petite sexy self made him hard. With the prim and proper way she carried herself, he never would have expected her to be so uninhibited in bed. He suspected not many people saw that side of her, but he had enjoyed every moment. In and out of bed.

He finished his meal, set the plate aside and made a few more changes to his drawing. Just as he started, Christian called. He activated the FaceTime. "What's up, Chris?"

"Hey. Just checking in with you about Nelson."

"What about him?" Nelson Atkins had given his notice the day before Jeremy left for Madrid.

"Instead of leaving in three weeks, he came in this morning and said today is his last day."

Jeremy muttered a curse. "Did he at least finish his part of the motion-control system like he promised?"

"Ah, that would be a no. Which is why I'm calling. I uploaded the open position to all the job sites we use and made sure to note it was a thirty-day trial to determine the best fit."

"Thanks. I'm probably going to have to do some overtime to pick up the slack until we fill the position." He had figured they would be able to hire a replacement before Nelson left to avoid disruption in their schedule.

"Hopefully, we'll be able to find someone soon. I already have three applications. Also, I'm putting together a bid on another project."

"It sounds good, but will it be feasible with the limited staff? I don't want to put us in the position of having to work overtime to meet any deadlines."

"Which brings me to my next topic."

"What?" Jeremy asked warily. Chris had always been a go-getter, which was how he'd made his first million dollars at age twenty-two. He applied the same work ethic to their company.

"I'm thinking we should hire four for the trial and keep the two best. It would give us an extra person, so we could take on one or two more projects."

He mulled it over. "Okay, but can we afford it?"

"I ran the numbers and we'd be good financially. And if we get this next contract, it would give us a fair amount of breathing room."

"Alright. Let's go with it."

"How's Madrid?"

He smiled. "It's great. I met an incredible woman."

Chris laughed and shook his head. "Are you still talking about being able to know on sight if the woman is for you?"

"Yes, and I think it's her."

His laughter faded. "*What?* Jeremy, you can't be serious. I know you don't believe that kind of thing really exists."

"Of course I believe it. Why wouldn't I?"

"Because…because… This is reality and not some fantasy romance that you read in books."

"You don't think you could meet a woman and feel

like she's the one you've been waiting for?" As crazy as it might have sounded, that was how he felt.

"No," Chris said emphatically. "I think you've got a serious case of sexual attraction going on, nothing more."

Jeremy laughed. "Yeah, that, too."

"Oh, hell. You slept with her already?" He dragged a hand down his face. "Jeremy, this isn't like you."

"You're right, which is why I know she's special." She stimulated his mind just as much as his body.

"If you say so. What's going to happen once you come back home? I assume she's not local."

"She lives in Reno and I'm more than willing to keep getting to know her, but I won't know how she feels about it until I ask tonight."

"Well, I hope it works out. With the way things are today, you might want to proceed with caution. People aren't always who they say they are. You almost need to do a full background check."

Smiling, he shook his head. "I'll take my chances." He heard a knock. "Someone's at my door."

"Probably your mystery woman."

"Yep."

"I'll talk to you later. Hit me up when you get back on Sunday."

Jeremy nodded. "Later." He cut the connection and went to open the door. His smile widened when he saw Serita standing there. "Come in, baby." He bent to kiss her. "How was dinner?"

Serita rolled her eyes. "Ugh. I should've canceled. Caroline took it upon herself to invite these two guys to join us. They ran the bill up to several hundreds of dollars and had the nerve to suggest we split the bill."

He smiled at her annoyed expression. "I take it you weren't too happy about that."

"You take it right. I wasn't paying one dime more than what I ate."

Chuckling, he pulled her into his arms. "See, if you'd accepted my dinner invite, you wouldn't have had to deal with that kind of foolishness," he teased.

"Tell me about it. Anyway, enough of that." She backed out of his arms. "Are you working?" She pointed to his laptop, which still had mechanical parts displayed.

"A little bit." He gestured to the chair. "Have a seat."

She sat and picked up the mystery thriller on the desk. "I have this book, but haven't had a chance to read it yet."

He sat on the edge of the bed. "I just started it. How about we discuss it once you're done? We can do it over a dinner *date*."

Serita laughed softly. "So is that your way of letting me know up front?"

"Yep." Jeremy figured this would be a good time to bring up his proposal. "I've really enjoyed spending time with you this week and I'm hoping we can continue once get home. I have no problem driving to Reno to see you." He had his place in Tahoe, as well, and could see them spending a weekend there. However, he would rather do it before it got too cold and the snow started.

"I appreciate what you're saying, but how do you know it'll be the same or whether things will work out?"

"I don't know, but I'm willing to find out." What he did know was that this woman moved him like no other and he would do whatever it took to find out whether she was *the one*. "What do you say?"

"I would like to say yes, but you need to know that relationships don't seem to work out for me."

The tone of her voice gave him pause. Had she been hurt...and how many times? Jeremy left the bed, hunkered down in front of her and grasped her hands. "We've all had relationships that didn't work out, but we won't ever find the right one if we don't keep trying."

"True." She appeared to be weighing his words. Finally she said, "Okay."

Jeremy leaned up and kissed her, wanting to assure her that he would do everything in his power not to hurt her. He reached behind her, picked up his phone and opened the contacts. "Can you put your info in?"

Serita took the phone and started typing. As she handed it back, the cell rang.

He frowned. He rarely used his phone when he traveled out of the country to minimize costs and fees. Seeing his cousin Lorenzo's name on the display made his frown deepen. "Can you excuse me a moment—it's my cousin." He hit the button. "Hey, Zo."

"I know this is long-distance, so I'll keep it short. Randi went into labor an hour ago and is in the hospital."

Jeremy slowly rose to his feet, his heart pounding. "What do you mean she's in labor? She's not due for almost two months. What happened?"

"We don't know. She called Ced from her office and told him she'd been having contractions and he took off. He just called to tell me they're keeping her. He's not taking it well."

"How're my parents?"

"Worried, but they seem to be holding up okay. My parents are here at the hospital, too."

"I'm going to take the first flight out." He could only imagine the fear Ced and Randi were experiencing. He had to get home.

"Email me your flight info and I'll pick you up."

"Thanks. Keep me posted." He disconnected and closed his eyes briefly. Then he turned to Serita. "I have to go home. My sister-in-law went into premature labor. She's not due for another two months."

Serita stood and wrapped her arms around his waist. "I hope they can stop the contractions."

"I know we were supposed to spend the day together tomorrow. I'm sorry."

"No apology is necessary, Jeremy. You need to be there for your family."

"I promise to make it up to you. Let me give you my number." He had hoped to have that last day with her, and had planned for them to rent a boat and take a ride on the lake, then have a picnic. She handed him her phone and he inputted the information.

She took the phone back and dropped it into her purse. "I'll get out of your way. I know you need to make your flight arrangements."

Jeremy placed a staying hand on her arm. "No, don't leave. At this hour, I probably won't be able to get a flight out until morning, and I want to spend as much time with you as possible."

She nodded.

He smiled faintly. "Thanks." He used the hotel phone to call the airline and it took more than fifteen minutes to find a flight. Thankfully, he didn't have to pay an additional fee due to his A-list rating. He hung up. "My flight leaves at six in the morning."

"That means you're going to need to be at the airport at O-dark-hundred. It's after ten. You need to be going to bed."

He laughed. "Yeah, *early*. How about we go get your café con leche and talk for a little while? I'll be okay." And he could sleep on the long flight.

Chapter 5

Jeremy grabbed his luggage off the carousel and made his way through the airport terminal. On the way, he called Lorenzo, then exited to the pickup area. Obviously, several planes had landed around the same time because the he could barely find a spot to wait in the crowd. Luckily, his height gave him an advantage, and less than four minutes later he saw Lorenzo's Lexus SUV and waved him down. His cousin popped the trunk, and Jeremy tossed the bags in, then got in on the passenger side.

"How was the flight?" Lorenzo asked as he merged into the traffic.

"Long." He laid his head against the seat and closed his eyes. He had not been able to sleep on the plane as planned and was beyond tired. "How's Randi?"

"They have her on some meds that'll, hopefully,

stop the contractions. They've slowed, so that's a good thing."

"It is."

"You want to stop by the house first or go straight to the hospital?"

"Hospital." He could imagine the fear she and Cedric were experiencing and Jeremy needed to see with his own eyes how they were doing. Besides, if he went home, he might not make it back today. His thoughts shifted to Serita. Strange as it seemed, he missed her already. While waiting for his luggage, he had sent her an email like she'd asked to let her know he'd made it home. However, he didn't expect a reply. With the nine-hour time difference, it was already after midnight there. She'd be flying home tomorrow and chances were they wouldn't connect until sometime during the week. Jeremy didn't realize he had drifted off until he felt the tap on his shoulder. He opened his eyes and sat up slowly.

"Maybe you should've gone home to take a nap," Lorenzo said with a chuckle as he got out of the car.

Jeremy followed suit and stretched. "I'm not staying long and, yeah, I need some sleep." Inside the hospital, they took the elevator to Randi's floor. Cedric was standing in the hallway talking with their mother. Both looked up with surprise.

"Oh, my goodness! You're home early." His mother rushed over and engulfed him in a crushing hug. "I didn't expect you until tomorrow night."

He kissed her cheek. "Zo called about Randi and I took the first flight out. You know I had to come." Family meant everything to him, and he couldn't *not* be there during a crisis.

She nodded in understanding and patted his cheek.

"I'm so glad to see you. You can tell me all about your trip sometime later in the week. I'm going to go in and see if Randi is awake."

Jeremy embraced his brother. "How're you holding up?"

Cedric dragged a hand down his face and blew out a long breath. "I've been better. Hey, Zo."

Lorenzo clapped Cedric on the shoulder. "Hang in there. I know she's going to be fine." He turned to Jeremy. "I'm going to chill in the waiting room down the hall. When you're ready to go, come get me."

"Okay." Jeremy studied his brother and could see the lines of tension and fatigue lining his features. "How is Randi doing now? Zo said the contractions are slowing."

"They are, but not enough right now. She's worried. I put up a good front with her, but I'm scared to death something's going to go wrong. The doctors were talking about lung and brain development and a whole lot of other stuff that freaked me out." He let the wall take his weight. "I don't know what I'll do if anything happens to either of them," he said in an anguished whisper. "I feel so damn helpless."

"We've got to pray and believe that everything is going to be okay. You said the contractions are slowing. Let's take that as a sign things are moving in the right direction."

"Believe me, I'm trying."

"Do you need me to do anything?"

"No, we're good. You look dead on your feet."

Jeremy smiled. "So do you. I know the hospital is probably limiting her visitors, but I want to poke my head in for a minute."

Cedric waved him off. "You're fine. You should've

been here last night when the entire family showed up. We almost got put out. Mom and Aunt LaVerne scared those nurses so bad they just let us all in."

"I can imagine." When it came to their children—regardless of the fact that all were adults now—both women were very protective. As soon as Randi married Cedric, she became one of them and they guarded her as if she had been born into the family. "What about her parents?"

"They're flying in tomorrow." He pushed the door open and held it for Jeremy.

"Hey, sis," Jeremy said, approaching the bed.

"Hey, Doc," Randi said softly. "Aren't you supposed to be in Madrid wooing all the senoritas?" Even though she looked as if she had been through the ringer, she still had her wit.

He smiled. "I had to come and check on you and there's only one senorita I'm interested in wooing."

"What?" his mother and brother said at the same time. Randi stared at him.

He gave her a wink. "I'll tell you all about her when you get home. Right now, I need you to concentrate on resting." He placed a gentle hand on her belly. "Hey, little one, I know you're anxious to meet your family, but we need you to hang out awhile longer. I promise we'll all be here to greet you when it's time." He bent and placed a kiss on Randi's forehead. "Rest up, sis, and I'll check on you tomorrow."

She grasped his hand. "Thank you, and I'm sorry you had to shorten your trip."

"No apologies necessary." Saying those words reminded him of Serita saying the same thing to him. He hoped things would work out between them so he could introduce her to his family. He knew they'd love her.

His mother eyed him. "You get a good night's sleep because I will be calling you tomorrow."

Cedric laughed.

Jeremy had no doubt that she would call him by nine, generously allowing him that extra hour. He gave her another hug and kiss. "I'll be expecting it."

Cedric caressed Randi's cheek and kissed her. "I'll be right back, baby. I'm going to walk Jeremy out." As soon as the door closed, he said to Jeremy. "What do you mean wooing a senorita? Did you meet someone there?"

"I did."

"Look, bro, I know you're all into finding Mrs. Right, but Spain is a long way from Cali."

He grinned. "She doesn't live in Madrid. She's a lot closer—Reno."

Cedric's eyes widened. "Still long-distance, and how do you know she's going to go for that?"

"We already talked about it. Serita is a beautiful woman—about five-two or three, brains, sweet curves, all this curly hair and a pair of sexy glasses."

He shook his head. "Only you. So she's got some sexy nerd-girl thing going on?"

"Exactly. We spent a lot of time together this week and I really like her."

"Be careful that you don't get all caught up so soon."

Jeremy let out a short bark of laughter. "I know you're not talking to me, Mr. Slept-With-Randi-On-The-First-Date."

"Yeah, whatever. That wasn't unusual for me. You,

on the other hand, have always waited until you had
some kind of commitment first."

"True…usually."

Cedric held up a hand. "Wait. Are you telling me
you slept with this woman already?"

"I'm not telling you anything. I'll talk to you later.
Call me if you need me. Later, big brother." He laughed
at Cedric's shocked expression and left him standing
there. As he made his way to the waiting room, he
thought about the look of adoration Cedric and Randi
shared. The love between them was palpable and it
made Jeremy even more sure that he wanted the same
thing in his life. He just needed to know if Serita was
the one for him.

Sunday evening, Serita dropped down on Gabby's
sofa, closed her eyes and groaned. "Girl, I don't ever
want to move again." It was a fantasy because she only
planned to stay with her friend temporarily, until she
found her own place. Instead of moving in a month,
she'd had to put her condo on the market and pack up
to move in less than two weeks after returning from
Madrid in order to start her new job.

"You're more than welcome to stay forever," Gabby
said with a laugh, collapsing on the other side of the sofa.
"Well, if you had taken Jeremy up on his offer to help
you move, you wouldn't be so tired."

She cracked open an eye. "Shut up." When Jeremy
found out she had decided to relocate back to Sacramento, he had immediately offered to help with the move
and finding her a place. But she was used to doing things
on her own and didn't want to start depending on any
man, especially one she had known for only a short time.

Granted, she'd come to feel closer to him in that short period than she had with all the guys she'd dated combined. "He doesn't actually know I moved this weekend. I haven't talked to him since last week. He mentioned having to work overtime because someone at the company quit. And then there are the concerns with his sister-in-law's pregnancy. Thankfully, her contractions stopped, but from what he told me, the doctor's put her on bed rest for the duration of her pregnancy. We've been playing phone tag and exchanging texts here and there, but that's about all."

"How do you feel about seeing him again? I mean, it's easy to get wrapped up in the beauty of a foreign country and with all the romantic things you guys did, but do you think it'll be the same now?"

"I honestly don't know and that's part of the reason I didn't mention the move." She also didn't want it to turn into just a physical relationship. She wanted more and, at age thirty-two, didn't plan to settle for being anyone's plaything. She didn't sense that to be the case with Jeremy and, if so, he put up a good front.

"You're going to have to tell him eventually because I'm sure he'll ask. And I'm really curious about him. If he turns out to be the real deal, I need to know if he has any available brothers."

Serita chuckled tiredly. "He has just the one brother, who's married."

"Damn. Why are all the good ones taken?" Gabby asked with a mock pout.

"I don't know about you. Maybe he has a friend."

She perked up. "Ooh, yeah. I need you to get me the hookup. Just make sure the friend isn't one of those crazy men who has some whack belief system about women being barefoot, pregnant and in the kitchen."

"I thought you wanted kids."

"I do, but I don't want to have to quit my job to do it. I've got no issues cutting my hours, but I'm not the Suzie Homemaker type."

"Hey, you never know. You'll see those babies and end up being one of those women who attend every PTA meeting, coordinate all the bake sales and play chaperone on field trips."

Gabby shot Serita a look. "Bite your tongue. I. Don't. Think. So. Not in this lifetime or the next one." She shuddered.

She laughed and pointed. "I wish you could see your face."

"I don't need to see it to know what it looks like. I bet you'd say the same thing."

Serita nodded. "Yeah, no. Not quitting. I worked too hard to get where I am to just let it all go. I'd like to own a small company one day, and I won't be able to do that if I'm sitting on the sofa all day eating bonbons."

She lifted her hand and gave Serita a high five. "Amen, my sister!"

The two women fell out laughing. When they finally calmed, Serita said, "I've missed hanging out with you." There was never a dull moment with her friend around.

"Same here." Gabby yawned. "It's getting late and I need to be in the office at seven in the morning. Did you find out any more information on the company where you'll be working?"

"The website was down the other night when I checked and, with everything going on, I forgot about it. I guess I'll just wait and see in the morning. If it turns out to be a mess, I'll do that thirty-day trial and be out the door. I'm still applying at other places, just in case."

"I hope it works out."

"So do I." From the job description, it appeared to be exactly what she was looking for—challenging and cutting-edge—and it would give her a chance to sharpen her skills. She'd had little time to work in the field over the past seven years and this new opportunity gave her the same excitement she had felt when she started at her first robotics company right out of college. After working for four years, she'd gone back for her doctorate and had accepted the job in academia at the suggestion of one of her professors. "Thanks again for letting me crash here until I find a place."

Gabby stood. "Oh, girl. I'm glad I could help. I'll see you in the morning."

"Good night." She sat there a moment longer, then went to prepare for bed. After a long, hot shower, Serita felt a little better, but she hadn't used many of those muscles in a while and knew she'd probably be sore in the morning. She went through the closet, trying to decide what to wear, and settled on a pair of gray slacks and a short-sleeved black blouse. Even though the calendar read mid-October, the weather still remained near eighty degrees.

She fell asleep as soon as her head hit the pillow, and when her alarm went off at six thirty the next morning she swore she had just lain down. Serita dragged herself out of bed and got dressed. Gabby had already gone by the time Serita emerged and had left coffee. Since she didn't particularly care for it, she opted for a cup of hot peppermint tea. She had yet to find a recipe for the café con leche she liked, but vowed to search one out as soon as she had a moment. After a quick breakfast of fruit and a boiled egg, she Googled directions to the Roseville office and set off. Fortunately, Gabby's Antelope condo was less than twenty minutes away.

She arrived fifteen minutes before the scheduled eight-o'clock time and, taking a deep breath, entered the one-story building located in an office park off Douglas Boulevard. In the small lobby, a trio of chairs surrounded a coffee table filled with magazines, and photos of various types of robots hung on the walls. A young woman sat at the desk. "Good morning. I'm Serita Edwards and have an appointment with Christian Hill."

The woman smiled. "Good morning." She clicked a few keys on the computer, then said, "Have a seat and I'll let him know you're here."

"Thank you." Serita sat in one of the chairs and speculated what her job would entail. The company focused on medical robotics, and that could mean anything—surgery robots and instruments or prosthetics. A couple of minutes later, a man who looked to be around her age or a couple of years older rushed through the door. He smoothed his blond hair back and went over to the receptionist, then joined Serita in the waiting area.

"Are you starting today, too?" he asked.

"Yes."

"You must be a new grad." Smiling, he stuck out his hand. "I'm Wade."

She shook his hand briefly. "Serita." She purposely didn't respond to his assumption.

"Sorry to keep you waiting."

Serita turned at the sound of a deep voice. A tall, mahogany-skinned brother stood there with a warm smile. She stood.

"I'm Chris." He stuck out his hand.

"Wade Brewer."

Serita stifled an eye roll. The man jumped in front of her and nearly knocked her down.

Chris raised an eyebrow, then shifted his gaze to Serita. "And you are?"

"Serita Edwards."

"Nice to meet you. If you'll follow me, I'll get you all set up with the paperwork. Hopefully, the other two new hires will be here shortly and I can give the information once."

They went down a long hallway to a conference room holding a table that seated eight. She waited until Wade sat before taking a seat at the opposite end.

Chris handed them each a stack of papers.

"Chris, your other two candidates are here."

He turned. "Thanks, Nicole." He made introductions, then gestured the two men to the table and gave them the forms. "After you fill these out, I'll tell you a little about our company, and then we'll discuss the parameters of the position and the projects that you'll be working on."

"Will we be working under you?" Wade asked.

"No. I just handle the business. I leave the other stuff to the engineers." Everyone chuckled. "I'll be back in a few minutes."

Serita turned her attention to the paperwork. That was one thing she hated about starting a new job. It seemed as if employers wanted to know everything except the color of someone's underwear. *With all these papers, I wouldn't be surprised if they did ask.*

"Okay, everybody. If you're done, you can pass your papers to the end of the table. I want to introduce you to Jeremy Hunter."

Her head snapped up and she gasped. Jeremy seemed to notice her at the same time and his eyes widened for a brief moment before he schooled his features.

"How about you go around the table and introduce yourselves."

As usual, Wade jumped in first. Not only did he provide his name, he launched into a brag session of all the places he'd worked.

Jeremy cut him off. "We've gone through the résumés, so just a name will suffice for now." He reached out and shook Wade's hand.

The two other men introduced themselves as Darryl Ross and Scott Aldridge, and Jeremy repeated the gesture.

When it came to her turn, he came and stood so close to her she could feel the heat from his body mingling with her own, bringing with it memories of their week in Madrid. "Serita Edwards."

"Ms. Edwards."

Instead of the quick shake he'd done with the others, Jeremy held her hand a little longer and circled his thumb over the back of her hand. To keep from grabbing him down for the kiss she wanted to give him, she pulled back and folded her hands in her lap.

A slight smile curved his lips, as if he knew the effect his touch had on her. "Chris will start, then I'll give you a general overview of our projects. Afterward, I'll meet with you individually to determine where you'll best fit. You will only be working on existing projects, so please note that there is a form that you'll need to sign stating you understand our policy on design changes."

He spoke that last sentence while looking directly at Serita. Her pulse skipped. How was she going to get through the next thirty days working with him without wanting to be in his arms? How was she going to get through this first meeting with him?

Chapter 6

Jeremy could hardly contain his excitement, knowing that Serita would be working with him. He didn't need a month to know she would fit in with his company. He spent about half an hour detailing the various projects before talking with each person individually. He got good vibes from everyone except Wade. The man acted like he was the only one in the room with an engineering degree. Jeremy could tell right off that Mr. Brewer would be looking for employment elsewhere. Chris had also mentioned that Wade had jumped in front of Serita to introduce himself out in the lobby. Any man who disrespected a woman had no place in Jeremy's business. Typically, he would have had Serita introduce herself first, with her being the only woman in the room. However, saving her for last had been selfish in nature and given him time to linger over her nearness.

When she walked into his office, it took every ounce

of control to stand there, when all he wanted to do was hold her in his arms and show her just how much he had missed her. "How are you, baby?"

"A little shocked to be honest." Serita sat in one of the chairs opposite his desk and perched on the edge.

"Join the club," Jeremy said with a laugh. "I thought you were moving back at the end of the month. You should've called me, so I could help you."

"Things went kind of fast and I know you were busy. I had planned to call you tonight and let you know, but I guess the cat's out of the bag now."

"I guess so." He waged an inner battle with himself for several seconds. Unable to take it any longer, he rounded the desk and gently pulled Serita to her feet. "I know this is work and I'm going do my best to be professional around you, but I have to kiss you right now."

She studied him, then held up a finger. "One kiss, Jeremy. One time and that's it."

It was all he needed to hear. He traced a finger down her cheek and over her mouth. It had taken her just four days to get under his skin. Jeremy lowered his head and brushed his lips over hers once, twice. Her lips parted on a breathless sigh and he captured her mouth in an intoxicating kiss, feeding from the sweetness inside. He sat on the desk and pulled her to stand between his legs. He deepened the kiss while his hands roamed down her spine and over the roundness of her backside. It took a minute, but he finally ended the kiss. He rested his forehead against hers and their ragged breathing echoed in the office.

"We can't do this," she whispered.

"Maybe not here, but as soon as the workday ends, you're mine."

Serita's gaze flew to his.

The panicked look in her eyes gave him pause. "You didn't change your mind about us seeing each other, did you?"

"No. I just don't want to mess up this job opportunity."

"You won't."

"How long have you worked here?"

Jeremy debated whether to tell her the truth. She might change her mind about them. In the end he decided to be honest. "Since the day the doors opened three years ago."

"You know the owner well, then?"

He smiled. "From the day I was born."

She stared at him in confusion.

"HJ Robotics is my baby."

"You *own* this company?" Serita shook her head. "*Nooo.* I can't work here."

He frowned. "Why not? You're qualified."

She placed a hand on her hip and lifted a brow. "You're going to be the person deciding which of us stays after thirty days, right?"

"Yes," he answered slowly.

"Exactly my point."

It dawned on him what she meant. "You think I'll give you special preference because of our relationship."

"Yes."

"Serita, this is my business, my livelihood. I worked my butt off to get to this point. Don't think for one minute I'd do anything to jeopardize that. Now, I will admit I'd like to have you working with me because I believe you would be a great asset to the company, but I promise to judge you on your work only." At her skeptical look, he added, "I'll even put it in writing, if you want."

"I don't know."

"Come on, baby." He nuzzled her neck.

"See, this right here will have me walking out the door now."

Jeremy set her away from him and placed his hands behind his back. "Then I'll keep my hands to myself."

"And your lips."

He opened his mouth to say something, but her look made it clear there was no point arguing. "Fine. And I'll keep my lips to myself…between eight and five."

A smile spread across her lips. "I don't know what I'm going to do with you."

He wiggled his eyebrows. "I'm sure I can come up with a few ideas."

She pointed to his chair. "The only idea you're going to be coming up with right now is telling me which project you're assigning me to. You're on the clock, Mr. Hunter, so let's get to work."

He couldn't do anything but smile and do as she asked. Once seated behind his desk, he told her about the three project areas—a surgical arm, a console that incorporated the robots, instrumentation and other technologies, and a surgical system that would be used for eye surgery. "The latter has the closest deadline, so I'd like you to work on that one."

"Who else is working on the project?"

He chuckled inwardly, knowing what she was getting at. "What you really want to know is if I'm working on the project, right?"

Serita dropped her gaze briefly. "Yes."

"You don't think we can work together?" Jeremy

stood, came around the desk and took the chair next to her. "I happen to believe we'll work very well together. And I already promised you I'll be good while we're on the clock." They shut down at five and his staff was usually out the door right at that time. He, on the other hand, often stayed late. Maybe he could interest Serita in a little overtime—work *and* play. He rose to his feet and extended his hand. "Come on. Let me introduce you to Elena, and she'll put you to work."

She placed her hand in his and he helped her to her feet. "Thank you. I'm still not sure how I feel about this whole thing, but I will do my best to help you get your robot done on time."

"I have no doubt about that." He lifted his hand to touch her cheek, then remembered the agreement and let it drop to his side. He crossed the room, opened the door and gestured her forward. On the way to her assigned project, he pointed out the different work areas, bathrooms and break room. He stopped at a door at the end of the hall. "This is where you'll work." He led her over to the worktable where his two engineers stood. Both looked up at Jeremy's entrance. "Elena Arevalo and Shane Meyers, this is Serita Edwards. She'll be working with us, hopefully for a long time to come."

"Hallelujah! Finally, you hired somebody with a brain," Elena said in her Spanish-accented English. "Welcome, Serita."

Shane snorted. "Hey, I'm the only one in here with one. Glad to have you, Serita."

Jeremy met Serita's wary gaze and shook his head. "Serita, don't pay them any attention. It's never a dull moment with these two around." He told them, "Try not to scare Serita off before lunch, please."

Elena waved him off. "Oh, we'll be fine." She beckoned Serita over and said in a loud whisper, "The only one who's scary is that big man behind you."

"Sabes que puedo oírte, Elena?"

"Of course I know you can hear me." She snorted. "I don't want you to think I talk about you behind your back."

Serita laughed. "I think I'm going to enjoy working here."

He stared down at her. "I hope so." Because he was looking forward to working with her and more.

Serita enjoyed working with Elena and Shane. Contrary to Elena's teasing, Shane did have a brain, a highly intelligent one. He reminded her a little of Chris Hemsworth—minus the Thor muscles. Both had a wealth of knowledge, and she could see why Jeremy had hired them. It took Serita a short time to get her bearings, but by late afternoon, she was up to speed. The high-precision hybrid design would provide exceptional steadiness of the instrument while allowing surgeons to maintain close contact with a patient. She got so engrossed in her task that she had to suppress her disappointment when the day ended. She hadn't been this excited since her first job.

"If I get a vote, I say Jeremy needs to keep you forever," Shane said as they locked up. "I know you mentioned being out of the field for a few years, but you could never tell."

She smiled. "Thanks."

Elena patted Serita's arm. "You'll definitely get my vote. We need another woman around here to keep these men in line. Have a nice evening."

"You do the same. See you guys in the morning." She smiled. *Not bad for a first day.* Over lunch, Serita had learned that the fortysomething-year-old Elena had gone back to school and got her engineering degree a decade ago, after her youngest child turned three. It made Serita think about the conversation she and Gabby had had the night before. If Elena could juggle marriage, children and an intensive degree program, surely Serita could do it. If it ever happened. Automatically her thoughts shifted to Jeremy. Where would they end up? She didn't even want to contemplate how awkward it would be if he hired her permanently, then sometime down the road their relationship fizzled out. She'd be back at square one because no way would she be able to see him every day and remember how it had felt to be with him. As it stood now, she was going to have a hard time keeping her hands to herself. Serita had extracted a promise from Jeremy and she needed to be sure to abide by her own rules, no matter how tempting it was to touch or kiss him.

Instead of heading to her car, she went back down the hall to see if Jeremy was still there. She poked her head in the open door and saw him seated behind his desk and working on his computer. She knocked. "Are you busy?"

Jeremy grinned. "Nope. Just playing an online *Jeopardy!* game while I wait for you."

"Are you any good?"

"Of course I'm good. I can wipe the floor with you anytime." He spread his arms. "We can do it right now."

Serita chuckled. "Hmm, tempting, but maybe some other time."

"What? You scared?" he teased.

She rolled her eyes. "Please." She found herself enjoyed the silly bantering between them.

"So how was the first day?"

"It went pretty well. I think I'm going to like working with Elena and Shane."

"They're cool peeps. That's why I hired them. I had a few classes with Shane back in undergrad and we kept in touch over the years. He had gotten downsized from the other company where he worked just as I was launching mine, so I took that as a sign."

"What about Elena?"

"I met her when I went back for my doctorate. She was just returning after having her kids and I tutored her for a couple of classes. My love of Mexican food is because of her. I wouldn't take any money from her, so she repaid me by fixing some of the best enchiladas, tamales and tacos I've ever eaten." He smiled as if remembering. "She told me I was too old to be her son, so she'd think of me as a younger brother."

Serita laughed softly. "I like her."

"She's special. At one point, she had been discouraged about her ability to get through the program."

"I can understand. It's no joke." She had spent her fair share of nights, fussing, cussing and crying. But she had made it through near the top of her class.

"I told her she could do it and promised her that whenever I started my company I would hire her."

"And you made good on that promise." She was liking this man more and more. He appeared to be almost perfect, but no one could hold that title. He must have some faults.

"What are you thinking?"

"Just that you seem to be too good to be true. You're

generous, a gentleman, you tutor people for free… Everybody has at least one blemish."

Jeremy burst out laughing. "Oh, I have a few. I can be pretty anal at times, especially when it comes to my business. I've been known to stick my foot in my mouth a time or two. I work toward perfection and I expect everyone around me to do the same."

"Nobody's perfect, Jeremy."

"You're right, and I remind myself of that daily so I don't walk in one morning and find that everybody's quit." He pushed back from the desk. "Come here, for a minute."

The look in his eyes left no doubt in her mind what he wanted. She told herself they were still at the job, but somehow her feet missed the memo and she ended up right where he wanted her—on his lap. "Jeremy—"

"It's five twenty, baby, well past professional hours," he murmured as he trailed kisses along her jaw and throat. "I know it might sound crazy, but you have no idea how much I've missed you."

She wanted to tell him that yes, it sounded crazy, but she had missed him, too. But the sensations evoked by the heated kisses and slow pass of his hands down her body stacked up like lightning and made speech impossible. The best she could manage was a soft moan. She slid her hand up his magnificent chest and over his strong arms and heard his own groan of pleasure.

"I guess this is one way to ensure you get past the thirty-day trial period."

Serita's eyes snapped open and she tried to jump off Jeremy's lap. "Let me up," she whispered through clenched teeth. This was exactly what she wanted to avoid.

"You're fine right here, sweetheart. Chris already knows about you."

Her gaze flew to his, then Chris's.

Chris angled his head and lifted a brow. "Ah, no, I don't think I do."

"My mystery woman from Madrid," Jeremy said.

Chris's mouth fell open. "Oh, damn, you hired your... I mean, did you know she was one of the candidates?"

"No, and remember you did the ranking." To Serita, he said, "We rank each person by education, experience, leadership skills without knowing who they are. I have Nicole remove the name and gender before giving it to us."

She felt a measure of relief knowing that he hadn't tried to manipulate the situation. She'd had enough of that from a previous relationship.

"Well, you can thank me for your good fortune by giving me a raise," Chris said with a wide grin, leaning against the door frame with his arms folded.

Jeremy shot him a glare. "Get out of my office."

"See how bossy he is, Serita?"

Serita just smiled. "I'm not in this. In fact, I have to go."

"You don't have to leave. I was—" Jeremy glanced over at Chris. "Do you mind?"

"Oh, my bad. See you in the morning, Serita." He tossed her a bold wink and departed.

"This is why you never hire your best friends."

"How long have you been friends?" she asked.

"Middle school. Sometimes I think we've been friends too long," he said, shaking his head. "Do you want to have dinner?"

"I already made plans with my friend Gabby. She's

letting me stay with her until I find a place. Can we do it another time?"

"Sure. Do you want to go out or eat in?"

"Whichever you prefer." She knew he wouldn't consider letting her pay, so she left the choice up to him. Serita didn't want him to think she was one of those women who liked to spend a man's money.

"Eat in. I'll cook for you. Just let me know when you're available."

She leaned back and studied him. "You can cook?"

"Of course I can cook. How do you think I've been eating for the past fourteen years—going over to my parents' house every night or existing on takeout?"

Serita elbowed him playfully. "That's not what I meant and you know it. I mean do you cook well?"

"That's the same question in my book," he said with amusement. "I offer to cook for you and this is what I get. Fine, I'll just order some takeout."

"Oh, no, you don't. I want a five-star meal." The last word was said on a squeal because he started tickling her. She slapped at his hands as she laughed hysterically, but his grip was too strong. "Okay, okay, I won't dis your cooking." Finally he released her and she hopped off his lap, still trying to catch her breath. "And I'm available on Saturday."

"Saturday, it is." Jeremy shut down his computer, stuffed the laptop and some folders into his bag and stood. "I'll walk you out." He reached for her hand. "I can hold your hand, right? Or is that against the rules, too?"

She glanced up at him. "Whatever." But she couldn't stop smiling.

Chapter 7

"You look like you made it through the first day just fine," Gabby said as soon as Serita entered the condo.

"I did. Well, after I got over a major shocker about the owner this morning."

"Oh, no. Is it something bad and will it impact your ability to do the job?"

"It's not bad, per se, and it could have an impact." Although Jeremy had promised her he would judge fairly.

"Girl, if you don't just spit it out."

"Jeremy."

Gabby's hand flew to her mouth. "He works there?"

"He owns it."

"Well, damn. I wasn't expecting that."

"Yeah, neither was I. By the look on his face this morning, he wasn't, either."

A slow grin spread across her lips. "And I don't see one thing bad about it. All I see is *job security*."

"That wouldn't be fair."

"It's not like you're unqualified for the job, Serita. You got the position on your own and you already like your boss, so it's a win-win situation for both of you."

"We'll see. Let me change into something comfortable and we can go."

"I'm thinking Arden Fair Mall because I've been craving those catfish nuggets from Delta Soul in there."

"Sounds good to me," she called over her shoulder while heading down the hall.

Thirty minutes later, Gabby circled the parking lot at the mall searching for parking. "I can't believe all these people are here. It's Monday at seven."

"Maybe they all had the same idea as you. I think someone's coming out a few spaces up," Serita said. They ended up parking near the JCPenney entrance, which was in the center of the mall. "There are a lot more restaurants than what I recall." She saw a BJ's Brewhouse and Seasons 52. "And new stores."

"The latest one is Alex and Ani, and I really don't need one of those here. Hmm, we might have to stop in, so I can see what new bracelets are in."

"Are we shopping or eating first?"

"We should probably eat first and then walk off some of the food, but tonight I want my meal to settle in real good."

They burst out laughing. "Shopping it is." They started at the jewelry store, since it was on the first floor and Gabby ended up purchasing two more bracelets to add to her collection and talked Serita into getting the rose-gold Path Of Life two-bracelet set. "This is exactly why I don't shop with you."

"You have to admit they're pretty."

"I'm not admitting anything." She pivoted on her heel and strode out the store with Gabby's laughter trailing. Serita hadn't bought herself anything in a while. Her mother and Gabby always said Serita needed to spoil herself every now and again, but Serita's practical self rarely did. "Where to next?" she asked when Gabby caught up.

"I want to go upstairs to Bath & Body Works to get another lemon mint leaf candle. I love the clean scent and it does wonders for eliminating that stale smell."

They took the escalator up to the store and ended up staying for a good twenty minutes smelling candles and lotions, spraying body mists and trying out the different types of hand soaps from exfoliating to nourishing. She bought a few soaps for the bathroom she'd be using, as well as two of the smaller candles for her room. Once they had accomplished that, the two of them walked farther down the mall to the food court and ordered the catfish nugget meal and lemonade.

Gabby opened her container when the food came. "Look at all this. And they cook them the old-fashioned Southern way with cornmeal, instead of that batter." She immediately opened some packages of tartar and hot sauces, mixed them together and dipped in a piece of fish. She popped it into her mouth, closed her eyes and moaned. "So good."

Serita chuckled and tasted a piece. "Oh, my goodness. It *is* good."

"You have to mix the sauces together and try it."

She made a face. "I don't think so." The combination looked like a pink mess.

"Don't knock it until you try it."

"I'll just stick with the hot sauce." They ate in silence for a few minutes. "Have you heard from Jodi and where she's staying?"

"That girl. She said something about staying with another friend. The thing is she was supposed to be saving up her money to get her own place. That's why I didn't charge her much. If she couldn't handle the four hundred dollars at my place, I don't how she thinks she can make it on her own."

She shook her head. "That's a bargain."

"I know. I was trying to help her, and she had the nerve to tell me she didn't understand why I was getting so upset about her not paying, since I'd been paying the full mortgage before she came."

"That's not the point."

"I said exactly that and told her she wasn't going to use extra water, gas, electricity and everything else for free. This ain't her mama's house." She rolled her eyes and ate a french fry.

Serita laughed. She couldn't believe Jodi. "I promise you won't have to worry about that with me." She had already paid her for three months, the amount of time Serita figured it would take her to find a place. She hoped to move by the start of the year.

Gabby patted Serita's hand. "You can stay for free. I haven't forgotten the semester you let me stay in your dorm room when my dad got laid off and I couldn't afford housing. If it wasn't for you, I would've had to drop out."

She dropped her head and shrugged. "It was nothing." Silence rose between them and they continued to eat.

"How do you think things are going to go with Jeremy?"

"I don't know." She sipped her lemonade. "I really like him so far. When I'm with him I feel like... I don't know. Somebody different." Thinking back, she realized her past relationships had centered around dinner or theater dates where they dressed up. Nothing as simple as taking a walk or talking for hours about everything and nothing. She had never teased with those other guys, or been so open and playful as she was with Jeremy.

Gabby angled her head thoughtfully. "I think there's something about him that makes you feel free to be the real you, and that's a good thing."

"Maybe."

"You'll know one way or another because I don't see him walking away from you so easily. He sounds like he might be a keeper."

Serita's mind went back to the moments in his office earlier when they had been interrupted by Chris. Jeremy had made his intentions quite clear and she agreed with Gabby's assessment. Each thing she learned about him only added to her attraction, and she didn't think it would be easy to walk away from him, either.

"I've been so busy with work and making sure Randi is comfortable that we haven't had a chance to talk about the woman you met in Madrid," Cedric said, handing Jeremy a box containing metal scraps, nails and bolts. "How's the long-distance thing working out?"

"Thanks for this." Three times a year, Jeremy conducted a six-week robotics camp on Saturday mornings for middle school students to get them interested in pursuing the sciences. He set the box on the floor in front of where he sat. "It's working out just fine because she's not long-distance anymore. She's closer than I ever hoped."

"Are you telling me this woman just up and moved to Sacramento so you two could be together?"

Laughing, he said, "No. She actually grew up here and was planning to move back after her teaching contract didn't get renewed. I got the surprise of my life Monday morning when she showed up as one of the four people I hired."

Cedric shook his head. "I'm sure you both were happy about that."

"Actually, she wasn't. You know I told you that they'll all be under a thirty-day trial and I'd keep the two best candidates. Serita is concerned about me giving her preference and wants her work to stand on its own."

"And are you planning to give her preference?"

"I don't have to because the woman is phenomenal. After the first day, Elena and Shane were singing her praises and all but told me I'd better hire her. But it's going to be tricky. One guy I know will be out at the end. He's been a pain in the ass from the moment he walked through the door." Shane also worked on the surgery arm project and had complained about Wade trying to take over and make changes on parts that had already been completed. Wade had told Shane he needed to think outside the box. If it kept up, Jeremy would let Wade go well before the month was up.

"I know you'll come up with a way to get it done. Do you think she's the one?"

"I do. I just need to convince her."

Cedric stared. "All these years, I figured all this talk about knowing your Mrs. Right when you saw her and falling in love at first sight was just that—talk. But you're serious, aren't you?"

"I'm very serious." He had always held out hope that he would find the woman who was perfect for him, but was realistic enough to know that he might not find her all wrapped up neatly with a bow. Now, however, reality seemed to be lining up with his dreams. He picked up the box and stood. "I need to get going. Class starts in an hour."

"You owe me for getting up at eight o'clock on a Saturday morning."

Jeremy grinned. "Just helping you be prepared for what's going to happen when the baby comes."

"I just hope this baby gives us another couple weeks at least. By then, she'll be thirty-six weeks and if she goes into labor, it should be okay."

"I'm glad to hear it."

"You can swing back by after class if you want. She should be up by then."

His class ran from ten until one in the afternoon. "I'll try to stop by tomorrow. I'm cooking dinner for Serita tonight and I have a few things to do before I pick her up. You know she was hassling me about not letting her drive over to the house, talking about it being a waste of gas."

"Randi did the same thing when we started dating, but I didn't care."

"True that." They did a fist bump. "See you later."

The classes were held in the multipurpose room of one of the Roseville middle schools. Jeremy had gone to school in the district and when he approached his old principal—she had been a teacher then—about his idea two years ago, it had been met with enthusiasm.

With her support, it didn't take long for the program to take flight. The first several classes had been comprised solely of male students. Only in the last summer session did he have one female.

Today, as the twelve students filed in, he was delighted to see the same young lady, as well as three more. His thoughts shifted to Serita and he made a mental note to ask her to join him for one of the sessions. It was important to him that students of color see themselves represented in careers other than sports and entertainment—not that there was anything wrong with those careers. He just wanted the students to know they had other options, or could do both, if they chose. He knew seeing another woman in the field of robotics would go a long way in boosting their self-confidence.

"Hi, Mr. Hunter. Did you go on your trip to Spain?"

Jeremy smiled. Davon was one of his repeat students and always eager to learn. "I sure did. After class, I'll show you a few pictures."

"Cool."

"Alright, everybody. Take your seats and let's get started. We have a lot to cover." He waited a moment for the students to get settled, then began with the introduction and the learning objectives. "Understand that this is not a time for goofing around. We're going to have a lot of fun, but be prepared to work hard." He met each student's gaze before continuing. "There are some safety rules that are very important for you to abide by. I'm passing out a sheet for you to read and sign that says you understand and will follow. Anyone who does not follow these rules will be asked to leave the class." Jeremy saw surprise on some of their young faces. He gave them a few minutes to complete the form, then started the class. He ended it with a demonstration of a few types of simple robots and a question-and-answer period. The class ended up running over by twenty minutes because of all the questions, but that didn't bother him. Their bright eyes and excitement always made him glad that he'd chosen to do the class, despite the amount of work it took.

Jeremy took a few minutes to share some of his photos from Madrid and a couple of minutes from his presentation. "This is going to be you all one day and I'll be in the audience to cheer you on."

"Do girls get to teach at the conferences, too?" Briana had a sharp mind, but tended to be very shy.

"They absolutely do." He scrolled through his photos and found Serita's presentation. He had been so enamored by her voice that he'd recorded it. He held the phone out to Briana.

Her face lit up. "Wow!"

Yeah, wow. That was Jeremy's first impression of Serita, too. A vision of them teaching together surfaced in his mind. He definitely had to get her to come to the class. "You can do the same thing. Just keep working hard and doing well in school."

"I will." She hurried off.

"Okay, let's wrap it up. I know your parents have been waiting. I'll see you all next Saturday."

Once everyone had gone, he packed up and went grocery shopping. Serita had mentioned wanting a five-star meal, so he planned to give her one. He stopped at a local florist and picked out a bouquet with half a dozen pink roses and drove home to shower.

The drive to Antelope from his Roseville house took only twenty minutes and, by traveling the back roads, he didn't have to bother with the freeway. When Serita opened the door to Jeremy, his heart started pounding. She looked gorgeous in a pair of tight jeans and a tan short-sleeved top that dipped low and emphasized the seductive swell of her breasts. Her natural curls hung loose and framed her face. "Hey, beautiful." He placed a kiss on her lips and handed her the flowers. "These are for you."

"Hi, and thank you. They're lovely. Come in." Serita stepped back for him to enter.

He followed her through the short entryway to the living room.

She placed the vase on the coffee table. "I need to grab my jacket and purse. Have a seat."

Jeremy sat and watched her hips disappear down the hall. She came back a minute later with a curvy golden-skinned woman and he stood.

"Jeremy, this is my friend Gabriella. Gabby, Jeremy."

"It's nice to meet you, Gabriella," he said.

Gabriella smiled. "Same here. You wouldn't happen to have any other single brothers or cousins hanging around, by any chance?"

He laughed. "Unfortunately, I don't. I'm actually the last one."

"Pity."

Serita shook her head. "She's outrageous."

"I'm not mad at her. You won't know until you ask," he said.

Gabriella gestured his way. "See, that's what I'm saying. Thank you, Jeremy."

Serita hooked her arm in Jeremy's. "Let's go. Bye, crazy woman."

Smiling, she said, "You two have fun."

Once in the car, Jeremy said, "I like her. Where did you meet?"

"We grew up together and ended up at the same college. I'm an only child and she's like the sister I never had."

"That had to be lonely sometimes." Despite their two-year age difference, he and Cedric were close, and he couldn't imagine not having the friendship that came along with being siblings.

"It was, but you deal with it." She fell silent for a few minutes. "I thought you said we were having dinner. Four o'clock is kind of early to eat."

"We aren't eating until later. I just wanted to spend more time with you. The earlier we start, the longer I get to enjoy your company. Do you mind if we stop at the bookstore on the way? I ordered a book and it's in. The bookstore is on the other side of town in Oak Park."

"No, though I always get into trouble when I go into bookstores."

"Same. We're all readers in my family, but my library is probably three times that of everybody else's."

"I'd like to see that," she said, facing him.

His gaze left the road briefly. "I'll be happy to show it to you, once we get to my house." They shared a smile and rode the rest of the way in companionable silence interspersed with conversation.

He parked in the lot adjacent to the building housing Underground Books and they went inside. He spoke to Mother Rose, the manager and store operator, and waited while she retrieved his book. She, as well as the Black-owned bookstore, was a fixture in the Oak Park neighborhood. Jeremy watched as Serita wandered around the store, stopping here and there to pick up a book. He walked over to where she stood. "Find anything?"

"More like what haven't I found," she said with a chuckle. "Are you in a hurry? I want to sit for a few minutes and check these out." She held up the four books.

"Nope. Take your time." He loved the bookstore's comfortable and homey feeling. R & B and jazz flowed through hidden speakers, and a sofa, matching chair and coffee table sat on the far side of the store, beckoning one to stay and relax. They sat reading and talking about the different books for a good half hour. In Jeremy's mind, it added to his growing list of evidence that she was indeed the one for him.

Chapter 8

Serita strolled through Jeremy's two-story home as he gave her a tour. "This is gorgeous." Every room in the four-bedroom four-and-a-half-bath home, with the shiny wood floors, elegant furnishings and spacious size, attested to his success. But his extensive library set in an alcove on the second floor left her breathless. "How long have you lived here? It's rather large for one person, unless you just like having lots of space."

"Almost five years. And I figured once I got married and started a family, I wouldn't have to move."

She whirled around and narrowed her eyes. She ignored that last sentence, not wanting to read anything into it. "Exactly how old are you?"

Jeremy chuckled. "Thirty-six, and you?"

"Thirty-two." That would somewhat explain his reference to being in the field for so long. She had thought about purchasing a house when she lived in Reno, but didn't want to have to worry about the upkeep or paying someone to do it. Her condo had suited her fine. But, glancing around the room now, she thought she might change her mind when she started looking this time. Of course, she didn't think she'd need such a big house, especially since she'd have to clean it. She scanned the many bookshelves and saw genres ranging from robotics and thrillers to biographies and cookbooks, and even a romance title or two. "Romance?"

"What? Men can't read romance?"

"Yes, but I just didn't expect…um…think you read that sort of thing."

He wrapped his arm around her shoulder and dropped a kiss on her hair. "Well, now you know I read romance. You never know when some of those things heroes do for their women might come in handy."

In her estimation, he did just fine in that department. Actually, from what he'd shown her already, he could have written the manual. "Like maybe you don't already do some of those things."

"I had good examples to follow."

Serita recalled Jeremy mentioning his father's role in his upbringing and wondered if his parents' marriage factored into the way he approached his own relationships. Watching the way her father had treated her mother had certainly influenced Serita's thinking, and that was why she had decided to let men take a back seat in her life. She hadn't found one that measured up. Until now. She followed Jeremy back downstairs to the kitchen. "What's for dinner?"

"I'm making that five-star meal you requested— seared sea scallops in a wine-and-herb-butter sauce, sautéed broccoli and mushrooms, roasted honey gold potatoes and homemade French bread."

Her mouth dropped. "I don't know what to say, other than *wow*. Five-star, indeed. You're going to make the French bread, too?"

"Yep." Jeremy walked over to the refrigerator, retrieved a pan and peeled back a towel covering a rising loaf of bread. "All I have to do is pop it in the oven."

"Where did you learn to make bread?"

"My mom. Before I went to science camp, I had planned to grow up and own a bakery."

She smiled. "One out of two ain't bad. You own your business."

"True. Would you like something to drink. Since we're having seafood, I opted for chardonnay or champagne."

"Either is fine." He opened the champagne, poured them both glasses and held his aloft.

"To the beginning of something beautiful."

She touched her glass against his. Their eyes held as they sipped. Yep, this man was setting the bar pretty high. She watched him pull several things from the refrigerator. "Do you need my help with anything?" she asked, taking a seat on a stool on the other side of the island.

He glanced at her over his shoulder. "Not this time. First visit gets a guest pass, but next time, we'll do it together."

"There's going to be a next time?"

Jeremy placed the ingredients on the counter and came to where she sat. He tilted her chin and placed a sweet, lingering kiss on her lips. "There are going to be many next times." Straightening, he went over and started the dinner preparations.

Serita wasn't aware she had been holding her breath until she felt the pressure in her chest. The kiss and his words had shaken her. She was falling for him, and fast. The realization scared her on one level because her feelings for Jeremy had taken on a life of their own. Despite her best efforts to slow this headlong rush down a path that could lead to heartbreak, the emotions kept gaining speed and she felt like a car careening out of control. She took a long drink with trembling hands and prayed things didn't end as they always had for her. Soon, the combined smells of bread baking and the food cooking filled the kitchen. The wonderful aroma made her stomach growl. "It smells so good in here."

"Thanks. Hopefully, it'll taste even better." Jeremy slid the pan with the quartered potatoes into a second oven and wiped his hands on a towel. He picked up a remote and held it out. The smooth sound of Maxwell singing about a little "Sumthin' Sumthin'" flowed from hidden speakers. This one happened to be the remixed slower version that had been featured on the *Love Jones* movie soundtrack. "Come dance with me."

She met him halfway, and he pulled her into his arms and started a slow sway. With their height difference, her head came to the middle of his chest and she could hear the strong, steady beat of his heart beneath her ear. The scent of whatever bodywash or cologne he wore floated into her nostrils and she moved closer to inhale the potent, warm fragrance.

"From the moment I saw you sitting in the hallway in that hotel, I imagined us here just like this, me holding you in my arms. It's as if you were made to fit right here," he whispered as his hands made a slow path up and down her back. "Your soft curves pressed against my body… Can you feel what you do to me?"

Have mercy! His words sent a jolt of electricity through her strong enough to power a room full of robots. And, yeah, she felt *exactly* what she did to him. The hard ridge of his erection sitting at her belly left no doubt.

"This thing between us was meant to be, specifically designed for the two of us."

Serita's pulse skipped. What did he mean? She lifted her head and searched his face. She read naked desire in his eyes—and something else she couldn't define. Jeremy's movements slowed until they stopped. He framed her face between his big hands and kissed her until the room spun. Her knees went weak and only his strong arm kept her from sliding to the floor.

"I need to check the bread and potatoes, and start on the rest of the meal." He kissed her again, then went over to the oven.

She stood in the middle of the kitchen, her heart racing and her body trembling. She sucked in several gulps of air, trying to get her breathing back to somewhere near normal, but it took a while. Finally she trusted her feet enough to move. He was waging an all-out assault on her senses and she was losing. By the time they sat down to dinner, she had managed to regain some measure of control.

Jeremy placed the serving dishes on the table he had set on his enclosed patio, topped off their champagne and sat opposite Serita. "You go first."

"Everything looks so good. Thank you." She filled her plate, got a piece of the still-warm bread and added butter. She moaned with the first bite. The scallops were tender and flavorful, as were the vegetables and pota- toes. If she could get food like this every day, she might seriously consider never eating out at a restaurant again. "You wouldn't happen to be looking for a job as a per- sonal chef?"

He laughed. "No, and you wouldn't be able to afford my rates," he added with a wink. "You don't cook?"

"Sure, I cook. But not like this." Cooking had never been high on her list of things to learn, much to her mother's chagrin. Serita tended to spend her time in the garage working on her latest robotic invention instead of being in the kitchen. As a result, her skills were sorely lacking. And she didn't even think about baking beyond what it took to follow directions to make a boxed dessert. "What other secret talents do you have—famous musi- cian, world-renowned artist, sports star?"

Jeremy laughed so hard he choked on his champagne. He coughed and coughed. "You're going to make me hurt myself," he croaked. He cleared his throat and took a small sip of the drink. "None of those, although I did play saxophone in the middle school band and basket- ball in high school. Did you do any sports or band?"

Serita shook her head. "I led a pretty boring high school existence." She'd had friends, but not many dates. The boys had always considered her too nerdy for their tastes. She had pretended that it never bothered her, but in reality every time one of her girlfriends men- tioned some great date or how well some boy kissed, it did. She didn't get her first kiss until senior prom, and it had been an awkward experience, one she'd buried and tried to forget.

"It doesn't seem boring now. Where do you see yourself in the next five years?"

She ate another bite of the melt-in-your-mouth scallops before answering. "Eventually, I'd like to do what you did and start my own company. In a perfect world, I'd teach part-time for the next two or three years while working somewhere else, then stop teaching to start my business. The field is growing and I want to capitalize on it before the market gets saturated. I still haven't decided whether that'll be here or back in Reno."

Jeremy frowned. "I thought you'd moved back permanently."

"It could be. I just don't know for sure right now."

He nodded. "About starting your own company, you should do it. I won't lie… Running a business is tough, but the ability to be your own boss makes all the hard work worth it. I'd be more than happy to help you when you're ready."

"I'd appreciate that. You really should think about teaching. You'd be great."

"I already do. I run a six-week robotics camp for middle schoolers three times a year. If you're not busy next Saturday, I'd love for you to come. There are four young ladies in the class and seeing you would be a huge boost to their confidence."

"I would absolutely love to come. Just let me know the time and place." Gabby had said Jeremy might be a keeper. Serita was beginning to think her friend was right.

Sunday afternoon, Jeremy sat in Cedric's enclosed patio with Randi and her sister Iyana eating dinner. They had taken advantage of the midseventies temperatures and cooked a tri-tip and some corn on the grill. Iyana had made the potato salad and baked beans.

"How was your date with Serita last night?" Randi asked.

"Great. I cooked dinner for her."

"Aww, that's so sweet. Your brother cooked for me, too, when we started dating."

Cedric placed a bottle of water in front of his wife. "And he cooks far better than I do."

"Really?" Iyana divided a glance between the brothers. "Randi told me that Cedric can throw down in the kitchen. See, this just ain't right." She pointed her fork Jeremy's way. "It's too bad I think of you as a brother. Otherwise, I'd be figuring out how to build one of those robots you work with to carry her off to another planet." They all fell out laughing. "I'm serious. I need y'all to hook me up with a friend, distant cousin or whatever."

Jeremy couldn't stop laughing. He had found out that Iyana was the total opposite of Randi. Where Randi had some introverted tendencies, her sister gave outgoing a new meaning. She would probably do well acting in some movie instead of being one of the makeup artists. "I'll see what I can do."

"When are you going to introduce her to the family?" Cedric asked. "Mom stopped by yesterday afternoon and asked the same thing."

"I don't know, and I told her that I'd come this evening after I leave here." Though he and Serita had been intimate and were dating, he still sensed some hesitancy on her part. She had also mentioned the possibility of moving back to Reno, and he realized he needed to slow down. He would probably scare her to death if he told her what he was feeling. Last night, as they danced in his kitchen, he'd had to catch himself after telling her they were meant to be. He saw the fear. "Hopefully, soon. I'm trying to take my time with her."

"Yeah, I don't think telling her 'I know we just met, but you're the woman I've been waiting for' is a good idea. It'll probably send her running for the hills."

"Thanks for the confidence," he said sarcastically. "That's just what I want to hear from my big brother."

Cedric shrugged. "I'm just sayin'."

"I know I would have," Randi said. "I'd met so many frogs, I didn't think there was a prince out there. Maybe Serita has experienced the same thing. If that's the case, then slow is better. But if you ever need to heat things up, you should visit Desiree's shop," she added with a grin.

Cedric skewered her with a look. "Please don't bring that up. Do you know how long it's been since—"

"Cedric!"

"What? They know what we're doing…or *not* doing," he grumbled.

Jeremy and Iyana laughed. Iyana said, "Wasn't it that massage oil from Desiree's shop that got you two in your current predicament?"

"Yes, yes, it was." The satisfied look he sent his wife this time gave the impression that he couldn't wait to do it all again.

Jeremy made a mental note to pay a visit to the shop at his earliest convenience. He'd heard a lot about that oil—warming, edible, flavored—yeah, he was all for that. An image of him licking the oil off Serita's skin surfaced in his mind and his body reacted in kind. He hopped up. "I'm going to get another bottle of tea. Anybody else want one?" They all declined. "Be right back."

In the kitchen, he took several deep breaths. He'd never had a woman who invaded his thoughts the way Serita did or aroused him with just a mention. He reached into the fridge for the tea, opened it and drank deeply, hoping it would calm his body.

"You're going to need a little more than that to help you out."

He spun around and met Cedric's amused gaze. "What are you talking about?"

"You know exactly what I'm talking about. I've never seen you this obsessed with a woman. If I didn't know better, I'd swear you were falling in love with her."

He didn't respond. He'd wondered that himself several times. The logical part of him said it couldn't be possible this soon in the game, but his heart told him something entirely different. Jeremy had always jumped into his relationships with both feet, only to come away unfulfilled. But not this time. This time everything felt right. The notion didn't scare him—he'd been looking for love—but he didn't want to make one misstep that would cause him to lose Serita.

"I take it by your silence that I'm right. I can't say I'm surprised, and I really hope it turns out the way you want. I never thought I wanted to settle down with one woman, but you were right about finding that one special woman. I'm happier than I've ever been in my life."

"I know you are and I'm glad. You know, it's pretty ironic that you and our cousins were all against falling in love and every one of you has taken the plunge into matrimony."

"You were the only one who thought differently. Your time is coming, Jeremy, and we'll all be there to celebrate with you."

He smiled faintly. "I hope so." They went back out to the patio and finished dinner. Afterward he helped Cedric clean up and left to visit his parents.

Jeremy's father answered the door. "Hey, son. Come on in."

"Hey, Dad." They shared a hug and Jeremy followed him back to the family room. His mother was seated in her favorite recliner doing one of her word search puzzles. "How are you, Mom?" He placed a kiss on her upturned cheek.

"I'm doing alright." She put the pen in the book to hold her place and set it, along with her reading glasses, on the small table next to her. "How are things at work? I remember you mentioning needing to hire another engineer."

"It's going pretty good." He told them about his and Chris's idea about the trial period. "We're only planning to hire two of them permanently and, so far, three out of the four are working out well."

"Well, there's always that one who can't seem to get it together. How's Serita, and when are you going to bring her down to visit?"

Leave it to his mother to cut right to the chase. "I'm not sure. She doesn't live in Reno anymore."

"Oh, honey, I'm sorry. I'd hoped you would have some good news."

Jeremy smiled. "I never said I didn't. She lives here now and just happened to be one of our new hires."

"What?" His dad's eyebrows shot up. Then he laughed. "Talk about bringing fate to your door."

His mother beamed. "That's wonderful, sweetheart. Then it shouldn't take long for you to bring her around."

"Mom, you do realize Serita and I only met a about a month ago?"

"I know. But at the hospital, you made it sound like she's the special woman you've been trying to find."

"I still believe that she is, but that doesn't mean she shares the same feelings. As soon as I know where this is going, I'll be happy to introduce her because I know you'll like her."

"Just don't take forever. You young people today like to drag out relationships. Either you want to be together or you don't. I'm the only one left with an unmarried child. LaVerne brags about Desiree and Jabari all the time." Desiree was Lorenzo's wife and Jabari was married to Lorenzo's sister, Alisha. "And I'm not even going to start on Nolan and Dee."

He shook his head. Even if he got married today, he wouldn't be able to catch up with his LA aunt and uncle. All five of their children were married and, between them, they had seven grandchildren. And from what Lorenzo had told him on the way from the airport three weeks ago, two of his cousins might be expecting again.

"Theresa, it's not a competition," his father said. "He'll bring his young lady over when it's time."

"I know, I know. I just want Jeremy to experience the same kind of joy we have."

Jeremy had grown up hearing all about how his father had predicted his mother would be his wife before they had even been introduced. He had fallen in love with his mother a week after meeting her and their love continued to grow and deepen, even after all these years. That's what Jeremy wanted for himself. And he wanted it with Serita.

Chapter 9

"We're so happy to have you back home, sweetheart."

Serita hugged her mother. "I'm glad to be back." Even though she had only been two hours away, she'd missed being able to drive over whenever she wanted. She'd left for college at eighteen and, aside from summer visits, remained in Reno until now. She had especially missed Sunday dinners.

"Your dad is outside by the grill."

A wide grin spread across her face. "He's making ribs?" she asked excitedly.

"Yes."

She rubbed her hands together with glee. Nobody could make ribs like her daddy.

"Is that my baby girl I hear?"

"Dad!" She launched herself into his strong arms and tears misted in her eyes. "I missed you." She had always been a daddy's girl.

"I missed you, too, baby."

Serita glanced between the two people she loved the most. David and Gayle Edwards had nurtured her, loved her and encouraged her to reach for her dreams, even when others didn't believe in them. She couldn't have asked for better parents.

"Your mama tell you I've got ribs in the kitchen?"

"Yes, she did, and I'm going to hurt myself."

His booming laughter filled the air. "Well, come on and get it."

"You don't have to tell me twice." She led the way to the kitchen and piled her plate high with the ribs, sautéed corn, macaroni and cheese, green beans and her mother's homemade yeast rolls. After they were seated at the table, her father blessed the food and Serita immediately bit into a tender rib covered in a thick, sweet barbecue sauce. "Dad, you outdid yourself. These ribs are to die for."

"Mmm-hmm, I'm going to have to agree with you, baby girl. I stuck my foot in these."

The rest of the food tasted just as good. Growing up, she had been known to eat four or five of those rolls at one time. However, her thirty-two-year-old metabolism couldn't handle that now, so she settled for eating just one. "I haven't had food that tasted this good in so long." As soon as the words were off her tongue, she wanted to call them back. She *had* eaten some great food last night prepared by a man who seemed to be working his way deeper into her psyche as the days passed.

"Tell us about your new job," her mother said.

She finished chewing before answering. "It's temporary right now, but depending on how I perform over the thirty-day trial, I could be one of two the company hires permanently." She still didn't know how she felt about dating the man who had a say in her employment, but he had promised to be fair and she had to take him at his word.

"Do you think you have a good chance?"

"Yes. The two engineers I'm working with mentioned that they believed I'd be a good fit."

"And your boss?" her father asked over his glass of iced tea.

Complicated...really complicated. "It's only been a week and he hasn't said much." It wasn't exactly a lie.

Her mother patted her hand. "I'm not worried. With your background and personality, you'll get the permanent spot. Mark my words."

"Thanks, Mom."

"I have to say we were a little disappointed when you decided not to stay here. It would've been cheaper and you could save that money for something else."

"I know, but I wanted to do this on my own. Even though the cost of living is higher here, I got a good price for my condo, so I should be okay. I'll probably start looking for my own place in a week or two."

"How's Gabriella doing? I hope she's not still dating that man we saw her with last year. Something about him made me uncomfortable. I wanted to tell her so, but your father made me stay out of it."

Serita chuckled. "No, she's not. I think she dumped him not long after that." Her mother treated Gabby as if she were another daughter and that included getting into Gabby's business.

"What about you? Have you met any nice guys that have potential?"

She had hoped to avoid this conversation but should

have known better. Her mom knew about all the heart-breaks Serita had suffered and always said that in life, one had to wade through the bad ones to get to the right one. "I did meet a guy at the conference in Madrid and he's very nice."

Her mother narrowed her eyes. "We had a long chat about that trip. Not once did you mention a man. Where is he from?"

"Here."

"I see. You'll have to bring him over so we can meet him."

Serita's father had always been her ally, so she looked to him for some sort of reprieve but found none.

"Don't look at me. I'm with your mother on this one."

Of course, when it came to men, he'd side with her mother. "I think it might be a little too soon for that. It's only been a month or so." And she'd done more with him in that time than she had with her ex, whom she had dated for eight months.

"What's his name? I assume, since he was at the conference, that he's in the same field."

"His name is Jeremy Hunter and, yes, he's an engineer."

"At least you know he has a good job," her father said, saluting her with his fork.

"He does. He owns his own company." *Just tell them,* her inner voice chimed. "The same one I happen to work at," she mumbled. Two pairs of eyes bored into her. "Neither of us knew until I walked into the office, so…" She had no idea what to say after that. She forked up some macaroni and cheese, feeling all of twelve years old.

"Sometimes things happen for a reason," her mother

said. "That job brought you back home, so I can't be too mad, but I'm really curious about this Jeremy now. I do hope that means you'll be back for good."

"I won't know until I find something permanent, whether that's with this company or another one."

"With him owning the business, I suspect he's much older than you. I'm not sure how I feel about that."

"Mom, you do realize that I'm thirty-two, not twenty-two and Jeremy is only four years older. If things start to get serious between us, I promise you'll be the first to know and I will definitely bring him over."

Her mother nodded as if satisfied.

Serita sighed in relief. *So, having sex twice, spending an entire evening at his house and hearing the man tell you the two of you were meant to be isn't serious?* She wished that annoying voice in her head would just shut up. It didn't matter that it was the truth.

Jeremy had tried diplomacy when dealing with Wade, but by Wednesday morning, he'd reached his limit. Wade seemed to forget that it was Jeremy's name on the deed to the building and not his. He had a habit of talking down to the other new hires and taking extended breaks, which, in Jeremy's mind, meant that Wade would not be a good fit for the company.

"Jeremy, I think you need to come see this."

He glanced at the terse set of Shane's jaw and knew the day was about to get worse. *It is only nine.* He just hoped nothing had gone wrong with one of the designs in progress. Pushing to his feet, he followed Shane out and down the hall to one of the work areas. Nothing could have prepared him for the sight before him. On the table lay one of the sensor components, detached from the robot console. The same one that had taken him two weeks to perfect. He'd worked late nights and weekends to get the precise specifications of the foot pedal that would be used by his client during surgery and now... It took Jeremy several seconds to find his voice. "What the hell happened in here?"

Shane nodded toward Wade.

"Wade?"

"What happened was innovation. This simple sensor would do nothing more than flip a switch when someone put their foot on it. I took the liberty of drawing up something with a little more pizzazz." Wade held out a notebook opened to a page with a sketch.

Ignoring it, Jeremy said through clenched teeth, "My office. *Now!*" He strode out of the room. When Wade got to the office, Jeremy slammed the door. "Your job was to work on designing the console from the existing schematics, not create your own."

"Robotics is about being innovative and thinking outside the box."

"You can be innovative and think outside the box on your own damn time, not mine. As of this moment, you're done here. Collect your belongings and get out."

Wade's face contorted in anger. "You can't fire me. My contract says thirty days."

Jeremy opened a file, took out a sheet of paper and slid it across the desk in front of Wade. "Actually, I can. If you hadn't been so focused on one-upping everybody in the room last week, you would have heard me mention the procedures for design change. Do you see your signature on the bottom of that page?"

He snatched the sheet up and read, then tossed it aside.

"Now, we're done here."

Wade stormed out of the office.

Jeremy paced for a good two minutes, trying to calm himself, then went out to make sure the man had left.

Serita passed and placed a hand on his arm. "Hey, everything okay?"

"Fine," he said tersely, and kept walking. He stopped. He hadn't meant to snap at her. "Serita?" He reached for her.

She held up a hand. "Obviously, you have a lot on your mind right now. It's okay." She left him standing there.

Jeremy cursed under his breath and ran a hand over his head. He wanted to follow her but remembered the parameters they'd put in place for their relationship while on the job. However, he did owe her a big apology and would take care of it as soon as possible. For now, he continued to Chris's office.

"That bad of a morning?" Chris asked, glancing up from the papers on his desk.

"Worse. Wade decided to dismantle a part of the console and tried to call it *innovation*."

Chris's eyes widened. "I hope you fired his ass on the spot. We should've done it last week."

"Agreed. Now, I'm going to have to spend many hours redoing something that shouldn't need to be done." In order to keep his bottom line down, Jeremy, most likely, would be working overtime for the next couple of weeks to get back on schedule. He hoped that the reassembly wouldn't take as long as the original assembly had.

"Well, we'll be taking it out of his check and if he complains, I'll tell him it's either that or we can sue him for destruction of property." Chris stood. "You go back to your office, and I'll make sure that idiot is gone."

"Thanks." He started toward his office, then changed direction and headed for the room where Serita worked. He poked his head in the door. "Serita, can I see you in my office for a minute, please?" He could tell she wanted to say no but, with Shane and Elena looking on, didn't.

"Sure." Serita crossed the room and sailed past him without a backward glance. She didn't say a word until they'd reached his office and Jeremy closed the door. "Yes?" She folded her arms and glared at him.

He sighed. She'd asked him if he had any faults, and he'd told her about being anal and a perfectionist. What he hadn't revealed was that until the age of ten he'd had an explosive temper. He'd had to sit out more Little League games than he could count because of it. Jeremy didn't like losing and whenever his team lost, he'd thrown bats, balls, torn down backstops and more. Of course, his mother's shoe landed on his backside as a result, but it didn't help. He didn't know how it happened, but by the time he reached age twelve, the behavior had all but vanished. In its place was the relaxed, laid-back man everyone knew. For the first time in his adult life, that old anger had risen up in him with such force that he'd almost lost it. It had been stirred to a level where he wanted to tear something apart, preferably Wade Brewer. "I want to apologize for my behavior in the hall earlier. My anger wasn't directed at you, but I was still wrong and I'm sorry." She didn't say anything, and it was killing Jeremy. Even though they were still on the clock, he had to hold her in his arms. Pulling her into his embrace, he kissed the top of her head. "Please forgive me, baby. I'm sorry."

Finally she looked up at him. "This time, but don't make it a habit."

He smiled for the first time that day. Unable to resist, he placed a sweet kiss on her lips. "I promise."

She backed away. "What are you doing? No kisses during the workday."

"That wasn't a regular kiss. It was an apology kiss."

Serita shook her head, but a smile peeked out. "I need to get back to work. What had you so upset anyway?"

"Wade."

"Ugh, that man is a pain in the butt."

"Well, he's going to be someone else's pain in the butt because I fired him. He dismantled one of the foot pedals on the console and I'm going to have to put in extra hours to redo it."

"Oh, no. I'm so sorry. Let me know if you need some help. I don't mind staying longer." She reached up to touch his face and then, seemingly remembering where they were, snatched her hand down.

"Thanks. I might just take you up on the offer. What are you doing for lunch?"

"I have to make a quick run to Target, why?"

"I thought we could have lunch, but we can do it another day."

"Okay. Do you need me to bring you anything back?"

"Nah, I'm good." He reached around her and opened the door.

"See you later."

Jeremy stared after her with his smile still in place.

"Should I be dusting off my tux?" Chris asked, coming from the other hall.

"Maybe." Jeremy laughed at the shocked expression on his friend's face.

"Hold up. I was just kidding."

"I'm not." Just like his father, Jeremy knew who he wanted and didn't plan to mess around and let her get away.

Chapter 10

Serita parked in the lot in front of Target and got out. In reality, she could have made the pit stop on her way home, but she wanted to get out of the office. While she enjoyed the job and working with Elena and Shane, they kept up a constant stream of conversation during the day. Being a relative introvert, Serita needed a break. Inside the store, she pulled out her list, grabbed a basket and started up the aisle. It took only a few minutes to get what she needed, then she made her way to the line. While standing there, she spotted a package of Skittles—one of her favorite childhood candies—and tossed them in the basket.

A few minutes later, she was in the car and on her way back, leaving her a good thirty minutes to eat a quick lunch. She had only gone a block when she felt her steering wheel pulling to the right and the unmistakable sound of a flat tire. Sighing, she flipped on her hazard lights and slowly pulled into a nearby parking lot. Serita got out. Just as she'd suspected, her right rear tire was flat. For the life of her, she couldn't recall running over anything on the road. Going back to the car, she searched for her auto insurance card to call for road assistance. Then she decided to call Jeremy first to let him know she would be late getting back.

"Hey, baby," Jeremy said when he answered.

"Hey. I have a flat tire, so I'll be late getting back. I'm not sure how long road assistance will take to get here."

"Where are you?"

"In the Rocky Ridge Town Center."

"I'll be there in five minutes."

She opened her mouth to tell him she could just wait, but the line went dead. She should have expected that would be his response. The late-October temperatures had started to drop into the low seventies, but the slight breeze made it feel cooler. Serita got her jacket out of the car and put it on. A few minutes later, her phone buzzed in her hand. She saw Jeremy's name on the display. "Hey."

"Where are you parked?"

"Near the front, by Macaroni Grill." She searched and saw his silver Audi. She threw up a wave and waited for him to park next to her Elantra. Unlike her, he had on a short-sleeved button-down shirt and no jacket. "You're not cold?"

He grinned. "Nope. Pop the trunk."

She did as he asked, then stood off to the side. While waiting, she checked her emails. It would have been the ideal time to eat her lunch, but it was at the office in the refrigerator. By the time they made it back, her lunch would be over. She'd probably have to eat on her afternoon break. Serita turned around to ask Jeremy something and froze. He had taken off his shirt. Her gaze traveled down his body from his wide, muscular chest and defined abs to the low-hung jeans riding his trim waist and his black boots. A pulsing began in her core. She was about two seconds from jumping him right then and there. She closed her eyes to bring her rampant desire under control and opened them to find him standing in front of her, concern lining his features.

"You okay?"

She nodded quickly. "Why did you take off your shirt?"

"Didn't want to get it dirty."

It made sense, but still… Serita shoved her hands in her jacket pockets to keep from running them all over him. He needed to hurry up, fix that tire and put his shirt back on. To keep herself from doing something crazy like straddling him while he was on the ground, she went around to the other side of the car. Far away from temptation. It didn't help because her mind conjured up every possible scenario of her riding him—in the car, on the hood. Beads of perspiration popped out on her forehead and she removed her jacket. That old song by Nelly played in her head. It was definitely getting hot. Unable to resist, she poked her head around to the side of the car where he worked and snapped a picture. Glancing down at the photo, she smiled. Her selfie game might still need some work, but everything else was on point. Twenty minutes later, he stored the tire in her trunk and they drove back to the office.

"I can take you to get a new tire tonight, if you want," Jeremy said.

"Don't worry about it. I can take care of it on the weekend."

He grasped her hand. "Serita, I know you can take care of it, but it's alright to let a man who cares about you do something for you every now and again. It doesn't make you any less independent."

How he'd read her mind she'd never know, but he was dead-on. She appreciated his willingness to do things for her but didn't want to become dependent on him, or any man, for that matter. However, the sincerity in his voice made her relent. "Okay. Thank you."

"I know you didn't get to eat, so go ahead and take an extra thirty minutes."

Serita nodded a smile of appreciation and headed for the break room to warm up her lunch. She took the bowl holding the last of her leftovers from Sunday's dinner, the bag of Skittles and the mystery novel she had yet to start and walked into the small office she'd been given. The ribs and macaroni and cheese tasted as good as they had the first day. After opening the book, she started reading. Three pages in, she knew it was going to be good and wished she had held off beginning until she got home. Thirty minutes wouldn't be nearly enough time. She had just put the first Skittle in her mouth when Jeremy stuck his head in the door.

"Can I come in?"

"Sure." He entered and stared down at the desk curiously. "What?"

"Why do you have your Skittles all separated and lined up like that?"

She grinned sheepishly. "I like to eat them by color, starting with my least favorite." It was a quirk of hers, just like eating Craisins and almonds. She organized them on a plate or napkin to have one of each together, so she could taste the sweet and nutty flavors at the same time. Sure, she'd been teased about it, but she didn't care.

Jeremy laughed softly. "Hey, whatever turns you on."

"This does." Just like watching him change a tire while shirtless, but she kept that to herself. "Did you want anything in particular?"

"Yes. To see if you were serious about your offer to help me with the console."

"I was." Serita popped a green one into her mouth and frowned. *What the...?* She picked up the wrapper and checked the back.

"Problems?"

"They changed the green from lime to green apple. Didn't nobody ask me." It had to have been at least ten years since she'd purchased the candy. When did that happen? She met his amused gaze. "I'm serious. This throws off the whole taste of the pack." She moved them to the side and picked up a yellow one, then glanced up at him, waiting for him to continue.

"If you have about half an hour this evening, I'd like to go over the what needs to be done, then we can make a schedule. I'll probably have Shane help out, too, since he's familiar with the project."

"I have some time."

"Enjoy your candy." He gestured toward the book. "I see you started. When you're ready, we can have our own private book club to discuss it. We'll have food and everything."

"Sounds like a plan." She was still smiling when he left. She checked the time. Not wanting to take advantage of Jeremy's generosity, she put the rest of the candy back into the package—minus the green ones. Those she threw away. Then she cleaned up and got back to work.

At the end of the day, she went in search of Jeremy and found him talking to Chris.

"How's it going, Serita?" Chris asked. "The boss isn't working you too hard, is he?"

"It's going fine and no, he isn't." She tried to keep her smile hidden.

He shook his head. "You two are a pair. I'm going home. See you guys in the morning."

"Later." Jeremy shifted his gaze to Serita. "Let's get moving, so we're not here all night."

She led the way to the design room and stood engrossed as he explained the task. She studied the 3D image on the computer, rotating it one way, then another. "So the console will have foot pedals that control the different tasks. That means each sensor needs to provide specific feedback to make it easier for the surgeons."

"Exactly." He pointed out some of the parts both on the screen and on the actual console.

She adjusted her glasses and inspected the partially completed pedal. They went back and forth for a few minutes, discussing the best way to proceed. She had gotten so engrossed that it took her a moment to realize that Jeremy had moved and now stood behind her. He slid one hand around her waist and used the other one to push her hair aside before trailing kisses along her neck. "We're supposed to be working."

"I am working."

"No, you're not," she murmured, getting lost in the pleasure his warm lips against her skin evoked.

"Yeah, baby, I am." His hands came up to caress her breasts. "I'm working hard to please you."

His words almost melted her in a heap. He continued *working* until her body caught fire. He swept her into his arms and carried her to his office. Kicking the door closed, he placed her on the small conference table.

Jeremy locked the door. "No one is here, but I don't want to take any chances. Now, where was I?" He slanted his mouth over hers in a deep, passionate kiss. "I think I was here." He dropped his head down to the part of her chest visible above her blouse. He opened the buttons, one at a time, kissing each newly bared portion. He released the clasp on her bra and cupped her breasts in his hands, kneading and massaging them.

Serita's head fell back and she braced her forearms on the table. The heat of his tongue licking and sucking her nipples sent a flurry of sensations whipping through her. But he didn't stop there. He unfastened her pants, then tugged them and her panties off. At the first swipe of his tongue against her clit, her hips flew off the table and she let out a loud moan.

"Does this please you?" He continued the sweet torture, swirling his tongue deeper and deeper inside her. "What about this?" He slid two fingers inside of her.

Serita didn't think she could take much more.

"Tell me, baby. Am I pleasing you?"

He sped up the motion and the dual sensations were too much. *"Yes!"* she screamed as she came in a rush of ecstasy that snatched her breath and left her weak. Her body continued to pulse and she gasped for air.

"I think I like having you in my office."

She liked having him anywhere.

Saturday afternoon, Jeremy went with Serita to get a new tire. He had them check the other three and found out that the tread on the front two were worn and would need to be replaced pretty soon. He didn't see the point in buying three tires and told the man to replace all four.

"Jeremy, I don't need to get all four right now," Serita whispered. "He said I still have a month or two, depending on how much I drive."

"There's no sense in coming back three or four weeks from now when we're here now. The weather is changing and it's going to start raining soon. I don't want you driving on bald tires and risking an accident." He would never forgive himself if they waited to change the tires and something happened. His heart couldn't take it. "Baby, you're one millimeter off the recommended change time. I need you to be safe," he said.

"I want to be safe, too. Okay, go ahead." She hugged him. "I really appreciate you helping me out."

"I'll always be here to help you." They made their way to the waiting area. If he had his way, he'd be there for her forever.

"We should be done with the pedal by the end of next week if we keep up the schedule," she said.

"We could, but I don't want to have you and Shane working overtime that many days in a row."

"Darryl has been a great help. He doesn't say much, but he gets the job done."

He thought the same thing. Darryl had recently moved to Sacramento to be closer to his aging mother. He had more than twenty years of experience and it showed. When the time came to choose the two best candidates, it would be a tough decision. Scott seemed to be just as dedicated. He had only been out of school a couple of years, but Jeremy expected the young man to do great things in the future. "We'll see how it goes next week. After we're done here, do you want to grab a bite to eat?"

"That works. There are a few places not too far from here."

For the next several minutes, they continued discussing the different projects and what he hoped to accomplish. Then he turned the conversation to her. "I've been meaning to ask whether you've been checking out the colleges to see if they have any openings."

"Not much. I logged onto Sac State's website a couple of times, but didn't see anything. But that was a month ago. I should probably look at the page again."

"And if I see something, I'll let you know."

The mechanic came in and called them over. "We're all done. I just need your signature here." He rattled off the total.

Serita signed the form and placed her credit card on the counter.

He took it, handed it back and put his own up there. "I've got it." She looked like she wanted to argue, but Jeremy counted on her not wanting to make a scene to work in his favor. It did. But her beautiful brown eyes flashed with irritation behind the glasses. He expected her to let him have it as soon as they exited the building, and she didn't disappoint.

She threw up her hands. "You know, I do have my own money."

"I do know that, and you can pay for whatever you want when I'm not around."

"Jeremy—"

He cut her off with a kiss. "You're special to me, and this is one of the ways I choose to show it. Can you humor me, please?"

She didn't say anything for a moment. "Only because you said please." She strutted off.

Jeremy roared with laughter and caught up in time to open the car door for her. She tossed him the keys and he got in on the driver's side. Still chuckling, he leaned over and kissed her temple.

Serita eyed him. "I guess Chris was right about you being bossy."

"Just when necessary. Any particular place you want to eat?"

"I want a big, juicy hamburger."

"Mel's is right up the street. We can go there, if you like." His phone rang before he could say anything else. He saw Cedric's name on the display. "This is my brother. Let me see what he wants." He connected. "Hey, Ced."

"It's showtime."

Showtime? Then it dawned on him. "The baby?"

"Yes. We're at the hospital."

"It's still a month early, though. Are they going to try and stop the contractions again?" Even though it was closer to the due date, he still worried about all the issues that went along with a premature birth.

"With Randi being thirty-six weeks, the doctors are going to let nature take its course."

"Do Mom and Dad know?"

"No. I called you first. Can you call them? I'm going to call Iyana so she can let Randi's parents' know."

"Yeah. I'll be there soon. I'm about ten minutes away. Good luck, Dad."

"Thanks. I need to get back in there. Text me when you get here."

"Okay." He disconnected and turned to Serita. "The

baby's coming and I need to go to the hospital. Do you mind if we go straight there? If it looks like it's going to be a while, we can go back to your house and pick up my car."

"Of course. I hope everything goes well. It's still a little early, right?"

"About four weeks. I need to let the family know first. Ced knows my mom will most likely ask a hundred questions, so I'm sure that's why he called me first."

"My mom is the same way. She wants all the details even though she'll be walking out the door before I'm done talking."

"Exactly," he said with a laugh. Shaking his head, Jeremy called his parents and relayed the message. Just as he suspected she wanted to know everything about how long Randi had been in labor and what the doctors were saying. He told her he didn't have any information and that she'd be able to find out once she got there. He heard her telling his father they needed to leave, and Jeremy wouldn't be surprised if they made it to the hospital before he did, even though he was closer. Next he sent a text to Lorenzo and Alisha. He started the car and drove off. "I have to warn you that my entire family will probably be there."

She gave him a nervous smile. "I figured as much."

This wasn't the way Jeremy had planned to introduce her to his family, but it worked just as well, because he wanted them to meet the woman who had captured his heart.

Chapter 11

Serita observed the tense set of Jeremy's jaw as he drove and sensed his turmoil. A lot could go wrong, so she understood his apprehension. She didn't know how she felt about meeting his family at this stage in the relationship, though. She was honest enough to admit that her feelings for Jeremy were growing at a pace she had never experienced, and she couldn't help but wonder where it would all lead. The way he treated her and the things he did gave the impression that he might be far more serious about them. No man was going to foot the bill for a set of tires in a casual relationship. She enjoyed being with him no matter what they were doing—talking, working, making love—because he made her feel as if she were precious and a priority.

"You look deep in thought. Is everything okay?"

She glanced his way. "I'm fine."

Jeremy placed a hand over hers. "I hope you're not concerned about my family and whether they'll like you. If so, you have nothing to worry about."

"Maybe a little. We haven't known each other every long and it's kind of early for the whole meet-the-parents thing."

"That's true, but it doesn't change what I feel for you, Serita."

Serita contemplated asking him exactly what that mean, but she wasn't sure she was ready for the answer, or to answer the question herself. Fortunately, their arrival at the hospital gave her a reprieve. Taking a deep breath, she placed her hand in Jeremy's and they headed for the entrance. Inside, he took a moment to text his brother, then followed the directions Cedric supplied. They took the elevator to the maternity floor, and she saw a man coming toward them that had to be Cedric. The brothers favored each other more than a little bit. He was a couple of inches shorter than Jeremy, but shared the same muscular body structure and was just as handsome.

"How are you guys holding up?" Jeremy asked as he hugged Cedric.

"My baby's a trouper. It's been six hours and I know she's tired, but she's hanging in there. The baby's fine, so far."

"That's good to hear. Ced, this is Serita. Serita, Cedric."

"Serita, it's a pleasure to finally meet you. I've heard a lot about you." Cedric smiled. "And don't worry, it was all good."

What had Jeremy told his brother? "It's nice to meet you, too."

"I'm sure I'll be seeing you around a lot and we'll

have a chance to talk, but I need to go check on my wife and baby."

"I'll be praying everything goes well."

"Thanks." To Jeremy he said, "Iyana is on her way and I gave her your number. Let me know when Mom and Dad get here. I know Mom is going to want to come and check on Randi." He gave them Randi's room number.

Jeremy chuckled. "You got that right. She asked me a ton of questions." He clapped Cedric on the shoulder. "I'll handle the family, you just take care of Randi. You can text me with updates and I'll relay the info."

"Thanks, bro. See you in a bit." He smiled Serita's way and hurried back down the hallway.

"This is the same floor she was on last time and the waiting room is this way." He pointed and led the way. They joined three other people already there.

They hadn't been seated more than five minutes when an older couple entered. The woman's frantic gaze scanned the room and Jeremy stood to meet them. Serita guessed they were his parents. The nervousness she'd felt in the car returned in full force.

"Did you talk to Cedric? How's Randi?" the woman asked.

"I saw him briefly and he said Randi is tired, but doing well. And the baby is fine, too."

She sagged against the older man in relief. "Thank God."

Jeremy reached for Serita and draped an arm around her shoulder. "Dad, Mom, I want you to meet Serita."

"It's very nice to meet you, Mr. and Mrs. Hunter," Serita said.

His father smiled. "Nice to meet you, Serita."

Mrs. Hunter's eyes widened and she threw her arms

around Serita. "Oh, my goodness. I've been waiting to meet you, Serita."

She didn't know what she had expected—a handshake or polite nod maybe—but not the crushing, albeit warm, embrace. Again she pondered what Jeremy had told his family about her, about them.

"Jeremy will have to bring you over for dinner, so we can get to know you." She turned to Jeremy. "I'm so happy for you."

Jeremy chuckled. "Me, too, Mom." He gave Serita's shoulder a gentle squeeze.

On the heels of the introduction more people entered the room and another round of greetings ensued. Serita met his cousin Lorenzo, Lorenzo's sister, Alisha, along with her husband, Jabari, and three children.

"Uncle Jeremy!"

Jeremy reached down and swung the little girl, who looked to be about five years old, up into his arms and kissed her cheek. "Hi, Lia. How's my big girl?"

"I'm good."

He ruffled the head of an older boy. "Hey, Corey. I think you've gotten taller since I saw you last month. How's school?"

"It's fine. I have to do a paper on what I want to be when I grow up. I think I want to build robots like you or go into the Air Force like my dad."

"Those are some great choices. You can do both."

Corey's eyes lit up. "I can?"

"Absolutely."

"Cool!"

Serita watched Jeremy interact with the children. He was a natural. Someday he would make a great father.

"Uncle Jeremy, is Miss Serita your girlfriend?" Lia asked.

Every eye turned Serita's way and she felt her cheeks warm.

Jeremy didn't hesitate. "She sure is."

Lia giggled. "She's pretty."

"That she is." The way he stared at Serita made her heart skip a beat.

"I like your glasses, Miss Serita."

"Thank you, Lia."

Alisha came over and took Lia from Jeremy's arms. "Serita, I apologize for my nosy daughter." She tickled the little girl and Lia doubled over in a fit of giggles.

"She got it honest," Lorenzo said with a chuckle.

"Mom, Ced said you can pop in." Jeremy told her where to go and she rushed off.

Everyone took seats and soon the room was filled with lively conversation. Serita contributed when someone asked her a question, but was content to sit back and listen. They seemed to be nice and she could tell they were a close-knit family, as evidenced by them all showing up at the hospital. However, being an only child, it was a tad bit overwhelming. Her reserved personality didn't help.

Jeremy went over to the baby carrier, picked up Alisha's baby daughter and brought her back to where he'd been sitting next to Serita. "This little beauty is Kali and my goddaughter."

She touched the baby's hand. "Hi, Kali." The pride in his voice was evident, as was the love and adoration in his eyes. A vision of him holding their baby popped into her head. She had no idea where it had come from and immediately dismissed it. She needed some space. Now. "I'm going to find the bathroom. I'll be right back." Serita hopped up and made a hasty exit. After searching for a couple of minutes and not finding one, she asked one of the nurses.

Serita poked her head inside and, thankfully, it was empty. She leaned against the wall, took a few deep breaths and let them out slowly. Feeling her control return, she chalked up the wayward thought to the impending birth and being surrounded by the children. Serita allowed herself another moment of silence, then headed back. Jeremy was waiting when she opened the door. "Did something happen?"

"No. I came to see about you." He gave her a gentle kiss. "Are you alright?"

"Yes. Just needed a minute. You have a big family."

"I keep forgetting you're an only child and it can get kind of loud when we're together. My mom came back and said Randi is at seven centimeters dilated, and that it could be a few more hours or a few minutes. But we can go pick up my car and I'll come back."

She could see that he was torn between leaving and staying. "You don't have to do that. Besides, you told Cedric that you would be the point of contact for your family, and you can't do that if you're gone."

"You sure? I don't mind, and Lorenzo can do it."

"I'm positive."

Jeremy kissed her again. "Thanks. I can't tell you how much it means to have you here with me."

"By the way, what did you tell your family about me?"

"Just that I enjoy being with you and how much you're coming to mean to me. That I'm—"

He had such a serious look on his face. When he didn't continue, she asked, "You're what?"

"I'll tell you later. Come on. Jabari is going to pick up some food and you can tell him what you want."

She didn't want food. She wanted him to tell her what he planned to say...*now*. That was the second time he'd alluded to his feelings. Did she dare hope that this time would turn out different than her past relationships?

Between all the overtime hours to get the console back on schedule and Jeremy visiting with his new niece—who had finally come home after having to remain in the hospital an extra three days, until her temperature regulated—Serita hadn't seen much of him outside of work. She was looking forward to spending the entire Saturday with him. They hadn't made any concrete plans outside of her accompanying him to his science class. He'd mentioned some of the lesson might take place outdoors and that she might want to pack an extra set of casual clothes just in case. She took a bag and placed it on the living room sofa, then went into the kitchen to fix a light breakfast of a boiled egg and a bowl of fruit. "Morning, Gabby."

Gabby was seated at the table reading a magazine, eating a bagel and drinking coffee. "Morning. I guess things are really heating up between you and Jeremy. You've met his family and now you're helping teach his class. Next, you'll be moving in with him."

"First, I'm not helping teach his class. He has a few female students, and he thought it might boost their self-confidence to see someone who looks like them. Second, I will not be moving in with anyone, unless there's an 'I do' beforehand."

"I can see that happening." She took a sip of her coffee and started humming the "Wedding March."

Deciding to ignore her friend, Serita brought her food to the table, then went back for a glass of orange juice. "So when are you going to take that stroll down the aisle, Miss Gabriella?"

"As soon as I find someone worthy of my heart."

She conceded her that point and agreed wholeheartedly. They both had kissed enough frogs to last two lifetimes. Halfway through her meal, her phone buzzed. She dug it out of the back pocket of her jeans and read the text from Jeremy: Bring your book so we can discuss. Oh, and I have a few other things up my sleeve. Smiling, she let him know she would. She had only gotten halfway through the book, so she wasn't sure how much they'd be able to discuss. And she was very curious about what other things he had in store.

Gabby toasted her with her bagel. "Yeah, you're going down, sis. Goofy smile all the time, drifting off into space, giggling at those texts."

"I am not," she said with mock outrage. Yet, she couldn't stop the grin spreading across her face.

"Mmm-hmm. Whatever, girl."

Serita finished her breakfast, rinsed the dishes and stacked them in the dishwasher. She went to get the book and stuck it in her tote. "What are you doing today?" she asked Gabby when she came back to the kitchen.

"I told my mom I'd stop by and go with her to pick out some new bedding, towels and other stuff for the master bedroom and bathroom. Apparently, they painted and nothing matches now. It's going to be hard getting her to spend more than twenty dollars. She is the discount queen, but I'm not letting her get anything that'll unravel before they wake up the next morning."

She laughed. "Good luck with that."

"I'm going to need more than luck—more like divine intervention."

The buzzer let them know someone was at the front gate. Still chucking, Serita said, "I'll get it." It was Jeremy, and she hit the button to let him in. Minutes later, he appeared at the front door.

Jeremy gave her his full, dimpled smile. "Morning, beautiful."

"Good morning." She came up on tiptoe to kiss him. "I'm ready."

"Hey, Jeremy," Gabby called, passing by the living room on her way down the hall. "Y'all have fun and don't get into too much trouble."

"Morning, Gabby. No promises on staying out of trouble."

She paused, divided a glance between Jeremy and Serita. "Yeah, probably not. Well, if you're gonna do it, make it count."

Staring into Serita's eyes, he said, "I plan to do just that."

Serita's pulse skipped. "Um, we should get going." She picked up her bag from the sofa and Jeremy eased it from her hand.

"After you."

She led the way to his car. En route to the school, she shifted in her seat to face him. "So, what kind of surprises do you have up your sleeve?"

He slanted her an amused glance. "If I tell you, they won't be surprises. However, I'll make sure each one is worth every second."

She had never encountered a man like him, someone who could seduce her with a simple sentence. *I'm working hard to please you.* Every time she thought about that evening in his office, how he had pleased her, she knew he would make good on his promise and each second would be more than worth it. When they arrived at the school, she helped him carry in the supplies that the students would use to start building their robots.

"This session, we'll be building a robotic arm, and the students can choose which function they want it to perform—drawing or picking up items."

"Sounds like it's going to be a lot of fun…and hard work."

"It is, but most of the students are really plugged in and come in ready. I've only had two students in the two years that I've been doing this that I had to put out of the class." Jeremy shook his head as he positioned the parts on the long table. "Both were very bright, but saw this as a way to blow off time and I wasn't having it. I don't think they believed I was serious when I warned them what would happen. But after two weeks of them goofing off and using some of the parts for everything but the intended purpose, when their parents came to pick them up I told them they were no longer welcome."

"What did the parents say?"

"They tried to tell me that I couldn't kick their kids out of the class because they'd paid their money. I calmly reminded them of the guidelines that they signed, which stated specifically what would happen if the rules were broken. And they forfeited the fee."

His tone had hardened and Serita didn't know what to say. He seemed so easygoing most of the time, but she totally understood his viewpoint. The memory of him snapping at her that morning Wade screwed up rose in her mind. No, Jeremy did not play. The students drifted in one by one and Jeremy started the class pre-

cisely at ten. She marveled at his patience and willingness to answer each and every question, and just like
with his nieces and nephews, he had a great rapport
with the students.

"Okay, everyone. I'd like to introduce Dr. Edwards.
She's a robotics engineer and will be hanging out with
us today. Let's welcome her."

More than a few eyes widened at his pronounce-
ment, but they all greeted Serita with enthusiasm and
her heart swelled. She told them a little about herself,
her teaching at a college and some of the projects she'd
worked on. "Does anyone know what a prosthetic arm
is?" Only two hands went up. She pointed to a young
man sitting in the back.

"It's something they use when a person's arm gets
cut off."

"Right. Years ago, the hands and arms didn't do
much, but now we're able to build them so a person can
do some of the things they used to, like bending each
finger, picking up objects and tying shoes. And they
feel almost like real skin." Several hands shot up. She
smiled over at Jeremy and he returned one of his own.
"I don't have time to answer questions right now because you have a lot of work to do, but you can talk to
me afterward. How does that sound?" The students nodded in affirmation and Serita turned the class back over
to Jeremy. She thoroughly enjoyed herself and had no
problems sitting on the floor of the multipurpose room
to assist the students. More than once, she glanced up to
find Jeremy watching her with an expression that made
her heart race. Serita was falling and couldn't do a thing
about it. She wasn't sure if she even wanted to.

Chapter 12

Jeremy placed the bag holding their lunch from a nearby deli on his kitchen counter. He still couldn't get over the way Serita had interacted with the students. He wanted her as his partner in this and everything else, but he still sensed that she was a little skittish. They hadn't talked about it, but last week at the hospital when she'd bolted, he knew it had to do with more than his large family. Even though the way they all embraced her as if she was already part of the family might have been scary enough. Every one of them could tell how he felt about her—he didn't try to hide it. And something told him that Serita knew, as well, and it scared her. More than once, he wondered about the men in her past. Had someone hurt her and made her wary of relationships? He suspected that might be the case, but he planned to do everything in his power to let her know not all men were that way. *He* wasn't that way.

"Do you want to eat in here or out in the sunroom?" He preferred his deck, but with the considerable temperature drop, the season had definitely changed from summer to fall.

"The sunroom."

"Okay. It's a little chilly, so I'll turn on the fireplace."

"That would be great. I forgot how fast the weather changes here. Last week, it was almost eighty. Now, it's barely reaching the seventies and they're talking rain."

He carried the bag outside and set it down, then turned on the gas fireplace. "Isn't it colder this time of year in Reno?"

Serita followed with their drinks, took the food out of the bag and placed it on the table, along with the napkins. She sat. "Yes, but it's not the drastic ten-degree change like here."

Jeremy took the chair across from her. He unwrapped his turkey sandwich and took a bite.

"You're really great with those kids, Jeremy."

"So are you. Would you consider teaching with me? At least for the rest of this session. They were blown away by you, especially Briana. She's a little shy." He angled his head thoughtfully. "Actually, she reminds me a lot of you. Brilliant, yet reserved."

She dropped her head and stuffed the lettuce back into the sandwich. "I don't know about brilliant, but I will confess to being somewhat of an introvert."

"I can tell. Especially last week at the hospital. But I hope you'll think about what I said."

"I'll think about it."

As they ate, he continued to study her and toyed with telling her that he was falling in love with her—more accurately *in love* with her—but decided to hold off awhile longer. "Do you see yourself settling down and maybe having kids?"

Serita took a sip of her soda before answering. "Sometimes, but only if I find a guy who likes me the way I am. I don't like a lot of hoopla, I'm not into partying all the time and I like my glasses."

Her defensive stance confirmed that she had been hurt before. "There are men who appreciate all of that." He covered her hand with his. "I'm one of them. I like everything about you, Serita, and I think you already know what those glasses do to me. There isn't one thing I want you to change." *Except maybe your last name.*

"That means a lot, Jeremy, and maybe that's why I enjoy being with you so much. Most people think that I'm teetering on the brink of boring, but you let me be me."

He raised an eyebrow. "Boring? I don't think you're boring at all. You're pretty exciting in my book."

"Obviously, you don't get out much."

Laughter spilled from Jeremy's lips. "I get out plenty. Baby, you're a woman after my own heart."

She gasped slightly.

Their eyes locked. Yes, he had meant that literally, and she would find out soon enough. Smiling, he went back to his food. When they finished, he cleaned up, took everything inside and dumped the remnants into the trash. "Grab your book and we can get comfortable in the library."

"Okay, but I'm not done reading it yet."

"I'm not, either. So we can either talk about the first part or just read for a while."

"How about we do a little of both?" Serita said, taking her book out of her tote.

"Works for me." Jeremy led the way upstairs. "Have

a seat and I'll be right back." He went to his bedroom, took out his contacts and put on his glasses. Then he removed his shoes. Grabbing his book off the nightstand, he went to the library. He found her stretched out on the oversize chaise lounge with her shoes off.

"You wear glasses?"

"Yep. They're not as sexy as yours, but they've got a little style." The titanium rimless frame curved at the top, leaving the outer edges of the lens free. It twisted at the joint and reminded him of a robot arm.

Serita patted the space next to her. "I beg to differ. They're *very* sexy. And so are you," she added softly.

He sat next to her, covered their legs with the blanket that was draped over the back and slung an arm around her shoulder. They chatted for a few minutes about their favorite parts so far and who they thought the killer might be, then read silently. Serita rested her head against his shoulder, filling Jeremy with a contentment he had never experienced with any other woman. He had to have this woman in his life. No other one would do.

"This is getting good," she said after a long while, closing the book.

"Then why are you closing the book?"

"You said you had some surprises up your sleeve and you've got me curious."

Chuckling, he closed his book, sat up and swung his long legs over the side. "We're going to play a little *Jeopardy!* game so I can see if you're as good as you claim."

Serita snorted. "Claim? I'm going to wipe the floor with you, Jeremy Hunter."

"Let's go, Miss Thang." She preceded him down the stairs to the family room, where he already had the stack of questions waiting, along with another surprise she'd find out about later. Jeremy turned on the fireplace and cranked up the heat a couple of notches.

"Why are you turning up the heat if you have the fireplace going?" she asked, dropping down on the sofa.

"Because we're playing strip *Jeopardy!*, sweet baby girl, and I don't want you to be cold when I take all your clothes." He wiggled his eyebrows.

She held up a hand. "Wait a minute. You didn't say anything about that."

"Surprise." The look on her face was priceless.

"What happened to playing for pennies or something like that?" she asked, waving her hands around.

Her flustered state made him smile inwardly. He shrugged. "If you're as good as you say you are, it won't matter because you'll be fully clothed, but if you're scared…" He took a seat on the floor.

Determination lined her features and she joined him. "Bring it on."

"I'll even let you go first." He gestured to the waiting cards with a flourish.

Serita pulled a card and read the question. "'This man wrote *Jurassic Park*.' Who is Michael Crichton? Easy."

Jeremy grinned and took his turn. "'This word means to dislike strongly.' What is abhor?" They went back and forth for another three rounds and neither of them missed. It came back around to him. "'The elements on the periodic table are ordered by this characteristic.' What are atomic numbers?"

"Yeah, yeah. Of course, you'd know that." She snatched up the next card. "'Elements on the periodic table in Group 18 are often referred to by this name.' Noble gases."

"Wrong."

"What are you talking about? You know that's the correct answer."

"Maybe so, but you didn't phrase it in the form of a question."

She hit her palm against her forehead and groaned.

He rubbed his hands together. "Hmm, what do I want first? I think I'll take these." His hands went to the waistband of her jeans.

Serita hesitated briefly, then lifted her hands to the button.

Jeremy shook his head slowly. "Did I mention that the other person gets to remove the article of clothing?"

"No, you did not," she said with a soft gasp.

"My bad." He rose to his knees in one fluid motion. "Lie back, baby." He kissed her until she lay flat on her back, then teased her with caresses and kisses as he eased her pants down and off. His hands and his mouth made a slow path up her legs to her thighs and inner legs before grazing her core.

She moaned and her legs trembled. "We're supposed to be playing."

"We are." He helped her back to a sitting position. He was so aroused he promptly missed the next question.

"Well, now. Looks like Dr. Hunter is going to be without his pants, too. Your turn. Lie back."

He readily complied. Instead of immediately taking off his pants, Serita straddled him and ground her body against his, forcing a low groan from his throat. He gripped her hips and arched up to meet her.

She reached for his hands and removed them. "No, baby. You don't get to touch me. It's not your turn."

Jeremy went still. She had never called him *baby*

before, or used any other type of endearment for that matter. The implications made his heart pound in his chest. Gyrating in slow, erotic circles, she slid her way down his body, then ran her hands over his erection. His breath hissed out. "If you don't stop, we're going to be playing a different game called How Many Ways Can I Make You Come."

Serita smiled serenely. She undid his belt and pants, and he lifted his hips to facilitate their removal. The faster she got them off, the easier he'd be able to breathe. When she went back to her spot on the floor, he threw his arm over his face and lay there panting as if he'd run the anchor leg of a four-by-four relay. Finally he was calm enough to sit up. He met her gaze and wondered if they were actually going to be able to finish the game. The rise of her breasts let him know she'd been just as affected. "I believe it's your turn."

"'Traditionally made vodka is done by distilling this root vegetable.' *What is* a potato?" She made sure her answer had the correct form.

Two hands later, she lost her shirt, and right after that her bra. Jeremy took sweet revenge. She got a little payback of her own when she won his shirt, which made them even—both only had their underwear left— and tormented him until he thought he would explode. Breathing harshly, he drew the next card. "'This island country's landscapes represented Middle Earth in the *Lord of the Rings* movie trilogy.'" His brain was in such a sensual haze he couldn't think.

"Five seconds."

At the last moment, he said, "What is New Zealand?"

"Lucky."

"Just take your turn," he said with a smile.

"Okay. 'The general term for beverages which mix neutral grain spirits with sugar, glycerin and flavorings.' What is schnapps?" she said smugly.

After she'd answered her fourth question about alcoholic beverages correctly, Jeremy said, "Is there something you want to tell me? Either you're an undercover bartender or you've been doing some serious testing."

Serita threw her card at him in mock outrage. "I beg your pardon. Neither. I just read a lot. Take your turn." She rolled her eyes playfully.

They continued battling back and forth for several minutes. He had never played *Jeopardy!* or any other form of recreation quite like this. But he knew from now on it would be their special game. In the end, Serita lost her last piece of clothing. "I guess that means I'm the champion." Jeremy reached up and got the blanket off the sofa and spread it on the floor.

"What's that for?"

"It's easier to wash a blanket than clean the carpet." He saw the moment it registered in her eyes. "As the winner, I get the grand prize."

"Which is?"

"You." He picked her up and placed her on the blanket. Then he stood, quickly shed his briefs and donned the condom he had placed beneath one of the throw pillows. "Remember that other game I mentioned earlier? I'm going to see how many times and how many ways I can make you come *and* make you scream." His tongue teased the corners of her mouth before slipping inside. He took his time tasting and swirling his tongue around hers, then he transferred his kisses to her throat and her breasts.

"Ohh..."

He retrieved the bottle of strawberry massage oil

he'd purchased from Desiree's shop and drizzled some over her breasts. He blew on it lightly and watched Serita's reaction.

"Oh, my goodness! It's…getting hot."

"That's exactly how I want you," he murmured, latching on to a nipple and sucking it clean.

Serita cried out. "Jeremy!"

He made a path with the oil from the center of her breasts down the front of her body and the valley between her thighs, and followed with his tongue, savoring the sweetness of the oil and her skin. Jeremy gently pushed her legs apart, added some oil to her inner thighs and kissed his way to her center. He took his time, using slow, long licks to increase her pleasure. The sounds of ecstasy spilling from her mouth sent his desire soaring straight through the roof.

She gripped the blanket, writhing beneath his mouth, her vocalizations rising. A moment later, she screamed, calling his name over and over.

Jeremy slid two fingers inside her, taking up a lazy rhythm and rebuilding her passions. She came again, gasping and arching. He needed to be inside her. *Now.* And he knew just how he wanted her. He lifted her to straddle him and lay back on the blanket. "I liked it when you were here earlier. Ride me, baby."

"With pleasure," Serita said, lowering herself onto his rigid erection.

She started the same erotic swirl of her hips and he didn't think he was going to last a minute. His hands played over the curve of her hips, up her spine and around to her breasts. He cupped both in his hands, kneading and massaging as she moved up and down on him. His hands slid back down to her hips and he plunged deeper.

He leaned up and fused his mouth against hers. No other woman had come close to arousing the emotions in him Serita did. Resuming his position, he closed his eyes and let those emotions take over. He increased the pace, and her feminine muscles clenched him tight. He trembled slightly as the sensations intensified.

"I'm going to come," she panted.

"Let go, sweetheart." Jeremy whispered erotic endearments from a place he never knew existed.

Her nails dug into his shoulders and her body tensed all around him. She let out another scream as she shuddered with her release.

He tightened his hold on her hips, setting a rhythm with deep, powerful thrusts, and came right behind her, growling hoarsely as an orgasm ripped through him. Before he could recover, a second one overtook him, snatching his breath and making him yell her name loud enough to be heard throughout the neighborhood. It took every ounce of control he possessed not to blurt out that he loved her. She collapsed on top of him and he could feel her rapidly beating heart against his. The only sounds in the room were their ragged breathing. Jeremy wrapped his arms around her and kissed the top of her hair. *I love her.* He had to do everything in his power to keep her in Sacramento.

Chapter 13

Serita lay pulsing in Jeremy's bed Sunday morning after another round of lovemaking. She hadn't planned to spend the night, but it seemed that neither of them could get enough. And she would never, *ever* be able to watch or play *Jeopardy!* without remembering what had happened last night. They had fallen asleep on the floor, awakened two hours later and gone up to shower, which ended with him taking her from behind in the oversize shower stall. Both were too exhausted to move and she didn't protest when he suggested she stay the night. Part of her felt weird waking up in a man's bed— she had never done it before—but the part of her that was falling in love with him thought it the most natural ending to a perfect night.

"As soon as I catch my breath, we'll shower, get some breakfast, then I'll take you home."

"This time, I'm showering alone," she said with a tired chuckle.

Jeremy leaned up on an elbow and ran a hand over her hip. "You don't trust me?"

She stilled his hand. "I know you're not asking me that."

He nuzzled her neck and pulled her closer. "You can't blame a brother for trying. I find myself addicted to you in every way and I may not ever let you go."

She froze. "What did you say?"

Running a finger down her cheek, he said, "Meeting you has been the best thing that has happened to me and I don't want to ever let you go. If I could keep you here with me forever, I would do it in a heartbeat. I'm going to do whatever it takes to make that happen."

He stared at her with such a look of tenderness that myriad emotions surged through her, bringing tears to her eyes. The gentle kiss that followed made her fall a little harder. She was in deep and it frightened her. Not wanting him to see it, she schooled her features and pasted a bright smile on her face. "We should probably get moving. I have a few things to do today to prepare for the week."

Jeremy sighed heavily. "So do I."

They left the bed reluctantly and showered separately, then he took her home. She declined the late breakfast he had offered to prepare.

Inside the door, he held her tightly. "I'll see you in the morning. I decided to cancel overtime for tomorrow. We can pick it up on Tuesday."

"Okay." She leaned up to kiss him. He stood there a few seconds longer, as if he wanted to say something else. Instead, he kissed her once more and left. Serita rested her head against the closed door.

"That must have been some night."

She jumped and spun around, clutching her chest. "Gabby, girl, you almost gave me a heart attack."

Gabby scrutinized Serita for a lengthy moment. "Come on over here and spill it. I can see something's wrong."

She didn't bother to ask how Gabby knew. Gabby had always been good at reading people, especially Serita. She followed her friend to the living room and lowered herself to the sofa.

Gabby sat next to Serita. "Did something happen?"

"Yes. I'm falling in love with him."

She stared. "*O-kay*, so tell me how that's a bad thing. I mean, unless he doesn't feel the same way, which, for the record, I know he does. I can see it on his face every time he looks at you." She paused. "By your expression, I'm guessing you realize it, too, right?"

Serita nodded. "What if he's wrong and he just thinks he's falling in love. It's happened before." Her ex had confessed his love, then a month later said he'd made a mistake. It wasn't love he felt, just a strong case of lust and he didn't think they should waste their time continuing the relationship because they were too different. He had wanted her to change her look—straighten her hair, get contacts and wear clothes that *he* thought were sexier. He always wanted to manipulate her life, make it into something more in line with what *he* liked. She'd found out later that he'd been dating someone else at the same time. A woman who possessed all the traits Serita didn't, or one who could be influenced.

Gabby grasped Serita's hand. "Honey, I know where

this is coming from. I don't want to say I told you so, but the signs were there with Tate. He was a selfish bastard, and you can't punish Jeremy or yourself. I truly believe Jeremy cares for you a lot and you owe it to yourself to grab all the happiness he has to offer."

Jeremy had made her happier than she could have ever imagined when he'd waltzed up to her after her session in Madrid and asked her out. But relationships never ended in her favor and she was already in too deep.

"Did he say anything to make you think he's pulling away?"

"No, just the opposite. He keeps saying…*stuff*." Serita waved a hand. "Things like wanting to please me and never letting me go. He even paid for my tires last week." She buried her head in her hands. "I'm so confused," she said with a groan. "He's everything a woman could want, but there's this part of me that's afraid it's all going to go away." The emotions she had for him were stronger than all her relationships put together and she didn't think she would survive that kind of heartbreak.

Gabby let out a short bark of laughter. "If the brother is saying he's never going to let you go, you can bet he's in it for the duration. In case you didn't know, *never* is a long time. Like somewhere in the vicinity of forever."

Serita shot her friend a glare.

"Don't shoot those daggers at me. You know I'm right. Get yourself together, girlfriend, and let that man love you the way you should be loved." She stood. "Now I'm going to fix me some lunch. You're welcome to join me, if you haven't already eaten."

"I haven't."

"Ooh-wee! Any man who can make you forget about food is a keeper."

She shook her head and gave in to Gabby's whack sense of humor. The woman always knew how to make Serita smile. She stood and hugged her. "Thanks for being my friend."

"You're welcome. If you really want to thank me, make sure I'm your maid of honor at the wedding. And FYI, Gabriella is a great name for a girl."

Serita latched on to Gabby's arm. "Okay, you're getting out of control. We're done with this conversation." They broke out in a fit of laughter.

Hours later, as she folded the last of her laundry, Jeremy called.

"Did I catch you at a bad time?"

"No. I'm just finishing up laundry. What's up?"

"Nothing much. I wanted to hear your voice."

She laughed softly. "You just saw me less than eight hours ago." It had been just after noon when he'd dropped her off.

"And it feels like eight hours too long." Jeremy fell silent for a few seconds. "Do you think this is crazy?"

"Some parts of me do and I wonder if it's all still some fantasy left over from Madrid."

"And the other parts?"

"The other parts want it to be real," she answered softly.

"It is real, Serita. Very real. I'm far past the age of playing games, though I never have. I know what I want, and it's you. *All* of you. I want everything that makes you uniquely you—glasses and all. I realize this seems to be happening fast and I know you're afraid. I sense it every time I hint at my feelings for you. We can take this as slowly as you need, but understand that I'm not going anywhere. Rest well, sweetheart, and I'll see you tomorrow."

"You, too." She disconnected and held the phone against her heart. *Just maybe.*

Jeremy hit the ground running on Monday with two meetings from prospective clients in the morning and an afternoon visit to a manufacturing company looking to build industrial robots. Until now, he had dealt primarily with medical robotics, but industrial robots would expand his business into a new territory. When he got back to the office, he and Chris would have to hammer out the details and determine the feasibility of such a project. Before driving off, he took a moment to text his friend and ask him to leave an hour for them to chat.

As he drove, his mind drifted to his favorite subject of late—Serita. He'd caught a glimpse of her on his way out that morning, but hadn't gotten a chance to say anything to her. He was still blown away by their weekend, but he couldn't rid himself of the sensation that she was still holding back. Each and every time he came close to revealing the depths of his emotions, he sensed her retreat and didn't know what to do to convince her that what they had was the real thing. What she said about wanting to find someone who accepted her as is still resonated with him. He got the feeling that one or more of the men in her past had tried to change her instead of respecting the incredible woman she was. But she didn't have to worry about that with him. As Jeremy had told her, her uniqueness was what drew him. Cookie-cutter women were a dime a dozen, but finding Serita had been like discovering a blue diamond, a rare and precious jewel.

Jeremy arrived at the office and went straight to the work area where he knew he'd find Serita. He knew he couldn't kiss her like he wanted, but he had to see her and talk to her for a minute to see how she was doing after their phone call last night. Without saying as much, he'd pretty much told her that he loved her. He still didn't think she was ready to hear the words outright, but he wasn't sure how much longer he would be able to hold out. "How's it going, ladies?" he asked when he opened the door.

Serita and Elena glanced up, and Elena said, "Making good progress. Did I already say that you should hire Serita permanently?"

He smiled. "Yes, you did, Elena." Serita's face was unreadable.

"And since I know you were raised to honor your elders, I have no doubt you'll follow through."

"I'll take your suggestion under advisement."

Elena eyed him over the glasses she had recently begun wearing. "You'll do more than that. Serita, go ahead and take your break," she added with a knowing smile. "That's why Jeremy is here in the first place."

Serita's eyes widened. "I don't think… I'm sure he's just making sure we're progressing on schedule," she stammered.

She patted Serita's hand. "I may be a few years older than you, *chica*, but I'm not blind. You could do worse. He's a good man." She gestured to the door. "Go. We'll continue when you get back. And you can tell me the story of how you two met. I know it's going to be a good one," Elena said with a little laugh.

Jeremy couldn't do anything but smile. Leave it to Elena to figure it out. He had been very careful in his dealings with Serita, so he had no idea how Elena knew, but he planned to question her as soon as he got the opportunity. "I'll have her back in a few minutes." He didn't say anything until they were safely behind the closed door of his office. She seemed more beautiful each time he saw her. Today she wore her hair piled on top of her head, and a few errant curls had come down. "How are you, baby?"

"I'm okay. Did you mean what you said last night?"

"Every word, sweetheart. I'm not asking for details because they don't matter, but just know whatever he or they told you about who you are is wrong. You've enriched my life in ways I can't begin to describe."

Silence stretched between them. Finally Serita said, "I feel the same, but…" She ran a hand over her forehead and paced.

"But what?"

She stopped and held his gaze intently. "It never works out in the end. At least not for me. I'm not sure I want to put myself through that again."

Jeremy blew out a long breath. Seeing her so vulnerable made his heart ache. He wanted to hold her so badly it hurt. But he'd made a promise, and he would keep it even if it killed him. And at this rate, it just might. "What can I do to help you with this? I don't want to lose you, Serita."

"Don't change."

"I won't." He stood there warring with himself whether or not to go to her. In the end, he lost the battle and gathered her into his embrace. Neither of them spoke. After several seconds, he released her and went around to his desk. "I'm plugged in to several job sites and I received an announcement from Sac State that might interest you. I'll email it to you."

She perked up. "For an adjunct professor?"

"Yes. I wish I had seen it earlier, though. It closes tomorrow."

"No, no, that's okay. I'll get it done. Thanks for looking out."

"Hopefully, you'll get the position. It'll be a win-win situation for both of us. You get to work on that perfect world you mentioned and I'll be able to do the same."

"And your perfect world would be?"

"Doing everything I can to convince you to stay here with me." He rapped his knuckles on the desk. "I know you need to get back to work. We can talk later."

Serita shook her head. "Yeah, I don't want to give Elena anything else to talk about."

Jeremy chuckled and held up his hands in mock surrender. "For the record, I didn't say a word. I have no idea how she found out about us. I've been very careful. And I know Chris wouldn't say anything."

"She's a mother, so that probably explains it," she said, opening the door. "They always know everything."

"Right. See you later."

Smiling, she gave him a tiny wave and exited.

He stood there a few seconds longer, then went to check on his other two hires. He had only a couple more weeks before making a decision. He started with Darryl. "I just wanted to check in with you and see how you're doing."

"Good, good. This is one of the better companies I've worked for. I mean, I'm not saying that because I want any special favors or anything," he said. "But everyone here is nice."

"I'm glad to hear it."

"And I'm glad Wade isn't here anymore. He was pretty rude to Scott. I tried sticking up for him, but…" He shrugged.

"I appreciate that because we're like family here. Speaking of family, how's your mother doing?"

Darryl seemed surprised by the question. "She's okay and is glad to have me back home. I'm looking into getting her some in-home help because she can't do as much on her own."

Which meant he would definitely need a permanent job. He knew in-home care was expensive and insurance didn't always cover everything. "I hope you can find what she needs."

"Thank you, Jeremy. And thank you for giving me an opportunity."

Jeremy asked a few more questions before ending the conversation. He met with Scott next and the young man related the same incident regarding Wade. It made Jeremy even more glad that he had booted the man out.

"I really like working here. I'm learning a lot, especially from Shane."

Scott was only two years out of school, but Shane had mentioned that the young man was a quick study and showed great potential. "That's good to know." He glanced up at the wall clock. "It's almost five, so we can call it a day." His father had drilled into Cedric's and Jeremy's heads the notion of having a balanced work life and, as soon as Jeremy's business was on solid footing, he had cut back on his working hours. He still had to put in extra hours sometimes, but he tried to make sure his employees didn't stay beyond regular working hours unless absolutely necessary.

"Thanks. See you in the morning."

After Scott left, Jeremy rotated his chair toward the window and stared out onto the tree-lined street. It would be difficult to choose which two candidates to hire because they all possessed the skills he wanted and needed to grow his company. Serita was a forgone conclusion, even if he didn't factor in his emotions. But the other two men would be valuable assets, as well. Laughter in the hallway interrupted his thoughts. Through his open door he saw everyone leaving for the day. It pleased him to see Scott, Darryl and Serita blending so well with Shane and Elena. He stood and went to the door. "Elena, got a minute?"

"Sure." She said her goodbyes and walked over to Jeremy's office. "What's up, boss?"

"Just want to know why you think something is going on between me and Serita."

Elena reached up and patted his cheek. "I'm not blind, *mi amigo*. It's not anything you've said, but your eyes tell all. You love her, no?"

He dropped his head. "I do. Did Serita say anything?"

"Not one word," she said with a laugh. "She's a shy one. Smart as a whip, though."

"That she is."

"She's good for you."

He agreed wholeheartedly. "Thanks. See you later. Tell Eduardo and the girls I said hello."

"I will."

Jeremy watched her disappear down the hall and round the corner, then made his way to Chris's office. "Hey."

Chris leaned back in his chair. "What's going on?"

"I wanted to talk to you about the meeting I had with Archibald Manufacturing. They're looking to build a dozen dual-arm robots."

"Isn't that out of the scope of what we typically do?"

"Yes, but it'll give us the opportunity to expand into the industrial arena."

He scrubbed a hand down his face. "I don't know, Jeremy. Right now, we're pretty maxed out, timewise, on staff. Taking this on will mean increasing staff and pay, and I thought you wanted to keep the company relatively small."

"That hasn't changed." Unlike his LA cousins who owned a large in-home safety company and employed almost a hundred workers, he didn't want the increased responsibility that came along with that size business. Neither did he want a board of directors that would have input and make the decisions on the way he ran *his* company. "What if we kept Serita, Darryl and Scott?"

"Offhand, I don't know if we could offer full-time employment to all three right off the bat, especially when you factor in the benefits package."

He thought for a minute. "If we took this contract and sealed the deal for the exoskeleton, it would be doable."

"True," Chris said slowly, as if mulling it over in his mind. "If you're serious about hiring all three, I'd feel better if we offered a part-time position to the third one, with the possibility of increasing the hours. That way, we don't overextend ourselves at the outset. At the same time, we keep them away from the competitors."

"I like the way you think." They did a fist bump.

"That's why you pay me the big bucks." He made a show of thinking. "Wait. No, you don't, and I'm still waiting on that raise for reuniting you with your woman."

"Shut the hell up."

"Speaking of Serita, are you any closer to getting to your goal?"

Jeremy sighed. "Sometimes I think yes, then other times I'm not so sure. The more we get to know each other, the more I realize how her past failed relationships are affecting what we've got going on." He still couldn't believe what she'd told him about guys wanting her to look different, and he shared some of the details with Chris.

"Some men are asses. You know, when you first talked about the whole love-at-first-sight thing, I really thought you were crazy. But I've been watching you with Serita, and I have to admit I might be wrong in this instance."

He smiled. "You doubted me? As long as we've been friends, you should've known better. It's not like I've said anything different in all that time."

"True. I'm just amazed, I guess."

Jeremy stood and stretched. "Well, while you're being amazed, I'm going home. I'm serious about Serita being my one and only, and I'm going to do everything and *anything* I can to keep her in my life." *Whatever it takes.*

Chapter 14

Serita sat at her desk Friday afternoon eating her lunch and checking her emails and messages. She saw that she had missed a call from her mother and decided to return her call first, then listen to her other messages.

"Hi, honey," her mother said when she answered.

"Hey, Mom. I'm returning your call. Is everything okay?" Her mother typically didn't call during Serita's workday. She took a sip of her water.

"Yes. Nothing's wrong. I wanted to catch you before you left work to invite you and Jeremy to dinner tomorrow."

Dinner? She choked on the drink.

"Are you okay, Serita?"

"Yes," she croaked, coughing and trying to clear her throat. "Water went down the wrong way." It took a second for it to settle. "Dinner tomorrow?"

"We've been waiting to meet him, so I thought this would be a nice way to do that. And don't give me that tired excuse about you two just meeting and it's too soon. I'd venture to say you're a lot more serious about him than you've let on, and your father and I need to check him out."

Her mother knew her well. There was nothing to do but surrender. Besides, she'd met not only his parents but just about everybody in his family. She thought it only fair that he got a turn in the hot seat. "I'll see if he's free."

Her mother's soft laughter came through the line. "Oh, I'm certain he'll be free and, more than likely, already spending the day with you. I gotta run. Call me later to confirm. Dinner will be at six. Love you, sweetheart."

"Love you, too, Mom." Serita tossed the phone onto the desk and fell back against the chair. Why was she so reluctant to introduce Jeremy to her parents? He was a man any woman would be glad to bring home. She acknowledged that she continued to have doubts about whether she had another heartbreak in store, yet she'd made no attempts to end the relationship. She couldn't. She had to keep taking it day by day and praying that her fears would subside under the growing love she felt for him.

Picking up the phone again, she listened to her missed messages. Her heart rate kicked up when she heard the one from Sac State letting her know she'd made it to the interview step. She wanted to turn a cartwheel. After writing down the contact information, she called right then to schedule. Afterward she was so excited, she packed up the remainder of her food and went to Jeremy's office.

She poked her head inside his partially open door and knocked.

"Come in."

"Are you busy?"

Jeremy shifted his attention from the computer to her. "Never too busy for you. What's up?"

"I have an interview for the position next Tuesday," she said with a grin.

He stood and hugged her. "That's great. Congratulations."

"Don't congratulate me yet. I haven't gotten the job."

"But you will. They'd be foolish not to hire you."

She came up on tiptoe and kissed him. "Thanks for the vote of confidence." Belatedly she remembered they weren't supposed to be doing this during work hours, and she nearly jumped away from him. She hadn't closed the door when she came in.

He chuckled. "No one's watching, sweetheart. You're good. And you don't hear me complaining."

Serita swatted him on the arm. "You're supposed to remind me."

"Please. I haven't held you in my arms in almost a week and as far as kisses go, I'm way overdue." Jeremy moved closer to her. "So, what do you think I should do about that?"

Truth be told, she'd missed his kisses, too. However, with them working overtime, they hadn't been able to schedule any private time since last weekend. She still had some apprehensions but had resolved to work through them. She wanted to be with him and he hadn't given her any reason to think he would change. He'd promised he wouldn't. "Nothing right now." He gave her the smile that made her lose all reason and she knew she needed to leave. "I have to go."

"You don't like my kisses?" he asked with a sly grin, closing the distance between them.

She backed up and he kept coming. "What are you doing?"

Jeremy reached behind her and closed the door softly. "I'm going to kiss you." He slid an arm around her waist and dipped his head. "Any objections?"

Yes, yes, yes! She dismissed that voice of reason. "No."

He stared intently at her, then traced his finger down her cheek and across her lips. "Do you know how much you mean to me?"

Her pulse skipped. "Jeremy," she whispered. He touched his mouth to hers once, twice, then his tongue slipped between her parted lips, curling around hers in a long, drugging kiss. He drew her closer and deepened the kiss. After a tantalizing moment, sanity returned and Serita tore her mouth away. "I need to get out of here before you get me into trouble."

He took her hand and placed it over the solid length of his erection. "I'm already in trouble."

Serita snatched her hand away. "Yeah, well, you won't be getting into any more." She opened the door, then remembered the other reason she had come to talk to him. "I almost forgot. My parents want to meet you and invited us to dinner tomorrow evening, but if you're busy, that's okay."

"I'm not busy and I'm looking forward to meeting them. Just let me know what time to pick you up. Afterward, maybe I can interest you in another game of *Jeopardy!*"

His reference conjured up every erotic moment of that night and the space between her legs began to throb as if he were touching her. "Dinner is at six. Bye." She spun on her heel and strode down the hall, his laughter trailing. One more minute and she would have given in to everything he offered. *That man is too tempting for his own good.*

Saturday after his class, Jeremy drove over to see his new niece. He hadn't seen her in a week and wanted to check on her. So far, she was progressing well. He smiled thinking about how disappointed his students had been when he had told them Serita wouldn't be there. He didn't blame them because he had missed having her with him, as well.

Cedric answered the door. "Hey. Come on in. I figured you'd be spending the day with Serita, since you guys have been putting in all the extra hours at work."

He and Cedric went to the family room. "I'll see her later. Her parents invited us to dinner."

"More like they want to check you out over dinner." They shared a grin. "I remember meeting Randi's parents for the first time. She dropped the bomb on me on our way back from Tahoe and I had about an hour to prepare myself."

"I'm not really worried about it, but I can see why you were, since your hookups never lasted more than a month or two, *maybe*."

Cedric nodded. "For real. But I knew what I was feeling for Randi by that point and just told them the truth."

"And that's what I plan to do. Except I haven't told Serita how I feel about her. Well, not in so many words. I've hinted around but haven't come right out and told her that I'm in love with her." Jeremy filled his brother in on what he'd learned about Serita's past relationships. "She's still a little hesitant about us."

"It was the same with Randi and it didn't help that I had been adamant about it being a no-strings-attached affair. You situation is different and, hopefully, it'll make things easier. Tell Serita how you feel, Jeremy. That'll go a long way in showing her that you're sincere. And she definitely needs to hear it from you before you tell her parents."

He thought about the advice. Serita did deserve to hear it first, and he'd do it when he picked her up. "You're right."

"That's why I'm the big brother," Cedric said.

"You're the *older* brother. I've been bigger than you since high school." Jeremy flexed his biceps.

"But I can still kick your—"

"I thought I heard voices down here," Randi said, coming into the room holding the baby.

Jeremy and Cedric stood.

She laughed. "I still can't get over this whole standing-when-I-come-into-the-room thing."

Jeremy smiled. "Hey, what can I say." He kissed Randi's cheek. "How are you feeling?"

"Tired, of course, but I'm enjoying motherhood. I assume you came to see your niece." She transferred the baby to him.

"Yes, ma'am." Looking down at the small bundle in his arms filled him with all kinds of emotions. He placed a soft kiss on her forehead and reclaimed his seat. "Hey, Aniyah. She's so tiny." With her head in the palm of his hand, the length of her body on his forearm barely reached his elbow. She stared at him curiously.

"Ced, I hope you've got your shotgun ready because the boys are going to be beating down the doors to get to this little beauty."

"Hell, I'm going to have my shotgun, do a background check and a few other things."

"And I'll run their fingerprints," Randi added.

Jeremy chuckled and stared down at Aniyah. "Looks like you're going to be well protected. Uncle Jeremy is going to keep all the knuckleheads away."

"You look like a natural holding her."

He glanced over at Randi. "And I'm looking forward to holding my own little girl."

Randi's eyes widened. "Okay, back up. I know I've been busy for the past few weeks, but did I miss something?"

"You didn't miss a thing, baby," Cedric said. "Baby brother is in love and says that Serita is his Mrs. Right. He's going to meet her parents tonight."

"Wow. Things are moving pretty fast, aren't they? Are you sure about this, Jeremy?"

"Surer than I've been about anything in my life. Yeah, it does seem fast, but I know what I feel."

Randi stared at him with concern. "And her?"

"I think she's on the same page, but she has some past hurts that are holding her back." She might not have said the words, but he could see what seemed like love whenever she looked at him, feel it when she touched and kissed him.

She placed a hand on his arm. "I hope it turns out the way you want."

"So do I." His cell rang and he shifted Aniyah so he could pull it out of his pocket. He checked the display and held up the phone. "It's Mom." He connected. "Hey, Mom."

"Hi, honey. Are you busy?"

Jeremy's senses went on alert. Whenever she asked that question, she wasn't calling for idle chitchat. "I'm over at Ced and Randi's right now and will be going over to Serita's parents' house for dinner later." The moment the words left his mouth he wanted to call them back. It was the absolute wrong thing to say.

"Humph. I've been asking you to bring her over for dinner, yet you're going to visit *her* parents."

"Mom, you've met Serita, but I've never met her parents. So, technically, you were first." He met Cedric's and Randi's smiling faces and shook his head.

"As if that makes a difference. That thing at the hospital was *not* an introduction." She fussed for a good minute.

"Mom," Jeremy cut in. "How about I see what Serita is doing tomorrow and, if she's free, we come over for dinner?"

"That's fine. Tell Cedric and Randi your dad and I will be by later this afternoon."

"I'll pass the message along."

"Make sure you call me back tonight so I have time to prepare."

"I will. Talk to you later."

"Bye, son."

Jeremy tossed the cell onto the sofa next to him. "You'd think I'd never even mentioned Serita's name with the way she was fussing."

Cedric grinned. "Glad it's not me."

He scowled at his brother. "I'd better get going. She said she and Dad will be by later. Randi, when are your parents coming?" He kissed Aniyah, then stood and passed her to Cedric.

"They're coming back on Wednesday and staying through the weekend. I wanted us to have a couple of weeks to bond before everybody started camping out."

"If you need me to help with something while they're here, let me know."

"We will. She's already hinting at having a little family get-together, since everyone will be here," Randi said.

"Whatever they decide, you won't be doing anything," Cedric said pointedly. "Jeremy, you should plan to bring Serita. She might as well get used to being with the family."

He thought about her reaction at the hospital and her admission that she was an introvert. If she came, he would have to make sure she had some quiet moments. "Keep me posted and I'll see." When Randi stood, he said, "You don't have to walk me out. I'll lock up." He kissed her cheek. "Take it easy." He and Cedric did a fist bump. "Later, big bro."

When he arrived home, Jeremy ate lunch and went through his mail. Afterward he went upstairs to shower and change. The dinner would be a casual one. Even so, he chose to wear a pair of slacks and a button-down shirt. He planned to make a good impression because he didn't want them to have one reason to doubt that he would be good for their daughter. While dressing, he thought about how to tell Serita he loved her. Should he make some eloquent speech first or just say what lay in his heart? After a couple of minutes going back and forth in his mind, Jeremy settled on the latter.

He left a little early to stop at the florist. The last

time he'd purchased Serita flowers, he'd chosen pink roses. This time he went for red and had them placed in a crystal vase, leaving no question about his intentions. He also picked out a mixed bouquet for her mother. Initially, he had experienced a small amount of anxiety at the prospect of meeting her parents, but by the time he made it to Serita's place, it had all but vanished. He didn't have any reason to be nervous and, if need be, he could pass any background check.

Once he had gained entry to the complex, Jeremy parked and went to ring the doorbell. Gabriella answered the door. "Hey, Gabriella."

"Hi, Jeremy. Don't you look nice. Come on in. Serita should be just about ready."

"Thanks." Serita made it into the living room as he entered. Gabriella smiled and disappeared down the hall.

"Hey, baby," he said, greeting her with a kiss and handing her the vase. "You look beautiful." She had on a pair of black pants, a black-and-white-patterned cold shoulder top and wedge-heeled sandals. She'd pinned her hair up and left a few loose curls to frame her face. The bronze color on her lips perfectly complemented her dark caramel skin.

"Hi and thank you. These are gorgeous." Serita gave him a bright smile. "I'll leave them right here for now, but when I get back, they're going in my bedroom." She placed them on the coffee table. "Ready?"

"Absolutely."

When they got into the car, she said, "I should probably warn you that my mom will probably ask you a million questions and my dad will most likely sit there with his arms folded while she conducts the interrogation."

Jeremy laughed. "I'm not worried."

"You're not?"

"Not at all." He took her hand in his and brought it to his lips. "I'm not worried because when they ask me what my intentions are toward you or how I feel about you, I'll already have the answer."

"Um…you do?"

"Yes. And I want you to hear it before they do. I love you, Serita, and probably have since I saw you sitting in the hallway of that Madrid hotel. You took my breath away then and have ever since."

Serita gasped softly. "I wasn't expecting you to say that. I…I don't know what to say."

"You can tell me what you feel. But if you're not ready, that's okay. I can wait." He hoped she would tell him that she loved him, too. However, the brief flashes of fear he'd seen since they'd been together let him know she might not be prepared to say it yet.

She glanced out the window then back at him. "I'm getting there, okay?"

He smiled. "Yeah, it's okay." Placing a gentle kiss on her lips, he got them under way. She didn't talk much on the drive and he didn't push the conversation. He sensed that she needed some time to digest what he'd said.

"You can just pull into the driveway," Serita said, when they got to the house. She blew out a long breath and fiddled with her hands in her lap.

Jeremy parked and helped her out of the car. "You seem nervous."

"A little."

"Hey, you already know them and they love you. I'm the one who'll be in the hot seat."

"Yeah, you've got a point."

"I'll be fine. I don't scare easily."

She looked him up and down. "No, I guess not with your height and size."

He chuckled and got the flowers from the back seat.

"And you brought flowers? That'll earn you some brownie points."

"I'm counting on it." He tossed her a bold wink, took her hand and started up the walk. They were laughing and talking when her father opened the door. The man stood a good half foot shorter than Jeremy, had the same coloring as Serita and a sprinkling of gray around his temples.

"Hi, Dad."

"Hey, baby girl." He kissed Serita's cheek.

"Dad, this is Jeremy Hunter. Jeremy, my dad, David Edwards."

Jeremy extended his hand and looked the man straight in the eye. "Mr. Edwards, it's a pleasure to meet you."

Mr. Edwards shook Jeremy's hand. "Nice to meet you, Jeremy. You two come on in."

Jeremy stepped back for Serita to enter first, then followed them inside to a home that was simply but elegantly decorated. Mr. Edwards led them to the family room. Jeremy studied all the photos lining the walls and smiled at a young Serita. Just like him, she'd started wearing glasses in elementary school. He wondered if she'd had to endure the teasing like he had. In his case, it had taken one bloody nose to his classmate in a blow delivered by Jeremy and a threat from Cedric and Lorenzo for the teasing to stop. Had there been anyone who had stepped in to help Serita? His gaze went to the large bookcase on the other side of the room and he spotted a couple titles he owned. Just as they sat, a petite older woman entered from the kitchen. Serita looked exactly like her mother. He stood.

"You must be Jeremy," she said, approaching with a wide smile.

"Yes, ma'am. It's a pleasure to meet you, Mrs. Edwards. These are for you."

Mrs. Edwards's eyes lit up in surprise as she accepted the flowers. "Why, thank you. That was nice of you. Serita, he's a charmer, and tall, too."

Serita glanced up at Jeremy. "Yes, he is."

"I'm going to put these in water, then we can sit down to eat. Serita, show Jeremy where he can wash up."

She led Jeremy to a half bathroom off the family room. "My mother likes you already."

"How do you know?" he asked, washing his hands.

"Usually, she's five questions in before you have a chance to sit, and she hasn't asked you one." She took her turn at the sink.

"I'm going for the gold medal."

Serita elbowed him but was smiling. "Whatever."

They joined her parents at the dining room table and Jeremy seated Serita before taking the chair across from her. "Mrs. Edwards, everything looks and smells delicious." She'd made roast chicken, green beans, mashed potatoes and corn bread. A pitcher of iced tea sat in the middle of the table.

"Thank you."

He met Serita's gaze and she did a mini eye roll. He chuckled inwardly. After her father recited a blessing, everyone filled their plates.

"Serita told us you have your own business," her father said, cutting into his chicken.

"Yes, sir, I do. I started it three years ago and it's

challenging and I have to work extra hours sometimes, but I have a great team and the company wouldn't be where it is today without them. Serita's been a great asset and I'm hoping she'll consider staying on permanently." He spoke that last sentence staring directly into her eyes.

Mrs. Edwards divided a glance between Jeremy and Serita. "Serita, how do you like working with Jeremy?"

He could tell by Serita's expression that she'd rather not answer the question.

"It's fine, but I thought this was supposed to be about you grilling Jeremy, not me."

Her parents laughed and her father said, "It is, but you're part of the equation, too."

They ate in silence for a while. The flavorful food reminded Jeremy of his mother's cooking, and the corn bread almost melted in his mouth.

Serita's mother sipped her tea. "Jeremy, you mentioned having to work hard. What do you do when you're not working?"

"I hit the gym, play basketball with my brother and cousin and read. You have a few of the same titles I have on my shelves. It's something Serita and I enjoy doing together." He didn't mind answering questions. He wanted them to get to know him because he planned to be around long term.

Chapter 15

Serita couldn't believe how easily Jeremy was charming her parents. The first and only guy she'd previously brought home had gotten nothing but glares and grunts from her father and a meal her mother made sure ended as soon as the last bite was eaten. She hadn't even served the dessert she'd prepared.

"Serita's been an avid reader all her life. She always had her nose in a book, and I'd sometimes have to pry her out of that room just to eat."

Jeremy laughed. "Same. It was either that or me building the next greatest invention to help me get out of my chores."

"I don't know why I didn't think of that," Serita said. As she listened to them talk, she learned more about the man who had openly admitted to being in love with her. She couldn't say that she'd been surprised. He'd been hinting at it from the beginning and everything he said and did backed up his words. Truthfully, she felt the same, but that nagging fear in the back of her mind and heart wouldn't allow her to jump into the deep end.

Her father smiled. "Do your parents live in the area?"

"They live in Granite Bay and are both retired."

Her mom said, "I'm giving nursing another two years, then I'll be joining the club."

Her father lifted his glass. "Retirement is a wonderful thing."

"So my dad says, but I have a few years to go," Jeremy said.

Serita's father had retired earlier in the year after working thirty-five years as a pharmacist.

"Serita, why don't you help me clear the table and bring out dessert," her mother said, rising to her feet.

Jeremy made a move to stand. "I'll help."

"Oh, no. You just relax. We'll be right back."

Serita didn't miss the nonspeaking glance her parents shared. The ploy was designed to give her father time to talk to Jeremy alone. A quick glimpse at Jeremy confirmed that he'd caught on, as well. To his credit, he didn't look bothered by the prospect one bit. She gathered their plates and carried them into the kitchen. "That wasn't too subtle, Mom."

"I wasn't trying to be subtle. It's clear Jeremy is very taken with you and we need to know just how much."

She opened her mouth to tell her mother what Jeremy had said, but changed her mind. Her father would fill his wife in as soon as Serita and Jeremy walked out the door. She helped her mother bring in the peach cobbler and ice cream and caught the tail end of her father's question.

"I can tell you like my daughter, so what exactly are your intentions toward her?"

"Mr. Edwards, I more than like your daughter. I'm in love with Serita and want her to be part of my life. Yes, it may seem like things are moving rather fast, but my feelings for her are very real."

Serita's mother gasped.

"Here, let me take this." Jeremy stood, relieved her of the glass dish and placed it on the table.

Still staring at him, her mother said, "People just don't meet and fall in love that quickly."

He smiled. "Actually, they do. My father, whom I respect and is a great judge of character, met and fell in love with my mother in a week. They've been married for forty years and their love has only grown stronger over the years. I'm not surprised that the same has happened to me, especially with Serita. Your daughter is amazing. How could I not fall in love with her?"

Serita couldn't move. She had never had a man declare his feelings for her so openly and boldly in her entire life. And in front of her parents. It overwhelmed her, and she fought the urge to do what came natural—run to her room, pull the covers over her head and shut down so she could process. Jeremy seemed to sense her plight—she didn't know how he had learned to read her so well in their short time together—and sent her a reassuring smile. With her parents still staring at her in what appeared to be shock, she placed the ice cream, bowls and spoons on the table and retook her seat. "Since you all are just sitting here, I'll start things off." She scooped a portion of the cobbler into her bowl, paused, then added more before placing it in front of Jeremy. She mouthed, *Thank you.* She fixed her own bowl and added some of the vanilla ice cream. "Dad, I was really hoping you made your homemade ice cream."

"I'll make some the next time you and Jeremy come over."

His smile let her know he approved of the relationship, and it gave her a measure of comfort.

Later, as Jeremy drove her home, Serita sat with her eyes closed.

"You okay?"

"Yep. Just need my bed for a while."

Jeremy placed a hand on her thigh. "The evening was a little overwhelming."

She rolled her head in his direction. Even in the shadows of the car, she could see the concern on his face. "I'll be alright. This is how I handle things. I have to shut down." She figured he should know that about her if they were going to be together.

"We all deal with our emotions differently. I used to disappear from home for about half an hour. Now, I run."

"Ugh. That would stress me out even more."

His laughter filled the car. "Like I said, we're all different." He paused. "Well, I'm about to stress you out a little more."

Serita sat up.

"My parents invited us to dinner tomorrow." He slanted her a quick glance. "The good thing is they've already met you, so I doubt you'll have to endure what I did tonight."

She viewed him skeptically.

"Trust me. My mom just wants to get to know you. If it gets to be too much, know that I'll make sure to find you a quiet place to regroup."

"I love you, Jeremy." The words were out before she could stop them and her heart pounded in response.

"And I promise to protect that love."

She knew he would.

Tuesday evening, Serita sat on the sofa reading with R & B playing in the background. She closed the book when Gabby came in. "You look exhausted. I thought the office closed at five."

"It did. I stopped by my parents' house to help with their home improvement project."

"Oh, yeah. They're redoing the master bedroom and bathroom."

Gabby dropped down in a chair and laid her head back. "The next time they mention fixing up a room, I'm hiring somebody, even if I have to work eighty hours a week. It was supposed to be painting and getting a few new items. Now, they're talking about changing the linoleum on the bathroom floor. My dad started pulling up the flooring and it's a mess. Then they had the nerve to start talking about replacing the tiles in the shower and got upset when I suggested using someone who knows what they're doing, saying it would be a waste of money." She shook her head. "I told them I'd send a list of contractors, packed up and left."

She laughed. "Well, it would save money."

"It won't when they have to hire someone to fix the mess they made and *then* do it right. Anyway, enough about that. I've been waiting to hear all about the family weekend drama and your interview."

Serita set the book on the sofa next to her. Because Jeremy had stayed around both nights after bringing her home and Serita had worked overtime yesterday, she and Gabby hadn't had a chance to talk. She decided to start with the easier subject. "The interview went well and I should hear something within a week or so."

"I hope you get it."

"So do I. The thirty days at Jeremy's company will be up at the end of next week, so I really need to have something."

Gabby eyed her. "You know as well as I do that man is going to offer you the job. And please miss me with crap about preferential treatment. You're probably the most qualified out of the group. You know it, I know it and *he* knows it."

"I didn't say I wasn't qualified."

"Thank goodness. Now what happened with your parents?"

She shook her head at her friend's ability to change the subject on a dime. "My parents took turns grilling Jeremy, but he didn't seem bothered by it at all. He brought my mother flowers and had her smiling, and my dad invited him back."

"I knew he wouldn't have any problems winning them over."

"Especially after telling them he was in love with me."

Gabby's mouth fell open and she bolted upright. "He did *what*? Oh. My. Goodness. I would've swooned under the table."

"It was impressive." The memory of his impassioned words still made her heart race. She told her what Jeremy had said, including the part about how his parents fell in love after a week and that he wasn't surprised about it happening to him. "You could hear a pin drop when he finished. I had never seen my parents left speechless like that before."

"I know you love him, too."

"Yes, I do," Serita said softly.

She placed her hand over her heart and said dreamily, "This sounds like one of those romance novels."

That's the truth. Only Serita had never been one to believe it could happen in real life. Now she knew better.

"What about his family? I know you were worried about dinner."

"Dinner turned out to be better than I expected. His parents are really nice and treated me like they've known me forever." When they'd arrived, Jeremy's mother had hugged her and gone on and on about how happy she was that Serita and Jeremy were dating and that she was looking forward to her and Serita getting to know each other. While Serita couldn't have been happier about their acceptance, the woman's exuberance eventually started to take a toll on Serita. True to Jeremy's word, he had made sure that she had those quiet few minutes to regroup.

"Where do they live?"

"Granite Bay. Their house is stunning and so big they could host a party for fifty or sixty people and it wouldn't feel crowded." She had told Jeremy the same thing and he said it had happened before, with most of the people being family.

"Maybe the next one will be to celebrate your engagement."

"I think you're getting *way* ahead of yourself."

"No, I'm not. It's about time you found someone who appreciates that cute nerd-girl thing you've got going on."

Serita smiled and picked up her book. "Yeah, you're right."

* * *

"Have you recovered from last weekend's meet-the-parents saga?" Jeremy asked Serita Friday evening as they worked on the console. Elena had been scheduled to work with them, but had to leave early to pick up her sick daughter from school. He had been secretly elated to know they would be alone.

"Barely."

"Just so you know, my family is planning a get-together to celebrate Aniyah's birth. I was specifically instructed to bring you."

Serita eyed him. "Exactly how often does your family have these gatherings?"

A smile played around the corners of Jeremy's mouth. "Do you want the truth?"

"As opposed to?"

"I don't want to scare you," he said with a chuckle. "We do it pretty regularly, but they're not always big gatherings. We have Sunday dinners with my parents about once a month, same with me, Ced, Lorenzo and Alisha. It used to be us four cousins, but now that includes spouses and kids. Then there are the times my LA cousins come up to visit. There are five of them and they're all married."

She held up a hand, bowed her head and closed her eyes. "Okay, okay, I get it."

Jeremy sympathized with her. It would definitely be overwhelming, but they would welcome and love her as much as he did. "It won't be too bad, but I have just the thing to relax you beforehand."

"What's that?"

He carefully removed the part from her hand and laid it on the table. "Come with me." He led her to his office, closed and locked the door. "I've been fantasizing about making love to you in my office ever since that interlude last week. I promise by the time I'm done, worrying about my family will be the last thing on your mind." He walked over to his desk, opened a drawer and took out a bottle.

Serita brought her hands to her mouth and giggled. "I know that's not the massage oil."

He nodded slowly.

"Jeremy, we cannot do…do…*that* in here."

"Sure we can. I even brought towels."

"I can't believe how scandalous you are."

"You'll believe it soon enough." He placed the bottle on the desk and whipped his shirt over his head.

Serita gasped. Then her expression changed. "Okay." She sauntered toward him and ran her hand over his erection. "Then you might want to hurry up and take these off."

He didn't need to hear anything else. In the blink of an eye, he had them both naked.

She picked up the oil. "You know, I think I want a turn this time." She drizzled it along the length of his shaft and slowly rubbed it in. She lowered her head and blew softly.

Jeremy cursed under his breath. The heat of the oil and the feel of her hands stroking him almost sent him over the edge. And when she took him into her mouth, he swore to let her have a turn. All. Night. Long.

Chapter 16

Monday afternoon, while on her break, Serita took a moment to check her email. She had been stalking it daily, looking for news about the job. Her stomach flipped when she saw it. Her thumb hovered over the link for a second before opening it. Her heart sank. She hadn't been chosen for the position. She placed the phone on her desk and leaned back in the chair. This was the last week of the trial and she knew Jeremy would offer her one of the positions. Serita did enjoy working there, but the rejection made her realize how much she really did want to teach. *Back to the drawing board.*

She went back to the design room where Elena and Shane were working.

"Good, you're back," Shane said. "Jeremy wants me to tag team on the surgical arm for the rest of the afternoon." He finished the part he'd been working on. "Okay, I'm out."

When he left, Elena asked, "Do you like working here?"

"Yes, but it's complicated."

"Not really. I've watched you work, Serita. You're the best person for this job and you won't find a better work environment. It's a great company and the boss ain't too bad, either," she whispered conspiratorially.

Serita agreed with that assessment wholeheartedly. The "boss" was wonderful and amazing. But it still didn't change her disappointment.

"Hey, ladies." Jeremy stuck his head in the door. "Serita, can I talk to you for a minute?"

She searched his face for a clue as to what he wanted, but his face was unreadable. After what had happened in his office Friday night, she had vowed to stay as far away from there as possible. He was too tempting and she didn't seem to have any willpower when it came to his magical kisses. "Sure. I'll be right there."

"Thanks."

Serita shared a look with Elena, who gave her an encouraging smile, then made her way to Jeremy's office.

"Can you close the door?"

She lifted a brow. He must have read her expression because he laughed.

"Relax, this is business. But I have to tell you every time I walk into my office I can't stop thinking about Friday night. It's going to be hard as hell not to seduce you, strip you naked and lay you on that table whenever you cross my path."

That was what worried her. It didn't help that she had been a willing participant in his seduction. She'd surprised herself the other night with her inhibition. Sex had always been just okay until she met Jeremy. He unleashed some carnal side in her she never knew existed. And she kind of liked it.

"Now that you know you're safe for the time being, you can close the door."

She complied, then sat in one of the chairs opposite his desk. "You said this is business."

"Yes." Jeremy studied her. "Everything alright? You seem a little down."

Serita sighed. "I heard back from Sac State and I didn't get the job."

"Baby, I'm so sorry. I thought for sure you would."

"Me, too."

"Is there anything you need me to do for you?"

"No, but thank you." He looked genuinely concerned. "Really. I'll be fine. What did you want to talk to me about?" she asked, changing the subject. She felt down enough and didn't want to dwell on it.

"Actually, there are two things I'd like to discuss. The first is I don't want to hide our relationship anymore. I love you and we are both consenting adults. It's nobody's business what we're doing and if they find about us, fine."

She understood his point of view and, most likely, everyone already knew. Elena had figured it out the first week and Serita was sure she'd mentioned it to Shane. More than once, she'd caught him smiling at her when he saw her coming from Jeremy's office. And Chris... She didn't even want to think about how he had found out. She had been mortified when he'd walked in and found her sitting on Jeremy's lap. "What exactly does that mean?"

"We won't be having desktop sex during the work-day, if that's what you're concerned about. But if I want to give you a good-morning kiss—nothing too heavy—then I want to be able to do it. I want to be able to hold your hand and take you out to lunch or eat lunch in here."

The things he'd asked for weren't anything other dating couples wouldn't do. She remembered a few of the professors and other staff members who dated doing some of the same things. They were affectionate, but not overly so. Serita really had no reason to be embarrassed. "Okay, we can do that."

A huge grin spread across his face. "Can we seal the agreement with a kiss?"

She laughed. "You don't ever quit, do you?"

Jeremy shrugged. "I can't help myself. I've never been this out of control with a woman in my life. This is all your fault."

Hearing that she could make him lose control put a smile on her face. She'd happily take the blame. "That makes two of us. I've never done the things we have with any other man, so you're just as at fault."

He placed a hand over his heart. "I will gladly take the blame," he said, echoing her thoughts.

"Didn't you want something else?" He brought out a side of her very few people saw.

"Yes. Hopefully, this will counter your bad news and make you feel a little better." He handed her an envelope.

Serita's brows knit in confusion. She withdrew the sheet of paper and read. "You're offering me the position." She was admittedly excited, but a small part of her still wondered if he had judged fairly.

"And before that beautiful brain of yours starts going places it shouldn't, I decided to hire all three of you."

"Can you afford to do that? I'm sorry, that's none of my business."

"You're fine. Chris and I talked about it and, with a couple of potential contracts in the works, we'll be able to handle it. You and Darryl will have the full-time positions because you have the most experience. Scott will work twenty-five hours to start, with the potential to transition to full-time once those contracts are secured."

She reread the letter. "I'm really glad. I didn't get a chance to work with either of them very often, but I like them."

"Better now?" he asked with amusement.

Smiling, she said, "Much. Do I need to answer now?"

"No. You can just tell me yes on Friday, like the letter says."

Her mouth gaped. "How do you know I'm going to say yes?"

Jeremy stood, came and gently pulled her to her feet. "Because I'm making you an offer you can't refuse."

"Oh, really?"

"Really." He brushed a kiss across her lips. "Would you like to have dinner tonight?"

"Yes, but I'd like to go home and change first."

"That works. We need to drop off your car anyway."

"Or I could just meet you at the restaurant."

He stared at her as if she'd lost her mind. "I'm not even going to reply to that nonsense."

She burst out laughing, having known that would be his response. Smiling, she walked over and opened the door. "Later, darling." Yep. She loved this man.

"You really lucked out with Darryl, Scott and Serita," Chris said to Jeremy as they stood outside the door of Jeremy's office.

"I did. And I'm sure both men will be accepting soon, and alluded to that fact. But Serita is the only one who hasn't given any indication whether she's going to accept." Jeremy had sensed her disappointment at not getting the teaching position and didn't want to add any more stress onto her.

"And her reason would be?"

He shrugged. "I didn't ask her for an immediate answer." He glanced up and down the hallway to make sure no one was coming, then lowered his voice. "She just found out today that she didn't get the job at Sac State and she's a little down. We're going to dinner tonight and, hopefully, I can cheer her up."

Chris grinned. "I bet you can."

"I also told her that we're done hiding our relationship."

"About time. It's not like everybody didn't know anyway, especially with the way you're always looking at her. I'm surprised you haven't set the damn building on fire."

"Hey, what can I say?" Jeremy straightened from the wall when he saw Serita approaching. "You ready, baby?"

"Yep. Are you leaving, Chris?"

"I am. Looking forward to seeing your pretty face around here permanently," he said with a wink.

Serita divided a glance between Chris and Jeremy.

Jeremy waved a hand. "Don't pay any attention to him." As he guided Serita toward the front, he shot Chris a lethal glare over his shoulder. Outside, at her car, he asked, "Any place in particular you want to go for dinner?"

She slid in behind the wheel and angled her head thoughtfully. "No, but I'll think about it on the way home."

"Okay." He placed a soft kiss on her lips, closed the door and got into his own car. As he followed her, he thought about everything he wanted to have with her and decided he needed some advice. He hit the Bluetooth button. "Dial Brandon."

Brandon answered on the second ring. "Hey, cousin. What's up?"

"A few things. I need your help."

He chuckled. "This wouldn't happen to have anything to do with the woman you met six weeks ago, would it?"

"Yes. I'm in love with Serita. I want to marry her and add her name as co-owner of the company." The line went silent so long Jeremy thought he'd been disconnected. "Brandon?"

"What the hell are you talking about? Look, I know you've been spouting that love-at-first-sight crap all your life, but this isn't some fairy tale. It's real life."

"Brandon, don't act like it doesn't happen. You do remember my parents falling in love within a week, right?"

"Yeah, but that—"

"And correct me if I'm wrong, but wasn't it *your* dad who walked up to your mother the day he met her while he was on a two-week military leave and asked for her name and phone number, then married her on the next one?"

"Okay, you've got me on that one."

"I also know that, had you not been acting like such a butthead, you would've acknowledged the fact that you loved Faith far sooner. Need I go on?"

Brandon's heavy sigh came through the line. "Damn, it's like that?"

"It's exactly like that," he said with a chuckle. "So, are you going to help me or not."

"You know I will, and I can't wait to meet this woman."

"I can't wait for you to meet her, too." If Jeremy had his way, it would be soon.

"What do you need to know?"

"As I said, I want to add Serita as co-owner and I want to know how you handle it with Faith." Faith's and Brandon's fathers were best friends and had started Gray Home Safety with a pact that the company would be passed down to their children. Only no one had known about Faith until her father found her after twenty-eight years. Brandon had had no idea that the woman he'd rescued during an accident and begun dating would be his second in command and he hadn't been happy about it. Now they were happily married.

"If you're serious about this, Jeremy, then you need to be able to say that you trust Serita with everything and I do mean *everything*. No second-guessing on decisions, always listening to her suggestions, and when they're better than yours, being man enough to accept them. It means that sometimes you won't be in control."

Jeremy mulled the advice over in his mind. Could he really allow someone else to come in to the company he had built from the ground up and make decisions?

"You're quiet, cuz."

"I'm thinking. Was it hard to give up total control?"

Brandon laughed. "Hell, yeah. And you know me when it comes to business." His cousin ended up with his foot in his mouth on more occasions than the family could count because of his intense nature. "But I'm learning it's okay. Of course, I still have issues, but Faith keeps me grounded."

"Thanks. That's what I need to know." He drove into the complex behind Serita and parked. "I just pulled up to Serita's, so I'll talk to you later."

"Let me know if you need anything else and I hope everything works out. Later."

He ended the call and got out. That was what he loved about his family—no matter what went on, he could always count on them to give him good advice. Smiling, he caught up with Serita.

Serita stopped and got the mail before going to her unit. She opened the door. "I still have no idea where to go for dinner."

"That makes two of us." Jeremy followed her to the kitchen, where she dropped off her lunch tote.

She flipped through the envelopes. "What would really be good is another one of those five-star meals that you cook," she said, smiling up at him flirtatiously.

"It's a little late for that tonight, but we can do it next time."

"And I can't wait." She opened one of the envelopes and read for a minute. "I don't believe it."

"What is it?" He leaned close and saw it was from a university in Reno.

"The college where I taught in Reno is offering me a position, this time as an assistant professor instead of adjunct." She smiled.

Jeremy's heart started pounding. "I thought you

didn't want to teach full-time, and typically assistant professor positions are just that."

"I know, but this is a great opportunity and would put me on track for tenure."

"I agree. But what about your job here? What about us?"

Serita's smile faded. "I…don't know." She tossed the letter on the counter and paced. "I need to think about this."

His heart pounded harder. "What is there to think about? You said you loved me." He couldn't believe what he was hearing. Was she just going to throw away everything?

"Jeremy, I do love you." She placed a hand on his arm. "I *do*."

He stepped away from her. "Yet you're willing to walk away."

She scrubbed a hand across her forehead. "I didn't say that. All I'm saying is I need time to process all this—two job offers in one day is a lot."

"If the shoe were on the other foot, I wouldn't hesitate because I know what I want. You. If I had a choice between taking a job and staying with the woman I love, you'd win, hands down." Jeremy observed her a long moment. "But, obviously, you don't know what you want," he said softly, his heart breaking.

"I do want you. I want *us*, but this is a big decision."

It came to him that maybe she didn't love him as much as he loved her. "Then I should probably go and give you the time and space you need to figure it out." He pressed a kiss to her forehead, pivoted on his heel and walked out.

Serita rushed out of the kitchen behind him and blocked the front door. "Wait."

"Can you tell me right now that you're not going to walk away from us?" When she didn't reply immediately, he gave her a bittersweet smile. "I didn't think so. I'll see you in the morning." He stepped around her and opened the door. "Be sure to lock up." Kissing her once more, he walked out. *Now what am I supposed to do?*

Chapter 17

Gabriella snatched the covers off Serita. "Okay, that's it. You've been in here for four hours and I've let you wallow in your self-pity long enough. It's time to get up and face the music."

Serita groaned, rolled over onto her side away from Gabby and tried to take the covers back. "I need more time." Ever since Jeremy had walked out the door, she'd been in bed with the covers over her head, trying to shut down so she wouldn't have to deal with the hurt she'd seen in his eyes or the mess she'd made of her life in a matter of minutes.

"No, you don't." She sat on the side of the bed. "You know I love you, right? We've been through pretty much everything together since sixth grade, but as your friend, I have to tell you, you're full of shit."

She flipped over onto her back and glared. "What did you just say?"

"You heard me. You found a great guy who loves you and wants to give you the world, and you're screwing it up. How many times have you cried about one man or another cheating on you or trying to change you?"

Too many times to count. "But I might not get another opportunity to land a tenure-track position. And I'm already established at the school and, if I went somewhere else, I'd have to start from the bottom again."

Gabby stared at her incredulously. "Don't insult my intelligence. You know as well as I do that you'll find another job, and one that will be even more perfect than this one. But you won't ever find another man who adores you the way Jeremy does." She placed a sisterly hand on Serita's shoulder. "Now, do you want to tell me what you're really afraid of, because I know it's more than just about the job."

Serita dragged herself to a sitting position. Why did Gabby have to know her so well? "It is partly the job." She released a deep sigh. "But it's also Jeremy. I love him more than I thought possible, and I'm so afraid everything is going to come crashing down and I'll lose him."

"So…what? You just walk away instead?"

"Every time I think I've found the right guy, something happens. It starts off wonderful, then somewhere down the line things change and the person I am is not the one they want to be with." She thought she had loved her ex, but in hindsight, what she had felt for him didn't hold a candle to the deep emotions that had consumed her with Jeremy.

"Serita, love always carries a risk, but you can't let your fears get the best of you. Remember that tenth-grade girl who built her own robot because the boys wouldn't let her be part of the team? You need to get her back."

She smiled at the memory. Those boys thought the only thing a girl was good for was writing down the data. When she'd refused, they'd kicked her off the team. She'd buried her head under the covers for two days crying until her mother did exactly what Gabby had just done—snatched the covers off. *So, I guess those boys were right, since you're lying here doing nothing.* She had been so outdone by her mother's words that she'd hopped out of bed and started her own design. She chuckled inwardly, recalling their faces when her project took first place. Serita had been risking it all in her field since that day. Not so much in her personal life, however.

"Sis, don't throw away what could be the best thing in your life because of fear. The worst thing you could do is look back and wonder. You don't want that regret, *trust me*. I know." Gabby fell silent. "I won't do it again," she added softly.

Obviously Serita had missed a few things while living in Reno. She'd get the story some other time, but right now she had more pressing issues.

"What are you going to do?" Gabby asked.

All the moments they had spent together from that first day until now ran through her mind. She would never forget his first words to her: *I don't know what impresses me more, beauty or your brains. It's the brains, I'm thinking.* He'd made her laugh, called her sexy, and he'd never once made her feel that being a nerd was a bad thing. And where would she find another man who would come to her rescue when she felt overwhelmed? Tears misted her eyes. "I messed up. I can't leave him." Deep down inside, she knew what she wanted, and when Jeremy had asked, she should have swallowed her fears and told him the truth. She wanted him. As much as she wanted to teach—and she did believe she would find another opportunity—she wanted, no, *needed* Jeremy in her life.

She hugged her. "Good girl."

"I need my laptop." Serita jumped off the bed, retrieved it from the desk and brought it back over to the bed. She searched for and found what she needed.

Gabby glanced at the screen. "What are you planning?"

"You told me to get her back, and I'm going to need your help to pull this off." Serita explained her plan.

"If you're going to do it, might as well go all out."

"I don't want to leave anything to chance. The cooking thing might be a little dicey but, hopefully, I can make it work."

She stood. "You're definitely going to need my help then."

Serita laughed. "That's why I love you. You tell me the truth, even when I don't want to hear it."

"You've got that right, my sister. Now I'm going to bed. I need my rest for this."

"Thanks for everything." Gabby was right. Serita loved Jeremy, and she'd be damned if she was going to let another woman take what she already had. His love.

Jeremy woke up Wednesday morning more tired than when he'd gone to bed. He doubted he had slept more than two hours straight all night. He replayed the conversation with Serita over and over, and each time he remembered her not being able to answer his question broke his heart a little more. He had no idea what to do. He did know that he needed to talk to the one person who had guided him his entire life. Picking up his phone, he sent a text to Chris saying he might be late, then called his father. Even though he had retired two years ago, he still got up early and had probably done two or three things by the time Jeremy showed up at seven.

When Jeremy arrived, his dad greeted him with a hug. "Come on in, son. I could tell by the tone of your voice you've got a lot on your mind."

"I do. Mom still sleep?" he asked, trailing his father to the kitchen.

"She was a half hour ago. Do you want me to get her?" He poured himself a cup of coffee and added sugar.

He shook his head. He met his father's concerned gaze. "I just need to talk to you right now. You can fill Mom in later."

"Then have a seat and tell me what's on your mind."

"Serita. I think I'm going to lose her." All the details of what had happened poured out of him. He told his father about Serita not getting the Sac State job and him offering her one at his company, and then Serita receiving the letter from Reno and saying she didn't know what she was going to do. "You know what hurt the most, Dad? I asked her to tell me she wasn't planning to walk away and she couldn't." Jeremy buried his head in his hands. He had never been this miserable. "What am I supposed to do? I love her."

"Jeremy, you're so much like me it's frightening."

He lifted his head. "What do you mean?"

You've always known what you wanted in every area

of your life and you went after those things with determination and never took no for an answer. Just like me when I was your age. The problem with love is you can't control the other person. No matter how much you love Serita, it will never work unless she loves you with the same passion."

That was not what he wanted to hear. His misery increased tenfold. "Are you telling me to break it off?"

His father chuckled. "No, unless that's what you want."

"It's not," he said emphatically. "I want to marry her."

"Well, the only thing you can do is continue to show her that you love her. Don't tell her, *show* her. Bring her flowers, and I don't mean some huge arrangement. Just something small, so she knows she's on your mind. What's her favorite beverage or sweet?"

Jeremy straightened in his chair. The flower thing he had on lock, and he would be stopping at the store to pick up a bag of Skittles—minus the green ones—and line them up just as she liked. As far as the drink, he drew a blank. Then it dawned on him that she'd mentioned not being able to find a good recipe for the café con leche she'd had in Madrid. He whipped out his phone and Googled recipes. He tried to recall which place had the one she liked best and what they'd put in it. It took him a few minutes, but he found it. "Dad, I need to use the espresso machine."

"I guess that means you're not giving up on her."

He smiled for the first time since leaving Serita's place last night. "You guess right."

"Let me get that machine out for you."

He wanted it to be hot, so with a promise to bring it

back later, Jeremy left. He stopped at the store for the ingredients and the candy, then the florist for a red long-stemmed rose. Jeremy planned to leave everything on her desk for her to find when she arrived at eight, and he had less than twenty minutes to get it done. Chris was already there when he arrived. He stuck his head in the office. "Morning."

"I thought you were going to be late."

"It didn't take as long as I anticipated." His father was a man of few words, but he made each one count. Had it been his mother, Jeremy would have been late. He walked to Serita's office, tore the corner off the Skittles and took out the ones she didn't like. He taped the corner closed and attached a small sticky note: *Because they ruin the whole pack.* In the break room, following the directions from the website, he made the café con leche and carried it down to the office. After arranging everything, he stood back and viewed his handiwork. Satisfied, he went to his office. He was going to give her every reason to stay.

Jeremy settled at his desk, powered up his laptop and checked his email. He always wondered how spammers got his address and sent more than a few to that folder. He clicked on one confirming the date to service one of their robots at an outpatient surgery center. He was glad he'd had the foresight to offer maintenance contracts. As he opened a folder to work on the proposal for the manufacturing company, Chris came in.

"Hard night?"

"You can say that."

Chris smiled. "Dinner didn't end the way you had hoped, I take it."

"We never made it to dinner." He got up and closed

the door, then reclaimed his seat. "When we got to her house, she had a letter waiting from the university where she taught in Reno, offering her an assistant professor position."

"Oh, wow. That's a great opportunity for her, but I assume she's going to turn it down and apply for something else here."

"I don't know."

He frowned. "What do you mean you don't know?"

"I don't know. She said she needed time to think about what she wanted to do." Thinking back, Jeremy could have been more patient and not demanded an answer right then. He understood her desire to teach, and she was right about it being a big decision to make. However, the only thing he had been able to focus on was the growing ache in his heart.

"I hate to say this, but you're going to have to let her figure it out on her own. The last thing you want is her having regrets ten years down the line because you pressured her."

"True, but that doesn't mean I can't plead my case in other ways."

"I'm not going to ask. Anyway, I've redone the budget with the added staff, so when you're ready to go over the numbers, let me know."

"We can do it—" A knock sounded. He got up and opened the door. His chest clenched when he saw Serita standing on the other side. "Good morning."

"Good morning. Do you have a few minutes to talk?"

"Chris and I were—"

"I'm leaving," Chris said, standing and crossing the room. "We can talk when you're done." To Serita, he said, "Morning."

"Good morning. You don't have to leave. I apologize for interrupting your meeting."

"You didn't." He exited and closed the door.

For a minute, Jeremy stood there marveling at how much she filled his heart. Even with the uncertainty swirling around their relationship, he couldn't turn off his emotions. "How are you?" She looked as tired as he felt.

"I've been better."

"Join the club. Would you like to sit down?"

"No, thanks. I'm not going to take up too much of your time."

Once again, alarms went off in his head. Had she come to a decision? And would it tear them apart? Remembering what she'd said about his height, he propped a hip on the desk to decrease the difference. She didn't say anything for the longest time, and it made him even more nervous that she had come to end it.

"First, thank you for the rose, the candy and especially the café con leche. It tastes just like the ones I had in Madrid. Maybe you can share the recipe with me."

"I'll text it to you."

"Second, I need you to know that I do love you, more than you know, and I'd like for us to talk."

"Then have a seat."

"Not here. Dinner at my place tomorrow night at seven."

He couldn't take another thirty-six hours of not knowing. Everything inside him wanted to shout, *Just tell me now.* But he didn't. She appeared to be barely holding it together, and he didn't want to overwhelm her any more than he'd already done. Besides, he needed her to be fully locked in when it came to the job. They couldn't afford any mistakes. "Dinner tomorrow at seven, it is."

"Jeremy…"

"What is it, baby?" He saw the tears forming in her eyes and, unable to stop himself, wrapped his arms around her and held her close. She held on to him as if she didn't want to let go. Neither did he.

At length, Serita backed out of his hold. She swiped at the moisture on her cheeks. "I'd better get started."

He nodded and watched her go. Then he smiled. Jeremy had waited for her all his life and he wasn't giving up that easily.

Chapter 18

Thursday evening, Serita and Gabby moved the kitchen table closer to the lone window. Serita had power shopped online after coming to her senses and tried to transform the kitchen to resemble the Dantxari Restaurant in Madrid where she and Jeremy had dined the first night. She'd found a similar patterned red plaid tablecloth and matching napkins, and white plates at one of the bedding stores, and she had ordered a stained-glass mirror panel and had it shipped overnight.

Gabby placed her hands on her hips and surveyed the area. "It's looking really good in here."

"I agree. I just hope the food is somewhat comparable." She had already warned Jeremy that her cooking didn't hold a candle to his, so she hoped what she had to tell him would make up for that shortcoming.

"The food is going to be fine. You want him to eat as soon as he gets here?"

"Yes."

"Then we'll start around six thirty. The croquettes will be fine warmed and the asparagus will only take a few minutes."

"It's the butter sauce and steak I'm worried about. I'd hate to serve him a steak that's either too rare or as hard as a hockey puck."

"Don't worry. I got you, girl. You're going to be cooking like a pro before it's all said and done. You'll need those skills once you two get married."

"Married? Let me just work on straightening out this part first." She draped the tablecloth over the table and set it according the restaurant's website photos.

Gabby went to gather ingredients from the refrigerator. "One more thing—there's no need for you to keep searching for a place. I have a feeling you and Jeremy are going to be under one roof sooner or later, so it makes no sense for you to go through the hassle of buying or leasing a condo."

Serita paused. "Gabby, I appreciate the offer, but even if we do get back on track, it could be a year or two before we take that step." Admittedly, the thought of being married to Jeremy made her heart skip a beat, but she didn't think that would be on the radar for a while.

"And? Still, it makes no sense. We can talk about that another time. Let's get this food started."

She and Gabby worked side by side and finished the meal at five minutes before seven. She covered the steaks to let them rest and stay warm, and placed the croquettes and asparagus in the oven drawer. They went into the living room and Serita turned on the stereo to a jazz station.

"Okay, I think you're good. I'll see you tomorrow. I decided to spend the night at my parents' house."

"I can't let you do that. This is your house. We agreed on ten o'clock and that's enough time for dinner and conversation."

"Uh-huh. If things go the way I think they will, you're going to need all night." She picked up her bag and hugged Serita. The buzzer rang and she pressed the button to open the gate. "That's my cue. Good luck and you can tell me all about it tomorrow."

Serita nodded. She needed all the luck she could get. Jeremy appeared a minute after Gabby left. When she saw him, it took all her control not to launch herself into his arms. "Hi."

"Hi." Jeremy bent and kissed her, then handed her the red rose. "It smells good in here."

It didn't come close to how good he smelled. She loved the warm, woodsy citrus blend he wore. "It probably won't be quite up to your five-star meal, but I hope it's not too bad." They shared a smile. "We're eating in the kitchen." She gestured with a flourish. "What do you think?"

His surprised gaze met hers. He stared and turned in a slow circle. "The restaurant in Madrid where we had our first date."

"I wanted to recreate the magic we had there because it was where I first knew I was falling for you."

Jeremy whirled around. "Are you saying what I think you are?"

"Although I didn't realize it then, I think I fell in love with you after my first selfie lesson."

A soft smile curved his lips. "I was already a goner by then, myself."

"Have a seat and I'll fix our plates." She went about the task, then brought them to the table.

"You cooked the meal we had, too? This is really special."

"Yep, but you might want to hold off on the praise until you taste it."

He laughed. "I'm not worried." He opened the bottle of wine she had in the bucket on the table and filled their glasses. He held up his. "To recreating the magic."

Serita touched her glass to his. "To recreating the magic forever." Their gazes held while they sipped. She set her glass down and waited for him to take the first bite.

Jeremy cut into the steak and ate a piece. His eyes widened. "This is really good."

Smiling, she started in on her own meal. Both were content to enjoy each other's company without speaking. The sounds of jazz filtered through the room, filling the silence. When he finished, she said, "I have dessert, too."

"The lemon sherbet?"

"Absolutely. Complete with champagne and vodka." As they ate the sweet, tart dessert, she tried to gather her thoughts for the forthcoming conversation. By the time she was done eating, her nerves were a jumbled mess.

He stood and extended his hand. "Let's talk, sweetheart."

She took his hand and let him lead her into the living room, where they made themselves comfortable on the sofa. He didn't say anything as he gave her hand a reassuring squeeze.

"I'm sorry I wasn't able to tell you the whole truth," Serita said.

Jeremy frowned. "I don't understand."

"You said that I didn't know what I wanted and that wasn't the truth. I knew, but I was afraid to hope for it." He opened his mouth to speak and she placed a finger on his lips. "It had nothing to do with you. This one is on me. In my mind, I thought it would be easier to walk away than to risk being hurt again. But not being with you hurt more. I love you, Jeremy, and I *can't* walk away from us. You have been one of the best surprises of my life and I don't want to lose you."

"I love you and I don't want to lose you, either. What can I do to show you that I'm going to be here always?"

Serita straddled his lap and cupped his cheek. "Nothing. From the day I met you, you've shown me what real love looks like. And I love the way you take care of me, not just with material things, but with the stuff that counts. You take care of my well-being, my soul… my heart, and that's all I'll ever need." She covered his mouth in a tender kiss, trying to let him know she was ready to risk it all for them.

"Then let me keep taking care of you."

"I will. There are a couple more things I need to tell you."

He lifted a brow.

"I turned down the position in Reno and I accept the job offer at HJ Robotics."

"I love you." Jeremy crushed his mouth against hers in a hungry kiss. "What time is Gabriella coming back?" he murmured, still placing butterfly kisses along her throat.

"Tomorrow."

His head came up sharply.

She smiled. "I took a drive to Old Sacramento and visited Scentillating Touch. So…"

He jumped to his feet with her in his arms. "Bedroom."

"Down the hall, second door on the right." She loved this man.

Jeremy unloaded the last of the supplies from his class and stacked them in his garage. "Another successful session."

"They were so excited about their robots," Serita said, getting into the car.

He'd been just as excited to have her there with him. Since their reconciliation dinner last week, they'd spent almost every evening together talking and growing closer. When she confessed to still having some fears, but told him that her love was stronger and that would be her focus, his emotions had welled up, and he'd thought his heart might burst from his chest. He got in on his side. "Do you want anything from inside before we get on the road?" He had wanted to take her to his Lake Tahoe home, but with it being mid-November, he didn't want to run the risk of getting snowed in. He hadn't seen it in the forecast, but with temperatures in the twenties, the weather could change in an instant. Instead, they were going in the opposite direction, to spend the weekend in Monterey. Barring traffic—he didn't hold out much hope—the drive would be about three hours. Jeremy had his mind ready for at least four.

"No. I'm good." She turned in her seat to face him. "You know, I just got this job—so I shouldn't be taking off a day already." They wouldn't be returning until Monday afternoon.

"I'll talk to your boss. I'm sure he's okay with it."

She punched him in the arm playfully. "I already agreed that we wouldn't hide anymore, but I don't want everybody to start thinking I can come and go as I please. Don't make me have to look for another job."

"Ha! It's too late. You signed on the dotted line and you're stuck now, baby. Didn't you see that clause about having to agree to stay for five years?"

"What clause?" A few seconds later, she said, "There wasn't any clause requiring five years."

Jeremy laughed. "But you weren't sure for a minute."

She turned away and folded her arms. "I don't know what I'm going to do with you, Jeremy Hunter."

"You will by the end of the weekend." She turned her questioning gaze his way, but he just smiled and kept driving. As he'd predicted, traffic came to a standstill in several places. It took them three hours just to get to San Jose, and it would take another one to reach their destination.

"Traffic has really gotten bad since I left. It never used to take this long to reach the Bay Area."

"I don't come this way often, but Cedric and Lorenzo do and they say it's bad almost all day now." They fell silent for several minutes, but he could hear her humming softly to the music. "Now that it's been over a week, how are you feeling about not going back to Reno?" Jeremy still harbored some concern that she would regret her decision.

"I don't feel as badly as I thought I would. I'm still wondering if I'll ever get another opportunity, but I'm happy with my decision. I have a great job, a pretty cool boss and a man who I am madly in love with, so I consider myself blessed. I'll have to trust that there will be something else down the line. And who knows, I may change my mind and want to go in a different direction by then. In the meantime, I'll enjoy shaping the minds of the next generation at this great science camp."

"What?" he asked excitedly, turning in her direction. He remembered he was driving and jerked back into his lane. With all the changes she'd been going through, he hadn't brought it up after asking her the first time. "Do you know how happy you've just made me?"

"Yes, but I'd like to be alive when the next session starts, so keep your eyes on the road."

"Yes, ma'am." Jeremy wanted to stop the car and get out and dance. "There's one other thing I'd like your help with. I'm working on a new prosthetic hand that will closely mimic natural function."

"Are you kidding me? I'd love to help you."

Jeremy slanted her a quick glance. "Great. We can talk about it when we get back." By the time they made it to the hotel, neither wanted to go out to eat, so they had dinner in the hotel restaurant and went back up to the room.

"Is it my imagination or did the temps drop by ten degrees while we were downstairs?" Serita asked, rubbing her arms.

"I'll turn up the heat." He adjusted the thermostat and turned on the gas fireplace. "Once it warms up, we can play."

She laughed. "I know you didn't print out more cards for *Jeopardy!*"

"Of course I did. Didn't you enjoy it the last time we played?"

"I'm pleading the Fifth," she said, trying to hide her smile. "We're playing strip *Jeopardy!* again, right?"

"Yes."

She rubbed her hands together. "Good, because I've been studying and this time I'm going to wipe the floor with you, and *I'm* going to see how many ways I can make *you* come."

Jeremy's arousal was instant. He folded his arms. "What happened to shy Serita?"

"She's still here, but I can be me with you, or who I want to be."

"Yeah, you can." He loved this woman so much, and he was glad that the men in her past had never taken time to know her. Their loss was his gain. He pressed a kiss to her lips. He'd meant it to be a short one, but the moment their mouths touched, passion took over.

Serita broke off the kiss. "Hey, no kisses until I'm done whipping you. I will not be distracted this time."

He roared with laughter. "We'll see." They sat on the sofa in front of the fireplace. "We're changing the game a little."

"How?"

"This time, whoever pulls the card will read it and the other person has to answer."

"Okay, I can go with that. Who's first?"

"Ladies first."

"Aw, you're such a gentleman," she said sweetly. "But that doesn't change how fast you're going to be naked."

"Oh, you're just all talk tonight, huh?"

"Oh, no. I'm going to be all action, too."

And he couldn't wait for that.

She pulled the card. "'Abraham Lincoln was shot here in 1865.'"

"What is Ford's Theater?" He smiled smugly and

drew the next one. "'This team was the focus of the 2014 Deflategate scandal.'"

"What is the New England Patriots? Bet you thought I wouldn't know that."

Jeremy shook his head and chuckled. She had indeed studied because, after four more rounds, she still hadn't lost a piece of clothing. He was missing his shirt.

"Ooh, I think I'm going to win tonight. Next question is—'This ends in two hearts being bound together.'"

He made a show of thinking. "I know what it is. Wait, wait."

"Five seconds." She started humming the *Jeopardy!* theme.

He snapped his fingers. "I got it." He slid off the sofa onto one knee at the same time as he opened the small black velvet box. "What is will you marry me?"

Her eyes went wide and she brought her hands to her mouth.

"Serita, I fell in love with you from the moment we met and I promise to keep loving and protecting you. My arms will lift you so you can soar and shelter you when you need a safe haven. You won't ever have to fear being alone because I will *always* be here."

"Oh, my goodness, *yes*!" She jumped into his arms with such force it knocked him backward on the floor. She scrambled up. "Wait, wait. You have to put the ring on," Serita said.

She held out a trembling hand and he slid on the blue diamond solitaire surrounded by brilliant white ones. He'd told her she was a rare jewel and he had wanted to choose something that matched her uniqueness.

"This is the most beautiful ring I have ever seen. And this diamond is blue."

"It's rare and precious, just like you."

"I am so happy I could scream. I love you, Jeremy." She waved her hand around. "Ooh, I have to take a picture to send to Gabby." She dug her phone out of her purse and joined Jeremy on the floor. "I gotta get the angle just right."

Jeremy pulled her onto his lap and smiled at her attempt to do a selfie.

Serita held her hand up, counted to three and hit the button. She checked the photo. "Yes! It's perfect."

"Yes, it is. I do belive you've reached pro status."

A grin covered her face.

"I do have one more thing to show you." He reached for the large envelope he'd placed on the end table and handed it to her.

She opened the flap and withdrew the papers. "What is this?"

"You said you wanted to own a company sometime down the road and I want to make your dream a reality. I'm having the company name changed to HJS Robotics."

She stared up at him, then back down to the papers. "You mean, you're making me co-owner?"

"Yes."

"Jeremy, I don't know what to say. You are… I think I'm going to need to lay down."

Jeremy chuckled. "We have the entire weekend for you to recover."

She leaned up and kissed him. "I'm so glad I accepted that first dinner offer." She went back to the papers, shaking her head as if in disbelief.

"I am, too. So when do you want to get married?"

Serita whipped her head around. "I have no idea. Um...do we have to have something big?"

He chuckled. "No, baby. You can have whatever you want." He knew she didn't like a lot of hoopla, as she'd put it, so something small would work for him, too. Though he didn't know how small it would be once all his family showed up. "What's your favorite holiday?"

"Christmas, why?"

"I have an idea. How about we get married on Christmas Eve? You're the only present I want under my tree this year."

Serita blinked. "As in *this* Christmas Eve...a month from now?"

"You said you don't like a lot of excitement. The sooner we do it, the less time our mothers have to try to turn this into a colossal event."

She gasped. "You're right. But it's too late to try to find a place."

Jeremy wrapped his arm around her. "I have the perfect place. Remember when you said my parents' house was big enough to fit fifty or sixty people? We can get married there. It can just be our families and close friends, and if need be, we can hide out in my old room for a few minutes."

"They do have a lovely house. But will they be okay with it?"

"You met my mother. She's going to be bragging to all my aunts for the next decade. So, is that a yes?"

"It's a yes."

"You know we have to celebrate." He picked her up and carried her over to the bed.

"We absolutely have to celebrate," she said, removing her clothes. "By the way, I won, so we get to play my game now."

He quickly shed his pants and briefs and rolled on a condom. He slid into her warmth and groaned. "Baby, we can play that game all night."

Epilogue

Jeremy stood in the kitchen with Cedric, Lorenzo, Alisha, their five Gray cousins from LA and all their spouses. In ten minutes, he would be a married man and he couldn't wait. Just as he'd thought, his mother had been beside herself with excitement when he had asked about having the wedding there. She had decorated the house in a winter wonderland theme worthy of any amusement park.

Cedric said, "You were the last to fall and the fastest."

Everybody laughed.

"I told y'all, but you didn't want to believe me. I should've made a bet so I could get my two hundred dollars back."

"Too late now, unless you want to bet how fast you'll be parents."

Siobhan, the oldest of the Grays and their generation of cousins, held up a hand. "We are not placing bets on babies. Jeremy, don't you need to be getting over to the stairway to wait for your bride-to-be? She is such a sweetheart, by the way."

"Yes, she is and, yes, I do."

"Before we go, we need to make a toast," Cedric said. They all picked up their flutes filled with champagne. "To love."

"To love," they chorused.

Minutes later, Jeremy took his place at the base of the staircase with Cedric by his side. Gabriella stood opposite them in a navy blue slim-fitting off-the-shoulder dress. Instead of the traditional wedding song, they had chosen "Setembro" by Quincy Jones. He remembered his parents playing the song when he was growing up, and when his mother suggested it, both he and Serita agreed that it would be perfect. Even more perfect was the woman who would become his wife as she descended the stairs on the arm of her father. The strapless white gown hugged her every curve and had sparkling jewels embroidered all over it. Her hair was up in an elaborate twist with rhinestones woven throughout. His breath stacked up in his throat and his heart raced with excitement. When she reached him, it was all he could do to stand there and not kiss her. "You're so beautiful." Serita smiled up at him, then they turned their attention to the minister. Less than fifteen minutes later, he heard the words he had been waiting for since they'd met.

"I now pronounce you husband and wife. Jeremy, you may kiss your bride."

Jeremy leaned down close to Serita's ear. "Get ready for some hoopla, sweetheart." He kissed her with all the love in his heart and would have kept right on kissing her if Cedric hadn't elbowed him.

Tears shining in her eyes, she said, "Thank you for loving me."

"This was destiny, *our* destiny." He finally had his Mrs. Right and she was designed specifically for him… *by love*.

* * * * *

SPANIARD'S BABY
OF REVENGE

CLARE CONNELLY

To Esther Scott and Hunter Smith – two of my favourite babies.

May your futures be as bright and sparkly as all the stars in the night sky.

PROLOGUE

Beneath him, Madrid sparkled like a thousand jewels, the night lights twinkling against the inky black of the sky. It was a city of history, a city rich with stories, but in that moment Antonio Herrera was conscious of only his own history.

A history that had been defined by a family feud, a hatred that was as ingrained in his heart and soul as any one man could ever have felt. Some might say that his life had been charmed, but Antonio knew the truth. Hatred for the diSalvo family ran through his Spanish blood, poisoned his mind, and he would stop at nothing to fight this war. No, to end it.

His father had been destroyed by diSalvos' machinations. A corporate empire, decades in the making, had been systematically pulled apart, and it had needed Antonio to set things to rights. At eighteen, he'd taken over the business, side-lining his father to arrest the financial bleed. He'd triaged their losses, strengthened their assets, and now, at thirty, he was a single man in charge of a billion-euro corporation, known the world over for being a titan of all types of industries.

His eyes drifted to the gleaming oak of his desk, and the file that had arrived that afternoon.

How strange the timing was. Less than a month after his father had died—a man who had been made to suffer at the hands of the diSalvos, a man Antonio would do anything for—and she had been found.

After a year of searching, a year of waiting for his elite investigator to turn over some hint of the elusive woman, and finally he had some answers.

Amelia diSalvo. Or Amelia Clifton, as she was calling herself. But a name changed nothing—she was still undeniably a diSalvo.

The missing piece of the puzzle, the woman in control of the vital shares he needed to take the jewel in the diSalvo empire into his own hands—Prim'Aqua—the shipping company that had, at one time, been owned jointly by the diSalvos and the Herreras, until both patriarchs had fallen in love with the same woman and bitterly broken their business alliance, turning friends into sworn enemies.

And now, this diminutive woman owned the shares Antonio needed, and he'd stop at nothing to convince her to sell them to him.

He stared at the photograph, looking for any resemblance to her half-brother Carlo.

There was none. Where Carlo was cast from a similar Mediterranean mould as himself, with dark hair, honeyed skin and jet-black eyes, Amelia was fair and slight.

Like her mother, he thought, remembering the world-famous supermodel who'd evidently, at one time, been the mistress of Giacomo diSalvo. Only Penny Hamilton had been tall and Amelia was tiny—as diminutive as some kind of fairy, he thought, looking at the way she was walking down the street in this photograph. It must have been a warm day, for she wore a simple cotton dress with thin straps and buttons down the front. It fell to just above her knees and the sun streamed from behind her, showing her tantalising silhouette through the dress's fine fabric.

A jolt of very masculine awareness splintered through him. Desire? For a diSalvo? How could that be, when she was part of the family that had set out to destroy his?

Regardless of his determination, his body tightened and

his eyes lingered a little longer than was necessary on the photograph, taking in the details of her pale peaches-and-cream complexion, a smile that was wide on a petite angular face, hair that was long and blonde—whether it fell naturally in those loose Botticelli curls or had been styled that morning, he would only be able to say after he'd met her in person.

And that would be soon.

In a small English village near Salisbury there was a billion-pound heiress, the daughter of a world-famous British supermodel and an Italian tycoon, a woman who'd been born into wealth and a blood rivalry. And she would be the key in winning this ancient family war.

His eyes dropped to the photograph once more. She was beautiful, but beauty was not uncommon. She was also a diSalvo, and for that he would always hate her. For one night, though, he would appeal to her sense of decency, he would implore her to return to him what should always have been his. And if she didn't, he'd find another way to secure the shares.

One way or another, he would succeed. Because he was Antonio Herrera, and failure simply wasn't an option.

CHAPTER ONE

IT HAD BEEN a perfect day. Warm and cloudless, so that the late afternoon sun filtered through the windows of her home, bathing it in a timeless golden light. But as the evening had drawn around her, the sky had clouded over and the air had begun to smell different, a portent of summer rain.

The first day of school holidays had been everything Amelia could have hoped. She'd slept late, read a book from start to finish, walked into the village for a cider at the local pub, and now she was home, making a fish pie with episodes of *The Crown* playing in the background. She'd seen the whole show already, but she loved to have the television on for company—and who better to keep company with than the Queen?

She scooped some flour from the canister in her fingertips and added it to the roux she was stirring, thickening it and breathing in the aroma gratefully—she always made a roux with garlic and saffron, and the fragrance caused her stomach to give a little groan.

Yes, the first day of school holidays had been deliciously perfect, Amelia told herself, ignoring the little pang of emptiness that pushed into her mind. It was only that a month and a half was a very long time to have off work, particularly when work was the purpose for one's life.

Teaching wasn't necessarily a calling for everyone, but it was for Amelia, and the idea of having seven whole weeks out of the classroom wasn't a prospect she entirely relished.

She'd been invited to Egypt with some of the faculty, but she'd declined. She'd done enough travelling to last a life-time—a childhood that had seen her dragged from pillar to post depending on where her mother's latest assignment or lover had taken them, Amelia preferred to stay right where she was, in this charming village in the middle of England.

Her bluebell-shaded eyes drifted around the cottage, and a rueful half-smile touched her pink lips. It was pretty safe to say that Bumblebee Cottage was as far from the life she'd experienced as a child as possible. Her first twelve years had been spent mostly in five-star hotels, sometimes for months at a time. School had been a luxury her mother hadn't seen the necessity of, and it was only Amelia's keen desire for knowledge and the never-ending string of questions which Penny had no patience for that had led to the hiring of a tutor for Amelia.

But then Penny had died, and twelve-year-old Amelia, already so like her supermodel mother, had been shunted into another life completely. As rarefied and glamorous, but so much more public. In the wake of the supermodel's drugs-related death, Amelia had been followed everywhere she went, and her father—a man she hadn't even known about—simply hadn't been able to comprehend what life had been like for the young Amelia.

Talk about going from the frying pan and into the fire! If being the daughter of a woman like Penny Hamilton made Amelia a magnet for paparazzi, then becoming a diSalvo made her even more so.

And she'd been raised, from that moment, as a diSalvo. Loved, adored, cherished, but she couldn't outgrow the feeling that she didn't really belong.

She hadn't belonged anywhere until she'd moved to this tiny village and taken up a teaching position at Hedgecliff Academy. Unbidden, her eyes drifted to the fridge and the artwork that covered it. 'Thank you' pictures from the students she'd taught, colourful drawings with their childish swirls and squiggles—happy pictures that almost always made Amelia smile.

Fish pie finished, Amelia slipped the dish into the old Aga—it had come with the cottage and she couldn't bear to modernise the thing when it worked perfectly—and then stared around the room for a few moments. It was ridiculous to feel so lonely already.

The summer holidays had *just* begun. Only the day before she'd been surrounded by twenty-seven happy, curious eight-year-olds. Besides, she was the one who'd turned down invitations for the summer break. She had elected to stay at home.

So what good was it to dwell on the gaping void of people and company in her solitary existence? She'd chosen this life.

She'd turned her back on her father, her half-brother and the world they inhabited.

And she wouldn't have it any other way. Would she?

The cottage could not have been quainter if it had been brought to life from between the pages of a Beatrix Potter storybook. Stone, painted a pale cream, roses in the front garden, wisteria scrambling over an arch that led to the front steps and a thatched roof that showed the house to be two-storey, with little dormer windows shaped into the roof. Lights were on inside, making the cottage glow with a warmth that did something strange to Antonio's chest.

He studied it for a moment, a frown on his face as, for a brief and uncharacteristic moment, he rethought the necessity of this.

He had already bought his way into—through shell companies and entities—many of Carlo diSalvo's businesses, giving him if not a controlling interest in their operation, enough of a stake to be difficult and a nuisance to the man he had been raised to hate.

But this was different. He would gladly let the rest go if he could only get this one company under his control. And if Amelia diSalvo proved difficult, if appealing to her sense of decency didn't win her over, then he'd show her what he'd been doing and how close he was to ruining her brother.

He crossed his arms over his chest as the first drop of rain began to fall, quickly followed by another. It was a summer storm that brought with it the smell of sun-warmed grass and the threat of lightning. Inside the cottage a shape moved and he narrowed his gaze, homing in on its location.

Amelia.

He held his breath unconsciously as, with blonde hair scraped into a bun, she moved into his vision. Her face was pale; at this distance it was hard to tell, but he would say she wore no make-up. She stared out of the window for several moments and then turned away.

Certainty fired in his gut.

She was a diSalvo.

That made her fair game.

It had been less than a month since he'd buried his father and in that moment Antonio's only regret was that Javier had not lived to see this final, deeply personal revenge be enacted.

With renewed determination, his stride long and confident, he walked up the winding path. Gravel crunched underfoot and the moon peeked out from behind a storm cloud for a moment, casting him in an eerie sort of silver light. Foreboding, some might have called it, but not Antonio.

Bumblebee Cottage, a brass sign near the door proclaimed, and he ignored the image it created—of sweetness and tranquillity. Amelia diSalvo might be playing at this life, but she was the daughter of a supermodel and the most ruthless bastard on earth. And she was also the piece of the puzzle he needed—victory was within reach.

As if her loneliness had conjured a companion, the doorbell rang. Olivia wasn't so maudlin and self-indulgent to forget all common sense. It was almost nine o'clock at night—who could be calling at this hour?

She'd bought Bumblebee Cottage because of its isolation. No prying neighbours, no passing motorists—it sat nestled into a cul-de-sac of little interest to anyone but her and the farm that bordered the cottage on one side. It was a perfect, secluded bolthole. Just what she'd needed when she'd run from the life she'd found herself living.

She adored it for its seclusion but a *frisson* of something like alarm spread goosebumps over her flesh. She grabbed a meat cleaver, of all things, from the kitchen bench then moved to the door.

'Who is it?'

A man's voice answered, deep and gravelled, tinged with a European accent. 'Can you open up?'

'I can, but I'm not going to,' she muttered to herself. 'Who are you?' she called more loudly. 'What do you want?'

'Something that is easier to discuss in person.' He was hard to hear over the falling rain.

'What is it?'

'I just said—' He released a soft curse in Spanish. When she was eight, she'd mastered curse words in French, Italian, German, Spanish, Greek, Mandarin and Polish. She'd been bored on a yacht and the staff—one from each of these nationalities—had spent one late night teaching her. 'It's important, Amelia,' Antonio said.

The fact he knew her name got her attention. With a frown on her face, she unlocked the door, keeping the chain lock firmly in place so that it only cracked open a wedge.

It was dark on the porch, but enough light filtered out to show his face and it was strong and interesting.

'How do you know my name?'

There was a beat of silence and then, 'I'm a business acquaintance of your brother's. I need to speak to you.'

'Why? What about? Is it Carlo? Is he okay?'

The man's eyes flickered with something and for a moment Amelia was worried, but then he smiled. 'So far as I know, Carlo is fine. This is a proposition just for you.'

At that, Amelia frowned. 'What kind of proposition?'

His look was mysterious. 'One that is too confidential to discuss through the door.'

'It's late at night. This couldn't have waited until tomorrow?'

'I just flew in.' He shrugged, his eyes narrowing. 'Is it a bad time?'

She wanted to tell him to go away, because something about him was making her pulse fire and her heart race. Fear, surely?

'It will not take long,' he said once more, appeasing, and her eyes lifted to his.

When had she become so suspicious? True, she'd had a baptism of fire when she'd gone to live with her father and half-brother. She'd learned that there were many people out there who would hurt you—not physically, necessarily, but with any means it took. His so-called friends had proved to be wolves in couture clothing. But she'd fled those people, that world. She'd moved across the earth, to the sweetness of a tiny village, and the homeliness of Bumblebee, and she'd become not Amelia Hamilton, nor Amelia diSalvo, but Amelia Clifton—her mother's real surname. A normal name. An unrecognisable name. A name that didn't attract attention or interest, a name that was all her own.

Intrusions from her other life weren't welcome.

'Fine,' she said crisply, pushing the door shut so she could unchain it and then opening it wide.

She did a double-take. Through the one inch of open door it hadn't been possible to see exactly how handsome he was. But now? His dark hair sat straight and spiky, enhancing the sharpness of his bone structure and, rather than looking as though it had been styled that way, it was more like he'd dragged his fingers through it enough times to make the hair stand on end. His was a face that was all angles and planes, symmetrical and pleasing, with a square jaw and a chin that looked as though it had been carved from stone. Only there was a divot in its centre, as if his creator had enjoyed pressing a thumb into it, a perfect little indent that drew her curious gaze.

His lips were broad and his jaw covered in stubble. His nose was long, straight and autocratic, but it was his eyes that robbed her lungs, momentarily, of the ability to pump air out of her body. They were eyes shaped like almonds, a dark grey in colour, rimmed in thick black lashes that curled in a way Amelia was both dumbfounded by and jealous of. They were eyes that seemed to tell stories, flickering with emotions and thoughts she couldn't decode.

'Well?' he asked again, gruff, but a smile on his lips softened the word. 'May I enter?'

'Yeah.' The word was breathy. She cleared her throat. 'Of course.'

He shrugged out of his jacket, revealing a shirt that had suffered several drops of rainwater. It was a simple gesture—showing the breadth of his chest and the sculptured perfection of his torso.

She swept her eyes shut for a moment and then collected herself, offering an apologetic grimace before moving in a little. 'I'm sorry; I don't get many visitors.'

'Apparently,' he drawled. And then his smile deepened to reveal even white teeth. Her stomach flipped in on itself. 'And so a meat cleaver is how you choose to defend yourself?'

She found herself nodding with mock gravity. 'I feel it's only fair to warn you: I have a black belt in kitchen instruments.'

'Do you?'

'Oh, you should see me wield a potato peeler.'

His laugh was a low rumble from deep in his belly and his eyes were assessing. She wanted to look away but found her gaze held by his, as though trapped. 'Another time,' he said.

'You can unarm yourself,' he added. 'I assure you I don't mean you any harm.'

'I'm sure you don't but I feel I have to point out that very few murderers announce their intentions, do they?'

'I suppose not.'

'So it's quite possible you're just planning the best way to kill me without making a fuss.'

'Except that I've already explained why I'm here,' he responded with a grin that seemed to breathe butterflies into her belly. He looked around her cottage with lazy curiosity.

Amelia didn't have guests often—a few of the teachers from school had come around for her birthday earlier in the year, and once she'd had a student after school, as a favour for the parents, but generally Amelia kept to herself.

What was the point of country solitude if you chose to surrender it?

She tried to see the house as an outsider might—the quaint decorations, the homely simplicity of her furnishings, the absence of any photographs, the abundance of paperback novels and fresh flowers.

'Ah, yes, your proposition,' she murmured. 'Please—' She gestured towards the lounge.

He moved ahead of her and she realised she was staring at his rear, distracted by the way his trousers framed his tight, muscular bottom. Distracted by the way just looking at him was making her nerves buzz into overdrive.

She had practically no experience with men, besides a few casual lunch dates with Rick Steed, the deputy headmaster. And those had ended with chaste kisses to the cheek, nothing particularly distracting or tempting.

As a teenager, she'd railed against the life she'd been sucked into, hating the expectation that because her mother had been renowned both for her beauty and sexually free attitude Amelia must be exactly the same.

She'd begun to suspect she was, in fact, frigid. Completely devoid of any normal sexual impulse or desire. That had suited her fine. What did she need a man for when she had all the men the books in her life afforded?

What indeed? she thought to herself as he turned to face her.

'Nice place.'

'Thank you.'

He was quiet, watching her, and ingrained manners and a need to fill the silence had her offering, 'Can I get you a drink?'

'Thank you.' He nodded.

'What would you like? Tea? Coffee?'

He arched a brow. 'At this hour?'

Heat suffused her cheeks at her own naivety. 'Wine?'

'Wine would be fine.'

'Have a seat. I won't be a minute.'

CHAPTER TWO

HER LOUNGE WAS even cosier—if that was possible—than the exterior of this country cottage had promised.

Delicate and pretty, and oh, so feminine, with soft cushions and blankets everywhere and pictures of flowers on the walls. It was cosy, homely and warm, but his mind was only half-focused on his surroundings. He was mulling over the proposition he'd come here to offer—and what he'd do if she refused.

Already he could see that Amelia diSalvo was different to what he'd expected.

Did that matter? Did it fundamentally change what he needed from her? And what she'd agree to?

His research showed that she'd been inactive in the business, not attending meetings of any kind. She was on the board but didn't contribute; it was clear she had no interest in the day-to-day operations of diSalvo Industries.

But would she be easily convinced to sell her shares to him?

Would she recognise his name and recall the bitter rivalry that had engulfed their families? Would she then have to launch straight into his backup plan? The idea of revealing his machinations to this woman hadn't bothered him an hour earlier but, standing in her living room, suddenly he wasn't in a rush to reveal his reasons for coming to Bumblebee Cottage late in the evening.

Which was absurd given that he'd had an investigator searching for her for over a year. Absurd given that he'd jumped on a flight as soon as she'd been located, with scant regard for the timing of things. If he'd been patient, he could have spent the night in London and driven into the countryside first thing the following morning, catching her in the daytime rather than on a rainy summer evening.

But he was here, and he wouldn't let himself get distracted by the fact that she wasn't the hard and cynical heiress he'd imagined. Nor by the fact she seemed kind of sweet and funny, and lived in a house that was like a tribute to quaint history.

He had spent his adult life setting things right, avenging this feud, and now he was within striking distance. All that stood between himself and success was this one tiny woman.

She was different to what he'd expected, but she was still a diSalvo and she still held the key to his ultimate revenge.

He had to remember that.

It was impossible to say why she felt as if she needed a moment to steady herself in the kitchen, but Amelia took several, sucking in a deep breath and then another and another as she reached for a bottle of wine and a corkscrew. All the wines she'd been given as gifts had actual corks.

She lifted it out easily enough and poured a measure into two glasses—her plans for a cup of tea falling by the wayside as she thought it would give her some fortifying courage.

Wine glasses in hand, she moved back into the lounge. And froze.

He was simply standing, staring at one of the pictures of hydrangeas she'd painted in watercolours, and it was that image of him that did something completely unexpected to her insides.

He was so utterly masculine in the midst of her living space and yet there was something strangely perfect about seeing him there. She stared at him, at the harshness of his face in profile, the strength of his body, broad shoulders and a narrow waist, legs that looked strong and athletic, and her pulse began to speed and her heart was trembling.

Oh, God, what was happening to her? Her mouth was dry and when she lifted her reluctant gaze back to his face she saw he'd turned and a hint of sardonic amusement danced in the depths of his eyes, bringing another flush of pink to her cheeks.

'Here,' she muttered, pushing the wine glass towards him.

He held her gaze as he took it, a smile playing about his lips. '*Gracias.*'

'You're Spanish?' she heard herself say and then winced. Why was she making small talk with him?

'*Sí.*' The word resonated with something spicy and mysterious and, despite the fact it was now raining, she was reminded of the day's sunshine and warmth.

She needed to focus. Why was he here?

'What's your name?'

'Antonio Herrera,' he said, and Amelia frowned, her eyes sweeping shut for a moment.

She felt his gaze, heavy and intent on her face, and her skin goosebumped once more. There was something in her mind, a memory, but it was distant and when she tried to grab it, to focus on it, the thing slipped away from her, like trying to catch a piece of soap that had been dropped into the bath.

'I know that name.'

'Do you?' he murmured, the words throaty.

He held his wine glass to hers, a salute, and she completed it on autopilot. Only their fingertips brushed together and it was as though Amelia had been thrown from an aeroplane. Her stomach twisted in a billion knots and she was in freefall, everything shifting and pulling and nothing making sense. The world was over-bright and her senses jangling. His eyes were merciless, pinning her to the spot, and from grey to black they went once more. She couldn't speak, couldn't move.

'Why do I know your name?' she asked when the answer hadn't come to her. Then, like a bolt of lightning, she remembered. 'Oh! Of course!'

Did his shoulders tighten? Or was she imagining it? 'Yes?'

Hadn't she realised he was a man used to being in command? A figure of dominance and assertiveness?

'You're that guy,' she said, clicking her fingers together. 'I read about you a while ago. You bought that airline and saved all those people from getting fired.'

'Being made redundant,' he clarified. 'And that's not why I bought the airline.'

'No?'

'It was going for a song.' He shrugged.

'I see,' she said thoughtfully, wondering why he was downplaying the altruism of the purchase. He didn't really care about twenty thousand people poised to be out of work if the airline went bust? Or did he want her to think he didn't care?

Her eyes narrowed speculatively. 'And you invest in schools in eastern Europe. And hospitals.'

He arched a brow. 'You seem to know quite a bit about me.'

'It was a long opinion piece,' she explained, her cheeks heating. 'And I like to read the paper. From cover to cover.' She was babbling a little. When she'd moved to her father's home, she'd been surrounded by men like this. Well, not *precisely* like this; he was somewhat unique. But men who were just a little too much of everything. Too handsome, too sharp, too rich.

And she'd never felt overawed by those qualities before.

Having seen her mother fall under their spell time and time again, she'd always been determined to remain immune to those charms.

Then again, she supposed it was a little like the aquarium effect.

'The aquarium effect?' he prompted, and Amelia was mortified to realise she'd been speaking out loud.

She turned away from him, walking unsteadily towards an armchair and sitting in it, then immediately wishing she hadn't when their height disadvantage became even more apparent.

'Please, take a seat.' She gestured towards the sofa.

'Sure. If you'll elaborate,' he drawled. 'I should like to see if you are comparing me to a shark or a seal.'

Her laugh was spontaneous. She watched covertly as he sat—not on the sofa but in the armchair across from hers, his long legs stretched out and dangerously close to her own legs.

'I didn't mean that,' she promised, sipping her wine. 'It's only that when you go to an aquarium you're expecting to see myriad fish, so that even the most beautiful tropical fish or the fluffiest penguin fail to have much of an impact. But if I were walking along the Thames and a beautiful penguin happened to cross my path I'd be basically breathless.'

'Speechless too, I should think, at finding a penguin in central London.'

She nodded, glad he hadn't taken her metaphor the vital step further. Because he was that spectacular piece of wildlife which, when surrounded by men of his ilk, might have left her cold. But here, like this, in her tiny cottage on the outskirts of a small village, smiling at her as though he found her fascinating and unique, how could Amelia fail to be breathless, speechless and hopelessly attracted?

'Have you lived here long?' he asked and she relaxed further as the conversation moved onto far safer ground.

She looked around the lounge, her heart warming at the comfort and beauty of this little room.

'I moved here straight out of University,' she said with a small nod. 'I thought I'd stay only a year or so, but then the cottage came on the market and, what can I say, it was love at first sight,' she said, looking fondly around the small lounge, with its low ceiling and unevenly rendered walls.

'I can see why,' he drawled cynically and she laughed.

'You sound just like my brother!'

Carlo had been just as scathing about the 'relic'. *'Why don't you buy some land and build something bigger? You're a diSalvo,* cara, *and this place isn't fit for a mangy dog.'*

'In what way?'

'Oh, only in so much as he didn't really like Bumblebee Cottage. He's far more into luxury and glamour.'

'And you're not?' Antonio enquired.

'What do you think?' she asked with a lifted brow and a half-smile, gesturing around the room.

'I think the house is charming,' he supplied, leaning forward a little, and his ankle brushed hers, probably by accident, but the effect was the same as if it had been intentional. She sat up straighter, her eyes finding his, a plea and a question in them. 'And so is the occupant,' he added, and now the charge of electricity that flared between them was unmistakably mutual.

She swallowed past the lump in her throat, her eyes round like saucers. His foot brushed hers and now she knew it wasn't an accident she told herself she should pull away. Remove her legs from his reach. Do something, *anything,* to show him she didn't welcome his presumptuous advances.

But oh, how she welcomed them. How she welcomed *him*.

'Thank you.'

It was hard to think straight in that moment. Her body

was charged, her senses in complete disarray, and she was left wondering at the bizarre circumstances that had brought this billionaire tycoon to her door right at the moment when she'd been at risk of sinking into thoughts of loneliness and the pervasive emptiness that came with being alone.

'Well, Antonio—' his name made husky by her too-dry throat '—perhaps you should tell me why you're here?'

He had come to Bumblebee Cottage expecting to hate her. She was a diSalvo; it was written in the stars that he *would* hate her. Only he didn't.

And not only did he *not* hate her; he was actually enjoying himself. He was finding it hard to keep his mind to himself, to concentrate on business when she was smiling at him and joking with him, and when her huge blue eyes kept dropping to his chest, roaming over his breadth as though she were starving and he the only meal around for miles.

And what would she say when he told her the truth of their relationship? What would she say when he explained what he needed from her?

Would she understand? Or would she tell him to get the hell out? Then he'd have to enact plan B, and her smiles would disappear when she realised how close he'd brought her brother to breaking point. And how much he was enjoying that knowledge.

How long had it been since he'd been with a woman? Months. Many months. His father's illness had been sudden and, between the company and Javier's demise, Antonio had barely had time for the distraction of women.

Did that explain the undercurrent of desire that was swirling around them? Was that the reason he was reluctant to tell her why he'd come?

It was the last thing he'd planned for, but now that he sat

opposite Amelia diSalvo he wanted to shelve business and his drive for revenge. Just for a moment. Just for a night.

A temporary delay, that was all, while he enjoyed her company. What was the harm in that?

'Antonio?' she prompted.

He sipped his wine thoughtfully. 'Our grandfathers were friends,' he said slowly, testing her, interested to see what she knew of the feud.

'Were they?' Her nose wrinkled, and his gut kicked. Damn it, she was distracting.

'A long time ago.'

'And that's why you're here?' she prompted.

'In part.'

Her look was teasing. 'Are we playing a guessing game?'

'We can do,' he murmured. 'Let me guess what you're doing in a village like this,' he murmured.

'You don't like it here?'

'It's a far cry from the life you must have lived in Rome.'

'Why do you say that?'

His eyes glittered and with effort he kept the disdain from his voice. 'You're a diSalvo,' he said with the appearance of calm. 'And this cottage is…not.'

She laughed again, a genuine sound of pleasure. 'True.'

Then her eyes fixed on his and he let the silence surround them, aware it was affecting her as much as it was him.

'I feel like I know you,' she said finally, simply, with a sense of surrender that made his body tighten. 'That's crazy, isn't it?'

Yes. It *was*. Everything about this was. She was a part of something he wanted, with all his being, to destroy, and yet in that moment all he could think about was her soft pillowy lips and how they'd feel beneath his. About the fact she was staring at him with huge eyes and her chest was heaving with the force of her breathing.

'I must be losing my mind,' she said, blinking her eyes as if waking from a dream. And then she sipped her wine before offering him a smile that was part self-deprecating and part the most beautiful thing he'd ever seen. What the hell was he thinking, letting himself be so distracted by her, and the way the air around them seemed to crackle and hum? He'd come here with a purpose—a plan he'd set in motion long ago, and *nothing* was going to derail that.

'My grandfather's name was Enrique Herrera. Has your father ever mentioned him?'

She blinked, her huge blue eyes showing obvious confusion. Outside, the rain was falling heavier now but he was barely conscious of it. 'No.'

That was strange. How could Amelia know nothing of a feud that had dominated both his and Carlo's lives?

'We weren't big on *tête-à-tête,*' she explained with a shrug of her slender shoulders that drew his attention to the fine, soft curve of her neck and the hint of cleavage revealed by her simple shirt. Then her eyes lifted to his and his body tightened, his arousal straining against his trousers.

Antonio had spent his adult life moving the pieces into place to destroy Carlo diSalvo, and this woman was a vital part of that. Only through her would he gain control of the one company he desperately wanted and finally avenge the feud that had destroyed his father. Only through appealing to her and then, if it came to it, blackmailing her, would he achieve his goal.

So why was he finding it impossible to sharpen his focus? Because he'd been celibate for months, he told himself. Because he'd been focused on easing his father's last few months of life, and then mourning him appropriately. And now, on acquiring the company that would set all of this to rights.

'My brother might know more about your grandfather,' she said softly, her lips parted. They were beautiful lips—

works of art. Pink and generous, and quick to smile. 'Have you ever spoken to him about Enrique?'

Twice. But conversations with Carlo never ended well. Their hatred was mutual. 'It doesn't matter.' He frowned.

'It must,' she countered, leaning forward a little, and beneath the small coffee table her legs brushed his and his body throbbed with all the awareness that was taking over his mind and soul in that moment. 'For you to have flown all the way here to ask me about him. Or was there something else you wanted to talk to me about?'

Madre de Dios. Antonio had built his company back from dust, he had single-handedly returned Herrera Incorporated to its position as a global powerhouse, and now this one woman was somehow threatening to bring him to his knees?

He stood abruptly and felt her gaze slide up his body. Hungrily. Needily. With the same kind of sensual curiosity that was powering the blood in his own veins.

He'd come to this quaint cottage in the middle of the countryside with one purpose in mind, but now that goal was at war with his body's more immediate needs.

Desire rushed through him as he imagined, for a moment, what it would be like to possess her. Where he was tall and dark, she was fair, all peaches and cream and soft and gentle. Their contrasts fascinated him. What would it be like to lay claim to her body, to drive her wild with desire?

She was a diSalvo! How could he even be thinking like this?

He heard the rustle of clothes as she stood, and then her hand was on his shoulder, turning him to face her. 'Antonio? Is something the matter?'

Everything was the matter! He was so close to bringing her family down, to destroying them as they'd sought to destroy his father, and this one woman was threatening his resolve.

'What is it?' she asked solicitously, her eyes running over his face.

Beautiful eyes in a face that was truly captivating, with long blonde hair he wanted to run his fingers through. He swallowed and then, finally, surrendered to this madness. She was so close, so enticing, and his body was screaming at him to act on his impulses—screw the consequences.

There would be time for revenge later. Afterwards.

With a fatalistic grimace, he lifted a hand and caught her cheek, holding her face steady beneath his. She gasped, her lips parting, a gentle sound of surrender.

And he took her surrender, and he surrendered along-side her.

Slowly, his voice husky, in his native Spanish tongue he murmured, 'You are the most beautiful woman I've ever seen.'

CHAPTER THREE

His words were heavy in the air, mesmerising, and she could only stare at him, and his beautiful body. She could only stare at him, lost to this and him and whatever was happening.

'I...' She frowned, unable to form anything more intelligible. And then her hand was lifting slowly, almost as though it were dragging upwards, pulled by the sheer magnetic force of his body.

She pressed her fingers to his chest, swallowing at the instant bolt of recognition that juddered through her system. Her eyes jerked to his, uncertainty laced with desire, and her fingertips moved across his chest then up to his shoulder.

He made a throaty, groaning sound and then his head dropped forward, or perhaps she pushed up onto the tips of her toes. Whatever it was, on autopilot their lips were meshing, bodies fused together, his broad and hard, his strength emanating from him. His lips moved over hers and she made a gasp of surrender, opening her mouth so that he could deepen the kiss. His hand lifted to the back of her head, his fingers curving around her, holding her where she was so that he could explore her until she was incandescent with pleasure.

'Antonio...' She kissed his name into his mouth, deep into his soul, and felt him answer. Her world was being blasted apart by a simple kiss.

No, there was nothing simple about this—it was crazy

and mad and she knew nothing about him, only his name and that their grandfathers had once been friends. And yet she was his for a song in that moment.

She didn't care what had brought him to her door; she cared only that he was there, and that he wanted her as she did him. Desire—something she had never known nor understood, was rampant in her system now.

As if the heavens were ratifying her surrender to something as elemental as passion, a loud clap of thunder rumbled around the small cottage and a moment later a blade of lightning sliced the sky apart and the house was plunged into darkness. Not complete darkness—Amelia had strung fairy lights generously throughout and, powered by batteries, they offered a golden glow, faint but enough to see by.

He didn't react to the power outage. But his hands roamed her body, running over her sides, finding the hem of her shirt and pushing it, so achingly slowly, up her body so that her skin was covered in goosebumps, her nipples tight against the simple cotton of her bra. He broke the kiss, pulling away from her just long enough to rip her shirt over her head and she pushed her arms skywards at the same time, as fevered as he. In that brief moment of separation their eyes met and something passed between them—an understanding, a commitment to this, come what may—and then he was kissing her again, this time dragging his mouth from her lips to her throat, flicking her with his tongue so that she whimpered with the strength of sensations he was stirring.

He pushed at his own shirt as his mouth claimed hers, dispensing with the fabric confines so his chest was bare.

Her fingers ran over his body without meaning or intent, certainly without forethought, and then her hands found his trousers and, of their own accord, her fingers were loosening his belt buckle then moving to the button and zip, pushing at them while his kiss held her body utterly captive. He stood out of his trousers as she pushed at them, and then her hands were curving around his naked buttocks, feeling his warmth in a way that was elemental and ancient.

He made a growling noise of awareness and dropped his hands to her back, pulling her hard against him so she could feel the strength of his arousal for herself. Surprise made her eyes flare wide and she swallowed, but then he was kissing her again, and now he lifted her as though she weighed nothing and she wrapped her legs around his waist and he rolled his hips so that his erection found her feminine heart, the pressure through the fabric of her jeans enough to make her cry out at what was to come.

He whispered words in Spanish and then he eased her to the ground, just for a moment, so he could retrieve his wallet from his trousers. He pulled out a condom. No, condoms, she corrected with pink cheeks, and she opened her mouth, knowing she needed to say something, to tell him that she was a virgin, because she was sure he wouldn't enjoy discovering that fact for himself. But then his hands came to her jeans and he was unfastening them, pushing them down her legs, and he crouched in front of her and brought his mouth to her inner thigh and she was lost again. She tangled her fingers in his hair, throwing her head back as he kissed her legs.

And then he dragged her simple cotton briefs down her body and she was complicit, stepping out of them. In the back of her mind, in the small part of her brain that was still capable of rational thought, she was surprised by how unselfconscious she was. She was almost naked in front of him and she didn't care.

He brought his mouth to the apex of her thighs and flicked his tongue against her womanhood and now Amelia cried out louder, harder, as pleasure licked through her like wild flames. She said his name over and over again, and her fingers ran faster through his hair before dropping to his shoulders and holding on tight. Pleasure was a rollercoaster and she was buckled in, riding it harder and faster, unable to stop the rush of momentum—not wanting to either.

His mouth drove her over the edge and she cried out as an explosion of delight, unlike anything she'd ever imagined, much less known, blew away the last vestiges of any idea that she might not be a sexual being. If this was sex, she could easily become an addict.

But there was no time to recover. He was straightening, lifting himself up, and in one movement he snaked a hand behind her back and unclasped her bra, and she pushed out of it at the same time. His head came crashing down to her breasts, his lips moving from one nipple to the next, circling her sensitive flesh, and desire was rampant in her bloodstream, running like a pack of leopards through her system.

She heard the opening of the condom and felt his hands move against her stomach and something, some thought, was pushing at her brain, but she couldn't catch it. Pleasure was her all—nothing mattered beyond the feelings he was invoking. She was a wildling, abandoned completely to this, and only this.

His hands on her hips were strong and commanding; he lifted her easily and, in her tiny kitchen, he pressed her against the wall and she cried his name, 'Please, please, please,' begging him for a release she couldn't articulate beyond knowing that it was a necessity.

His eyes, glowing in the soft light, burned into hers for several beats. 'You want this.' It was a statement but it dragged her out of the drugging haze of desire, if only for a second. He needed an answer.

An answer beyond her constant begging?

'Yes,' she groaned. 'Oh, God, yes, please, Antonio. I need this.'

And his dark eyes sparked with something new, something like relief and determination, and he moved his body forward and brought her down on his length in one swift, possessive movement.

She froze as the invisible barrier of her innocence was taken by him, and stiffened as an unwelcome and sharp pain pushed all pleasure aside.

He swore in Spanish, sensing what had happened, and she winced, and then his eyes held hers and he whispered softer words, Spanish words, and he wrapped his arms around her, pulling her from the wall, holding her tight, keeping himself inside her and holding her close to him as the pain subsided.

Pleasure returned and it was different and more demanding than before, because he was inside her and muscles she hadn't known she possessed were being stretched and taunted and desire was being stirred that demanded an answer.

'Please,' she said again and he lifted a hand to her cheek, curving it in his palm.

'You are sure, *querida*?'

'Yes.' She nodded.

And, with a look she couldn't interpret, he began to move again, softly this time, gently, and he pressed her against the wall, and he kissed her as his body stirred her back to fever pitch, and he watched her as she blew apart for a second time, this time in his arms and with his erection deep inside her.

And then he eased her back to the ground, her feet on the floor, but only for a second. He scooped down and lifted her, cradling her to his chest as he carried her upstairs, along the hallway. The lighting here was dimmer than downstairs; she had only a few strings of lights on the landing. He looked in one room first—her study—and the next was her bedroom, and apparently there was sufficient light for him to make out at least the shape of the bed. He strode in, laying her down on the mattress gently, then standing. She could just make out the silhouette of his body in the darkness of the house.

Her breath was rushed and she was grateful there was no lighting, glad he wouldn't be able to see the tangle of emotions swirling in her eyes.

'You should have told me,' he said simply, but there was no recrimination in the words, only regret. And then he brought his body over hers and his lips caught hers, and he kissed her as his arousal found its way to her core once more. She wrapped her legs around his waist and he pushed inside her and she groaned as pleasure already began to build anew.

'Your first time should not be with a man you hardly know,' he said, but she barely heard. The words were hoarse and she was way beyond logical, rational thought. When he kissed her his tongue duelled with hers in time with his body's possession of hers and this time, when she found release, he came with her, holding her tight, kissing her, passion saturating them both.

He stayed where he was, inside her, straddling her, but sat straighter; it was impossible to discern anything in his features owing to the blackness of her room.

But his hands found hers and his fingers weaved through hers, holding her, reassuring her.

'I had no idea,' he said.

'I know that.' Now that the bright burst of passion had receded, she had room to feel self-conscious. Not regret, not remorse, only a desire that she'd been better able to meet him on a level of experience closer to his. 'I probably should have told you.'

She was glad it was dark and that he couldn't see her blush and that she couldn't see his face—and the irritation she was sure would be there.

'Yes,' he agreed simply. 'If only so I could have made it perfect for you.'

She lifted her hands to his chest, running her fingers over his muscles thoughtfully. 'That was perfect,' she promised. 'I had no idea...'

His laugh was soft and, inside her, he jerked with the movement and she let out a soft moan as embers of pleasure began to stir anew.

'I mean it,' she repeated huskily. 'I never really got the whole sex thing.'

At that he sobered and when he spoke his voice was husky. 'I'm surprised to hear it.'

He might have meant it as a general throwaway comment, but that was unlikely. He came to her that night knowing who she was, knowing her name, because their grandfathers had been friends. He knew more about her than she did him, and that certainly included knowledge of her mother and her behaviour. 'I think lots of people expect me to be just like her,' she said with a small shrug. 'And I'm not.'

'You didn't want to be,' he clarified gently, and he pulled away from her and rolled them at the same time, so she made a squawking sound of surprise. He held her close to his body, tucked in one arm, and she relaxed against him. His fingers stroked down her back and she sighed softly. New pleasures were vibrating inside her.

'No,' Amelia agreed, hating that it still felt like a betrayal to admit that.

'You haven't dated?'

'Of course I have,' she was compelled to declare, hating what a novice she was! His fingers paused in their stroking for a moment before resuming their leisurely trail along her back. 'But never seriously, never for long.' She shrugged against his side. 'Whereas you, I imagine, have a *long* list of ex-girlfriends.'

'Not really,' he said, surprising her. 'I don't really date.'

Of course. How gauche of her. 'Lovers, then.'

He laughed. 'Enough,' he agreed after a moment.

She bit down on her lip. 'But I bet it's been a long time since you were with a virgin.'

'I've never been with a virgin,' he said simply. 'Not even my first time.'

She blinked at that confession. 'Seriously?'

'Yeah.'

So she was his first? She couldn't explain it, but she liked that. It was as though they'd both shared a new experience together, and it meant more to her than it should.

'How do you feel?' The gravelled question sent her pulse firing anew.

'Relaxed and satisfied,' she purred and he laughed, a throaty sound of wry amusement.

'I'm pleased to hear it. Stay here.' And he pulled away from her, standing and moving out of her room.

'What are you doing?' she called after him, but the words were soft, consumed by a yawn. And, instead of asking again, she collapsed back against the bed, closed her eyes and remembered. Remembered the madness in the kitchen that had brought his lips to hers, or was it the other way around? Remembered the way they'd exploded at that first touch and everything had seemed predestined in some way.

A moment later she had her answer, anyway. The sound of the bath running, then the bathroom cabinets being open and shut. She lay there, a smile on her face, listening, and a little while later he returned.

'Are you asleep?'

She squinted one eye open and then realised he couldn't see her. 'No,' she said, sitting up. 'Are you taking a bath?'

He laughed. 'No. You are.'

He reached for her hand and she wriggled off the bed,

standing on legs that had suddenly turned to jelly. He understood and he lifted her once more, so she joked, 'I could get used to this. Like some kind of Rajah.'

He stepped over the threshold, into the bathroom, and her breath caught in her throat. He must have found every candle in the house and the bathroom was glowing and warm, like something out of a fairy tale.

Don't! she alerted her subconscious.

Don't even think like that.

Fairy tales. Don't. Exist.

How many times had she seen her mother go down the rabbit hole of thinking a man was her Prince Charming and that their 'happily ever after' was at the end of the next party or vacation or new home or fresh start? Only to wake up alone, miserable, depressed and looking for consolation in the bottle or vial of whatever drug she was into at the time.

Amelia was not Penny—and that meant knowing, beyond a shadow of a doubt, that fairy tales didn't exist.

Still, fairy tale or not, the bathroom was beautiful in this lighting. The tub was half-filled and an extravagant layer of bubbles sat on top of the water's surface. There was an aroma of lavender in the air—so he'd found her bath oils.

He placed her over the edge of the tub, easing her feet into the water, and she smiled as the perfect warmth wrapped around her legs. She sank into it slowly, lying back against the edge and letting the water enfold her.

'Heaven,' she said softly and then blinked her eyes open to find him staring at her.

'Enjoy it.' His eyes sparked with something like promise and her heart turned over in her chest. 'I'll be waiting.' He retrieved a towel and placed it within easy reach of the bath, then moved to the door. 'Don't fall asleep,' he warned as he left and she smiled.

Fat chance.

She wasn't going to fall asleep all night. Not when she had Antonio Herrera as her own personal pleasure centre. Having discovered what her body was capable of feeling, she wanted more. She wanted everything.

And she wanted him to show her.

He collected his scattered clothes from the kitchen floor, and he dressed with true regret. He didn't want to put barriers up to more pleasure. He wanted to take her to bed and make love to her slowly, to seduce her all night long, like he would any other lover.

But there was danger in that—danger in forgetting why he'd come to her, why he'd spent a year trying to locate her. Why he needed her signature on the documents he'd brought with him, her agreement to sell her shares to him.

He had buried his father a month earlier and there was no way he was going to let his desire for a woman cloud his judgement.

He was so close to achieving his goal, and Amelia diSalvo was the key to that.

Sex with her had been a mistake. A stupid, careless mistake—because it had the power to confuse things between them. Because it muddied the water of what he needed from her.

With a grim expression on his face, he let himself quietly out of the house, walking towards his car with a growing sense of determination. The rain had stopped but the clouds were still overhead, covering the moon and the stars so everything was in pitch darkness.

The documents were on the front seat. He grabbed them out, tucking them under his arm before making his way back to the house. Silence came from upstairs.

He fought a desire to go and check on her, to see if she needed anything. A passionate encounter didn't a relationship make—there was no need for him to play the part of the solicitous boyfriend. It was better for both of them if he focused on his reason for being in the cottage.

Revenge was close—so close he could feel it. And it would be better than anything he'd ever known—even the pleasure he'd just felt in the bed of his arch-enemy.

CHAPTER FOUR

'I THOUGHT I heard the door.'

She appeared in the lounge and at that moment the lights flickered to life—a stutter at first and then a burst, and her expression showed bemusement.

'You're dressed?' She lifted a brow, padding across the room in only a silk robe. A robe that left little to the imagination, not that he needed to use it. He could remember every single curve and delineation of her body, every indent and hollow. Though he regretted now not making love to her in the brightness of this light, so that he could see her peaches and cream complexion all over, marvel at the contrast of her nipples to her skin.

Damn it—he tightened against his trousers, unwanted desire flooding his system once more.

'What's the matter? You're suddenly struck mute?' Something like uncertainty fluttered in her expression but she covered it quickly. 'I mean, I know that was good, but surely not enough to rob you of the ability to speak.'

His smile was tight on his face. Her easy nature was at odds with the direction of his thoughts.

'I came here tonight to talk to you about something important.'

Confusion clouded her expression. 'Oh. Right. I'd…forgotten. Something to do with our grandfathers?' She blinked, her expression still one of trust, and stepped across the room. 'Surely it can wait?' she implored, lifting a hand to his chest, her eyes meeting his in both a challenge and an invitation.

God, he wished it could wait. But being caught up in the moment, letting passion override common sense once was one thing. It would be quite another to keep exploiting her sensual need, an appetite he had awakened without realising her innocence.

'Not really.' He grimaced. 'Why don't you sit down?'

'I'm fine.' She shook her head as wariness crept into her expression. A wariness he couldn't help but resent.

He nodded, a stiff movement, and lifted his hand to rub his neck. He hadn't thought about what he would say. When he had come to Bumblebee Cottage, he'd expected this to be much like a standard business meeting.

She had something he needed, and he had something he could offer in exchange. Money, in the first instance and, failing that, a promise to bide his time with her brother's business, not to bring him to his knees in a cataclysmic fashion. Blackmail, yes.

Would he still stoop to that, given what they'd just shared?

He straightened his shoulders, his expression tense. Sex was beside the point. It didn't change the facts—he wanted what she had and he'd go to any lengths to acquire it.

Too much rested on his success here, and the hatred he felt for the diSalvo family went deeper than anything he'd shared with Amelia this evening.

'I need you to sign this.' He pulled the contract from his document wallet and placed it on the table—the coffee table they'd sat at only a couple of hours earlier, tension zipping through the room.

Well, there was tension again now, but a different kind altogether.

Her eyes showed confusion and then they skipped away from his. She crossed to the table, close enough that he could breathe in her sweet smell of lavender and vanilla, so close that he could simply reach out and pull her close, forgetting about the damned shares for a moment longer.

She pressed a finger to the contract, drawing it down the title page as she read, then silently flipped it over. She read that and then the next, and finally lifted her eyes back to his face. 'You want to buy my shares in Prim'Aqua? Why?'

'Because without your shares I can't assume a majority ownership.'

She blinked, his clear sentence apparently not making any sense to her. 'It's one of my family's business interests. Why would you want to assume a majority ownership?'

It was like waving a red rag in front of a charging bull.

'Because it was my family's company also,' he said with deceptive calm. 'And I will not rest until it is back in my hands.'

The words hung in the air like little daggers, but they made absolutely no sense. None of this made any sense.

He'd come to her house and, true, she hadn't exactly interrogated him about what he'd wanted but…how could she have known anything like this had brought him to her?

'I presumed you just wanted to talk about our grandfathers!' she said with a shake of her head. 'This can't be real.'

His eyes narrowed and a burst of adrenalin fired in her gut as she recognised in this man a latent power and determination that had been absent for the rest of the evening. He'd been charming and humorous and now she could see that there was a whole other side to him.

'I have acquired thirty-five per cent of the company,' he said, the words soft yet laced with iron-hard determination. 'Your father and brother will never part with their stake, but that does not matter. Not when your shares will give me the majority. I want them.'

'Why?' She pressed her hands to her hips, turning away

from the contract, then immediately wished she hadn't. Because he was wearing a suit and she was dressed in a silk robe and her body hadn't quite caught up with the fact that he was there for business. That she'd slept with a man, given her virginity to a man, who only wanted her shares in a family company. God knew *she* didn't want them—how often had she wished that her father hadn't gifted such a valuable portfolio on her eighteenth birthday? She'd always felt he was making up for lost time, trying to show her with money how valued and loved she was—but money was the last thing she ever wanted.

The assets she had made her feel even more vulnerable and exposed in that superficial world. With her mother's looks and a fortune at her fingertips—it had been a fast track to attracting all the wrong people.

It still was, apparently.

'Our grandfathers were best friends from the time they were boys.' He spoke slowly, as though she didn't have a tight grasp on English. That exasperated her further.

'I don't need to know the history,' she snapped. 'I need to know why these shares matter so much to you that you were willing to come to my home and…and…seduce me, just to get your hands on them.'

At that, he had the decency to look surprised. 'One thing had nothing to do with the other,' he said slowly and reached a hand out for her, a hand of comfort and reassurance, but she batted it away angrily.

'No.' She took a step back; her hip connected with the table. 'The part of the evening where you get to touch me is absolutely at an end.'

He compressed his lips in exasperation. 'I didn't come here intending to sleep with you. But you were so… It just happened,' he said with a shake of his head. 'I didn't plan it.'

'Oh, yes.' She rolled her eyes, shaking with pent-up rage and deep-down hurt. 'It was just convenient that I happened to fall into bed with you, right before you blindsided me by asking me for something worth millions of pounds.'

'You'll see on the contracts that I'm prepared to pay double their value,' he said silkily.

She put her hands on her hips then wished she hadn't. The gesture drew the robe across her front and his attention dropped to her silk-covered breasts, and nipples that were still tight and heavy with arousal.

'I don't need your money,' she spat. 'You think any amount would induce me to sell the shares to *you*?'

'Our grandfathers had a fight. No, it was more than that. It was war,' he said, returning to the original point. 'They'd started Prim'Aqua by joining together two shipping companies they'd inherited from their fathers, and it became the most powerful water-based logistics and transportation company in the world. Both of our families owe their prosperity to Prim'Aqua.'

'Fine, if you say so,' she snapped, moving towards the door. 'But it's *my* father's company now.'

'Your grandfather fooled my grandfather into signing it over—my grandfather trusted him implicitly and signed the deeds without reading.'

'More fool him,' she muttered.

His expression tightened. 'It was a mistake on his part to trust a diSalvo—and that is a lesson I will never forget.' His eyes glittered black when they met hers. 'But I can rectify this, if you will only be reasonable.'

'You dare ask *me* to be reasonable when you've just insulted my whole family? And me?'

'You come from a family of thieves and bastards, Amelia.'

She stared at him; it felt as if he'd morphed into some kind of alien. It took her several seconds to be able to find her tongue and push it into service.

'My God, get the hell out of this house,' she demanded, the words only slightly shaky. 'How dare you think I would give you *anything*? How can you speak of my family with such obvious disgust when you've literally come straight from my bed?'

'Sleeping with you has nothing to do with why I'm here. I did not plan for that to happen, and it is not going to derail me from my course.' His eyes narrowed warningly. 'Nothing will, Amelia.'

The light in the house was so bright, and she could see him clearly now. His ruthless determination was a physical force in the room, a dark shape she would never be able to grapple with.

Her skin paled, her heart lurched. 'You're a real piece of work, aren't you?'

He angled his head away from her and in profile his face was powerful, as if carved from stone, and a muscle jerked in his jaw, throbbing hard as he reined in his temper.

'You have no interest in the shares I want.'

'How do you know that?' she demanded, crossing her arms over her chest.

He turned to face her, his eyes pinning her to the wall. Oh, God, just like the wall he'd held her against when he'd thrust inside her. Her heart gave a strange little double-beat as memories threatened to swallow her whole.

'Since you inherited your stock portfolio, you have attended precisely zero board or shareholder meetings. You do not appear at corporate events…you do not have a bio on the website. You are absent in every way.'

'So?' She rolled her eyes. 'Ever heard of a silent partner?'

'It is not the same thing. You have holed yourself up here, as far as you can get from the seat of power in diSalvo Industries. You do not want to use your shares to control the company—'

'And is that any wonder? When getting involved in my family's business would mean running up against vultures like you?'

His nostrils flared as he expelled a rapid breath. 'You think I am a *vulture* for wanting to take back what was stolen from me? Prim'Aqua is my birthright…'

'As much as it is mine and Carlo's,' she interrupted firmly, her cheeks flushing pink. 'You have as large a stake in the company as I do. And larger than my brother's too. So what's your problem?'

'I do not want your family having *any* part of it,' he said with icy simplicity. 'Your grandfather stole it and I intend to take it back.' He softened his voice slightly. 'Only I am *not* stealing it. This is a business transaction, plain and simple. You have something I want and I'm prepared to pay you for it.'

'You're unbelievable. Do you realise that if you'd told me this when you first arrived I *might* have heard you out? But how can you think, after what just happened between us, you can lay all this at my feet and I won't be angry?'

'Because you're a sensible, mature woman,' he said. 'And I believe you capable of seeing that business is separate to the personal.'

'There is no business here!' she roared. 'We just had sex! Not even an hour ago! You took my virginity and it was… just a way to soften me up towards you, so that I'd agree to anything you wanted.'

He swore in Spanish and shook his head. His face was deathly serious, his face harsh with intent. When he spoke, the words were slow and grated from him, indignation heavy in each accented syllable. 'If you think I would ever stoop to something so low, then you have no idea who you're dealing with.'

'No, clearly I don't,' she agreed scathingly. 'Now, please go.'

'You do not want me to leave without those contracts,' he said, the words softly menacing.

It took a moment for the penny to drop, to make sense of the words he'd just issued. 'Are you threatening me?'

Something like sympathy crossed his face. 'No. I am threatening your brother.'

Now Amelia was frozen still, her breath coming in fits and spurts, her eyes holding his as she tried to make sense of what he meant.

'Carlo foolishly picked up our families' rivalry some years ago.' Antonio spoke calmly, emotions carefully blanked from his voice. 'In truth, I'm surprised he never spoke to you of it.'

'He knew I had no interest in that side of things.' She wrapped her arms around her chest.

Antonio's expression tightened. 'He wanted to ruin my father once and for all, to destroy my family's legacy as the final step in this feud. By the time I took over the company it was a shambles; my father was destroyed, his life's work ruined.' His eyes glinted with the harsh recollection, and there was something else there too. A grief that threatened to shake her sympathetic heart to the core. 'It has taken me a long time to rebuild Herrera Incorporated, but I have done it, *querida*, and then some.'

And then some.

The words sat between them and a *frisson* of tension ran down her spine because there was a threat in that word, surely. A threat and a promise.

'What does that mean?'

He seemed to be waging a war within himself, as though there was a part of him that wanted to spit the salient facts at her feet and a part of him that wanted to protect what they'd just shared. The former won, apparently.

'I have invested wisely these last few years, steadily amassing shares in diSalvo business interests so that I now find I own more than half of your brother's various companies.'

She sucked in a breath. Surely it was a lie, an exaggeration?

'I don't believe you,' she said after a beat had passed, her mind working fast to keep up. 'Carlo would *never* have allowed that to happen.'

'It is easy to acquire anything if you are prepared to bide your time.'

Her stomach twisted into dozens of knots. 'To what end, though?' The depth of his hatred made no sense to Amelia. 'Surely you don't *want* diSalvo investments?'

'Want them? No.' He lowered his voice. 'I want to destroy them. I want to take your brother's legacy and crush it into the ground, as he did my father's. Only I will destroy him beyond any hope of redemption. I will only rest when he is destitute and starving, so that the memory of having a wallet full of money is all he has to warm him in his old age.'

She stared at this passionate man who had only a short time earlier taught her body what it was capable of feeling, the pleasures he'd lavished her with! And now she saw the beast of hatred that moved within him and shivered, for there was such coldness there, such determination, that she didn't doubt him capable of carrying out what he'd threatened.

'You honestly think that's going to fix what happened to your father?'

He stayed quiet for a moment and then shrugged his broad, powerful shoulders. Her traitorous body gave a little jerk of awareness and she wanted to slap herself for feeling *anything* for this man except disgust. 'Carlo played with fire. I am simply making him feel the heat of those flames.'

She gaped. 'That's preposterous!'

But he was, apparently, beyond arguing. He spoke with a calm insistence. 'There are two options here, *querida*.

Sell me your shares in Prim'Aqua and it is over. Done. I will release the grip I have on his empire and he will be safe. Or, if you keep your shares and deny me ownership of a company that is rightfully mine, I will destroy the rest of your family's businesses. I have the power to tank them, and I will do it. And, what's more, I will damned well enjoy it.'

Her heart was thumping. 'You'll destroy a huge proportion of your wealth if you do that.'

'I have more than enough money,' he said carelessly.

'You're unbelievable.'

'Believe it.' His eyes locked onto hers and she shivered with the force of his power. 'And make a decision.'

'A decision? My decision is for you to get out of my house!' She wrenched the door open. 'Or I'll call the police!'

He stared at her for several moments, towering over her, and his breathing matched her own, then he shook his head. 'I do not want to fight with you.'

'I don't want to fight with you either,' she said and she shoved at his chest. 'Get out of my house! Right now!'

She didn't think he was going to go. And she hated that there was a very small part of her that didn't want him to go, that wanted him to stay and fight and plead with her. To apologise for what he'd done, or tried to do. To take it all back and say he didn't hate her family, that he wasn't actively working to bring down her brother and father's commercial interests.

But that was a very, very small part. Most of Amelia diSalvo hated Antonio Ferrara with every single bone in her body in that moment and couldn't wait to see the back of him.

'This isn't over,' he said, but it was soft, almost apologetic, and then he stalked out of the door and, she hoped, out of her life.

* * *

Antonio wasn't surprised to receive a call from Carlo diSalvo the next day, but he was surprised at the effect the call had on him.

He could not speak to Carlo without thinking of Amelia, and the way her body had responded to his. He couldn't close his eyes without seeing her tiny cottage and the fairy lights she'd decorated almost every surface with—and there was something so *her* about that design choice.

'You're a bastard,' Carlo snapped down the phone line. 'Did you really think I wouldn't find out?'

Antonio stared at the view of London he had from his penthouse, Mayfair sprawling with all its Georgian beauty before him, opening up to a verdant Hyde Park. 'I didn't much care,' Antonio said, not completely honest. Because he *did* care about something.

Amelia.

It was ridiculous, but he hadn't been able to get her out of his head since leaving Bumblebee Cottage the night before. Nor could he shake the feeling that, for the first time in his life, he might not have handled things in the best possible way. He hadn't achieved his aim, and he'd made things monumentally more difficult by sleeping with the enemy.

'So what's your plan?' Carlo demanded, switching to his native Italian.

Antonio followed him effortlessly. 'To destroy you. No, to do more than destroy you. I will eviscerate you. I will take everything you care about and destroy it, just for the satisfaction of seeing you suffer. My life has become a testament to your ruination.'

Carlo cursed down the phone line. 'You actually think you'll be able to succeed in that?'

'It is already done,' Antonio said, a wolfish smile spreading across his features. He disconnected the call and pushed all thoughts of Amelia from his mind. Sleeping with her hadn't been part of the plan, but that didn't matter. It was beside the point, just like he'd said to her. Sex had nothing to do with business, and this business was something he'd spent long years planning for.

He scrolled to his personal lawyer's number and held the phone to his ear.

'Herrera,' he spoke without preamble when the call connected. 'I need to see you. It's about the diSalvo situation.' He reclined in his chair, staring straight ahead and seeing only the gleam of success. The satisfaction of long-awaited revenge.

And the pair of big blue eyes that haunted him as he told his lawyer to begin tanking diSalvo interests?

They were just eyes—he would forget them soon enough. He would forget her too. Because nothing mattered more than righting the wrongs of the past. Nothing, and no one. For his father, he would succeed.

CHAPTER FIVE

AMELIA STARED AT the name across the foyer, emblazoned in solid gold letters: Herrera Inc. Her tummy was in knots as she waited in the echoing silence.

Not knots of anxiety, she hastened to remind herself. Knots of anger. Fury. Panic. Disbelief that six weeks after spending the night with a wolf in sheep's clothing—or no clothing, as the case had been—it had been necessary to fly to Spain and wait in his office on a day that was hot and sticky, when she would have far preferred to be home in her lovely little cottage with only her books and an enormous pot of tea for company.

She'd thought about calling him and breaking the news to him over the phone. It would have been satisfying to have the power to deliver the life-changing words and then disconnect the call, letting him stew on the discovery as she had been for almost a week. But this wasn't news one delivered over the phone, and she'd accepted that, even when it meant she would need to see Antonio once more.

Her face was pale and, though she didn't realise it, the immaculate secretary of Antonio Herrera was watching her from beneath hooded eyes.

'He won't be much longer, madam,' the woman assured her.

Did she really look that bad?

She'd mostly escaped the dreaded morning sickness, but of course it had reared its head that morning and she'd been feeling queasy all day.

She'd be better once this part was over. She had a plan, and it was simple.

Antonio, I'm pregnant, but I'm sure you won't want any part of the pregnancy or the baby's life, given that it's the devil's spawn.

Or, *Antonio, I'm pregnant, and you can't offer any amount of money that will induce me to sell this baby to you. Not everything is for sale.*

Then there was the option where she just blurted names at him, every single one she could think of, obscenities and curses, in all the languages she knew.

She ground her teeth together, her hand curled around the strap of her bag, her mouth dry. She thought about getting another cup of water from the dispenser, but she must have already drunk a litre since arriving in his office almost an hour earlier.

If he'd known she was coming, she would have blamed him for keeping her waiting. But she'd intentionally used a fake name to see him, pretending to be a journalist writing an opinion piece for a broadsheet newspaper. Eventually the assistant had cracked, offering a fifteen-minute slot. But apparently Antonio viewed journalists with disdain, if his inability to stick to the schedule was anything to go by.

Another fifteen minutes later and the door cracked open. A man emerged first—not Antonio. Blond, with green eyes and tanned skin, wearing a suit but looking like he'd much prefer to be in board shorts and riding a wave. When he spoke, it was with an American accent. 'Great to see you again, brother.' He grinned, and he was film-star-handsome. Sigh…

Damned hormones. She stood up, knowing Antonio's appearance was imminent and that the last thing she wanted was to be at a height disadvantage from the outset. Strength was imperative, even when it was simply a fraud.

Sure enough, a moment later he was in the doorway,

only he wasn't alone. A young boy was in his arms—only four or five, she guessed, but with the unmistakable facial features of a child born with Down's Syndrome. And the young boy was smiling at Antonio as though he were the second coming.

'You give your mother a high five from me, okay?'

And the little boy, on cue, lifted his hand and whacked it against Antonio's. 'Again!'

Antonio laughed, his eyes crinkling in the corners, and obliged, and Amelia had to dig her fingernails into her palms to stop from reacting.

Hormones! Tears were stinging her eyes suddenly at the sight of this man she *hated,* who happened to be the father of her baby, looking so perfectly at home with children. She blinked the tears away, assuming a look of passive impatience that was at odds with the lurching in her gut. And she felt it, the moment his eyes began to move to hers.

She glared at him, her expression icy.

'Amelia?' He looked genuinely surprised, and she was glad.

His friend followed Antonio's gaze and then reached for the little boy.

'We'll get out of your hair, man. Just don't leave it long before you get out to Venice Beach, yeah?'

Antonio didn't respond. He was staring at Amelia, not speaking, simply looking. Did he think he could intimidate her? That he could make her feel anything at all any more?

She squared her shoulders and straightened her spine, staring at him with all the disdain she felt.

He'd used her.

He'd come to her house and charmed her into bed and she'd fallen in with his plans like the naïve, innocent fool she was, and hadn't she learned her lesson? The reason she'd kept men like this at bay her whole life had unravelled before her.

The blond man and child left, the latter waving enthusiastically at Antonio as he went. But Antonio didn't notice. His gaze was fixed squarely on Amelia.

After several moments, he crossed the foyer, his stride long, and in that time he pulled himself together.

'I didn't realise you were in Madrid,' he said conversationally, as though they communicated regularly and she had simply omitted to mention the detail.

'I came to see you,' she said, glad when he didn't hold a hand out to shake hers, nor attempt to kiss her cheek. There was ice between them now.

'Really?' He arched a brow and she wanted to slap him then, and his smug assumption that she'd come for personal reasons. For sexual reasons.

Her glare, she hoped, would put paid to any such ideas.

'I presume you have an office in which we might speak privately?'

'Of course,' he murmured throatily, putting a hand in the small of her back.

And trumpets flared in her mind, bleating 'hallelujah' at the simple touch and she ground her teeth together in utter rejection of that. 'I'm quite capable of walking, thank you very much,' she said flatly and stepped to the side, away from him.

She only just caught the look of bemusement on his secretary's face before she spun on her heel and stalked towards his office.

So she was still furious with him, obviously. But she was here, in his office, and he had to think it had something to do with Prim'Aqua. No doubt the moves he was making against Carlo were starting to worry her family—and so they should. So had she chosen to come to him, like a lion to the slaughter? To beg him to back off?

It was pretty obvious she hadn't turned up in Madrid

looking for round two of their off-the-charts sexual chemistry. His body jerked with disappointment because, no matter what he told himself about that night, there was a reason it had been tormenting his dreams.

Physically, they made some strange kind of sense.

Their bodies had moved as though they'd been designed for one another, but that meant nothing. Sex was sex. He walked a pace behind her, hating that he was staring at her as though she was a dessert on a buffet, knowing he could hardly stop himself.

Instead of the jeans and casual shirt she'd been wearing that night at Bumblebee Cottage, she'd chosen a pair of sleek black pants and a silk blouse that was a dangerous reminder of the robe she'd pulled on after her bath. She wore heels too, thin and spindly, giving her an extra few inches of height.

She'd dressed up.

For him?

At the door to his office she stepped aside, waiting. He pushed the door open then held it for her, noting with what he wished was amusement that she gave him as wide a berth as the doorway allowed.

His office was everything she'd expected. Just like her father's. And her brother's. And no doubt all the other dictatorial, selfish corporate tycoons who ruled the finance world. Enormous, with huge windows that framed a stunning view, impressive oak desk, state-of-the-art computer screens, a wall-mounted smart TV for conferences, a boardroom table of shiny timber surrounded by leather chairs, and white leather sofas. Different materials perhaps, but the same essence as the offices she'd been in before.

There were some indications of his personal taste. A black and white photograph of the Millau Viaduct, a small pottery *toro* on his desk, a stunning modern sculpture that was gunmetal grey and silver, and utterly striking.

She ignored these details though, and all the ostentatious signs of wealth, placing her handbag on a chair and turning to face him.

And she felt as if she'd been kicked in the gut.

God, he was handsome.

So handsome, with eyes that were laced with enquiry and hair that she ached to run her fingers through.

Stupid, stupid traitorous body.

Pushing any such thoughts from her mind, she tried to summon the words she'd prepared.

'Would you like a drink?'

Her stomach heaved at the very suggestion. 'No.' The word was abrupt, and she winced. 'No, thank you,' she corrected softly.

She paced to the window overlooking Madrid and stared out at the ancient city. In the distance, she could see a slice of Gaudí poking impishly from behind a far more sensible high rise, and she was reminded of a child hiding around the corner, awaiting a scolding. Gaudí's irreverence was one of her favourite things about Spain.

'Well,' he said quietly, and the word ran down her spine like warm honey. 'What can I do for you, Amelia?'

Her name on his lips tripped her heart up a thousand gears and she took a steadying breath, reminding herself that she was in control of her body, not the other way around.

When she hadn't spoken, after a moment, he said, 'I have an appointment any minute.'

'No, you don't.' She swallowed. 'I'm your appointment.'

When she turned to face him, she could see he was analysing this, examining her statement for meaning. 'You pretended to be a journalist, simply to see me again?'

She nodded crisply.

'Why not just give my assistant your name?'

'Because I took a perverse pleasure in surprising you,' she said honestly, and was rewarded with the hint of a smile at the corners of his lips.

It was too familiar—too familiar for what they were to one another, and what they'd shared. Theirs had been no love story; it had been two strangers in a thunderstorm. She'd been caught up in the romance—the storm had raged and he'd arrived, offering refuge from a clawing sense of isolation. She'd been a means to an end for him, her virginity unimportant collateral in his quest to draw her under his spell.

'You have surprised me,' he agreed.

You haven't seen anything yet, she thought to herself with a wry shake of her head.

Was she really going to do this?

Of course! What was the alternative? Have his baby and never tell him? Just like her mother had done to her father?

No way would her baby know the pain of that. Amelia had grown up with no idea who her father was—half the time she wasn't even sure her mother knew. She'd been a secret baby, a shameful love-child, unwanted, an accident, and there was no way her baby would ever grow up feeling like she had.

And didn't Antonio deserve to know? Not just for the sake of their baby, but because this was his baby too?

Amelia might not have liked what had happened with her and Antonio; she certainly didn't like the fact that he'd come to her cottage and seduced her without telling her they were part of an ancient blood feud, then expected her to hand over thirty per cent of a family business to him, but he was still a person. A person with inalienable rights. A man who would soon become a father and of course he deserved to know that.

Heaven help her if he decided he wanted to be a part of the child's life on a regular basis, because that would mean she would also have to see him too, she supposed.

But Amelia doubted he'd want much to do with their child. It would be, after all, a diSalvo.

The thought had her tilting her chin, her eyes sparking defiantly with his. 'This won't take long,' she assured him, thinking gratefully of the return flight she'd booked for later that same day.

'Go on,' he encouraged, perching his bottom on the edge of the desk, stretching his long legs in front of him, crossed at the ankles.

She ignored the throb low in her abdomen, the instant recognition of power and strength, the memory of how those legs had held her to the wall, pinning her with total ease, or straddled her body as he moved inside her. She looked away, her mouth dry. 'Perhaps I will have some water,' she said, stalking across the room to where the drinks were set up. She poured a small glass with hands that weren't quite steady and sipped from it, then shut her eyes as her stomach instantly rejected the offering.

Damn it. She pressed her fingertips to the bench, blinking, willing her insides to calm down, not to be ill. Not here! Not now!

'At the risk of appearing rude, I don't have all day.'

It was exactly what she needed to bring herself back to the moment. She spun around, then wished she hadn't when the room swayed a little. 'You're so far past appearing rude,' she promised firmly. 'And I won't take much of your time.'

His eyes were studying her and she hated that. She hated that he could probably read every emotion that crossed her face, every feeling that was shredding her insides.

'Go on,' he prompted.

'Don't rush me.'

His laugh was sardonic. 'You just told me this won't take long.'

'Yes, well, it doesn't help when you're staring at me as though you'd like to...'

* * *

She didn't finish the sentence but that didn't stop the immediate flash of desire in response to her suggestion. His expression softened as he allowed himself to do exactly what she'd said—to stare at her openly, to run his gaze over her body, remembering it precisely, and then lift to meet her eyes.

'I'm staring at you,' he corrected finally, 'like a man wanting a woman to get to the point.'

That wasn't completely true. Like Scheherazade's King, he was willing her to spin out a story to elongate this encounter.

He was, frankly, still reeling from the fact she was here, in his office. In the weeks after that night, he'd thought about calling her. Hell, he'd contemplated flying back to England, driving to Bumblebee Cottage and demanding she listen to him—ideally in bed.

If she understood the nature of their families' dispute, perhaps she'd look more sympathetically on his offer.

But he'd done neither in the end. Because he couldn't think of seeing her again without seeing her as she'd been that night. The look of betrayal and hurt on her face had made him feel, almost for the first time in his life, ashamed.

And he'd hated that.

So he'd relegated her to the back of his mind, to his 'past', and told himself he'd forget about her.

Because she was a diSalvo, and what point was there in trying to get her to forgive him?

There were more issues between them than a simple one-night stand.

Wrong thought. Wrong thought. His mind threw up the memories and he sank into them, remembering her body, the sounds she'd made as pleasure had caressed her, the way she had kissed him as if her very life depended on it.

'Have you reconsidered?' he prompted, thinking of his more than generous deal to buy her shares in Prim'Aqua—and the way he was deliberately tanking diSalvo interests around the globe. Did she know?

'No—' she narrowed her eyes '—my shares aren't for sale. And I don't think you'll be able to do anything to hurt Carlo either. He's very shrewd, great at what he does. You're no threat to him.'

Antonio almost smiled. She wasn't the first person to underestimate him, but truly she couldn't be more wrong.

'We'll see.' He shrugged with the appearance of calm.

Her eyes narrowed and he had the sense that she was analysing him now, looking for hidden meanings. 'You really hate my family, don't you?'

He expelled a soft breath. 'Is it any wonder?'

Her neck moved delicately as she swallowed, and he realised suddenly that she looked tired. Beneath the make-up she wore—another change since the night in Bumblebee Cottage—he detected the hint of darkening beneath her eyes and a pallor that hadn't been there before.

'So that night, when we slept together, you knew that we could never be more than that one experience?'

The question floored him. But only for a moment—he was Antonio Ferrera and he recovered quickly. 'Do you want it to be more?'

She pulled a face and her answer dripped with sarcasm. 'Yeah, right.'

He smirked to cover his irritation. He didn't like the ease with which she rejected that suggestion. Hell, at that moment he could barely remember that she was a diSalvo, let alone muster enough enthusiasm for their rivalry to care. She was simply Amelia and he was hungry—starving—for her.

'So you are not here to sell me your stake in Prim'Aqua,' he said, straightening, pushing off the desk and taking a stride towards her. 'And you say you are not here to rekindle what we shared that night.' Another stride, bringing him level with her, and the sweetness of her scent almost had him reaching for her and kissing her. How he wanted to relive that experience!

But every line of her body was a warning and a rejection. She was mentally distancing herself from him and he hated that.

'So why have you come?'

Amelia clamped her lips together and dug her fingernails into her palms and she stared at him and reminded herself that he was just a man! There was no need to feel so anxious! Besides, she was absolutely certain he wouldn't want to be a part of her life—or her child's.

'You look pale,' he added with a frown, and inwardly she groaned. She'd done her best to hide the evidence of the past few weeks, but apparently hadn't succeeded.

Some women glowed when they were pregnant and it seemed Amelia wasn't going to be one of them. This very recent bout of nausea combined with a sudden insomnia—no doubt brought on by the realisation she had to tell the father of her baby that she was pregnant—had left her looking drained.

'How I look is hardly relevant,' she murmured.

His frown was infinitesimal. 'Are you sick?'

'Yes, in a sense,' she said, and an urge to laugh, maniacally, overcame her. She ignored it with effort and reached for her water glass once more.

It wasn't that she was afraid of him, but she knew that once she spoke these words aloud, her world would change for ever. Up to this point, she hadn't mentioned her state to a soul, and she'd been allowing herself time to absorb the news and make her own plans.

She had decided she would need to have her own wishes

firmly in place before meeting Antonio. This was her baby, her body, her life and, while she knew she had a moral obligation to inform him of her pregnancy, she sure as hell wasn't going to let him think he had any right to weigh in on the situation.

'I don't like you,' she said, her eyes locking to his with a defiance that underscored her feelings. 'I think you're cold-hearted, ruthless and manipulative.'

He didn't visibly react, save for a slight tightening around his jaw.

'Go on.'

'You're a Ferrera and I'm part of the diSalvo family, but this is hardly some real-life *Romeo and Juliet* situation. I have no interest in being dragged into a crazy feud that should have ended two generations ago.'

'It is your brother who sought to ruin—'

She lifted a hand to silence him and though he obliged, closing his mouth, his eyes sparked with hers, his impatience obvious.

'He did something. You did something back. What a waste of energy—for both of you!' she denounced scathingly. 'You could have stopped at shoring up your own business interests. But you didn't. Instead of taking the high road, you've sought to ruin him right back. And there's no way I will *ever* be a party to that.'

Antonio's expression tightened further. There was a look of such ruthless determination in his features that many people might have been afraid. Not Amelia. She'd come up against arrogance and cold-hearted ruthlessness before. No, now, she was angry!

'You made this position clear already,' he said finally, the words cold and more heavily accented than usual.

'True. But I feel the need to underscore it.'

'For what purpose?' he demanded. 'Our business together was concluded six weeks ago. There is nothing to be gained from you being here now.'

Her eyes narrowed and for the briefest of moments she thought about leaving. How much easier it would all be if she were to turn on her heel and stalk out of his office, insisting that he never contact her again!

But how could she live with herself? A baby wasn't something you could hide—she was living proof. To know that she'd spent twelve years being raised with her parentage a mystery, that her father had had no idea of her existence. What had they both been denied? Would she have had an actual *family* if her mother had made a different decision?

Memories and past hurts had her straightening her spine, staring at him with renewed intent.

'I'll go soon,' she promised. 'In fact, I'm booked on a flight in a few hours,' she added for good measure, liking the safety and security that fact offered.

His frown was one of non-comprehension. 'You're flying commercial?'

At this, Amelia rolled her eyes. 'As opposed to?'

'DiSalvo Industries has many planes...'

She angled her face away from his. He was right. She could have flown in a private jet, but that wasn't—and never had been—Amelia's style. 'What an environmental nightmare,' she stated disapprovingly. 'Any billionaire gets a whim to go here or there and they power up their own plane, when there are dozens of flights scheduled to that same destination every day.'

'But then you have to fit in with someone else's schedule,' he pointed out with infuriating logic—and despicable arrogance.

'Oh, heaven forbid a little inconvenience.' They were getting off-topic and she didn't particularly want to stand in Antonio's office, arguing the merits of flight timetables with him.

'My schedule allows very little room for flexibility,' he said with an arrogant shrug of his shoulders.

And now Amelia did laugh, just a soft, panicked noise of utter disbelief. 'You're going to hate this, then.' Babies were the very definition of inconvenience, and this one particularly so, given how little either of them could have expected her pregnancy.

'Hate what?' He was wary.

When it came to it, there was no need for any preamble. Like ripping off a Band-Aid, she was simply going to tell him—to get it over with and then go home. With a deep breath and a voice that shook ever so slightly, she said into the silence: 'I'm pregnant, Antonio. And you're the father.'

CHAPTER SIX

'THAT IS IMPOSSIBLE.' His arrogant assertion was the last thing she expected and in other circumstances she might have found that amusing.

'Oh, okay,' she murmured sarcastically. 'Have it your way, then. I'm not pregnant.'

She glared at him, her arms crossed over her body, her expression one of disdain.

'You *can't* be,' he corrected, and Amelia almost felt sorry for him, because Antonio Ferrera didn't strike her as a man who was used to having things happen beyond his control. 'We used protection.'

'Well, you're the only man I've ever slept with and I am most definitely pregnant.' She pinpointed him with an icy glare. 'So I guess it didn't work.'

He was uncharacteristically lost for words.

'Anyway,' she said after a moment's silence, 'I thought you should at least know.' He remained silent. 'But you should also know that I don't need anything from you. I have the financial means to raise this child without worry, and I will be a good mum, all on my own.' She stiffened then, her spine straightening as she forced herself to finish the offer she came willing to extend. 'You may, of course, choose to be involved, if you'd like.' She let that sentiment hit its mark before barrelling forward. 'But I understand why that would be difficult for you and I'm okay—more than okay—with that. This is my baby. You don't have to worry about it.'

'I see.' He seemed to have relocated his voice. He spoke crisply and, though it was a genial enough agreement, it filled Amelia with a sense of wariness because she could feel a 'but' coming. 'And do you think I will let you return to England to have my child? And what, confer upon it your surname? Raise my son or daughter as a diSalvo?'

At that, a surge of anger beat inside her and she pushed at his chest, surprising them both with the violent outburst. 'Don't you dare draft my baby into this damned feud!' she exploded. 'Yes, this child will be a diSalvo because it's *my* child! But I won't be raising it to hate the Ferrera name, so you can relax.'

His expression was one of barely concealed fury.

'And as for you "letting" me do anything, I have a newsflash for you, Antonio. I don't answer to you. I'll leave when I want to leave, and there's not a damned thing you can do about it.'

Her threat was a gauntlet that she really shouldn't have issued. Because he wasn't afraid to run it. Hell, he was relishing the prospect of running it, in fact, and unsettling her attitude of unconcern. As though she could tell him she was pregnant and then waltz out of his life once more! Pregnant, and with his baby.

'You know, there's not even a legal requirement for me to tell you about this,' she continued, apparently oblivious to how close his patience was to fraying.

'And yet you're here,' he snapped.

She opened her mouth and then clamped it shut, before nodding. 'I thought you should know.'

'Thank heavens for small mercies,' he murmured, stalking away from her towards his desk, where he pressed a red button on his phone. 'Cancel my afternoon schedule,' he clipped and then disconnected the call before his assistant could respond.

'You don't need to do that,' Amelia muttered, a hint of panic flaring in her expression now. 'As I said, I'm flying home soon.'

'We have to discuss this,' he murmured, bracing his palms on his desk and dipping his head forward. The reality of this hit him in the solar plexus and a strange metallic taste filled his mouth. Adrenalin. Fight or flight.

He'd tasted it before: when his father had been staring down the barrel of bankruptcy and Antonio had known it was all down to him. That he alone could save his father's legacy: that he alone could salvage the ruins of the once-great Herrera Incorporated.

And he felt that again now. Fight or flight responsibility.

This was his baby, but she was offering him an out. She didn't want him to be involved. She didn't need him.

And God knew he didn't want to have a child. Not now, probably not ever, and sure as hell not with a diSalvo.

But when he lifted his gaze to Amelia, the door to escape swung closed.

Wanted or not, this baby was reality and there was no way he was going to ignore that.

'I intend to raise my child, *querida*,' he said, the words forged from iron.

It was obvious that she had not been expecting that. She took a small step backwards and made a sound of confusion, then shook her head from side to side. 'But…you… Didn't you hear me? You don't have to be involved. You don't need to have anything to do with him.'

'Do you truly believe that? This is my child and, while it is far from ideal that you are to be the mother, it does not change the fact that my flesh and blood is growing in your belly.'

'Gee, thanks. I'm so warm and fuzzy right now,' she clipped.

He ignored her ironic assertion. 'Obviously there is only one solution to this situation.'

'I swear, if you'd said "problem" I would have walked straight out of here.' And then her eyes flew wide and a slim hand lifted to her mouth, covering a gasp. 'You can't be serious?'

'Completely.'

Her face paled—if that was possible, and she staggered back once more. Then a hand came to curve protectively over her still-flat stomach. 'You can't actually expect me to terminate my pregnancy just because you don't want to have a child with a diSalvo?'

Her words seemed to come from a long way away, and took even longer to process. 'What?' he said eventually. And though his English was perfect, he presumed he must have misunderstood something in the translation.

'You want me to have an abortion? How *dare* you? I came here as a courtesy, to tell you that you're going to be a father and that I will allow you to be some part of our child's life and you actually try to bully me into getting rid of our baby?'

She sent one final glare in his direction and then strode purposefully towards the door. She grabbed her bag from a chair as she went and it took Antonio vital seconds to process both her accusation and the certainty that she was about to walk away from him.

He moved quickly, reaching the door first and putting his back against it.

'Move,' she demanded, not meeting his eyes.

And, heaven help him, he knew tears weren't far away for Amelia and he fought a ridiculous urge to comfort her. That was not who or what they were.

'I was not talking about an abortion,' he said in a tone that was carefully wiped clear of emotion.

'Then what exactly did you mean? What "solution" is there to this?'

'We'll get married.'

The relief that had glanced across her features was swallowed by another look of abject panic.

'You're kidding?'

'Do I look like I am kidding?'

'No,' she said, 'but you must be *crazy* if you think I would *ever* marry you.'

'It was not a suggestion,' he said, moving away from the door and returning to his desk.

It was a calculated risk—she would either leave, now he'd given her the opportunity, or she would stay.

And Antonio's instincts, finely honed through his experience in business and trade, told him that she would stay and fight. Because Amelia was not a coward, and she was also not a fool. She might be pregnant with his baby but he held all the trump cards. The perfect bargaining chip to get everything he wanted. Not just their baby, his heir, but Prim'Aqua as well. A primal sense of accomplishment made him want to roar like an animal in the jungle. He pictured his father, pictured all he'd lost, the grief he'd known, and he swept his eyes shut for a moment and simply breathed it in: the certainty that all was about to be righted, once and for all.

'And why is that?' she asked: he'd been right. She wasn't running. She was staying, because she knew as well as he did that this marriage was inevitable.

He took his time, savouring the moment, and then delivered the final blow to her insistence that marriage was a bad idea. 'Because if you don't marry me you know I will destroy your brother once and for all.'

She drew in a sharp breath but then seemed to rally. 'You *wish* you could do that. But you forget, Antonio, I've had time since that night to think, and I've told Carlo about you. He knows what you're up to, and he's not worried.'

'No, he doesn't,' Antonio said simply.

Amelia's eyes narrowed. 'What do you mean?'

'Come and see.'

She glared at him, as though moving close to him was the last thing she wanted.

But Antonio simply loaded up a spreadsheet on his computer and waited with a veneer of patience. Sure enough, a moment later, accompanied by a heavy sigh, Amelia closed the distance between them, pausing just behind him.

'What am I looking at?' she demanded.

'How much of your family's portfolio I have absorbed over the years,' he said, running his own eyes over the spreadsheet with a sense of triumph.

It was all laid out in simple black and white and it painted a stark picture. Several of the companies, if he clicked on them, would show dramatically declining stock prices.

He heard her breathing change, grow faster, and he closed his eyes for a moment before flicking off the computer screen.

In the reflection, his eyes met hers.

'You're saying,' she asked quietly, 'that you'll leave Carlo alone if I marry you?'

Antonio was at a fork in the road. The anger he had felt for a long time was balanced against a child he was determined to raise, and he found he couldn't turn his back on either. 'No,' he said, standing and surprising her by being right there, so close they were almost touching. 'I'm saying that if you marry me and hand over your Prim'Aqua shares, I will leave his remaining businesses alone.'

Indignation shaped her features as the full force of his words sunk in. 'You're blackmailing me?'

He made a sound of disagreement. 'I am offering you a chance to potentially save your brother from financial ruin,' he corrected. 'And I am offering us both a chance to raise our baby as a family, which is, surely, your preference?'

'My preference is never to see you again.'

He arched a thick dark brow. 'Let us stick to the realm of reality, hmm?'

She turned away from him and he fought an urge to lift his fingers to her chin and angle her face back to his. He didn't like it when she hid her expressive face. 'I will *never* give you those shares.'

Determination flashed in the depths of his black eyes. 'Then I will continue to destroy your brother in other ways. And believe me, Amelia, I do nothing by half measures.' He slashed his hand through the air to emphasise his point. 'Already I have wiped half a billion dollars off the value of his business interests—in a little over a month. What do you think I will have achieved by the year's end?'

She drew in a sharp gasp and lifted her face to his. 'You can't be serious?'

'Does it look as though I am joking?'

He was a study in humourless, dark intent.

'But…why?'

'Because I hate him,' he said through gritted teeth. 'And because he deserves this.'

She swept her eyes shut and his gut fired with adrenalin.

'A week after I turned eighteen, I came home from college to discover my father crying.' Sympathy clouded Amelia's expression. 'He'd lost everything—because of your father and your brother. A liquidator had been approached to step in. I honestly believe he wanted to end his life rather than live with the shame of his bankruptcy.'

Pink bloomed in her cheeks. 'I'm sorry he experienced that.'

His eyes lifted to hers, firing with the same strength that had led him then. 'I took over the company that same day. Bit by bit I rebuilt it. It was not easy, *querida,* and it did not happen fast. Every day when I woke up and stared down the barrel of uncertainty and doubt, when I knew my father's life and pride were riding on my success, I swore that I would win. And that I would make your brother pay for what he'd almost done.'

Amelia drew in a sharp breath.

'I hate him.'

'I can see that,' she whispered unevenly. 'But that doesn't give you the right to ruin his life…'

'*He* gave me the right.' Antonio closed his eyes for a moment and he was back in the past, remembering the bleakness in his father's eyes that night, many years earlier.

'He made an enemy of me long ago, and nothing will change that.'

'You talk like this about my brother,' she said stiffly, 'yet you actually expect me to marry you?'

'Yes.' His answer was instantaneous.

'And you'd be happy with the fact you're blackmailing me into it?' she countered, her eyes narrowed. 'You haven't even asked how I'm feeling. You haven't asked about the baby, the due date, nothing! You are heartless and selfish and so damned focused on revenge against my family that you don't even see me as a flesh and blood woman, do you?'

At that, his eyes flared and every cell in his body that was noticing only her womanly self pushed him forward. 'You ask if I see you as a woman?' he demanded fiercely, and now he cupped her cheeks and held her mesmerised face still. His voice was gravelly when he spoke. 'You think I don't want you even now, in the midst of all this?'

Her eyes lowered and he could feel the rushing of her blood; he could see the way she was as affected by this as he.

'That's not what I meant,' she whispered after a moment, but his words were turning her blood into lava. 'You don't see me as a person with my own desires and wants, as someone who deserves to be able to steer her own fate; to make her own decisions.'

'Of course you can decide,' he contradicted gently. 'But one of those choices is better for everyone.'

'Another ultimatum,' she grunted.

He sighed and dropped his hands, walking a few paces clear of her, to where the air was less thick with Amelia-ness and he could think a little straighter.

'Fine,' he said. 'Let us look at this differently. The circumstances of our meeting were unfortunate.'

She snorted her agreement.

'But I am not actually a bad person.'

Her eyes rolled heavenwards and when she spoke her words dripped with scathing sarcasm. 'You're determined to ruin the only family I have.'

'I am *determined*,' he corrected coldly, 'to be a father to this baby. Why can't we create a new family? Yes, I'm a Herrera and you're a diSalvo, but we are also a mother and a father now. I want us to live together and to raise this baby side by side, giving it everything we can in life. Tell me this is not what you want, Amelia. Tell me you don't want our child to grow up with a loving mother and father always at hand.'

The words were dangerous because they were so, so achingly true.

Her own childhood flashed before her eyes. The absence of any kind of family structure or regular home, the absence of time and love and affection. A mother who saw Amelia at times as an inconvenience and at others as a pet, and eventually an accessory, when Amelia was old enough, at eleven, to be dragged to parties that were, in hindsight, woefully inappropriate for a girl on the cusp of womanhood.

The things Amelia saw at her mother's side! The drugged-out state of various guests, the orgies, spectacular fist fights. More than once she'd had to call an ambulance when someone had become so high they were a danger to themselves or others. Then there were the nightclubs, when Penny would park Amelia with the bouncers and she'd listen to them swearing and ogling women all night—it was a wonder she'd reached adulthood with any semblance of normality.

In the midst of it all, she had desperately wanted someone who would just be *average. Boring.* Someone who would read her books and make her pasta for dinner, who would take her to the playground or on long walks, who would ask her about *her* life, her hopes, her dreams.

She had wanted a mother—and *not* a mother like Penny.

And oh, how she'd craved a father. In her mind, she'd probably idealised what role a father might take. Her knowledge had been fleshed out from the pages of her books, but she'd imagined a sort of Mr Bennet type figure, benevolent and kindly, strict when necessary.

And Antonio? What kind of father would he be to their baby?

'We hate each other,' she said quietly, trying to remind herself of all the reasons this marriage was a stupid idea. 'No child should grow up in a house where two parents can't stand one another.'

'We have more than seven months to find a way to co-exist,' he said sensibly. 'I think we can achieve that.'

'And if we can't?'

His eyes glittered with determination. 'I do not see failure as an option here, *hermosa.*'

Frustration curdled inside her. 'It would never work.'

'You cannot say that with any certainty.'

'Oh, yes, I can,' she insisted. 'You're the last man on

earth I would ever choose to marry, and it's quite clear the feeling is mutual.'

'This marriage wouldn't be about us, though,' he said simply. 'It's about giving our child a family from the moment of his birth...'

Something else occurred to Amelia and it had her fixing Antonio with a stone-cold stare. 'You just want him to have your name, don't you?' she demanded.

'Of course that matters to me.' Antonio shrugged, and she was torn between despising his motivation and admiring his honesty. 'But I would insist on his taking my name, married or not.'

She let out a sigh of exasperation. 'God, you're an old-fashioned, patriarchal jerk.'

'Perhaps,' he said with a lift of his shoulders. 'But I am also a man who wants to marry you, and I think you should think very carefully about the situation you find yourself in.'

'No way.' She shook her head but the words lacked conviction.

He moved towards the door and wrenched it inwards, his eyes holding hers with steely determination. 'Think about it,' he said simply, as though he was asking what she'd like for dinner, or which was her favourite song.

'I don't need to think about it,' she insisted, walking towards the door and pausing when she drew level with him. 'I know my answer.'

'Then think about what happens if you don't marry me.' He moved closer. 'Think about what happens if you make an enemy of me.' And, because he couldn't help himself, he leaned down and whispered into her ear, 'And think about the silver lining of a marriage between us, *querida*. Night after night in my bed as my wife...'

His words chased her all the way home, rattling around inside her shocked head. In a million years, and not for a million pounds, would she have thought Antonio Herrera would suggest marriage. He wasn't the marrying kind! And he clearly had major issues with her family! Surely it was the last thing he *wanted*.

Him? What about her?

She'd run as fast as she could from the kind of life he lived and she didn't regret that decision. Not for a moment. To marry a man like him and be swept up in his world—she'd regret it.

And yet...this baby! *Their* baby. This baby was as much his as it was hers. She had no interest in trying to pretend that wasn't the case.

This baby wasn't hypothetical. It was an actual being, a little person who would be a part of her life before she knew it. And she didn't want to look back on her baby's childhood and wish she'd done more, given him or her more. She didn't want him to feel lonely, as she had. Scared, abandoned, worried—she wanted this baby to have everything!

She wanted perfection—she wanted a fairy tale, but that was never going to be her future.

Her thoughts became a screaming choir in the background of her life. Every morning she woke with visions of Antonio filling her mind, and she heard him all day—his suggestion of marriage, his insistence that it would be best for their baby.

But she remembered his rage too. His hatred for her brother and father. His insistence that their families' feud was still very much an ongoing affair.

So when Carlo called one evening, clearly drunk and upset, she knew what it would be about even before he'd spoken.

'Jesus Christ!' he spat down the line, and then hurled several more expletives in fiery Italian. 'That bastard's done a number on me, Amelia. He's got his hands on *ev-*

erything! He's going to absolutely *ruin* me! Why didn't I realise?'

Because Antonio is very, very good at what he does, Amelia responded inwardly, her eyes swept shut as, for the millionth time since leaving Madrid, she conjured an image of the Spaniard in her mind's eye, and her body reacted predictably.

Night after night in my bed as my wife...

His words made her pulse speed up and her heart race, even now, a week after he'd whispered them like a sexy caress against her ear.

'How am I going to tell Dad I let this happen?'

Her heart sank because the plaintive note in his voice was the only thing that could have brought her to her knees. For twelve years she hadn't known she had a brother or a father, but then she'd turned up on their doorstep and they'd taken her in. They'd loved her, accepted her, and been the closest thing to a 'normal' family she'd ever known. What wouldn't she do to repay them that kindness? What wouldn't she do to protect them from this kind of grief and worry?

She soothed Carlo as best she could, placating him with hollow promises, and all the while her own future sharpened before her eyes.

When she disconnected the call some time later, Carlo was calmer but her own insides were quivering with emotion.

There was also a kernel of strength. She was resolute.

Because the answer to all her concerns was staring her in the face and she could—and would—be brave enough to admit that.

She could marry Antonio and she could give their child a family and a home, and the stability she'd never, ever had. She could give their baby the start in life she wanted, and that he or she deserved.

And she could solve Carlo's worries for good. At least she thought she could.

She would marry Antonio, but only if he agreed to her rules. Because Amelia diSalvo wasn't a fool, and Antonio was going to learn that the hard way…

CHAPTER SEVEN

'TWICE IN ONE WEEK—lucky me,' he murmured, crossing the marble floor of the foyer, his eyes fixed on Amelia diSalvo. As with the last time she'd come to his office in Madrid, she'd dressed to impress, this time in a pair of white trousers and a simple silk camisole top, pale blue in colour. Gold bangles covered one wrist, so many that they ran towards her elbows. Her skin had the hint of a tan and her face was sparingly made-up. He took his time studying her appearance, not least because he sensed her impatience and enjoyed provoking that reaction in her.

'Antonio—' her voice was clipped, her eyes cold with a silent warning '—can we speak?'

He tilted his head in silent agreement and gestured with his hand towards his office. She shot him one last look, a wary appraisal and a warning all wrapped into one, and then she walked ahead of him, just like the last time she'd been here.

As he passed his secretary he said, 'Hold my calls. No interruptions.'

'Yes, sir.'

Yes, sir. That was the response he was accustomed to. He spoke and people listened. His suggestions were universally obeyed because his suggestions made sense. Because he knew what he was doing. Because he was Antonio Herrera.

That seemed to hold little sway with Amelia, however. She didn't wait on the threshold of his office this time. She pushed the door open and walked inside, so that when he joined her she was pouring two glasses of water.

'I take it you've reconsidered my proposal,' he murmured and she jerked her face towards his, her eyes zipping with resentment and anger.

'I've reconsidered it and reconsidered it again a thousand times,' she muttered. 'In fact, right now I'm wondering what the hell I'm doing here.'

He waited. There were times for arguing and convincing, and there were times for simply being silent and letting a person explain their mindset. This was a time for the latter.

'*If* we were to get married…' she said

Something in his chest heaved with relief. No—not relief. It was a sense of victory that flared in his gut, because she was going to agree with his suggestion after all. This was her own version of *Yes, sir*.

'I would have some rules.'

'I see,' he murmured, unconcerned. The war was about to be won—so what if there were final skirmishes? 'Go on.'

She nodded, but there was anxiety in her features. 'This wouldn't be a normal marriage,' she said, a small frown creasing her brow. 'We don't like each other. We don't even know each other. But if the whole purpose of it is to give our child a family, we'd have to…redress that.'

He was silent.

'I mean, we would need to get to know one another—make an effort to be civil.'

That was simple enough. He nodded his agreement.

Her eyes narrowed, and he saw something beyond her anxiety. A steeliness that he hadn't expected.

'And, to that end, you'd need to give up whatever you're doing with Carlo's business interests.'

His eyes narrowed imperceptibly and danger whipped through the air. 'I will not do that.'

'Then I can't marry you,' she said firmly, crossing her arms over her chest in a classic gesture of rejection. 'So we might as well start talking about custody.'

He held a hand up, his nostrils flaring. 'You would honestly be happy to give up without even trying?'

He noticed the way his accusation landed; she winced, her face scrunching up, and she looked away from him. 'I'm here, aren't I?'

A familiar rush of victory throbbed inside Antonio. 'Yes.'

'But I can't marry a man who hates my brother and my father. They're—' her voice cracked unexpectedly '—they're important to me.'

He couldn't help the snort of derision. 'So much so you change your name and hide from them in England?'

'I'm not hiding from them!' she retorted swiftly. 'I'm… living my own life. And is it any wonder? With men like you waiting for me as part of the diSalvo legacy?'

He ground his teeth together, refusing to analyse why her words bothered him. 'Fine. You love them. I hate them. That doesn't matter.' He slashed his hand through the air. 'Our baby is separate to that.'

Her expression was pure exasperation. 'Our baby is separate to that? You can't seriously—'

'What?' he demanded, waiting for her to finish her sentence.

'You're like a child,' she snapped, lifting her fingertips to her temple and rubbing.

He might have laughed were it not for how ludicrous her statement was. No one had ever called him childish. Even when he was a child!

'Careful, *querida*, or I might be tempted to remind you of how very adult I can be…'

He was rewarded by a hint of a blush spreading through her cheeks. 'That won't be necessary.' The words were so clipped and cold, yet he smiled. A wolfish smile, because he could see the fine tremble in her knees and the flush of her cheeks and he knew that whatever had drawn them together in the first instance was still electrifying the air between them.

'I won't raise a baby in an environment of hate.'

'Then let's not hate one another,' he proposed.

'You know what I mean,' she said, shaking her head so pale blonde hair flew around her shoulders, catching the afternoon sunlight in a way that made him think of the beach and lazy afternoons on the deck of his yacht. 'My father and brother will be a part of this child's life.'

That, he hadn't considered and the suggestion was immediately unwelcome.

'What's the baby's first birthday going to be like, with you and Carlo glaring at one another across the cake?'

'We shall have two parties.' He shrugged, as though her concern was really so easily solved.

She rolled her eyes, a habit he should have been bothered by but instead found strangely addictive. 'So you're just going to pretend my family don't exist?'

'I didn't say that,' he responded instantly.

'Oh, of course!' She slapped her palm to her forehead in an exaggerated gesture of recollection. 'You're going to be busy eviscerating them financially.'

He shrugged. 'What I do with my business has nothing to do with our child. He will not be affected by this.'

'So you won't raise him to hate all diSalvos, as you were raised?'

'I was *not* raised to hate your family,' he ground out. 'Your brother almost broke my father. Your brother, your father. This is their doing.'

'Fine,' she snapped, crossing her arms once more. 'They started it. So you can still be the bigger person and walk away.'

He narrowed his eyes. 'It's too late for that.'

She opened her mouth to say something but he shook his head, lifting a hand into the air to silence her.

'Marry me. Marry me because you want to give our child a stable family. Marry me because you know it is the right thing to do.'

She swallowed, biting into her lower lip and turning away from him, pacing over towards the windows. Madrid glistened in the distance, and her shoulders slumped forward a little as she—apparently—lost herself in contemplation. Seeing her weakening, realising he could push home his advantage, he took a step closer.

'You didn't know your father until you were a teenager. True?'

He knew it was—he'd read the file his investigator had put together.

'Yes.'

Antonio's expression tightened and something heavy landed in his gut. He'd known about his own child for a week and already he couldn't imagine what kind of man he would have to be to neglect him or her like that.

'And didn't you wish he'd been more involved in your life?' he pushed, watching the way her features visibly contracted, showing pain and hurt.

'There's no sense wishing for what's not possible,' she said with a shrug. It was an imitation of nonchalance, he could tell. He wished she'd turn to face him so he could see her eyes, see her mouth, see all of her.

'But I knew my father,' Antonio continued, his voice thick with unexpected emotion—the loss was still fresh, he supposed. 'He was a busy man but he always made time for me. He talked to me each evening, telling me stories, and on weekends we went hiking through the forest that surrounded our home. We fished in a stream and ran until our lungs threatened to burst. When I was little, if I had a nightmare, it was my father who comforted me. He was an excellent man.'

Amelia turned to face him and her eyes were like the ocean on a turbulent day. 'Why are you telling me this?'

'Because you should know what kind of father I intend to be for our child.'

Her eyes swept shut, her long silky lashes forming perfect fans against the pearly whiteness of her cheeks.

'Don't you want our child to have that?'

Her expression showed anguish when she opened her eyes, blinking to face him. 'Yes.'

He admired her for not prevaricating, and he admired her even more when she visibly pulled herself together, extinguishing the flames of anguish and assuming an expression of calm.

'Yes, I do,' she agreed more firmly, as though she were convincing herself. 'But I can't marry a man intent on destroying my family. That's obvious.'

He understood her need to negotiate on this point, but Antonio wasn't a man to give concessions. Not when it came to getting what he wanted. In a battle of wills with Amelia he would back himself every time. 'Then give me Prim'Aqua. Agree to marry me.'

'And you'll stop going after Carlo's other businesses?' she whispered, the words haunted.

He looked at her long and hard and finally nodded. 'For now.'

She frowned. 'What does that mean?'

'Only that I expect you to try to make our marriage work,' he said. 'If you don't, if you walk away from me, then the deal is off.'

Her breathing was raspy and shallow. 'You're serious?'

'Deadly.'

Her complexion paled.

'I am the father of your child, and I want to marry you.

I want the marriage to be a success because I am not used to failure, *querida*. This is what I want. What is it that you want? What matters most to you?'

Amelia blanched, his ultimatum horrifying because she already knew that she was going to agree. She pressed a hand over her stomach, and her heart squeezed at the thought of the little life growing inside her. Would it be a boy? Or a girl?

She didn't care—she just wanted a healthy, happy baby.

She turned away from Antonio—looking at him made it almost impossible to think straight—and paced towards the window. The same Gaudí was peeking back at her, this time bathed in gentle sunshine.

Antonio hated the diSalvo family, and the same could be said of Carlo and the Herreras. But her child wouldn't feel that bitterness. This child had the power to heal those breaches. Surely once their baby was born, and was an actual little person rather than a hypothetical concept, Antonio would see for himself how damaging it was to continue this ridiculous blood feud? Surely he'd wish to put paid to the last vestiges of resentment, for the sake of their child?

It was a gamble.

Because he hadn't said or done anything to give her the impression that his attitude might soften. But was it possible that over time, and as he got to know her, he would see the futility in hating Carlo the way he did? Particularly when the object of his acrimony was his own child's relatives.

She spun around, her eyes pinning him, her gaze unknowingly forceful. 'Promise me you'll…be reasonable,' she said instead.

His brows lifted upwards. 'I'm always reasonable.'

She made a scoffing noise of disbelief. 'I'm serious, Antonio.'

'As am I.'

Amelia shook her head. 'This is ridiculous. There's been nothing reasonable about how you've behaved with me. Nothing. You're the most intractable, difficult...'

'Bastard, yes, you've said this.'

She ground her teeth together. 'I'm not going to be trapped into a marriage that makes me miserable, and so far you've done nothing to show me that you're the kind of man I can even vaguely bear to be around.'

His expression was pure sensual challenge and it had the desired result. Her pulse notched up a gear and her breath burned in her lungs.

She pushed on before he could speak. 'You're asking me to marry you and stay married to you, and you're giving me nothing in return.'

'I am giving you,' he said so softly it was dangerous, 'an assurance that I will leave your brother's other business interests alone. And, believe me, Amelia, this is not a concession I make easily.'

She *could* believe it. In that moment, she felt his hatred and rage and she wondered how he'd managed to conceal those emotions so well when he'd come to the cottage.

It was so far from ideal! If only there was a way she could wrest some control back from him—show him that she wasn't going to be pushed around. 'I won't sign my shares of Prim'Aqua over to you,' she said quietly, 'until the baby is born.'

He frowned, his expression showing he didn't fully comprehend the distinction.

'Why the delay?'

'Because—' she spoke slowly, logically '—once I give you Prim'Aqua, you hold all the cards. Even if I do decide to divorce you.' She tilted her chin defiantly. 'And I will not stay with you unless I truly believe that our marriage is in the best interests of the baby. Understood?'

It was obvious from his expression that he hadn't expected a challenge on this point. He was cool and calm again almost instantly, but for a moment she saw surprise flare in his expression. What she didn't register was the look of grudging admiration. 'Fine,' he said, shrugging with apparent indifference. 'Seven months is not so long to wait.'

'And you won't touch my brother's businesses in the meantime,' she demanded, waving a single finger in the air to underscore her point. The silk of her camisole strained across her chest, emphasising the gentle curves there, so Antonio's eyes momentarily dropped lower. 'Swear you'll leave Carlo alone.'

Antonio's jaw clenched and he slowly drew his eyes back to hers in a way that set her pulse racing. 'You do not trust that I want to do what is in our child's best interests?' he asked after a moment. 'You are not the only one making a sacrifice here, *querida*. Believe it or not, marrying you is the last thing I would have wanted.'

'Gee, thanks,' she drawled sarcastically.

'Marrying *anyone*,' he corrected with a shrug of his broad shoulders.

'That makes it so much better.' She couldn't help rolling her eyes, but frustration and impotence were burning through her.

'You came to me today,' he reminded her after a moment. 'And I believe we have discussed what we are each willing to give to make this work. So? What is your decision, Amelia?'

'I...' What was the conclusion to that sentence? He was right: she'd come to his office today, and with every intention of marrying him. And, while she desperately wanted Carlo to be immune from this man's vengeance, there was a far greater consideration.

Their baby deserved the very best. Materially, she could provide everything the child needed, but what of that gaping hole in the middle of Amelia's heart, from her own child-hood? What of her own desperate yearning for a father?

Her eyes landed on Antonio's face, his devilishly hand-some face, and she expelled a soft, slow breath. And then, with every sense that she was making a deal with the devil, she nodded. 'Fine. I'll marry you.'

There was a momentary response of triumph, a flare of reaction in his jet-black eyes, and then he moved on, with that rapier-sharp mind he was renowned for.

'You'll move to Madrid?'

Amelia blinked. She was still processing the monumen-tal agreement she'd just entered into and he was already firing onto the next point of negotiation, without giving her so much as a moment to breathe.

'But… I live in England. I have a job…' she pointed out, but weakly, more weakly than she would have liked. Damn it, this was supposed to be on her terms and he was push-ing all her buttons to get what he wanted.

'The same could be said for me.'

She bit down on her lip, swallowing past a lump of un-certainty. Her whole world was about to change—she was having a baby. Fighting change was going to get her pre-cisely nowhere. Leaving her job was inevitable—did it make a difference if that was in six months or now? From the perspective of the children she was teaching, it would be better for them to have a new teacher at the start of the year rather than halfway through.

She could leave her job—temporarily. But to move to Madrid?

She'd run a mile from this very world he inhabited.

Her time in Italy, as a diSalvo, had been harrowing. She thought of the women who'd befriended her as a teen-ager, using her as a way to get to her brother. The 'friends' who'd only been jealous—one in particular who'd got Ame-lia drunk and then taken unflattering photographs of her passed out and shared them across social media. Men who'd seen her as a new, shiny toy on their society scene and done whatever they could to get her into bed. Only she'd learned her lesson from Penny: Amelia was no one's plaything.

And marriage? Marriage to a man like this? How many of the men who'd flirted with her and tried to tempt her to become their mistress had been married? Was that the kind of future she had in store? Marriage to a man like Antonio, but marriage in name only?

She'd run a mile from this world, and with very good reason. Her time in Italy had been miserable. And though she'd loved her father and brother, they couldn't see that the way they lived wasn't something she wanted any part of. They couldn't see how ill suited she was for that lifestyle.

Her eyes swept shut as she thought of the life she'd carved out for herself and felt it disappearing from her, like a ship sinking into a silent, deathly ocean.

Perhaps her distress showed in her face because he was suddenly solicitous. 'You will like Madrid, *hermosa.*'

'It's not about Madrid,' she said frankly, worrying at her lower lip.

'Then what is it?'

How could she tell him? To admit vulnerabilities to a man like Antonio was to give him a weapon with which to wound her. And she was smarter than that!

'It's just a lot to ask of me,' she covered awkwardly. 'Particularly when you aren't even willing to consider moving to the UK.'

'I cannot do my work from the middle of nowhere,' he said simply.

'And what of my work?' She couldn't resist asking, though she'd already made her peace with the sense of leaving her job sooner rather than later.

'You are going to have to stop working at some point,'

he said with infuriating logic—as though six months was the same as six days! 'Why not now?'

'Because I love my job,' she said, aware that she was being stubborn purely for the sake of it. She expelled a sigh and ran a hand through her hair, not noticing the way his eyes followed the simple gesture as though transfixed. 'But I will think about it.'

His eyes glowed. 'Good. Then it is done.'

Amelia blinked rapidly. 'What's done?'

He walked away from her, towards his desk, and retrieved something, then a moment later was standing in front of her. 'Our engagement.' He reached for her hand and she was too shell-shocked to react. He put something in it and she looked down to see a small velvet box. She flipped it open on autopilot and couldn't help the small sound of admiration that escaped her lips at the sight of the ring.

An enormous turquoise gem, square-shaped, sat in the centre and it was surrounded by sparkling white diamonds on each side, so that it glistened and shone. The band was platinum and there were delicate swirls on either side.

'It's beautiful,' she said with a frown, because it was so much lovelier and more elegant than she would have credited Antonio with choosing.

He made a gruff noise of agreement then slid it onto her finger. They both stared down at it, and she was mesmerised by the sight of it on her finger.

'It was my grandmother's,' he said after a moment. 'She had eyes like yours.'

Amelia blinked at this reference to his forebear, as it reminded her obliquely of the feud that lay between them.

She didn't want to think about it in that moment. It was hardly a romantic marriage proposal, but it was still a proposal and she would have preferred it not to be tainted by talk of the animosity that flowed between their families.

'Thank you.' She frowned. It was hardly an appropriate sentiment—he'd blackmailed her into this marriage, no two ways about it.

'I've had the papers drawn and a judge has offered a special dispensation. Our marriage can take place within a week. I presume that's long enough for you to wrap things up in England?'

'You make it sound like finishing a meal, not resigning my job and shutting up my house.'

'I know it is more complex than that, and yet I would prefer to be married as soon as possible.' And with a sigh, and as though the words were being dragged from him against his will, 'If your employer requires more notice, then I suppose you could return once we are married. We could stay in your house *for a time*, if we must.'

'Gee, great,' she said with an upward shift of her eyes. 'Seeing as you're clearly so willing...'

He interrupted her, his words spoken with the same strength as a blade of steel. 'I am willing to do what it takes to make you my wife.'

She swallowed, the intensity of his statement almost robbing her of breath. This was about possession, she reminded herself, nothing more. Possession, ownership, control. He wanted their baby: she came with it.

She couldn't have said why the thought was unpalatable to her. 'Do you just have engagement rings sitting in your desk drawer on the off-chance a woman might drop by?'

His eyes smouldered when they met hers. 'I got it from the family vault the day after you left Madrid.'

'Why?'

'Because I knew you'd be back.'

She made a groaning noise in acknowledgement of that. 'What if you'd been wrong?'

He caught her hand and ran his fingertips lightly over the ring. 'Then I would have come to England and helped you see sense,' he said, the words simple, light, and yet a shiver of anticipation and adrenalin coursed through her veins.

Was she seeing sense? Or had she moved into the realm of insanity by agreeing to this?

Amelia couldn't say: only time would tell.

Antonio stared at his desk, his expression brooding.

It was all laid out before him: the totality of his aggressive investment in diSalvo Industries, the way he'd been slowly, meticulously devaluing them, ruining them for the sake of destruction alone. Businesses that had little interest to him beyond one aspect: their ability to wound Carlo and Giacomo.

His fiancée's family.

I can't marry a man intent on destroying my family.

And yet she was, and he was. Destroying the diSalvos had obsessed him for so long, and now, since his father's death, it had become his reason for being.

For so long, he had planned it: he would take what he could from them, and he would enjoy standing over them, seeing the shock on their faces when they realised how completely he'd masterminded their downfall.

He'd thought Prim'Aqua was the sum total of what he wanted, but now there was Amelia. Was it possible that in marrying her, creating a family with her, raising the child as the Herrera heir, he held the greatest key to destroying them?

Carlo hated Antonio—just as Antonio hated Carlo. So what would this child's existence do to the diSalvos? His smile was one of dark pleasure. It would destroy them, that was what. They would possibly even believe that Antonio had planned it—the seduction, the pregnancy—planned it all. His grin spread. And wouldn't that kill them? They'd hate it.

So much the better.

A light on his phone blinked, signalling a call, but he ignored it.

Amelia would be on a flight by now. His brows knitted into a gesture of silent disdain at her insistence that she fly commercial—yet again. To his disbelief, she hadn't even booked first class.

It was clear that she was engaged in some kind of protest against her wealth and situation, but to ignore all the luxuries she had at her disposal, and then the luxuries that he could furnish her with, beggared belief.

Then again, didn't everything about this situation?

Sleeping with her had been a mistake. A beautiful, heavenly mistake. Because, while the sex had been unforgettable, he'd returned to Madrid knowing he *had* to forget her. He had to put that misstep in the past and refocus his attention on his need to avenge the insults inflicted on his father.

And he'd been doing that, destroying the diSalvos and relishing his success.

But her pregnancy... He frowned, thinking of the unlikelihood of that. He was religious about using contraceptives. He was no monk. Sex was a part of his life, and he knew children weren't on his wish list. But the second Amelia had dropped her bombshell he'd felt an explosion of protective instincts, a primal, all-encompassing need to do whatever he could for that child.

That it was a child he would be raising with a diSalvo was something he would have to accept.

That had nothing to do with business—what he and Amelia shared, the life they would make for their baby, was all personal.

CHAPTER EIGHT

'*I NOW PRONOUNCE you husband and wife.*'

The words swum around Amelia's mind, heavily accented, and ever so slightly like a death knell.

Only that was stupid and dramatic. She was no little lamb, being led to the slaughter. She'd chosen this marriage, and she had to remember that. She wasn't a piece of detritus being drawn into an ocean's current—she had gone to Antonio and told him of her pregnancy, and she had chosen to at least try to create a life with him.

A real life?

Anxiety gnawed at the edges of her stomach as she came to the crux of the question that was tormenting her.

What exactly did a 'real' marriage look like, to Antonio Herrera?

She barely knew him, she thought, sliding a sideways glance to the man beside her. He drove the car through the streets of Madrid with effortless ease, the afternoon sunshine warm and golden, the powerful car eating up the distance between the utilitarian courthouse in which they'd said their vows and…

And what?

His home.

Another thing she had no idea about. Would it be a luxurious penthouse? A mansion? A yacht? Trepidation at the unquestionable glamour and luxury that awaited her had her remembering the life she'd fled, a life she'd sworn she'd never return to. Yet here she was: as far from her life as a primary school teacher as it was possible to be.

He wore a tuxedo and she wore a dress—simple, white, no lace, no pearls, no beading, no zips. The only concession to the fact it was a wedding was a little bouquet of white roses Antonio had presented her with when the limousine had brought her, straight from the airport, to the town hall. To any passers-by they might have even looked like a normal couple, sneaking off to quickly marry, happy at the prospect of the future that awaited them.

But this was far more like a business arrangement than anything else.

So who exactly had she got into bed with? No, not bed! Her cheeks infused with pink heat and she focused her gaze on the city streets as they passed.

He was ruthless, if his behaviour towards Carlo was anything to go by. But then, there were his charitable works—was that just an excuse, though, to soften his reputation as a hard-hearted bastard? Good PR work, the strings being pulled by an agency focused on rehabilitating his image rather than being motivated by any genuine social concern?

It was hard to believe Antonio particularly cared about his image, or how people might perceive him.

And it was better for her to believe that the man who would be a father to her child had good in his heart, somewhere.

I am not actually a bad person, he'd said, right before suggesting this marriage.

A marriage you agreed to, her memory pointed out sharply.

Her eyes dropped to her finger, and the rings she wore now. A simple diamond band accompanied the engagement ring, sparkling back at her encouragingly.

'Having regrets?' The words surprised her. They hadn't spoken in at least thirty minutes, since leaving the town hall.

She angled her face towards his and wished she hadn't when she found his eyes momentarily scanning her. Only for a scant few seconds, then his attention was claimed by the road, but it was enough. Heat seared her, expectation lurched in her gut and memories—oh, the memories! The way he'd kissed her, the way it had felt for his lips to press against hers, the urgency of their lovemaking, as though each had been waiting for the other all their lives. What madness had driven them into bed?

'Because it is too late to change your mind, you know,' he said, a tight smile stretching across his too-handsome face, the expression shoving more pleasurable thoughts from her mind.

'Not at all.'

'So you have been twisting your fingers to shreds because you are relaxed?' he responded with scepticism.

Had she been? It was a nervous gesture she'd had since childhood: lacing her fingers over and over as worries tumbled through her mind. She'd thought she'd conquered it but old habits, apparently, died hard.

'I'm thinking about our marriage,' she said honestly. 'And about the fact I know very little about my husband.'

He turned to face her again, slowing down at traffic lights.

'And what I do know,' she said quietly, 'I don't like, at all.'

His expression was one of grim mockery. 'I'm a big, bad Herrera,' he pointed out. 'Of course you do not like me.'

'It has nothing to do with this ridiculous feud,' she returned. 'I had no idea about that when we slept together; I hadn't even heard of you, except for an occasional mention in the papers.' Her teeth dug into her lower lip. 'This is all about your behaviour. To my brother, my father—your attitude to my family, and now me...'

'And what is my attitude to you?' he enquired, looking back at the road and easing the car into gear when the lights changed to green. The city had given way without her realising it, and now there was green on either side and he slowed as they approached a large gate. It flashed as the car neared and swung open, allowing Antonio to drive through.

She didn't answer that. It was hard to pinpoint what was bothering her, when actually he hadn't done anything but argue for this marriage. And she had understood his reasoning, had even agreed with him. But she knew why she'd done this—she wanted to give their baby everything she'd never had.

Why had he married her? Was it something so simple, and barbaric, as insisting that their child have his surname? He'd claimed that was a part of it, but what else was there?

Many possibilities came to mind; none of them relaxed her.

At the base of all her worries was the likelihood that Antonio saw this baby as yet another pawn in his war with her family, and there was worry there—worry that he might end up hurting the child. That her hopes for this baby having stability and love would be destroyed by his need for vengeance. And what would she do then?

A sigh escaped her lips without approval. She didn't see the answering look of impatience that crossed his face: her attention was captured by the view they drove past.

On one side of the car, heavenly grass and enormous oak trees spread for miles, with a lake at the centre. On the other? Mansions. Enormous, palatial homes with tall fences, stretches of darkly tinted glass, infinity pools, landscaped lawns.

She knew the drill.

She compressed her lips, disapproval filling her body.

Of course he lived somewhere like this.

Only his house wasn't one of the homes lined up in a fancy row, overlooking the park. His house was *in* the park. What she'd taken to be a public area was, in fact, part of Antonio's garden. The house itself was like a twenty-first century palace—all white walls and blue glass, with sharp lines and bright flowers tumbling out of terracotta pots on the endless balconies.

It was beautiful, she admitted grudgingly to herself. 'If you think we're raising our child in this museum, you're crazy,' was what she said. And when he drew the car to a halt at the front of the mansion she continued to stare at it.

'What's wrong with it?' he asked, the words flattened of emotion.

'Well, for one thing, look at the terraces. Do you have any idea how risky that is?'

His tone was curt. 'Yes, if only there were some handy way to keep children off terraces. I don't know, something flat that could be pulled to create a barrier. Something a bit like, oh, what's the word for it…a door?'

She scowled. 'Sarcasm doesn't suit you.'

He laughed then, a husky sound. 'And pettiness doesn't suit you. The house is fine, and you know it, so stop complaining for the sake of it and come and have a look.'

Only the fact he'd stepped out of the car and was coming around to her side had her pushing the door open and making a hasty exit before he could open the door for her. It was symbolic of the marriage she wanted—separate, but together. She nodded to herself at that description. It was perfect.

Marriage didn't mean they had to know everything about one another. Courtesy, civility, distance.

That could work, right?

Only his look showed he knew exactly what she was doing and she was left with a sense of having acted childishly, and she hated that! Her fingers knotted together before she realised what she was doing.

'The house itself is gated,' he pointed out, 'so there is little worry our children would find their way into the lake.'

'Children?' She stopped walking, pressing a flat hand against her stomach. 'This is one baby, so far as we know.'

He shrugged. 'So far.'

'You mean…?' She gaped. 'We aren't having more children.'

He gestured towards the house. 'Lots of rooms to fill…'

'That's a great reason to compound this situation,' she muttered, to cover the way her heart had speeded up at the very idea of a big, happy, noisy family—with this man.

'You want to give our child everything, don't you? Does that not include siblings?'

She stared at him, her eyes sparking. 'No.' Not if it means sleeping with you again, she added inwardly, but her traitorous body surged at the very idea and she spun away from him to hide her reaction. The dress was a fine cotton and her nipples were hardening at the mere thought of being possessed by him once more.

'We'll see.' He simply shrugged and the hand he placed at the small of her back might have been intended only to guide her forward, but her body was already on fire, her pulse racing, spurred on by memories of that night, so that she was electrified by the simple touch.

But pride held her steady; she wouldn't give him the satisfaction of knowing how he affected her by jerking out of his reach.

'The door opens with a code,' he said, tapping in some numbers. 'Raul will programme yours.'

'Raul?'

'Head of my security and operations.'

'You have security?'

He shot her a look of impatience. 'Yes, *querida*.'

'What the heck does someone like you need a bodyguard for? You're six and a half feet of muscle. Are you telling me you couldn't defend yourself?'

His smile showed both amusement and something else, something darker and more dangerous, because it spoke of a desire in his bloodstream that answered her own.

She blinked it away.

'Raul is not a bodyguard,' he said with a shake of his head. 'His purview is the security of my properties, the safety of my staff, and protecting my cyber interests. He monitors the alarms, ensures staff are vetted appropriately. And he will oversee your protection as well, from now on.'

'I don't need protection.'

'Amelia—' He expelled a heavy breath, clicking the door shut behind them. It was impossible not to contrast this phenomenal space with the cosiness of Bumblebee Cottage. They were standing inside a door now, as they had been then but, instead of quaint lighting and pictures drawn by her students, here there was all white marble, high ceilings, crystal chandeliers and world-famous pieces of art hanging from the walls. Mondrian, Dali and—of course—Picasso. She stared at the bright modernist piece with a growing sense of awe.

'Amelia?' he repeated. 'Are you okay?'

She blinked, her nausea nothing to do with the baby in that moment so much as the enormity of what she'd done. Marriage to Antonio was one thing, but until she'd stepped into his lavish home and been confronted with the sight of millions of pounds' worth of artwork within the hallway alone, she hadn't completely grasped what she was doing: the world she was moving back into.

'I'm fine,' she lied. 'Just hot.' And it *was* a hot day, stiflingly so, but the house itself was perfectly climate controlled. Other urges were responsible for the heat that ran rampant through her veins...

'Come, have a seat,' he urged, gesturing deeper into the house. Three steps led down into a sunken living space that showed views of the park they'd driven alongside. The windows were floor to ceiling and several of them slid to open completely, so that the enormous terrace beyond could become a part of this room with ease.

The sofas were white leather, large and soft. She sank into one and wished she hadn't because it was comfortable and she didn't want to be at ease. She needed to keep her wits about her.

Antonio disappeared, then returned a moment later with a bottle of ice-cold water. 'Drink this,' he said, handing it to her.

'Yes, sir,' she couldn't resist clipping back, diminishing his act of concern to one of dictatorialism.

He crouched down in front of her and, God help her, her eyes fell to his powerful haunches and the way the fabric of his trousers strained across them. He'd discarded his jacket somewhere, presumably in the kitchen or wherever he'd pulled the water bottle from, so her eyes roamed upwards, to the flat tightness of his stomach and, finally, up to his face. He was watching her but his expression gave little away.

'Do you have any idea how much you're worth?'

The question surprised her. She brushed it aside. 'Not precisely.'

He arched a brow, as though he couldn't believe this, and then shook his head. 'A small fortune. No, a *large* fortune. You were worth millions of pounds before you married me, and now? Do you not see that there is *some* risk you have to accept with being so financially advantaged?'

'I don't consider my finances an advantage,' she said seriously.

'Obviously, to have been earning a pittance working as a teacher.'

'How do you know what I earned?' she asked, lifting a brow.

'Do you think teachers' salaries are secret?'

She shook her head. 'It was more than enough to live on.'

At this, he regarded her through veiled eyes. 'So you chose not to access your vast trust fund?'

Feeling that there was more weight to the question than was obvious, she stuttered, 'W-why does that matter?'

'I'm curious as to why anyone would turn their back on a life of such privilege.'

She considered not answering him, but hadn't she been the one to insist they go into this marriage with the aim of making it work? And didn't that involve, at some point, opening the lines of communication? Besides, her feelings were no huge secret. 'I didn't want money to define me,' she said gently. 'I…found…people treat you differently when you're an heiress.' Her smile was grim. 'I didn't like that.'

His eyes roamed her face and she hated that he seemed to be reading her as one might a book. But after a moment he straightened, standing and holding a hand down to her. 'You experienced this when your mother died? And you went to live with your father?'

He wasn't touching her and yet his proximity was doing crazy things to her body. She was breathless and her tummy kept flopping, as though she'd crested over the high point of a rollercoaster. She nodded, not sure her voice wouldn't shake if she spoke.

'But money is just a part of who you are.'

She cleared her throat. 'The most important part, to many people.' Her lips twisted. 'Money, shares—even my marriage comes down to what I own, not who I am.'

At that he frowned, just an infinitesimal flicker of his lips, but he said nothing to dispute her summation. How could he? It was the truth.

'Do you feel up to finishing the tour?'

She sipped her water and nodded. 'Yes. I don't suppose you've had a map printed?' she said, only half joking. The place really was enormous.

'You'll get the hang of it,' he promised, holding a hand out to her. She put hers in his and he pulled her from the sofa. His fingers curled around hers and the pulse that had already been frantic went into overdrive. At this height, her gaze dropped to his lips and her mouth was dry as memories slammed into her from all angles.

'There are three bedrooms on this level,' he said, apparently oblivious to the tension that was zipping through Amelia. He gestured to their left as he guided her through the living space. Another step down and they were in yet another entertaining area, this time with a grand piano polished to a high sheen and panoramic views of the city in the distance. 'One can be for the nanny, and the other will be set up as a daytime nursery for the child.'

His words landed against her like little thuds. 'What nanny?'

He frowned. 'The child's nanny.' And at her darkening look he grimaced. 'There is no need to pull that cross face. I haven't hired anyone—you can do that. I'm simply saying this is where she will be accommodated. The third room along has its own kitchen and bathroom and is perfect for a live-in position.'

'Why in the world do you think I'd want to hire a nanny?'

He stopped walking, releasing her hand so he could thrust his hands into his pockets. 'Seriously?'

'Yes, seriously.' Her eyes narrowed. 'Did I ever say or do anything that implied I mightn't want to raise my child?'

'You *will* be raising him,' Antonio said with a frustration that belittled Amelia's feelings and caused anger to surge defensively through her, even when she knew she was possibly being a little over-sensitive. 'But you'll have help. Help for sleepless nights, help for long days, help with feeding or if the baby is restless or ill. Help, Amelia, is not the end of the world.'

'You sold me on this marriage by claiming you'd be a hands-on father and you're already trying to outsource the raising of a baby who hasn't even been born yet!'

He expelled a hiss of impatience. 'I am doing no such thing,' he said. 'A nanny just makes sense. When you go to work, who do you imagine will look after our child?'

'Work?' She blinked at him, the question so surprising it took her a moment to frame any kind of response.

'Yes, teaching. I presume you will want to return to work when our baby is older?'

'I…' A frown crossed her face. 'I thought you wouldn't want that.'

Now it was Antonio's turn to look confused. 'Why?'

Good question. 'Because you're…you. And I guess I thought you'd want me to be home with the baby, you know, being a mother…'

'You will still be a mother, I imagine,' he said, arching a single brow 'And I do not care if you work or not. My assumption was based on what I thought your preference would be. It's not a reflection of my wishes.'

'So you *don't* want me to work?'

'I just said I don't care either way,' he said with the appearance of patience. 'But if you are to return to work, we will need a solution to help, and I thought it would be better for the child if that person was someone they'd known from birth.'

It was all so damned logical and in her hormonal state that simply irritated her further. 'Where would I even work? I only speak Spanish curse words.'

At that he laughed and, ridiculously, she did too, and the tension that had been curling around them shivered a little and then gave way, like a dam bursting its banks. 'There is an international school,' he said quietly, 'just a few miles away. Lessons are conducted in English.'

'Teaching the children of rich moguls and tycoons?' she asked, still smiling.

'Teaching *children*,' he emphasised. 'Or are you so bigoted against wealth that you would judge the children who happen to be born to it?'

Another fair point that had her mood darkening once more. 'I'll think about it.'

'Fine,' he said. 'We have time to make a decision.'

Yes, that was true; time at least was on their side.

'The baby's room,' he said, opening the door to a room that currently housed little more than a bed and a small chest of drawers. 'Obviously we will have it decorated suitably once we know the gender.'

'I don't think I want to know what we're having. Not until it's born.'

'Why would you choose not to know?'

'I want the surprise,' she said with a shrug.

'You do not think the baby will be a surprise in and of itself?' he teased.

She tried to fight the temptation to banter with him. To succumb to his many, many charms. She'd done that once before and it had been disastrous.

'You're missing the point,' she said with an attempt at coldness.

'No, *querida.*' He shook his head. 'You are missing the point. We will decorate the room. We can paint it yellow. We can paint it green. We can paint it black, for all I care. We will make it a baby's room rather than this. Just as I do not care if you go back to work or not. I am showing you my house, and showing you how I think it can accommodate you and our family, and your future. I am trying to show you that I have thought this through, that I want this to work, just like you asked of me, yet you seem to want to argue with me at every turn. Why is that?'

She couldn't speak. Her heart was pounding, her mind was racing and her body was in flux. She was hot, despite the air-conditioning, and her cheeks felt flushed.

He took a step towards her, and then another, so that his strong body was almost touching hers. She stared up at him, her pale blue eyes meeting his stormy black ones and charging with electrical awareness. 'You are nervous,' he said simply.

'I'm not nervous,' she lied, her tongue darting out and licking her lower lip.

'You are nervous,' he said again. 'Because you are my wife, and I am your husband, and you do not know what that means. We married for a baby, but we never talked about this.'

'About what?' The words came out as a husky croak.

'About the fact that whatever madness drove us into bed that one time is still here, flaming at our feet.'

She drew in a sharp breath, surprise making her skin flush with goosebumps. 'No, it's not,' she said, raising her chin in a gesture of defiance that was completely belied by the way her eyes clung to his lips. 'Believe me, Antonio, I'm not so stupid that I'd make that mistake twice.'

His expression was scepticism itself. 'Really?'

'Really.' She nodded sharply. 'Sex has no part of this marriage.'

His smile was slow to unfurl and deadly in its danger to her. Because her heart began to beat off-rhythm and her pulse was thready. Legs that had been perfectly fine only minutes ago were wobbling now, threatening to give way.

'Do you realise how easily I could disprove that statement?'

She swallowed but it was useless, her mouth remained dry, as though coated with sawdust.

'Perhaps not,' he said, closing the distance between them. He didn't touch her, but oh, his body was so close she could feel his warmth through the fine fabric of her clothes and her body swayed forward of its own accord, so that her too sensitive nipples brushed against his chest and a soft, husky moan escaped her lips unbidden.

'You have no real experience,' he said, low and throaty. 'But what you're feeling now is desire.' He rocked his hips a fraction, so his arousal brushed against her and her eyes swept shut at his nearness and her needs.

'I'm feeling...' she said, searching for something, anything she could offer that would dispel his assertion. But nothing came to mind.

'Desire,' he supplied and then lifted a hand so he could smooth the ball of his thumb over her cheek.

'I don't...want you, like that,' she denied, so much more weakly than she would have liked. Her body—traitor that it was—pressed closer to his and when she blinked up at him her eyes were awash with desire and invitation.

His smile showed cynicism at her words, and then he stepped back. 'Yes, you do, *hermosa*, and I'm going to enjoy proving that to you.'

CHAPTER NINE

AMELIA FELT AS though she'd slept for three weeks and on a cloud. She awoke the next day completely relaxed, her body comfortable, her mind blank.

And then she looked around the room and it all came rushing back to her.

Holy heck, she was in Antonio's house. *Her* house. Their house! Because they were married!

The brief, but legally binding, ceremony came to her, and all that had taken place afterwards. She pushed out of bed, reaching for her phone—it sat on the bedside table. It was almost mid-morning!

She'd never slept so long in her entire life!

She was still wearing her wedding dress—if it could be called that. She'd worn it on the flight from England, and it wasn't even something she'd bought new for the event. She'd refused to observe any such kowtowing to tradition when their wedding was little more than a contractual agreement.

Yes, you do...and I'm going to enjoy proving that to you.

Awareness, hot and undeniable, pooled low in her abdomen. She galvanised her legs into action and made her way to the en-suite bathroom, where she freshened up. Her suitcase had been brought to this room at some point during her long rest. She cracked it open and pulled out a pair of shorts and a simple T-shirt, uncaring at how casual they were, refusing to feel the same insecurity when compared to Antonio's usual choice of lover.

Did it matter that the women he routinely slept with would probably swan about, draped in the latest couture dresses, all elegant and unapproachable, like this house?

Not to Amelia.

She wasn't going to let the ghosts of lovers past undermine her sense of self. With a nod to that commitment, she ventured out into the villa in search of Antonio.

Only the tour he'd given the day before, which had seemed to make perfect sense at the time, was a jumble in her mind. She found her way to the room he'd proposed using for the baby, and she saw it now with fresh, rested eyes and could admit it made perfect sense. In addition to being large, it was L-shaped, and she could imagine it with a small sofa and an armchair for nursing and, as he grew older, a little desk for his books and at which he could sit and do craft. It also lacked a terrace, and her concern for his safety made her glad for that.

The space beside the baby's room wasn't familiar to her. She pushed the door inwards and let out a gasp of surprise.

It was a library! A proper library. With thousands and thousands of books!

Antonio temporarily forgotten, she pushed deeper into the room, her breath unconsciously held as she scanned the spines. Many of the books were in Spanish; her heart dropped, but then it lifted once more.

So what? She had to learn the language—more than the bad words—at some point. Their son would be born in Spain, and his father was Spanish. In fact, their son or daughter would need to learn English, Spanish and Italian—all his heritages mixed together.

If they hired a nanny she would ensure it was someone bilingual, and perhaps she could include her own language tuition in the nanny's job description.

Only it was the second day of her marriage, she still knew barely anything about her husband—except that he was apparently more reasonable than she'd expected him to be—and she was most definitely getting ahead of herself.

She stepped out of the library and continued her walk through the house, heading downstairs and checking his office—empty—before moving to the ground floor.

A noise alerted her—splashing—and she went towards it.

It wasn't a particularly surprising discovery that he should be in the pool, but when she stepped onto the timber deck she stopped walking abruptly and could only stare.

Antonio was doing laps, and he wore only a skimpy pair of black briefs. As his legs kicked and his arms pulled him through the water, she stared at him, her eyes chasing his movements, her body hot all over.

He turned underwater and when he came up for breath, midway through another length, his eyes met hers and he stopped, standing in the pool water. The look he sent her was a more powerful aphrodisiac than even the image of him pulling through the water.

It was a look of absolute speculation, and something more. Something else altogether, like fierce masculine possession. Her fingers knotted in front of her, echoing the knots in her stomach. 'I thought I was going to have to wake you,' he said after a moment. 'It is almost midday.'

She nodded, moving closer to the pool and dipping her toe in. The water was delightfully cool. 'I know. I can't believe it. I guess that's pregnancy.'

He was watchful, his intelligent eyes moving analytically over her face. 'The books I read all say exhaustion is a symptom.'

'You've read pregnancy books?'

He frowned then shrugged, so water droplets ran over his shoulders and her eyes dropped to his smooth caramel flesh. 'Of course.'

He swam across the pool, coming to the coping right beside Amelia's feet. 'Have there been any other symptoms?' he asked, looking directly up at her.

She sat down, dropping her legs into the water and kicking them forward. The relief was heaven against her warm skin. 'A bit of nausea.' She shrugged. 'A headache, from time to time. Nothing remarkable.'

'How did you discover you were pregnant?'

'I went to the doctor,' she said simply.

'But why? Were you ill?'

'Oh, no. I just…the dates.' She shook her head, remembering that surreal moment. 'I couldn't believe it.'

'Did you think about keeping it from me?'

She looked away from him, swallowing. 'Not for even a second,' she said honestly.

She didn't see the way his lips pulled downwards at the corner. 'That surprises me.'

'Why?'

'You hardly know me, as you pointed out. And our family situation…'

She shook her head. 'I think what's surprising is that any woman would keep a baby from its father. A child isn't solely a mother's or a father's. To deprive someone of being a parent, for whatever reason…it seems wrong.'

'I agree,' he said, steel in the words. 'From the moment you told me I was a father my world changed. I cannot imagine how I would feel if you had elected to keep this to yourself.'

She swallowed past a lump in her throat as memories of her own childhood taunted her. 'To raise our baby to think either that their father didn't want them, or wondering at who and why… I wouldn't do that.'

Perhaps the words were laced with her own pain because, beneath the water, one of his hands wrapped gently around her ankle and he stroked it, so that heat flared in her skin. 'You weren't close to your own father, growing up.'

They both knew the truth of that statement.

But Amelia sighed heavily, regarding him with eyes that were unknowingly wary. 'No.' She bit down on her lip and focused on the small patterns formed in the water's reflection. 'I didn't even know who he was until my mother died.'

'You mean you'd never met him?' he enquired with obvious disbelief, moving to stand in front of her now, transferring his grip so he had a hand clamped around each of her ankles.

'I mean I'd never met him, and I didn't even know his name.' Her eyes dropped to the water. 'My mother never told me about him.'

'But he knew of you?'

'No.'

'No?' The word was bitten out with shock.

'No. She never told him about me. And any time I asked her about my father she'd get angry, and then say she couldn't remember, as though falling pregnant was something trivial and unimportant.'

Her face flashed with emotion. 'When she died her lawyer gave me the answers I'd wanted all my life—and, because I was a minor, I was sent to live with my father—a man who was as blindsided by my existence as I was his.'

A muscle jerked in his square jaw and her gaze fell to it instinctively. 'How could she have been so selfish?'

'That was my mother,' Amelia observed drily. 'She was the absolute definition of selfish. I suppose she thought she'd never die—utterly juvenile, given her lifestyle. Or maybe she thought she'd tell me when I was older. More likely, she just didn't think it through at all. She definitely knew who my father was, though, because in her will—and, believe me, I was shocked to discover she'd had the maturity to even draft one—my parentage was clearly noted. To this day, I have no idea why she chose to raise me on her own. God knows there were about a thousand things she'd have preferred to do with her life.'

The pain-filled invective lay around them, dark and spiky. Antonio's fingers stroked the flesh at her ankles and he stood at her legs, looking up at her contemplatively. 'And did your father take you in straight away?'

Her cheeks stained pink as the mortification of that summer wrapped around her anew. 'You make me sound like a puppy,' she said with a shake of her head, in an attempt to lighten the conversation.

He didn't smile. 'Did he?'

'More or less,' she answered, her eyes sparking with memories. 'He had a DNA test to be sure. I can't blame him,' Amelia was quick to offer in defence. 'Their relationship was brief, and he never heard from my mother again. His scepticism makes sense.'

'Perhaps. But I imagine his caution hurt you, as a young woman?'

Her expression was wary. 'I understood,' she said sharply, unable to admit the deep pain she'd felt at his decision.

'And once the results came back?'

Now her smile was brittle. 'I was a diSalvo, beyond a shadow of doubt,' she said. 'He laid proud claim to me in much the same manner you are to our baby. That's the way it works in dynasties like this, isn't it? Children are heirs more than they are people.'

Antonio's face was a mask of careful consideration. 'I think children are both.'

Amelia shifted her gaze away from his. 'Perhaps. In any event, I was no longer a child.'

'You were twelve?'

Twelve—still so young, she realised now. 'Nearly thirteen. And I'd been living with my mum so I'd seen a lot.'

Her smile was a rejection, a way of shutting the conversation down. 'It's all water under the bridge now.'

It was unusual for Antonio to have a conversation shift away from him, even more unusual to have it purposely pulled. He didn't want to allow the change in direction. There was too much he wanted to know.

But it was the first day of their marriage—an interrogation could wait, surely? He had all the time in the world to find the answers he wanted.

So he smiled calmly and then scooped some water up and flicked it at her. Her surprise was obvious and he wondered how she'd react, watching her, waiting.

Then she laughed, and returned volley, reaching down and lashing him with a heavy spray of pool water before reaching down once more. This time he caught her wrist and pulled, so she fell into the pool with him. She went underwater, then bounced back to the surface, dashing her hair away from her eyes.

She blinked, clearing her eyes, and the air between them seemed to charge. Her breasts were clearly visible beneath the saturated cotton of her T-shirt, bobbing on the water and, out of nowhere, he remembered the way they'd felt in his palms, the way he'd taken her nipples into his mouth, and his body was tight and hard beneath the water.

'Race you to the other side,' she challenged and, before he could answer, she was off. He watched her stroke for several seconds before powering to catch up with her. Yes, an interrogation would wait—there were better ways to spend the first day of their marriage.

Dinner was a surprisingly easy affair. Antonio was a skilled conversationalist and he kept things light, enquiring about her time at university and her job at Hedgecliff Academy.

It was no hardship for her to talk about her pupils and her work, the school she'd come to love.

What she didn't say was the part it had played in her recovery—she'd lost her mother and she'd chosen to turn her back on her father and her brother. Oh, there was no scandal, no unpleasant estrangement, but she'd walked away from them and all they stood for, choosing to live the life she'd always fantasised about.

A quiet life, with simple pleasures and easy friendships.

She didn't say how Hedgecliff had pulled her back together when she'd been searching for her real identity, separating herself from the girl who'd been the daughter of a supermodel and then a billion-pound heiress.

And whether he had questions or not, she didn't know because he moved their talk along, sharing his own stories of his time at university—his degree at Cambridge, and then he'd done postgraduate study at Harvard, which explained why his English was so perfect. And all the while he'd been overseeing his family business.

She knew from previous conversations that these years would have involved a time when Giacomo and Carlo were actively trying to ruin Herrera Incorporated, but he glossed over that too, undoubtedly for her benefit.

It was a pleasant night, and if Amelia had been asked two weeks earlier if that was possible she would have sworn until she was blue in the face that there was nothing on earth that would induce her to spend a nice quiet evening with Antonio Herrera—and especially not to enjoy it.

But dinner drew to a close and the sun dipped low over Madrid, setting late in the evening owing to the time of year. They were just two people then, with night before them, and all she could think about was the way he'd looked at her earlier.

She'd said she didn't want him, and he'd contradicted that.

Yes, you do, hermosa, *and I'm going to enjoy proving that to you.*

'Well,' she said, awkwardness in the small word, 'I might go to bed.'

She couldn't quite meet his eyes.

He didn't respond directly. 'Have you told your family about this?'

She was very still, her heart heavy inside her. 'Not yet.'

At that, she felt him stiffen. 'You haven't mentioned our marriage?'

'Nope.'

'Your pregnancy?'

She shook her head from side to side.

'*Dios mío!* For what reason?'

She chewed on her lower lip, reaching for her water glass and sipping from it to bring some moistness back to her dry mouth. 'It's complicated,' she said after a moment.

'Complicated? To tell them you are pregnant?' He stood, and her eyes dragged up his frame, drawn to his strength and breadth as though he were a magnet.

'You're not just some man to them, though. You're the devil, remember?' Her brows knit together. 'The fact I'm in some kind of relationship with you would be enough to kill them,' she muttered. 'Let alone when they realise it was just a stupid one-night stand from which I ended up pregnant.'

His expression was inscrutable as he came to crouch beside her, his trousers stretched over his powerful haunches.

'Come on,' she said with a roll of her eyes. 'You hate them; obviously they feel the same about you. And the last thing I want is for me or my baby to become some kind of pawn in your feud. If they knew I was pregnant, they'd have absolutely refused to let me marry you.'

He arched his brows and reached a hand for her chin, holding her face still when she would have turned away from him. 'And you'd have let them control your life in that way?'

'No.' Her eyes sparked with his. 'Because I'm doing this for the baby, because I want him or her to have a family, remember?' She sighed. 'I didn't want them trying to stop the wedding, and I didn't want them making a huge deal out of this.'

He frowned. 'It's ironic that you are attempting to keep our marriage a secret,' he said with a grimace.

'Why is that ironic? Can't you see that it makes sense?'

'No,' he said firmly, with a shake of his head.

'I obviously plan on telling them some time. I just... don't quite know when,' she finished vaguely.

In truth, the idea of having that conversation sat heavily on her shoulders. Nothing about this pregnancy was straightforward. Not the circumstances, not the baby's father, and certainly not the family history that shrouded their child, even before birth. And yet, in spite of that, one emotion had overridden all others: happiness. And, selfishly, she didn't want anything to detract from that. Giacomo and Carlo would be furious—and she understood why. But she didn't want to have that discussion yet. There was enough to adapt to—marriage to Antonio, getting to know him, settling into life in Madrid, dealing with her pregnancy.

Her family would have questions, and she'd feel better answering them when she knew exactly what those answers were! To have to defend her marriage, to explain her reasoning, to permit intrusions into what was a private matter—she didn't want that. She wasn't ready for it.

'Then you will not wish them to join us.'

'Join us?' She stared at him with alarm. 'What for?'

He dropped his hand away from her face. 'I've arranged a small wedding reception to take place next week. My friends and business associates, nothing big, but I thought you should meet them, and that they should meet you. I had wondered if you'd like your family to be there too. I must say, I'm relieved this is not the case.'

Amelia's heart began to race in her chest. Ignoring any suggestion of her father and brother coming face to face with the father of her child, a man they already hated, she focused on the rest of his statement. 'A party?'

'A cocktail party,' he agreed, making it sound civilised when she knew what these things were like. God, she'd been to more than her fair share, first with her mother and then courtesy of her second life as a diSalvo. 'Some music, food, champagne, fifty or so people. It will be over within a few hours but, vitally, it will cement our marriage.'

'Cement our marriage?' She scraped her chair back, standing with a sense of panic. 'I thought the document we signed did that. You know, the ceremony in front of a judge, the fact our marriage has been registered with the Spanish court?'

'I mean socially.'

'Socially? You actually care about that?'

He reached for the plates, carrying them through to the kitchen. She followed out of curiosity.

'I care about your life here in Madrid,' he surprised her by saying, stacking the dishwasher then turning to face her. 'I don't want you to be lonely and, the truth is, I work long hours. I thought you'd like to make some friends—there'll be women at the party, friends of mine. You'll like them.'

She gasped in a hot, angry breath and pushed away any thought that his gesture was one of kindness. 'You're actually trying to make my friendships for me? You really do have the most insufferable God complex.'

'And you have the ability to twist any gesture into some kind of insult,' he volleyed back, crossing his arms over his chest. She refused to analyse his words, nor to see truth in them. 'What did you think marriage to me would entail? Did you presume we would have no social life whatsoever?'

'I…presumed you'd go about your business as always and I'd be free to do my own thing.'

His eyes sparked with dark emotions. 'You believed wrong. You are my wife. You could do me the courtesy of at least trying to act like it, so far as the world is concerned.'

Her jaw dropped at this demand, so too did her heart speed up at his blatant claim of possession. *You are my wife.* How those words trickled down her spine like warmed honey, filling her with pleasure and pain all at once.

'But this isn't a real marriage,' she said weakly, when other words and pleas were swarming through her mind.

'You want to bet?' he volleyed back, and now his hands were braced on either side of her body, his palms pressed into the bench, his frame a perfect jail for her. She stared up at him, helpless and lost, and there was a threat in his eyes that filled her with desire.

'I…'

'You what?' he asked, dropping his head so his face hovered only an inch above hers.

'I…'

'Yes, *querida*?' he demanded, lowering his face still, so his lips brushed hers and a jolt of electricity fired up her spine. 'Tell me again how this marriage of ours is not a real one.' And his lips did more than buzz against hers then, they pressed to her mouth and she whimpered, low in her throat. Her fingers, of their own volition, grasped the sides of his shirt and he deepened the kiss when her lips parted on another moan. His tongue slid into her mouth and then he lifted her as though she weighed nothing, sitting her on the benchtop so he could stand between her legs and plunder her mouth as if he was the only man on earth.

And, God, wasn't he? For her at least?

But she'd fallen prey to this desire once before. It had flashed into her life and she'd been weak—too weak to realise that he could use this sensuality like a drug. She couldn't submit to it again—it would be foolish.

His fingers found the bottom of her shirt and he lifted it just enough for his fingertips to graze her bare flesh and every cell in her body cried out in relief and delight, and hope. Hope that he would strip her naked and make love to her once more.

With a guttural, desperate cry, she pulled away from him, moving back on the bench and lifting her fingers to her lips, lips that were bruised and throbbing with desire.

'How dare you?' The words were strangled from deep within her, and they were saturated with self-recrimination because she had wanted him to kiss her. She hadn't wanted him to stop kissing her!

He narrowed his eyes, and they were as clouded by desire as her own. 'How dare I what? Kiss you as you have been wanting me to all night? Kiss you as though you are my wife?'

'I haven't,' she denied hotly, but it was a lie and they both knew that.

He spoke without responding to her denial, but his voice was husky, filled with the passion that had flamed between them just now. 'How *dare* I want you to have friends? To have a social life here in Madrid? People to catch up with when I am travelling for work? Other mothers to talk to about babies and nappies and bottles and I don't know what else?'

She was glad to return to their argument, rather than have to defend the way she'd melted in his arms. 'That's up to me!' she snapped from teeth that were clamped together. 'I'm perfectly capable of making my own friends.'

'But you don't want them to be my friends,' he surmised, his expression shifting.

'I didn't say that.' She bit down on her lip, trying to find words that would defuse this, that would explain her hesitation. 'This has all happened so fast. I just need a moment to catch my breath before I start thinking about everything else.'

'It is a party. My friends, some food, music, dancing. You will enjoy yourself.'

It was the wrong thing to say. Panic filled her mouth with a taste of adrenalin. Everything was happening too fast. 'I can't do that.' She thought of all the parties she'd been to—first with her mother, then as a diSalvo heiress, and a shiver scratched over her spine.

'I'm sure it seems inconsequential to you, but it's not to me. It's too much, too fast.' She shook her head. 'No party. Please.'

His eyes narrowed and she was reminded that one of the many facets of this man was the ruthless, hard-nosed tycoon. That he conquered whatever he turned his hand to in the corporate world. That he was determined and he was fierce and that he was used to getting his own way.

'When you agreed to marry me, you told me you wanted me to be reasonable. Is there anything unreasonable about what I'm proposing?'

'Yes!' she snapped, and then shook her head because there wasn't.

'What is it, Amelia? Do you think you can keep this marriage secret for ever?'

'I…' She shook her head. 'This is not negotiable.' The words trembled with the strength of her emotion.

He exhaled softly and his warm breath fanned her temple, so her body swayed forward infinitesimally of its own accord. 'You're saying you wish me to cancel it?'

'Yes,' she responded quickly, too quickly, as her throat constricted. Her breath was hard and fast. How could she explain to him what her life had been like? At least, with Penny, Amelia had been dragged to events with an eclectic, artsy crowd. With the diSalvos it had been designer chic the whole way. Designer drugs, designer cars, designer everything. Amelia had never belonged, hadn't wanted to belong, and she'd fled that scene as soon as she could. The thought of being right back in the midst of it was impossible to countenance.

'Fine,' he said darkly, his disapproval obvious. 'Consider it cancelled. Now, if you'll excuse me, I have work to do.'

CHAPTER TEN

ANTONIO STARED AT the document and reread the contents for the tenth time in as many minutes. It was a simple feasibility study, the kind of thing he usually ate for breakfast, but on this night his mind simply wouldn't focus.

His eyes drifted to the clock above his desk: it was into the small hours of the morning and he was still seething over their argument. Over her intractability, yes, but also over his own actions. And something else niggled at the back of his mind—the way her eyes had flooded with emotions he couldn't quite unravel. It had made him want, more than anything, to understand her.

He'd organised the party out of a desire to smooth her transition into his life. Where the hell had that concern come from?

Why had he bothered?

True, she was pregnant with his baby, but had that fact completely erased all others? She was a diSalvo, and their family rivalry wasn't likely to be forgotten easily. Not with a party, not with a baby, not with anything.

His attempts to pretend otherwise were futile. He was better to focus on what they had, and what they were, and forget anything else.

She was a beautiful woman and their chemistry was off the charts. If she chose to join him in bed, then so be it. He wasn't going to lose sleep over her choice there. Their kiss, though, forced its way into his consciousness and his arousal strained against his jeans. She had wanted him then, and he had wanted her. Pleasure had been within reach. Only she'd pushed him away, as though the heat that flamed between them wasn't going to demand an answer at some point.

And it would: the call of their bodies was too strong to resist. But he would bide his time and let the desire between them swamp her, drive her to the point of madness, and then he would be there, when she was so desperate for his touch that she couldn't think straight.

And in the meantime nothing would be allowed to derail his reasons for marrying her. He wanted Prim'Aqua. He wanted the men who'd hurt his father to pay—and his marriage would bring that about, one way or another.

He kicked back in his chair, his fingers interlocking behind his head as he closed his eyes.

And saw Amelia, her huge blue eyes accusing in her face, her lips pulled downwards, a look of bewilderment on her expression.

She'd hate him, but he'd cross that bridge when he came to it.

Nothing could be allowed to alter his course. Nothing, and no one...not even the woman who was carrying his baby. She'd made it obvious she didn't welcome his involvement in her life, and didn't want his help. *So let her be,* he told himself. *Let her find her feet, have her breathing room and space.*

What the hell did he care?

Three weeks into their marriage and Amelia would have given her left arm for some civil conversation. It wasn't exactly that her husband *was* uncivil, he was perfectly polite, but the easy rapport they'd established on that first day had completely evaporated. So too the sexual tension that had threatened to unzip her completely.

They hadn't shared a meal together either. He'd made

a point of explaining his absences—he was working on a big deal and needed to be in his office late. It made sense for her to eat without him, he'd explained, giving her the number for the woman who prepared his meals so she could order whatever she wanted.

But three weeks into their marriage and she knew she had to speak to him. She'd tried to organise things herself but, with her limited language and no car at her disposal, she was hampered in a way she found utterly frustrating.

He worked late into the evening, not returning to the house until almost eleven o'clock. But, unlike previous nights, when she'd been in her own room, either fast asleep or pretending to be, Amelia was awake when he returned, dressed, sipping a cup of chamomile tea.

He clearly wasn't expecting it, if the look on his face was anything to go by. And he looked...tired. She only had a moment to glimpse that before he flattened his face of any emotion and looked at her with mild curiosity. As though she were a creature who'd wandered into his home, a unicorn or narwhal, utterly mystical and somewhat novel.

'Amelia? I thought you'd be asleep.'

'I need to speak with you,' she said softly, then cleared her throat. Her body screamed at his closeness, her lips throbbed and a drum began to beat low down in her abdomen, demanding attention.

'Oh?' He moved deeper into the sitting area, placing a document wallet down on the front hallstand. 'Is there a problem?'

'No.' She shook her head. 'Not really.'

'Good.' He expelled a breath, a sound which might have been one of relief or impatience. But she ignored it. This was important.

'I need your help.'

That had his attention. His eyes narrowed and he strode closer. 'You are sure everything is okay? The baby...?'

'The baby's fine, so far as I know.'

'What do you mean?'

'I'm twelve weeks into the pregnancy,' she said. 'I remember the doctor I saw in England telling me I'd need a scan around now. And some other tests. Only I don't speak Spanish and I have no idea where to go. I've tried to use online translation to find somewhere but it's pretty impossible, to be honest. And anyway I don't have a car here, though I guess I could get a taxi—but where would I get a taxi *to*?'

He stared at her, his expression shifting from confusion to something else, an anger that was self-inflicted. 'Of course,' he said, and his frown deepened. 'I'm sorry to say that hadn't occurred to me.'

'Why would it?' she asked shyly. 'It's not like you've had a baby before. This is all new to both of us.'

He frowned. 'Still, it's not exactly rocket science.'

'The doctor in England referred me to a clinic in London. Obviously that's not much good here.'

He turned away from her, striding towards the panoramic windows. His hands were on his hips and his back moved with the increased pace of his breathing.

'I have many cars. You are welcome to drive any of them.'

She frowned, following the thread of conversation. His cars were all fast, expensive, sleek and powerful. She shook her head gently. 'I'd prefer to buy something myself, something that's not got the horsepower of a wild beast beneath the bonnet. Except I don't even know where to do that.'

He turned to face her, his expression grim. 'Fine. We'll buy you a new car.'

'I can buy myself a new car,' she chided softly. 'I just need your help to...do that.'

'Fine.' Frustration zapped in the air between them, like lightning hitting a river.

'Thank you.' She cleared her throat and tried to break the silence with a smile. It felt strange on her lips—she hadn't smiled in a long time. Not since leaving England?

His eyes flashed in warning. 'Don't thank me for this, Amelia. I should have thought of it. I am truly sorry I overlooked all these practicalities—it's not like me to overlook anything. You must have felt like my prisoner here, after all.'

'It's fine. I've been reading, and swimming, and...' Her words petered out as he took a step closer, and then her breath grew heavy and her eyes swept shut.

'It is *not* fine,' he said simply, his accent thick. 'Please accept my apology.'

What she would have preferred was an apology for his absence.

'Fine, apology accepted,' she agreed unevenly. 'Now, about the appointment. I've been searching online and I *think* I've found a good obstetrics clinic.' She held her phone out to him and he took it, but his eyes remained locked to hers.

The air between them was charged and yet she was powerless to look away. Her eyes were held to his by an invisible magnetism, too strong to ignore. 'I just can't read the reviews,' she said, the words husky.

He held her phone but didn't look at it. 'How are you feeling?' The question was husky, drawn from the depths of his soul.

She blinked, but didn't shift her gaze.

'I...' Of their own accord, her hands lifted to her stomach and, as always, her heart lifted at the thought of the life that was growing there. 'Good.'

Now their eyes parted as his moved briefly to her gesture, and then his free hand was lifting like hers, moving over her stomach slowly.

Surprise was in his eyes, surprise and wonderment. He

curved his palm over the very faint hint of roundness, and when he spoke it was with a voice thickened by emotion. 'Are you well?'

Inexplicable tears formed in Amelia's eyes. She tried to blink them back, but one escaped unbidden and slid down her cheek.

Irritated by it, she grimaced. It was just that she'd been so lonely, and seeing him now, feeling him touch her stomach and feel the life that was growing there—how could she not be affected?

'I'm fine.' The words were slightly uneven.

He nodded slowly, then dropped his hand and, finally, the spell was broken. He turned to her phone, scanning the page she'd shown him, and nodding curtly. 'It looks fine. I will make enquiries in the morning and organise an appointment.'

'Thank you.' She turned on her heel, ready to leave the room, her brain unable to supply anything else to say.

But he forestalled her with a softly voiced, 'Would you like something to drink? A cup of tea?'

Her eyes swept shut and she was glad she had her back to him, so that he wouldn't see the complex knot of emotions that passed over her face.

'I haven't eaten,' he said. 'Join me.'

It was a simple invitation, spontaneously given, but it set off a cascade effect in Amelia. She'd missed him. Not him, *per se,* so much as a person to speak to, and laugh with. Or maybe it was all him—Antonio Herrera, the man who seemed to breathe life into her dreams and torment her sleeping body with memories of his touch.

Temptation was the devil and she knew she needed to fight it. To fight the desire to lean into him and ask him to hold her tight, to have him smile at her as he had that first night—even if she knew it would be a lie.

'I'm tired,' she said, turning to face him for a brief moment, heat warming her body, memories making her ache for the past. 'I… I think I'll just go to bed.'

She *had* looked tired, he admitted to himself, staring out at the shimmering surface of the pool, Scotch cradled in the palm of his hand. The moon was high overhead, casting a silver light over the water.

He'd spent the last three weeks holed up in his office, working late, yes, but also actively avoiding his wife.

Avoiding her enormous blue eyes that showed him the galaxy, avoiding the softness of her body, the addictive properties of her smile. He'd been avoiding her and tonight he fully understood why.

One look at her and he knew he'd run in front of a freight train to protect her and the baby that was growing inside her. One word from her and he was at risk of turning his back on everything he'd worked towards.

One word and he could almost genuinely forget his hatred for her family. It wasn't personal. It had nothing to do with Amelia. It was the baby; that was all. Some ancient, ingrained primal instinct was firing inside him, demanding he fulfil his duty and keep her and the baby safe and well. Even if that made him willing to surrender his own needs.

Weakness was foreign to him, and it sure as hell wasn't welcome. She wore his ring; she carried his baby, but she was still a diSalvo—and he couldn't forget that.

He shut his eyes and tried not to think of his wife. He forced his mind to erase her image momentarily, and replace it with the image of his father. He brought to mind painful memories that he generally chose to disregard, memories of his father's stress and grief and the first time Antonio had confronted Carlo with what he'd done, and Carlo had laughed in Antonio's face. Carlo had made an enemy that day—and Antonio knew he'd never be able to forget that.

Forgiveness might have been divine, but it was nowhere on Antonio's radar.

'Seriously, though, was the helicopter really necessary?' Amelia asked as the chief of the obstetrics wing of the Hospital Internacional de Madrid exited the exam room for a moment.

The room was dark, the lights off, a heavy blackout curtain blotting out all of Spain's sunshine. Medical devices surrounded them, casting a very soft glow—one that was almost eerie.

He tilted her a sardonic glance. 'Of course. I wanted to see how long it would take to get here in an emergency.'

And, despite the fact she'd told herself she would remain distant from him, she found herself rolling her eyes teasingly. 'A car would suffice.'

'You never know,' he said, and he was serious now, his eyes showing a strength that made her tummy flip and flop.

'Mr and Mrs Herrera.' Dr López returned, a kindly smile on his face. He must have been in his sixties, with steel-grey hair and a lined face, and his experience gave Amelia confidence. 'I have this,' he said, holding up a bottle. 'It will feel cold at first, okay?'

Amelia nodded, lying back on the narrow bed.

Dr López pushed Amelia's shirt up, right to the ridge of her bra, and he wiggled the waistband of her skirt lower, exposing her gently rounded stomach. The gel he applied was ice-cold but it wasn't unpleasant, given the heat and humidity of the day.

Once he'd finished, he smiled reassuringly and moved to the other side of the bed. 'Let us take a look.'

Amelia was inexplicably nervous and, almost as though he understood that, Antonio reached out and curved his hand over hers, squeezing her fingers in his. She blinked up at him and a throb of strong emotion passed between them. She wrenched her gaze away, hating that her hormones made her so close to tears at present.

Dr López pressed the ultrasound wand to her belly, firmly enough that she was slightly uncomfortable, and now she squeezed Antonio's hand.

'Okay?' he asked huskily.

'Yeah,' she whispered.

'The baby is playing hide and seek,' the doctor reassured them both. 'Just a minute.'

Amelia held her breath, waiting—tense, nervous, anxious, delirious with every emotion she could imagine.

'And you have not been unwell?' Dr López asked, his expression infuriatingly blank.

Amelia swallowed. 'No. I mean, I've been a little sick sometimes.'

'Good.' He nodded, and Amelia relaxed. Beside her, though, she was aware of tension emanating from Antonio that caused her heart to twist in her chest.

'You can see here your baby—' Dr Lopez pointed to the screen '—lying on its back, see?'

'Whoa…' Amelia blinked, tears filling her eyes now, and Antonio squeezed her hand tight '…that's our baby.' She blinked up at her husband and the sight of him, still as a rock, his own eyes suspiciously moist, made everything hurt.

'Yes, looking quite happy, you'd have to say.'

Their baby was still so tiny, just a blip on the screen, but already her heart was bursting with love and total vulnerability.

'You will need to come back in a month or so,' Dr López said, pushing the screen away and handing Amelia a soft towel. She wiped her stomach clean of gel and then placed a hand over her belly.

'And this is my card, with my personal number,' he addressed Antonio.

Her husband took the card with a curt nod. No gratitude, nothing to express that the chief of the hospital giving his private number to a patient was anything unusual. Because he was used to that kind of treatment. Doors opened for Antonio. He got what he wanted, when he wanted it.

'If you have any concerns at any time, you may call,' Dr Lopez continued. 'Otherwise, I'll see you in another month.'

He pulled some small square pieces of paper from beneath the screen and handed them to Amelia. Fresh tears welled in her eyes as she stared at the grainy first photographs of her baby.

And then, slowly, she looked at Antonio and bit down on her lip. Because, whatever doubts she'd had about this marriage, whatever had come before, in that moment— she had none. No doubts, no reservations, no regrets. She reached for his hand and squeezed it, her smile brighter than a thousand suns.

'Can you believe it?'

He shook his head slowly. 'Not even for a moment.' He rubbed his thumb over the back of her hand and then leaned down, pressing a kiss to her cheek, so close to the corner of her lips that a small nudge of her face in that direction would have connected lips to lips. But she stayed still, her eyes blinking closed as she breathed him in.

'Shall we go for lunch, Mrs Herrera?'

Right on cue, her stomach gave a low grumble and she nodded slowly. 'That sounds like a fine idea.'

Just a little way from the Parque del Retiro, down a small side street with brightly coloured buildings on either side, lined with large trees and small colourful shrubs, was a restaurant so exclusive there was no visible name. Just a black door—easily missed unless you knew where you were going—showed the entrance.

Antonio pressed a hand in the small of Amelia's back, the touch purely civil—it was a gesture that wouldn't have been out of place between colleagues, yet it was like a match being sparked low in her abdomen, and tiny flames burned in every single nerve ending. He pressed a button and a minute later a waiter appeared, wearing jeans and a white shirt, with a butcher's apron tied around his waist. He addressed them in rapid-fire Spanish, so Antonio responded in English.

'For two, on the terrace.'

'Immediately,' the waiter said, switching effortlessly to Amelia's native language.

The small door opened into a huge room, so light and airy it was like being in the countryside. Windows that should have looked out onto the street had been screened with green, creating the illusion of being in a garden paradise, and the ceilings were at least three storeys high.

There was a lift at the back and the waiter pressed a button, waiting beside them for it to arrive. Once the doors had opened, he held the doors then reached inside to press a button, before nodding and spinning on his heel.

The lift ascended swiftly—it took only seconds—and then they were on a terrace that exceeded all of Amelia's expectations. It overlooked the park, showing verdant rolling hills in one direction, and large trees grew in huge pots, jasmine scrambled over a pergola and the tables were placed haphazardly—scattered at random, so that no one table was near another.

It was perfect—private, intimate and clearly exclusive without being off-putting.

'Ah, Mr Herrera.' Another waiter appeared, this one a little older, with his dark hair thinning at the temples, his eyes holding Antonio's before transferring to Amelia. 'Lovely of you to join us again.'

Amelia ignored the instant surge of jealousy at that—because of course Antonio had frequented this restaurant before, and presumably not alone. It was the perfect place to bring a date—hadn't she just been thinking so? She straightened her spine, telling herself she didn't—couldn't, shouldn't—care.

'This way, please.' The waiter smiled at Amelia and then guided them to a table right at the edge of the terrace. Here, the fragrance of jasmine was exquisite and a nearby citrus tree in a pot was in blossom, so there was a faint humming of feeding bees, their pollen collectors glistening yellow in the afternoon light. The sun was high in the sky yet it wasn't unbearably warm. Amelia took the seat Antonio had held out for her, letting her gaze chase the details of the view.

For the first time, she felt a kernel of excitement for this—her new city. There was so much to explore, so much to learn!

'It's beautiful,' she said after a moment, her breath fast.

He looked towards the park, and pushed his sunglasses up onto his head. She transferred her attention from the park to Antonio, marvelling at how easy it was to forget just how intensely attractive he was.

'Yes.' He ran a hand over his stubbled chin. 'When I was a boy,' he said, turning to look at her and smiling an easy, companionable smile, 'my father used to take me there, almost every weekend.'

'Really? What for?'

'Football,' he said with a shrug so his shirt drew across his shoulders and she bit down on her lip to remind herself not to stare. 'And puppets.'

'Puppets?'

A waiter appeared with some sparkling water, placing it on the table before them.

'Puppets,' Antonio agreed, once they were alone again. 'There are puppet shows on, all the time, and I used to love them.'

Her heart turned over in her chest at this unexpected detail from his childhood—so mundane, so regular, and completely perfect.

'You're surprised?' he prompted, despite the fact she'd said nothing—and she knew it was because he could read her more easily with each day that passed.

'I'm…yes,' she said on a curt nod. 'I am.'

'Why?'

'Because you don't strike me as a man who was ever really a boy,' she said, and then wrinkled her nose on a small laugh, which he echoed.

'You think I was born like this?'

'No.' She rolled her eyes, her smile not fading. 'I guess you must have physically been a boy at some point. But one that played and had fun?'

He wiggled his brows. 'I assure you, I was both those things.'

'You weren't determined to take over the world, even at six?'

'Perhaps a little,' he said, lifting his hand, his forefinger and thumb pressed close together.

The waiter returned, brandishing menus, and Antonio took them without looking in the waiter's direction.

'Thank you,' Amelia murmured, flying the flag of civility for both of them.

'And you?' Antonio pushed, after the waiter had left. 'Was your childhood full of fun?'

Amelia bristled. 'I'm sure you know the answer to that.' She reached for her water, sipping it, turning back to the view. Inexplicably, her heart was racing.

'I have an impression,' he agreed with an air of relaxation. 'But you have not told me specifics.'

'With good reason.' She tilted a small smile at him. 'I don't like to speak about it.'

Speculation glowed in the depths of his eyes, eyes that were—at times—dark black, and now showed specks of amber and caramel. 'Then make an exception on this occasion. For me.'

CHAPTER ELEVEN

HE WATCHED AS she considered those words, wondering at the sense of reserve she wore like a cloak. It hadn't been there on the night in her cottage, when she'd brandished a meat cleaver and made him laugh, despite the seriousness of his business with the diSalvo family. Was it him that unsettled her?

The nature of their marriage?

Inwardly he cringed—how could it be anything else? Blackmailing someone into marriage was hardly a way to encourage closeness. Yet here they sat, husband and wife—as much an enigma to one another as the day they'd first met.

'I think,' she said, and he didn't realise until then that he'd been holding his breath, waiting for her to speak and half believing she wouldn't, 'some people would characterise it as fun.' She wrinkled her nose and his gut twisted, hard. He made an effort not to move, to appear natural, but it was as though he was hyper aware of every movement he made, every movement she made.

'But not you?' he asked, the words low and husky.

'No.' Her eyes met his and there was that thread of defiance, a whip of strength, that made his body arc up in immediate response. 'Not me.' She smiled, a tight smile, as she reached for her water glass, sipping from it slowly, her eyes landing on the view beyond them. 'I think the novelty of freedom is exactly that—a novelty. As a child I was always afraid.' She cleared her throat, and said no more.

So he prompted, 'Afraid of what?'

'What my mother would do.'

As though screws were being turned in every joint, his body tightened. 'She hurt you?'

'Oh, God, no.' She spun back toward him, her eyes enormous, and he could see so much of the famed supermodel in his wife's face that he wondered if they were alike in ways other than the physical. 'My mother was the kindest person you could ever meet. *Too* kind.'

'Is there such a thing?'

Amelia's frown was instantaneous but it was as though a storm cloud was moving in front of the sun. 'Modelling is a hard business. You can never be the prettiest, the skinniest, the best. She spent her life trying.' Amelia shook her head. 'She was a "good-time girl"—that was her reputation anyway, and it came to define her. She could never grow out of it, never shake it free. As I've got older, I've come to realise that she was living in fear, that she was afraid people wouldn't like her any more if she wasn't always the life and soul of the party.'

'I'm sorry if she lived with that fear.'

'I am too.' Amelia swallowed. 'But I spent a long time being angry with her.'

'Why?' he asked, though he had his own reasons for feeling anger towards her too.

'She shouldn't have kept me,' she said with a wry twist of her lips. 'I used to wish she'd put me up for adoption, you know.'

Sadness for the young Amelia flooded him—a surprising reaction, and not entirely welcome. 'Why were you afraid of her, then?' He reframed their conversation to her original statement.

'Because she was erratic, and almost always drunk or high. She'd invite random people back to whatever hotel we were living in at the time. I can't even tell you how often I woke up and found she'd left the hotplate on or taps running.'

Oh, *Cristo.*

Tears sparkled on Amelia's lashes, making her eyes shine like the ocean on a sun-filled day but, instead of letting them roll down her cheeks, she ground her teeth together, her expression almost mutinous. 'New boyfriends every few weeks—some of them creepy or not very nice, some of them fun but bad for her. I resented them all.' She shook her head. 'No, I hated them all. I hated them for taking her away from me. She was never a great mum, but at least when she was single, she'd try. Not very hard.' She frowned. 'Or maybe she did try hard and she just wasn't wired that way.'

And—he couldn't help himself—he reached out, pressing his hand over hers and squeezing it. 'And yet you turned out okay,' he said, the praise too faint, too light, but he wasn't sure what else he could offer.

She wrinkled her nose again and shrugged. 'I had examples of everything I didn't want to become. It was odd, growing up that way. Lots of people might think fame is aspirational, but oh, how I hated it.' She shook her head. 'Photographers going through our trash, Mum being in those gossipy magazines every time she got dumped or stumbled out of a nightclub. When I was old enough, I did my best to protect her from it, but there was only so much I could do.'

'You must have still been a child, even then.'

'Why do you say that?'

'You were only twelve when she died...'

'Yes.' She shook her head. 'But I think having a mother like mine forces you to grow up a lot sooner.'

With a visible effort to clear her thoughts, she stretched an uneven smile across her beautiful face. 'So that's my story. What of yours?'

He didn't want to stop talking about her—having opened Pandora's Box, he wanted all the secrets, all the mysteries. 'Far less interesting,' he promised.

'I doubt that.'

The waiter appeared and they ordered—a simple lunch, vegetarian for Amelia and seafood for Antonio—and then they were alone once more.

'Your mother died when you were young?' she prompted.

Antonio expelled a breath, wondering if it was impolite to discuss such a thing with a pregnant woman. 'In childbirth,' he said at length—there was no way to sugar-coat it. 'But from *very* rare complications.'

'Oh, I hadn't realised,' she said, looking away from him. 'That's awful.'

'As I said, it was extremely rare.'

'I'm not worried about myself,' she rushed to assure him, angling her face to his, and now she turned her hand upside down, capturing his and lacing their fingers together, templing them on the table.

She looked at their interwoven fingers as she spoke—it was an intoxicating contradiction—his fingers so tanned and long, hers fair and small, with the wedding ring he'd given her sparkling back at him. 'But how awful, that she never got a chance to know you. To be a mother. And she must have been so excited.'

That had him arching a brow. 'Are you excited?'

'Are you kidding?'

He laughed then. 'No. I'm curious.'

'Of *course* I'm excited!' Her free hand curved over her stomach and his eyes followed the betraying gesture with curiosity. 'Aren't you?'

It was an excellent question. At no point had he stopped to analyse his feelings. He had discovered her pregnancy and known only that he had to make her his, and that the baby would be raised a Herrera, right here in Spain.

'I'm...'

'Yes?' She blinked at him, a smile tickling the corners of her lips, as though she were trying to suppress it—and failing.

'I'm curious.'

She burst out laughing. 'That's it?'

'Well, is it going to be like you, or like me?' he said, uncharacteristically sheepish. 'A boy, a girl, tall, short, with blue eyes that shine like the Aegean? Or dark like mine?'

She sighed. 'And isn't that...exciting? I mean, we have no idea about any of this, and yet this is our baby! No matter what, they'll be part me, part you. I can't wait to meet them.'

Her excitement was contagious and he found himself nodding, trying to fathom what their baby would be like. Their food arrived and she pulled her hand from his— he regretted the separation, and wondered at that. But for weeks he'd kept his distance and then, after last night and the magic of seeing their baby's heartbeat on the screen, suddenly, he didn't want to keep his distance any longer.

'And you were close to your dad, obviously,' she murmured, bringing the conversation back to something calmer and more grounded in the present. 'I mean, the park, the puppets, football...'

'Yes,' he agreed. 'We were close. I idolised him.'

Her eyes were speculative, loaded with questions she didn't voice. She was tentative in a way he couldn't stand. They'd been sharing so much of themselves a moment ago, he didn't want her to withdraw from him again. 'You look like you wanted to ask me something,' he said softly, and her eyes widened with surprise.

She nodded gently. 'Is he...?'

'Yes,' he confirmed, unprepared for the rush of emotion that filled him. 'He's dead.' He frowned. 'Saying that is strange. I haven't...talked about him in the past tense yet.' A frown stretched across his handsome face. 'My father was an incredibly dynamic man—larger than life. I still find myself forgetting that he is gone sometimes.'

'I'm sorry.' She speared a small tomato and lifted it to her lips. 'You must miss him a lot.'

'Yes.' He reclined in his chair, taking in the view, his expression unknowingly sombre. 'When your brother set out to destroy Herrera Incorporated, it was very hard on my father. He'd spent his life building the company up, making it bigger and better than it had been under his father, and to have that in jeopardy—' He turned back to face her and for a moment he recalled she was a diSalvo, and he remembered all the reasons he had for keeping her at a distance.

But then she sighed, a soft, small noise, and she was so sympathetic that he couldn't throw her in the same box as her brother and father. She was different—lacking the killer instincts that had brought his father to his knees.

'I imagine that must have been very difficult for you.'

'Yes,' he drawled, and at her look of pain he grimaced, making an effort to soften his expression. 'The markets were weak and confidence was low. His investors deserted him—he was left with barely anything.'

'But you rebuilt it,' she said.

His nod was short.

'That must have taken an incredible amount of work.'

He shrugged laconically. 'It's what I'm good at.'

Her smile was just a shiver across her lips. 'I can see that.'

'I needed him to know that Herrera Incorporated was valuable again. It's more than a business, *hermosa*. This is a birthright. A legacy. No one wants to leave something worse than when they inherited. But my father...' he said, breaking off, not quite sure why he felt so free to confide in Amelia when he generally made a point of holding his private matters close to his chest. But she waited patiently, her enormous eyes promising him discretion, encouraging him to finish his sentence. 'He was a gentleman,' he went on, smiling as he surrendered to the memory. 'He believed in honour and decency. He came from a time when a man's handshake truly was as good as his word—and a word between decent people meant more than a contract. It was naïve, in hindsight, but it's how he'd always done business. It was easy for your brother to target him.' He cleared his throat. 'The despair almost killed him.'

She blanched visibly. 'You couldn't do anything to stop it?'

'Not at the time. My father didn't realise what was happening until it was too late. Their plan was ruthless, meticulous and executed with brilliance. Within the space of a fortnight, he'd lost almost everything.'

'I'm sorry,' she said gently, her eyes showing the sincerity of her words. 'I wish...that hadn't happened.'

How long had he been waiting for a diSalvo to apologise? A long time. But not this diSalvo—and not now. It was too late for apologies, too late for forgiveness. The die had been cast long ago: his hatred and need for vengeance had been forged in fire. No words could weaken those feelings.

'It is part of our history now,' he said, sipping his drink, his eyes holding hers.

'But not our future,' she ventured, her look one of hope.

He stayed silent—how could their future be anything but?

'When did he die?' she asked, turning the conversation away from their blood feud when he didn't respond. And he was relieved by that—another out-of-character feeling, for Antonio Herrera *never* shied away from a conflict.

'Not long ago.'

A frown flickered across her face. 'When?'

'Four months,' he said.

Her frown deepened. 'That's right before we met?'

'A month before,' he agreed.

'You didn't tell me.'

'Why would I?' he prompted, as though it didn't matter. As though his father's death hadn't invigorated his passionate need for revenge. As though it hadn't scored through his flesh like acid with new resentments, fresh pains.

'Because,' she responded with exasperation, 'we talked about stuff and because it feels like something your wife should know,' she said simply. And then, less simply, infinitely more pleasurably, 'Because I *want* to know stuff like that. Because maybe I could help you. Maybe talking is important.'

Her kindness was unexpected and touching—it was also unsettling. Because he suspected he didn't deserve kindness—particularly not from Amelia.

'Perhaps seeing you put all thoughts of my father from my mind,' he said, aiming to lighten the mood.

Her cheeks glowed pink, but she dropped her gaze, suddenly pretending fascination with the meal in front of her.

'I doubt that.'

'Do you?'

'Yes.' And she looked him square in the eyes, and something in the region of his chest tightened. 'You came to me because of your father. Why else would you act then? Shortly after his death, you enact this revenge plan of yours?'

'It wasn't that,' he said, although of course the timing had seemed fortuitous. 'It took my detective some time to locate you.'

'Detective?' she repeated, scandalised. 'You had a detective looking for me?'

His shrug was more relaxed than he felt. 'You weren't in Italy, as I'd presumed you would be. Nor were you in London. Who would have thought you'd take up a job as a teacher in a school in a town in the middle of nowhere, using an assumed name? It was as though you were trying to disappear from the face of the earth.'

Her lips twisted. 'I suppose I kind of was.' Her expression assumed a faraway look. 'I love my family, Antonio.' She sent him a look, and he heard the words she hadn't said: *Enough to marry you to save them*. 'But I never fitted into their way of life. I didn't like the sense of being a commodity rather than a person. All my life, I've wanted to be normal. Just a regular person with a real job, who can do normal things. That's why I was in tiny village in the middle of nowhere. It's why I became a teacher.'

His chest compressed at the picture she painted, of a girl always out of place and time, and he couldn't help the surge of guilt that rushed through him. Because he'd dragged her back into the spotlight, and deep down he knew she would have been happier if only he'd left her alone.

'But a detective?' she teased, turning their conversation back to his method of locating her.

He took her lead, but his mind was raking over her admission of having felt so out of place, and making a new kind of sense of that. Her refusal to take part in a wedding reception suddenly made sense, and he marvelled at his insensitivity. Her reaction had been unusually panicked. Now he understood that. Pity clouded his eyes but he kept his voice light.

'Why does that surprise you?'

'I suppose it shouldn't. You wanted my shares in Prim'Aqua; you did what you needed in an attempt to procure them—including sleuthing me out with a private eye. You don't let anything stand in the way of your dreams.'

But her words rankled and he needed to reject them instantly. 'I didn't come to your home to seduce you, Amelia,' he said throatily. 'What happened between us that night was as simple as me wanting you and you wanting me.'

'It wasn't simple,' she said softly. 'Not with all this between us.'

Never had truer words been spoken, yet still he sought to refute the statement. 'I wasn't thinking of our families when I took you to bed.'

And more heat suffused her cheeks and, *Cristo*, he wanted her in that moment. He wanted her, but not just because his body was tight with desire. He wanted her because he longed to kiss her, to make her cry out for him; he ached to seduce her slowly, to show her how it could be between two people completely in sync. Their single night together had been too short; had he known he would not have the pleasure of her company again, he would have lingered over their lovemaking, enjoying every move and thrust, every shift of their bodies in that primal heat. He would have helped her learn the ways of her own body, the pleasure she was capable of feeling, what she longed for most.

'I'm glad to hear it,' she said, but the words hitched in her throat and there was a breathless quality to them that spoke of her own desires and needs, and how he ached to indulge those!

And, despite the fact this was all new and different, and he didn't know what they were doing, he reached for her hand and lifted it to his lips, pressing a kiss against her fingertips as his eyes held hers.

Her lashes fluttered closed, but not before he saw the desire swirling in their cornflower-blue depths. Not before her lips parted on a sharp intake of breath.

Sensual heat was in the air around them, and he had no intention of ignoring it this time.

Did he have any idea what he was doing to her?

She tried to focus on the page of her book, but with Antonio doing push-ups on the terrace just beyond her, wearing a pair of black bathing briefs, his broad, tanned chest on display, his powerful legs, his dark hair slicked against his head like a pelt after his early evening swim—she was lost, powerless, completely entranced. The words in her book swirled before her eyes and she valiantly made an effort to read the paragraph once more.

It was her own fault, she supposed, for picking up *Anna Karenina*. Having read it before and suffered through a more in-depth appraisal of nineteenth-century Russian agriculture than anyone truly needed, she wasn't exactly sure why she'd felt compelled to pick it up once more.

It was hardly engrossing.

Not as engrossing as her husband, in any event. Their conversation over lunch had got deep under her skin. His insistence that he had come to her to buy shares but had then wanted *her*, not because of Prim'Aqua, not because of anything. Except desire. Lust. Need. Passion.

She hadn't realised until lunch how desperately she'd needed his assurances on that score and, now that she had them, how empowering it was. Because it legitimised what she felt—it showed that, no matter what else they were, this desire was real. It was true. He hadn't seduced her because he'd thought it would lead to her compliance. He'd been unable to resist her.

For the hundredth time in a handful of minutes, her eyes lifted towards the terrace. He wasn't looking at her. She allowed herself a moment to stare, to savour the lines of his body, the sleek, smooth masculinity that was all hard edges and beautiful planes, and then turned back to her book.

Two sentences later and her eyes lifted and finally, with an exasperated sound, she dropped the book and stood.

Did he have any idea what he was doing to her? Surely he did.

And couldn't two play at that game?

With a small smile on her lips, she slipped upstairs and

strolled into the enormous walk-in wardrobe. He'd filled it with designer clothes, but she'd assiduously ignored them, preferring to wear clothes she felt most like herself in, to wear the clothes of her old life like a uniform.

Only she hadn't brought a swimsuit with her, and she knew there were several stashed in one of the drawers. She opened the first—it was filled with jewels, so she snapped it shut and went lower. The next drawer revealed what she was looking for.

She pulled out a simple navy-blue bikini and dressed quickly, pulling her hair over one shoulder as she crossed the room on her way back downstairs. Only the sight of herself in the full-length mirror arrested her step for a moment.

She curled her hands over the hint of a curve, a smile stretching her lips from one ear to the other.

She began to walk once more, but the smile didn't shift. So as she stepped out onto the terrace she'd almost forgotten that a small part of her had wanted to go and get into a swimsuit just to repay the sensual distraction Antonio had been subjecting her to for the past hour. He was doing sit-ups now and, as he pulled towards his knees, he stopped, holding himself there, his body sheened in a light layer of perspiration so that he glistened all over, his expression burning her with its intensity. He dragged his eyes from her face, down her body, over the soft curve of her breasts to her newly rounded stomach, her legs and then back up, until her skin was covered in goosebumps and her heart was racing.

He stood slowly and, with the same pace, she took a step towards him, her eyes unable to pull away from his.

'You are…' He spoke with a voice that was husky, words that were dredged from deep inside his soul.

She held her breath, waiting for him to finish the sentence, but he shook his head, as if to clear the thought.

'Yes?' she asked breathlessly.

'You are beautiful,' he said finally and moved a hand to curve around her cheek, tilting her face towards his.

She could hardly swallow, so dry was her mouth. 'Thank you.'

'I cannot believe this.' And he dropped his hands to her stomach, discovering the roundness there for himself.

'I know; it's kind of surreal,' she said, trying to sound light and breezy.

But the look on his face rid her of any such notion. There was such an acute watchfulness in his expression, a sense of powerful, passionate possession, that she took a step closer, as close as she could get without touching him, and then he went the rest of the way, closing the gap and wrapping one arm around her waist. He held her, vice-like, to his body and she made a soft sound of surrender before his lips dropped to hers and he kissed her, his mouth demanding, as though everything was hinged on this kiss.

She tilted her head, giving him more access, and she lost herself in that moment but she found herself too.

Emotions surged inside her but Amelia couldn't have described them—not happiness, not doubt. She was a mix of everything and nothing; she knew only that answers lay within this kiss, within this touch, within him.

He lifted her easily, cradling her to his chest and carrying her towards the pool. And, despite the fact he was moving in that direction, the feel of cool water against her sun-warmed and passion-heated body still made her gasp. He swallowed the gasp and kissed it right back to her, and she laughed softly as the water rose higher and higher.

She spun in his arms, wrapping her arms around his neck and her legs around his waist, and then she kissed him with all the pent-up hormonal needs that were ravaging her common sense and making her need Antonio more in that moment than she'd ever needed anyone or anything.

'Make love to me,' she demanded, her hands weaving behind his back, interlocking and holding him tight.

He groaned, a guttural noise that was empowering to Amelia for it spoke of his desperation and slavery to this feeling, and she was so glad for that! Glad he was as lost to this as she. Glad he was as in her thrall as she was his.

'Why?' he asked, but his hands were curving around her rear, lifting her so she felt the strength of his arousal and tipped her head back. Her hair fell into the water, saturated, and he kissed the exposed column of her neck then found the tie for her bikini.

'Because you're my husband,' she said as he stripped the bikini top from her, discarding it in the water. His eyes devoured her breasts before his lips took over, his mouth moving over one of her nipples and then the next.

It wasn't a reason. At least, it wasn't as simple as being her husband: there were so many other factors. Having known this pleasure only once, she wanted to feel it again. She wanted to feel everything he could show her. She ran her hands over his body, delighting in the feel of his skin beneath her touch and the way he responded to her inquisitive exploration.

'Make love to me,' she whispered again, like an incantation, a demand that needed fulfilling, dropping her lips to his shoulder and nipping the flesh there with her teeth.

And there was a look of intense understanding in his eyes, a look of fierce determination too. 'I intend to, *querida.*'

Relief soared inside her and she found his mouth with hers, kissing him as though there was nothing between them but this passion, this heat. She kissed him as though this were a new beginning, and all the old hatreds and resentments were nowhere to be seen. In that moment, she wasn't a diSalvo and he wasn't a Herrera, and there were no storm clouds threatening on their horizon.

Her hands roamed his body in all the ways she'd been wanting to do since that night in the cottage. Movements that her dreams had crystallised became real. She pushed at his shorts, a low, keening noise in her throat when her fingertips grazed the strength of his arousal, the promise of his possession.

He pulled his head from hers, his expression one of utter need when he stared down at her. And awakening too, as though he were shifting out of a dream state and discovering this new reality.

'Why the hell haven't we done this sooner?' he demanded gruffly, finding her bikini bottoms and pushing them down at the same time she kicked out of them.

'Because we're stupid,' she said, the words intended as a joke but coming out seriously. There was nothing funny about the intensity of their desire.

'Sí,' he grunted, lifting her legs and staring at her for a long, intense moment before wrapping her around his body and sinking his powerful arousal deep into her moist core.

She groaned as he swept inside her, remembered sensations kicking to life along with new ones. It was so overwhelming! And as he thrust deep into her feminine centre, he brought his mouth to hers and his kiss mirrored the movements of his body, so her blood stirred to his tempo, gushing fast and desperately. She writhed in his arms, her ankles crossed behind his back, her hands tangling in the dark pelt of his hair, and then pleasure turned to something far harder to quantify—something earth-shattering and mind-blowing. She dug her nails into his back, scoring red marks over his flesh as the pleasure became unbearable and finally she exploded, holding onto him for dear life as everything she'd ever known seemed to fade into a distant, faraway pinprick of light.

She was high above the earth and there was only this— blinding, inconceivable light.

Amelia held onto him as slowly she sunk back down to earth, her eyes blinking open in disorientation to find she was in the pool, held by Antonio, his body tight against hers, his arousal still rock-hard inside her. He was watching her, and heat bloomed in her cheeks to recall what madness she'd just succumbed to. How lost she'd been to the feelings he could stir within her so easily.

But realisation didn't last long before he moved within her once more, this time watching her, their eyes locked in an ancient, primal examination. He watched as he drove himself deep inside her, he watched as her teeth sunk into her lip to stop herself from crying out, and he shook his head, lifting his thumb and rubbing it over her lips. 'Do not censor yourself.' The words were heavy with his exotic accent, thrilling over her nerve endings, setting little fires beneath her blood.

Before he could pull his hand away, she sunk her mouth around his thumb and his eyes flared wide at the sight of her pink lips swallowing a part of him.

His own groan was loud then, and power surged inside her to know that she could drive him every bit as wild as he could her. *'Tentadora,'* he growled, his strong, virile thrust sending spasms of awareness spiralling through her.

'Right back at you,' she whimpered, digging her nails into his shoulder as another wave of pleasure built.

But he stilled suddenly, his face wiped of anything she could discern, his expression unrecognisable. 'I want you to be my wife, Amelia,' he said, and the words were foreign and confusing when all she could think of was sensual pleasure.

'I am.' She rolled her hips, needing him to keep doing what he had been, needing him to keep pushing her towards the edge of what she could bear.

'No. I want you in every sense. In my bed, by my side. From now on. *Entiendes?*'

Something other than pleasure punched through her, something that set her soul on fire, that she couldn't analyse and couldn't comprehend, beyond knowing that it mattered more than the world to her.

'*Sí,*' she moaned, rolling her hips once more. And, satisfied with her agreement, he gave her what she needed, his body resuming its rhythm, driving her higher and higher into the heavens. And as she stood on the precipice, preparing to dive into an unknown heaven, he was there with her, his body vibrating alongside hers, and they clung together as they fell apart, into a billion pieces of what they had once been.

CHAPTER TWELVE

ANTONIO HAD ALMOST forgotten about the interview. It had been given months ago—shortly before their wedding, when Amelia had still been, for the most part, simply a diSalvo to him. A month before they'd slept together again and formed a new kind of relationship, one that existed outside the bounds of their blood feud.

Since that day in the pool, something had shifted for them. She'd come to his bed each night and he'd slept wrapped around her, a hand possessively curved over her stomach and a certainty in his chest that she was right where she belonged.

He stared at the newspaper spread over his desk and the photo they'd chosen to print of her, and his gut twisted with a mix of fury and disgust. She was only young in this picture—ten, perhaps? And her mother stood beside her, wearing a skimpy dress and huge sunglasses, looking every bit the drugged-out supermodel he had discovered her to have been.

Perhaps if he didn't know Amelia as he did now, he wouldn't have noticed the fear in her eyes. Nor the panic stretched across her beautiful young face.

But he understood every cell in her beautiful body, he *knew* her, in many ways better than he did himself. And even though they'd met only eight months earlier, seeing her in this picture, he understood exactly what she was feeling. There were photographers in the background of the photo, paparazzi, and her small fingers were curved around her mother's, as though she were the protector, the adult.

He swore a guttural oath into his office as he reached for his phone and dialled her number on autopilot. His eyes took in the headline to the left of the article: *Tycoon's Marriage Merger!*

His gut clenched.

> *In a move the billionaire businessman himself describes as 'fortuitous', the marriage of Amelia diSanto to Antonio Herrera brings together two warring dynasties—and a merging of assets that will form one of the biggest financial powerhouses in the world.*
>
> *'Prim'Aqua will be at the heart of my business operation going forward,' Herrera says. 'It gives me great satisfaction to bring the company back into the fold. The future is bright.'*

He hadn't even been misquoted. He *had* said that, and myriad other self-congratulatory statements lauding his own success in reacquiring Prim'Aqua. At the time, he'd thought only of Carlo's reaction on reading the news. He'd taken pleasure from imagining his sworn enemy having to see evidence of Antonio's success—and the marriage that would add insult to injury.

He hadn't thought of Amelia. Not when he'd given the interview.

He hadn't *known* her then. He hadn't known that she'd wish to keep this marriage secret, to give herself time to adjust to it. He hadn't known that she would turn out to be every bit as sweet as she'd seemed that night, long ago, in Bumblebee Cottage. He hadn't known that he would come to depend on her, that she could answer every single one of his needs.

His eyes dived to the next page, where there was a photo with him and one of his ex-lovers. A woman whose name he struggled to remember in that moment. *Billionaire Bachelor!* ran the second headline, and there was a list of his famous past lovers.

His chest felt as though it were being split in two.

'Answer your phone,' he snapped, then hung up and dialled her number again.

It rung out, but he kept trying, all the while reading the article.

Every paragraph showed it to be so much worse.

Hell, he'd forgotten about this interview, because it hadn't mattered to him at the time. He'd given no thought to Amelia, and how she might feel. She'd agreed to marry him, she'd agreed to give him Prim'Aqua once their child was born, and that had been the end of it.

But now?

Dios, please let her not have seen it.

With another oath, he grabbed his suit jacket and swung his arms into it as he walked, stalking towards the door of his office and slamming it in his wake.

'Sir? You have an appointment in ten…'

'Cancel my afternoon,' he bit out, jabbing a finger against the door of the lift. 'Cancel it all.'

He barely recognised himself in the shimmery reflection of the lift. His face was white beneath his tan. So this, then, was what true fear felt like.

Amelia stirred her tea, a gentle smile on her face. She daydreamed a lot lately. And she smiled a lot too.

Her hand curved over her rounded tummy—now so big she couldn't sit in properly against a table. She could use it as a table, she thought with a grin, as she balanced a book on it just for fun.

She stifled a yawn, then looked towards the clock. It was

still the early afternoon. She'd taken to napping, to catch up on sleep, because her nights were hardly as restful as they could be. Warmth suffused her body as she remembered the way Antonio had kissed her all over the night before, his mouth finding her most intimate core and his tongue driving her beyond wild, until her nails had almost torn shreds in the silk sheets of his bed and heat had threatened to burn her from the inside out.

He knew exactly how to touch her, to kiss her, to hold her, to give her more pleasure than she could put into words.

She stood slowly, stretching her arms above her head before reaching for her tea and carrying it with her towards her bedroom.

Her phone screen was glowing when she stepped inside and she moved towards it on autopilot, scooping it up to see a screen covered in alerts.

Missed calls—lots of them. From Antonio's office phone and Carlo's mobile.

Her heart began to trip faster and faster. She hadn't spoken to Carlo in months, except via text. It had been too hard to talk to him, knowing that she was lying to him, and she still hadn't been ready to face the reality of her brother and father's outrage. And they *would* be outraged when they discovered she'd married Antonio—that she was pregnant with his baby.

She needed time—and wanted to protect the marriage that they were building. A marriage that, in her heart, she suspected couldn't have been more perfect if their meeting had been a true love match. Because she loved him with all her heart and every inch of her soul, and she suspected he felt the same.

He had to.

Love didn't exist in a vacuum. One person couldn't have enough love to create this abundance of feeling.

She skipped into the voicemail section of her phone.

None from Antonio, several from Carlo. Concern for her father came to the forefront of her mind—it would make sense that both men would try to contact her if something had happened to Giacomo.

She lifted the phone to her ear, bracing herself for whatever was to come. But she couldn't have imagined it would be anything like this.

'Amelia? What the hell is going on?'

Several curse words in Italian.

'You're pregnant? Tell me that bastardo *is not the father. I swear, I'll kill him.'*

Her skin shivered with goosebumps as she tried to make sense of how Carlo had learned the truth. She'd been so careful, and she knew Antonio understood her desire to keep their marriage quiet. So? How had Carlo learned of this?

She clicked into the next voicemail; it was even angrier.

'Call me back, damn it! What the hell is happening? You married Antonio Herrera? He'll eat you alive and spit you back out for breakfast. How could you be so stupid? The man is a bastard, capable of only hatred and revenge. He is the devil.'

The next one was just a string of angry Italian, finishing with, *'How could you do this to me? He's using you, Amelia—and, damn it, you're letting him. He's using you to get to me!'*

She was ice-cold and dropped the phone to the bed just as it began to ring anew. Carlo.

She lifted it to her ear. *'Digame.'*

'Damn it, where have you been, Millie?'

'Not near my phone,' she said, sitting down on the edge of the bed, numb.

'Well?' The word was bitten out and she swept her eyes shut. 'Is it true?'

'I…'

'You're married to him?'

'I…'

'Damn it! Do you know who he is? He hates us, Millie. How could you do this?'

'It wasn't…' She bit down on her lip and stared at her hands, her wedding ring glinting as she looked at it.

'He's using you!'

'No, it's not like that. Our marriage isn't…anything to do with this feud.'

He swore in disagreement. 'He told me he would take everything I care about and destroy it, just for the sake of it. I thought he meant my businesses; I had no clue he was speaking of my own sister. He seduced you and convinced you to marry him purely to hurt me. Can't you see that?'

'No!' She shook her head, her mind clinging to the intimacy she shared with her husband, to the truth of what they'd become.

'Yes. Do you doubt him capable of it? He who has set out to bring down our whole empire?'

'You did the same to him,' she fired at him, her stomach in knots.

'To get him to back off!' Carlo grunted. 'But this was always about him—and his ability to destroy us. His sick need to avenge a generations-old feud. This is the man you've married. Is this *bastardo* to be the father to my nephew?'

She wanted to dispute what he'd said, but memories of conversations spun into her mind—his description of his childhood, the love he'd felt for his father. A father who'd suffered as a result of Carlo's machinations.

It was all too hard to process.

'How did you find out about us?' she asked, turning to the one thing she could attempt to make sense of in that moment.

'The article,' he snarled. 'Tell me you've seen it?'

'I…no.'

'Then you are in for a wake-up call. Your *husband*—' he spat the word '—couldn't help boasting about taking over our family empire. "A perfect merger", he calls it. You are little more than an afterthought—a bride for the sake of business. *This* is the man you married.'

Her chest felt as if it were being washed with acid. Panic was curving around her, and the baby in her belly began to flip and flop in response to the adrenal surge.

'I can't believe it.'

'It's online.' There was a pause. 'There. I've sent you a link.'

'*Gracias.*'

She disconnected the call without knowing if the conversation was at an end. Her forehead was hot and clammy as she clicked into the text message link and the article expanded on her device.

Tycoon's Marriage Merger! the headline screamed.

She read the article with a growing sense of panic and a lessening ability to breathe, then stared at her phone, the whole world seemingly made of shards of a broken mirror that she had no idea how to safely traverse.

'Amelia.' She hadn't heard him come in and the sound of his voice startled her. She lifted her gaze towards him and saw the tightness in his expression. The wariness too.

'You gave an interview?' Her words were low and throaty, her sense of betrayal evident in each sore syllable.

A muscle throbbed low in his throat and she stared at it, then shifted her gaze sideways, to the corridor beyond the door. Their baby kicked against her ribs but she didn't react.

'A long time ago,' he conceded, nodding, stepping into the room but pausing when she stiffened.

'When?' She looked at him, a plea in her features.

'Before we were married,' he said. 'I had forgotten about the damned piece.'

'Don't.' She shook her head, standing, nothing making any sense any more.

'Don't what?'

'Don't lie to me. Don't act as though this wasn't all a part of your plan.'

His brows knitted together as he stared at her, then he closed the gap between them, his stride long and purposeful. 'I am sorry the article ran. I am sorry I couldn't prepare you for it. I gave the editor an earful on the drive over here,' he said with a shake of his head.

'He's just doing his job! What were you doing? Bragging to all and sundry about how clever you are to have acquired the company you've always wanted through this…*marriage merger* of ours! That's all this is for you, isn't it?'

'I have *never* used those words to describe what we are,' he contradicted fiercely. 'And you know as well as anyone that the reason I married you is for our baby, not because of Prim'Aqua.'

She recoiled as though he'd slapped her and breath burned in her lungs. She *did* know the reason they'd married, but it still hurt to be reminded of how calculated this had all been for him. 'And somewhere between my agreeing to marry you and us actually getting married, you had time to gloat to a journalist about the controlling stake in Prim'Aqua you'd scored?'

He ground his teeth together. 'It is a statement of fact, not a gloat.'

'And the hurt this article caused my family? Can you imagine how they felt, waking up to read this?'

His expression tightened, his eyes glistening black. 'I do not care what your family felt,' he said finally, coldly, and then, with a noticeable softening of his features, 'I care about you. About any hurt this stupid journalism has caused you to feel.'

She bit down on her lip and turned her back on him. 'Hurting my family does hurt me. You've known that all along.'

He was silent.

'Nothing's changed for you, has it?'

'What do you mean?' he queried from right behind her, so his breath was warm against her flesh and her stomach twisted at his nearness and the distance she felt growing between them.

'You still hate my family—even though they're a part of me, and our baby is a part of them.'

He made a growling sound of dissent. 'Everything's changed. We are married. When I gave that interview, I didn't see you as much more than a means to an end, it's true.'

She winced.

'I have never hidden my feelings about your family.'

She frowned, knowing this to be the case and still somehow finding it impossible to process. An ache began to throb, deep in her chest. Or was it more like a ticking—incessant, unstoppable, louder and louder, speeding up and echoing the frantic racing of her heart?

'What's going to happen when our baby is born?' she whispered, curling her hands over her stomach. 'And I want to take him or her to Italy to see his grandfather? Or his uncle? Are you going to resent that? Are you going to hate me being there? Are you going to refuse to come? Or will you come and fight with two of the people I care about most?'

He ground his teeth together. 'I've told you, your relationship with them has nothing to do with me.'

She shook her head painfully. 'But what of our child's relationship with them? I will be raising our baby to love their whole family—that means my family—to talk about them with love, to speak Italian and understand his or her heritage. My child will have your last name but it will still be my child, of my family, with all that implies.'

His expression was shuttered. 'But around me he will be Herrera,' Antonio said simply. 'As you are now.'

The ache in her chest grew. 'I'm not any part of this feud,' she said. 'And I can't believe you're continuing after all this!'

'I am doing no such thing,' he said, his expression sombre. 'I have made *no* move against your brother since we married. I have left his business interests alone, even though I have had opportunity to destroy him ten times over. What is this if not proof that I am standing by our agreement?'

'Our agreement?' She paled. 'That's why you've backed off from Carlo's companies?'

He spun her around in his arms, his eyes searching hers. 'Why else?' The question was asked as if from the depths of his soul, as though he truly couldn't comprehend what was wrong with that statement. 'I am doing what you asked of me.'

And suddenly she needed to sit down. She collapsed onto the edge of the bed, pressing her fingertips into her temples.

'*Hermosa*, what is it?'

She ignored his apparent concern. 'That damned deal we made way back then is why you've left Carlo alone? You've let him be only because I'm giving you Prim'Aqua.' Her eyes glistened when she lifted them to his. 'That's all you care about.'

He swore softly. 'Not all I care about.'

'Yeah?' she demanded, scoffing.

'You know I care about you. It is why I'm here, Amelia, in the middle of the afternoon. Because the thought of you reading that article and thinking I had just given this interview...'

'But you don't love me,' she interrupted curtly, gnawing on her lower lip.

His eyes showed consternation when they locked to hers, impatience too. 'Love is beside the point,' he intoned flatly, and the words seemed to come from a long way away. 'I respect you and value you. I desire you and I have chosen to make a life with you.'

'But *love* would be a reason to leave my family alone. Love would be a reason for you to forget your hatred of them.'

'Nothing will allow me to do that,' he said gently, crouching down so his eyes were level with hers. 'I have hated them for ever and, no matter what role you play in my life, I can't simply forget how I feel.'

'You strike me as a man who can do anything he wants. So what you're saying is that you don't *want* to forgive them.'

His jaw was square, and the room was heavy with angst and sorrow for a moment before he nodded curtly. 'No,' he said at length. 'I do not want to forgive them. I want to hate them. I like hating them.'

'Even when it hurts me.'

He shook his head curtly. 'They are separate to us.'

'No, they're not.'

'They have to be. For our child, we must separate your family…'

'No, for our child, you must forget your need for revenge…'

'No.' A simple, final word that was like a nail in the coffin of all of her hopes.

'So your hatred for them is greater than anything you feel for me,' she said with a nod, as the truth of their relationship crystallised in her mind. 'You still expect me to hand over my shares in Prim'Aqua when our child is born?'

A muscle jerked in the base of his jaw and he didn't answer for a beat. Then, 'It's what we agreed.'

Her throat thickened with the threat of tears—tears she

refused to let fall. 'And you'll take Prim'Aqua to devastate Carlo? You'll take it and you'll use me to hurt him. Yes?'

He didn't answer and, quite demented by her grief, she stood and shoved at his chest, her hair whipping her cheeks as she pushed him. And he stayed where he was, impenetrable and strong, and then finally he tilted his head, just a tiny movement.

'Yes.'

Silence fell, condemnatory and grief-laced.

'And you can't even see how wrong that is, can you?'

Antonio gripped her wrists, holding her hands still against his chest. Her words were like blades in his side. 'I want Prim'Aqua,' he said, as though it were simple. He didn't need to be looking at his wife to know she was close to tears. He heard it in her voice, when she spoke next.

'More than you want me?'

'I want you both,' he said finally. 'I want you, I want this baby. And, yes, I want Prim'Aqua. That was our agreement.'

'I know that.' Her voice sounded husky, scored by sadness. 'But we were different people six months ago. I thought we were going to try to make this marriage real—'

'In what way is it not?' he interrupted, wishing he hadn't turned to look at her when he was confronted with such obvious despair on her features.

'There's no love here,' she said simply. 'Not from you.'

Her words filtered through his brain and something like an alarm bell sounded. 'Are you saying you've fallen in love with me?' he asked, incredulous, surprised, and not sure what else.

'Yes.' It was a simple answer, one that made his heart jump and panic all at once. 'I love you,' she said, and there was a part of him that rejoiced at that, and a larger part that wanted her to take the words back because they were undeserved and unasked for. Because they complicated a situation that should have been straightforward—an agreement between two parties, just like he was used to. 'But I can't do this.'

'Do what?'

'You can't actually think this marriage will work, with you hating my brother like this? With you intent on destroying him, determined to hold onto your revenge and your anger and your hatred. Not if there's a chance you're going to poison my child against him.'

The bottom was falling out of Antonio's world. Her words might as well have been spoken in Swahili for all the sense they made. There were very few facts in life he knew for certain, and one of those was that the diSalvo and Herrera families were enemies, to the death. He had no compassion for Carlo, no room for forgiveness for Giacomo. They deserved whatever fate he could conspire to give them.

And Amelia? What of her pain and hurt?

He faced the prospect of Amelia walking away from him and he wanted to assume super-human form, to build a wall as high as the sun to keep her in his home. To trap her? *Dios*, had he not already done that with this marriage?

Apparently not, if she was threatening to leave him. 'Your reasons for being married to me haven't changed,' he pointed out, falling back on his skills as a negotiator to silence the panicked drumming of his heart. 'We want the same things for our child—'

'No, we don't.' She fixed him with a level stare, icy determination in her own eyes now. 'I want my kids to have what I never did. I don't want them to live with uncertainty and insecurity, doubt, and a lack of love. And I'm sure as heck not prepared to bring my child into a war zone.'

Her words cut him to the core. 'You and I aren't a war zone! Look at how well things work between us!'

She sucked in a shallow breath. 'Because we haven't been tested! We work because we've existed as an island, totally separate from the reality of our situation. But we can't raise our child in a void! I won't deny them their heritage, and the love they can know from my family. You have no one left—no parents, no siblings, nothing you can offer them by way of an extended family. Carlo and Giacomo are it.'

'Better to have no family than those two *bastardos*—'

Her eyes fluttered shut, her lashes two dark fans against her pale cheeks. 'I can't accept that.'

'You have already accepted it,' he pointed out softly. 'You married me and you knew how I felt, and what I wanted. Carlo was bound to find out about us at some point, so now he knows. This is not the end of the world.'

She made a scoffing noise. 'He's *devastated*. He thinks you're using me to avenge your father. He thinks our marriage is just the next step in your revenge plan.' Her skin paled visibly. 'And the worst thing is, he's right.'

'*Madre de Dios*, you cannot actually believe this is all about revenge.'

'Not all of it, no,' she conceded softly. 'But it's a part of our marriage, and it shouldn't be.'

He ignored the compulsion to point out that their marriage *had* been born out of a desire for revenge—the words were lodged inside him, yet he couldn't speak them.

'Our marriage is immune from this.'

Scepticism showed in her expression. 'So you're telling me I can walk away from you without consequence? That you'll let me go and not set out to destroy Carlo?'

He ground his teeth as he processed her request and finally shook his head. 'No. The only thing stopping me from eviscerating him is you.'

'No, not me,' she said flatly. 'The fact I'm willing to go along with this charade.'

'You just said you love me,' he responded tautly, ignoring the throbbing deep in his chest. 'How can you then call our marriage a charade?'

'Because love doesn't exist in a black hole. My love means nothing without yours in return.'

His eyes sparked with hers but he didn't give her what she needed—and his words would have been meaningless, in any event. Meaningless when he was showing her with his actions how little he cared for her.

Sadness for the path he was set upon curdled her blood. 'Can't you see that you're pursuing revenge even when it's destroying your life? You are letting this feud become the whale to your Ahab.'

His eyes locked to hers and his chest felt as though a slab of bricks had been laid over it. 'I am doing what is needed.'

She hissed like a cat in an alley. 'Don't be ridiculous! To what? Avenge your father? I'm sorry, Antonio, but he's dead.' She winced apologetically. 'And I don't think he'd want you to use his death as an excuse to ruin your life. I don't think he'd want you to destroy your marriage in his name.'

He straightened his shoulders, staring at her down the bridge of his nose, nostrils flaring with his attempt to stay calm. She was his wife, but now she was taking it too far. 'You do not know anything about him.'

'I know that he was a man who took you to the park on weekends. Who cleared his schedule to read you books, to play with you. I know that he was a man who loved you and wanted you to be happy. Don't you owe it to him to try to move on from this?'

A beat of silence passed, heavy with her words, her hopes, his darkness. And then he spoke clearly, coldly and with finality. 'I am doing this *for* my father. I promised myself I would make Carlo pay for what he did and now I have the means of doing so. Do you think this won't make me happy?'

She took a step back, her expression like a wounded animal.

'Even when that means I'll leave?'

He stared at her, his eyes roaming her face, and then he shrugged—he appeared so cold, so measured, when his insides were shredding. 'If you truly love me, then you will understand what motivates me. You will accept this anger is a part of me, and you won't seek to change me.'

'I want to help you!' she denied hotly. 'No one should live their life with so much hatred. This is so pointless! So futile! I'm not saying you and Carlo should become best friends, heaven forbid, but can't you at least try to put the past in the past?'

'It is a part of who I am,' he said simply. 'As sure as I have two arms and legs, hating him is in my soul.'

'And loving him is in mine. I won't have my child be torn between us—feeling as though he's betraying you because he adores his uncle.'

'I've told you, I have no intention of letting our child be caught up in this.'

'How can you possibly prevent it?' She didn't wait for an answer . 'And what of me? You said last night you'd never do anything that would upset me. Can't you see how this is pulling me apart?'

A muscle spasmed low in his jaw. 'Have I spoken to you of your brother since we married? Have I brought up our feud, even once?'

She blinked, her expression one of bafflement. 'You haven't needed to! It's been in every conversation with us, every day! Why do you think I never speak of them?'

'Because they are nothing to us!'

She ground her teeth together. 'It's my *father*. He took me in when I was completely alone—'

'And you were miserable with him! That's why you hid away in that tiny village…'

'Yes, I wanted a different life, but that doesn't mean I don't love them!' She closed her eyes for a moment, sucked in a breath, hoping it would breathe strength into her. 'It doesn't mean I'll let you destroy them.'

His eyes narrowed and the threat she was making struck something in his chest, like a match to petrol. 'I don't need your permission.'

'You need my shares,' she pointed out.

'No. I have enough to ruin him, remember? To make him crumble into nothingness. Prim'Aqua is my first preference, but without it I will still succeed, *querida*.'

'Don't you dare call me that,' she spat. 'Not when you can be so ruthless and vile.'

His face flashed with surprise at her insults, and when she pressed her palm to her stomach, his eyes dropped to the gesture.

'I can't do this.' She reached for her wedding band and slid it off her finger, then her engagement ring—that had belonged to his grandmother. She held them out to him but he refused to take them, so she placed them on the table instead.

'I can't be your wife, I can't raise this baby with you, and I can't give you Prim'Aqua.' Her voice cracked. 'Our deal's off, Antonio. Destroy him if you will, but know that I will never, ever be able to forgive you if you do. Know that you will turn my love to hatred. It's your decision.'

CHAPTER THIRTEEN

HE SWORE UNDER his breath, watching as she disappeared into the wardrobe of their room. The last few minutes seemed like a dream—he could barely believe she was threatening to end their marriage.

She was upset, her shoulders shifting with silent tears, and his gut twisted with the knowledge that he'd done that to her. He'd hurt her, he'd brought her into something she hadn't even known existed.

But why? Why had this feud torn him apart, fuelled Carlo's actions, and yet Amelia had known nothing of it? Was it simply that she'd shown no interest in the business side of her family? Or was there something more to it? How could she fail to see how deep these wounds ran?

Her face, when she'd told him she was leaving, had been so full of certainty, resignation, as though that was the end of it. As though he wouldn't be able to change her mind.

That thought alone galvanised him into action—he couldn't accept the finality of that. He pushed his legs forward, carrying himself towards her, pushing into the large dressing room to find her taking clothes from drawers and laying them in a duffel bag.

And he groaned because, no matter what he felt for her family, he didn't want to lose her.

'Don't go,' he said simply, moving towards her and wrapping his arms around her waist. She swallowed a sob then, and it was a sound that tore him apart.

'Why should I stay?' she asked after a moment, pulling

away and looking at him with a challenge. She reached behind her for another stack of shirts and pushed them into the bag.

'Because you're my wife,' he said, as though it were simple.

'Yes. And I love you.' She nodded, but it was clear she didn't welcome that fact. 'But I have a track record of loving people when they can't love me back. And it destroys me—just like it did with my mother. If I stay, and pour all of myself into this marriage and our family, knowing you will never be able to give me what I need, then I'll be broken. And I won't be broken again.'

Her words landed against him like bricks. He stared at her, with no idea what he could say to change her mind.

'Tell me you love me,' she said softly, her eyes challenging him. 'Tell me you love me enough to forget your hatred for Carlo. Tell me you love me enough to leave the past alone and concentrate on our future instead.'

Silence. Her words were foreign, dipped in arsenic. He couldn't, wouldn't, soften in his resolve to destroy her brother. Never. Not even with his dying breath.

There had to be another way to get through to her. He reached for her gently, bringing her to him, and kissed her, intending to seduce her into seeing sense—or at least dependence. But he tasted her salty tears in his mouth and wrenched himself away, spinning on his heel and stalking across the dressing room.

That wasn't right either.

'I want you to stay,' he said simply, the words torn from him.

'Not enough.' She slid her feet into shoes and looked around for her handbag. She was tired—she wore no makeup and her skin was so pale, her eyes red from the sting of tears. 'And I won't stay for what you're offering.' She looked so incredibly haunted, so miserable yet so brave as she glared at him with every appearance of strength and determination, that the heart in his chest splintered apart, shattering into thousands of pieces.

'Stay because you want to,' he said softly.

She recoiled as though he'd physically hit her and his chest heaved.

'Please, stay.'

But she shook her head, and bit down on her lip. Her hands pressed to her stomach, and she moved towards the door. 'I'll let you know, when... I'll message you.'

The idea of hearing about the birth of his child through a text message sliced through his soul. How could he possibly bear to be distant from such an event? How could he be on the outside—not knowing how her delivery was going, not knowing that she was okay, that she was well?

He shook his head, opened his mouth to tell her that wasn't good enough, but she was gone, and he couldn't find any words.

What could he possibly say that would change her mind? Nothing.

And so he let her go, when it was the very last thing he wanted.

When it felt as though he were being beaten over the head. He let her go because he knew it would be best for her. And she deserved that.

Three days later and he hadn't acted. He held the shares in his portfolio and the ability to crush Carlo, and yet he still hadn't dropped the axe. Renowned for his ruthless instincts, he was hesitating at the final hurdle of a plan that he'd formed long ago. Long before he'd even met Amelia and seen her smile.

And the reason was simple.

Every time he imagined the crushing destruction of diSalvo Industries, instead of the rush of jubilation he'd expected, he felt only pain. Pain at how Amelia would respond, at how she'd judge him. Pain at how it would be the death knell to any future with her and their child.

And so he waited, and he wondered about her.

He didn't go to work. He had no interest in his office. Instead, he stalked through his home, seeing her in every room, the memories—though happy—slicing through him with their perfection. She had been everywhere, taken over everything, so that after such a short time he felt her absence completely.

The fresh flowers she had arranged in every room were beginning to wilt—that never happened while she was in the house. She always changed them before they could grow limp.

Antonio was a man who had rebuilt his crumbling family empire from the ground up; he didn't take defeat easily. But this pain was unlike any he had ever encountered.

He had failed in the one thing that mattered to him almost as much as destroying the diSalvos. He had wanted to be a good father, a great husband, yet he'd driven his wife away.

He closed his eyes and tried to picture her in Bumblebee Cottage, imagined her with all those fairy lights and her pregnant stomach, and he cursed loud and clear into the emptiness of their home. Outside, a bleak winter's day threatened rain, just like that first night he'd gone to Amelia, back in England. Only then he'd been so sure of himself, sure of his plan of attack.

Now? He knew only one thing with certainty: he couldn't let this be the end of it. He couldn't accept that their marriage was over.

Amelia would have liked to stay in bed all day, every day. She would have liked to ignore the demands of her body, to refuse to eat, to sob until her broken heart finally grieved and became light again.

Were it not for the baby inside her hugely rounded stomach, she would have indulged every single maudlin fantasy and abandoned herself completely to the grief that had saturated her soul.

She would have wept until her tear ducts dried up and her throat was red raw.

Only for her baby did she give up on self-indulgent mourning. For their baby, on a cold yet sunny winter's day, she forced herself to eat a piece of toast and a banana, to sip a cup of tea and then to dress warmly so she could go for a walk.

A small walk, she promised herself, and then she could go back to bed. Curl up as though the day weren't happening, and ignore the fact that in a matter of weeks she would have a baby, and would have to face the rest of her life without Antonio.

Her heart gave a painful squeeze as his image floated into her mind and she gasped audibly, hating how much she missed him. Hating how tempted she was to throw caution and common sense to the wind and return to Madrid, tail between her legs, pride in tatters, and tell him she would take him—on whatever terms he offered.

But she couldn't do that.

She weaved down a lane, reaching above her and grabbing a twig of jasmine as she went, lifting it to her nose and smelling it, the fragrance so perfectly intoxicating that the ghost of a smile crossed her face.

Not for long, though. Sadness and bleakness were back and she dropped the flower a few steps further.

It was colder than she'd realised and her face was icy, despite the winter sunshine. After a couple of miles, she turned back towards her cottage, already relishing the idea of being back in bed and blotting out this world for a while longer.

A sudden movement when she approached her house caught her eye and she squinted, wondering if she were hallucinating.

A man at her door looked almost exactly like… Antonio. She breathed in sharply just as he pulled his body from the door and then slammed himself against it, in an attempt to break through the ancient timber.

'Antonio!' she said sharply, moving up the small path towards the front door. 'What are you doing?'

'*Dios mío*, you are okay?'

'Of course I'm okay. Why wouldn't I be?'

If anything, he looked indignant, and as though he were controlling a temper. 'Because you weren't answering your door or your phone, and yet your car is here.'

She frowned. 'I went for a walk.'

Consternation creased his brow. 'In this condition?'

'My legs work fine,' she said softly.

'I was concerned,' he explained.

She struggled not to react. Not to let her heart throb hopefully, not to let her pulse fire. It had only been a week, but it might as well have been three years, for how desperately she wanted to stare at him and touch him. Fresh pain perforated her heart, because she couldn't give in to those feelings. He was wrong for her, wrong in every way. His hatred would poison their baby—and enough had been lost to the ancient feud. She was done.

'I could have just been ignoring you, you know,' she pointed out with a coldness she was proud of.

'I worried you could be passed out inside,' he said, and she saw for the first time that his skin was pale, as though he'd been shocked. Worried.

She forced her heart not to register that.

She was pregnant with his child; concern was natural.

'I wasn't.'

She moved to the door but he put a hand out, just lightly, brushing her forearm. 'I need to speak with you.'

Her eyes swept shut at this and she shook her head instinctively. Her voice shook when she spoke. 'I feel like we've said everything that needs saying.'

'You have,' he agreed, dropping his hand. 'But I have some way to go. I want to fix this, Amelia. If you'll let me.'

She shook her head again and lifted her fingertips to her lips, and then she took another step backwards, almost as though she were afraid of him. 'Not everything can be fixed.'

Antonio acknowledged her statement, and the truth behind it. He *couldn't* fix everything. Sometimes things were broken beyond repair and whenever he looked back on that last day in Madrid he saw the fractures he had forced into their relationship.

'I can try.' His voice was gravelly.

She turned to look at him, huge blue eyes in a face that he knew so very well. 'You shouldn't be here.'

She was pulling away from him, building up to telling him to get the hell out of her life. He had to make every word count.

'I've just come from Carlo's.'

And she paled, gasping and lifting her hands to cover her mouth. 'Oh, Antonio, *no*. What did you do?'

She was clearly terrified of him setting his plan in action—of what he might say or do to the brother she obviously loved. He'd done this to her—he'd made her think destruction was all he cared about. Wasn't that true? Destruction at any cost—and he could clearly see the cost his need for revenge had inflicted on the woman he'd married.

Shame at his actions threatened to suffocate him.

'He and I have come to an agreement.'

This she wasn't expecting. 'What kind of agreement?' Her eyes narrowed and he felt a wave of animosity bounce off her. 'Have you blackmailed him in some way? Or are you here to offer me a fresh bribe?'

'I'm here to offer you my heart.' He waited for the words to sink in. 'And to beg you to forgive me, Amelia, *querida*.' She swallowed, her neck knotting visibly. He fought an urge to reach out to her, to touch her, to comfort her in some way. 'I had been angry for so long, it was all I knew. I didn't realise I could feel any other way, until I lost you. You walked out of my life and I was filled with this huge ache, right here.'

He pushed his hand into his chest. 'I was alone and lonely for the first time in my life—and all the hatred I felt towards your family, my need to make them pay for what they did to my father, *Dios mío*, it seems so petty now. That I was willing to sacrifice our happiness to an ancient feud... That I laid my actions at my father's feet, when you were so right about him: the last thing he would have wanted would be for me to push you away.'

She swallowed, the slender column of her neck moving visibly, her chest inflating and deflating at speed. And then, after a moment, with a tiny shake of her head, 'I'm not giving you my stake in Prim'Aqua, no matter what you say.'

He couldn't blame her for believing that was all he was after, but her suspicion ripped through him nonetheless, tearing a hole in his chest. 'Good. I no longer want it.'

Her eyes showed her disbelief.

'Your brother and I have agreed to put our shares in trust—for our baby.'

At this, Amelia drew in a small, sharp breath. Surprise crossed her face. 'Why?'

'It's their birthright. It should pass to them in one piece.'

'Yes, of course.' She nodded slowly. 'I'll do the same.'

And then with another soft sigh, 'I only wish you'd thought of that right at the beginning.'

'It wouldn't have been enough,' he muttered, regretting his own stupidity. 'I wanted to destroy your brother, and nothing else would do. Not then.'

She bristled, visibly rejecting him. 'And now?'

'I no longer wish to destroy him, *hermosa*.'

Her expression showed wariness. 'Why not?'

'Because he is your brother, and you love him, and he will be the uncle to our child, just like you said. But it's more than that. I want, more than anything, to make you happy.'

She crossed her arms, the gesture one of scepticism and disbelief. 'Why are you saying this now?'

But she was tired, her skin pale. 'Come inside. Sit down,' he urged softly.

'No.' She was resolute. 'Why now? What happened?'

'You went away,' he said simply, but the words were punctuated by gravelled pain. 'And I saw everything clearly for the first time in a long time. Without you, nothing matters. It's that simple. Everything I was fighting for—to avenge a historic wrong—seemed so trivial. I just wanted you. To hold you and wake up with you, to make you smile and fetch you tea.' He stroked his thumb across her cheek, and she watched him as he studied her. 'I just want you back, so badly. I thought ours was a marriage of convenience and common sense—I had no idea until you left that I had become addicted to you—to all of you. I didn't realise that I had fallen completely in love with you.'

She was silent, her beautiful face pinched as his words settled around them, and he waited, even when anxiety was ripping him apart from the inside out.

'I don't know if you're capable of feeling love.'

The accusation hurt, but she had every reason to feel that

way, he acknowledged. Panic flared in his gut because he'd lost her once and he couldn't lose her again.

'I loved you, I think, even on that first night, when you threatened me with a meat cleaver. When you confounded all my expectations. When you made me laugh and look beyond my own stupid prejudices. When you gave yourself to me so sweetly, so willingly, and with all of the generosity that is so much a part of you.'

Tears filled her eyes and, God, he wanted them gone! He never wanted her to cry again, unless from sheer joy.

'You used me that night, Antonio. And you've been using me ever since.'

'No.' He shook his head emphatically. 'Our families had nothing to do with why I wanted you—they never did.'

'You blackmailed me into marriage—'

'I know that,' he interrupted gruffly, ripping his hand through his hair so it spiked at odd angles. 'I have been a bastard to you and I hate myself for that. I hate everything I have done to you, and yet I cannot say with confidence that I would not do it all again. I fell in love with a woman I wished I hated, and I have spent the last eight months pushing you away rather than face the fact that you're everything I've ever wanted in this life.'

Her eyes held his for a brief second before flitting away, and the sadness in them was enough to make him crumble. 'I don't deserve another chance with you, Amelia, but I am begging you for one.'

Her sharp intake of breath showed that he was hurting her and yet he couldn't stop.

'I want you to come home, to be my wife, to live with me again. I want to hold you in my arms as you sleep, to run my fingers over your hair and wrap my arms around your body. I want to kiss you every morning and make love to you every night. But I know that is a fantasy now.' He cupped her face, desperate for her to look at him, but she kept her eyes averted, staring at their feet. 'So please let me stay here, with you. In a spare room, on the sofa, anything. Let me in, just a little, so that I can show you I'm willing to work at this, that I'm prepared to be everything you could ever want. Our marriage was all on my terms—and now it can be all on yours. Just please, do not send me away, Amelia. I am begging you…'

Amelia shook her head and stepped backwards, moving away from him a little, but at least now she looked at him. Her expression was guarded; it was impossible to know what she was thinking and feeling. He waited, knowing he'd said his piece, knowing this decision was hers now, and that he had to respect her wishes.

'Why are you here?'

The question surprised him.

'Because I love you.'

Her eyes swept shut. 'But why now?'

'Because I missed you.'

'But that's not enough,' she said, and now she sobbed, and his gut twisted. 'I've been missing you too, like crazy. Walking out on you was the hardest thing I've ever done. Our marriage was just a fantasy, Antonio. There's nothing here but revenge and hatred, and a baby. If I hadn't fallen pregnant, you would never have come looking for me, right?'

'And do you know how much I hate that? Do you know how terrifying that is? I cannot imagine my life without you, not for even one more day. Call it fate or destiny, for whatever reason this child was conceived, I thank every star in the heavens.'

'A baby isn't enough to make a marriage work.'

'Our marriage,' he said, taking a step closer and curling his hand behind her neck, holding her face towards his, 'works.' And he brushed his lips over hers, almost groaning at the taste of her, the familiar feel of her.

And she swayed against him, her body softening, and he kissed her again, relishing this—the familiar, the perfection. 'Remember everything we are, everything good we have shared, and ignore this bitterness of mine towards your family. That is the future I promise you, *querida*. From this day forward, there is no anger, no resentment, no hatred. Our child is a Herrera and a diSalvo, and we are family.'

She sobbed into his mouth and he swallowed it, and kissed her deeper, harder, with all the urgency he felt in his chest, clawing at him, ripping him to pieces.

And when she pulled away it was as though he were drowning, and everything was dark and he was panicked, until she smiled and the sun burst into his life once more.

'I don't want to stay here,' she said, and she brought her lips to his and kissed him and his heart exploded with the perfection of that moment. 'Take me home, please.'

'To Madrid?'

'To our future.'

He stooped down and lifted her up, holding her against his chest as he moved back towards his car. He walked away from a home that had, that night, been wrapped in rain and storm clouds and was now bathed in milky afternoon sunshine.

And he smiled against her lips, because he had all he could ever want in life—and it was only going to get better.

EPILOGUE

'*YOU'RE* CARRYING THE next baby!' she groaned, squeezing his hand so hard he could almost feel bones crunching.

He laughed softly. 'You said that last time.'

'And I was right!'

'You're almost there,' the doctor promised. 'One last—'

'*Puuuuuuush!*' Amelia finished, a primal, guttural word. And then she collapsed back as a baby's cry sounded.

'Well?' Antonio asked, impatient. 'What is our son to have? A sister or a brother?'

'On your way to a soccer team,' she whispered, like her normal self now, a weak smile on her face.

'It's a girl.' The doctor grinned. 'And she's got quite a kick already.'

'A girl?'

Antonio smiled down at his wife, emotions surging through him. 'A little version of you.'

She grinned, holding her hands out for the baby. 'Javier won't be happy. He was desperate for a little brother.' And then tears sparkled on her lashes as she held her daughter, seeing her shock of black hair and honey skin.

'Maybe next time,' Antonio teased.

Amelia looked daggers at him. 'Next time? Unless you really are going to become a marvel of modern medicine and be the pregnant one, then let's not talk about "next time" right now.'

'But why not? When we make such perfect babies?'

He smiled at his wife, and then at their daughter.

'She is divine.' Amelia sighed. 'Just perfect.'

'Just like her mother.'

'Will you text my family?'

Antonio nodded. Giacomo and Carlo had been eagerly awaiting news of the new Herrera—strange that he rarely thought now of the feud that had first brought him to his wife's door.

So much water had flowed under the bridge since that night—so many good memories had overwritten all the bad.

And it was a truth, he decided, that it was impossible to dislike anyone who adored your children from the bottom of their heart—and there was no doubt in his mind that the diSalvo men loved this new generation of Herreras.

'I'll let them know,' he agreed. 'Soon. But for now, let's enjoy this time with our little princess.'

'Your wish is my command,' Amelia agreed softly.

'I think that's the other way around.'

'Yes, perhaps you're right.' She stifled a yawn, and love, pride and fierce adoration burst through him.

'I'm always right.' He grinned, but there was a serious note underneath, because he very nearly hadn't been.

At one time he'd almost made the biggest mistake of his life and let this woman walk out on him.

And he'd never be so foolish ever again.

He intended to do everything in his power to live happily ever after—with the love of his life and the family they'd made.

And because he was Antonio Herrera and he always got what he wanted, they did.

* * * * *

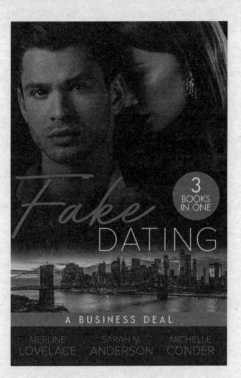

OUT NOW!

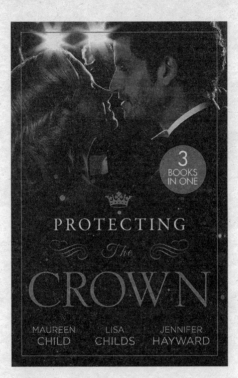

LET'S TALK

Romance

For exclusive extracts, competitions
and special offers, find us online:

 MillsandBoon

 @MillsandBoon

 @MillsandBoonUK

 @MillsandBoonUK

Get in touch on 01413 063 232

MILLS & BOON

THE HEART OF ROMANCE

A ROMANCE FOR EVERY READER

MODERN

Prepare to be swept off your feet by sophisticated, sexy and seductive heroes, in some of the world's most glamourous and romantic locations, where power and passion collide.

HISTORICAL

Escape with historical heroes from time gone by. Whether your passion is for wicked Regency Rakes, muscled Vikings or rugged Highlanders, awaken the romance of the past.

MEDICAL

Set your pulse racing with dedicated, delectable doctors in the high-pressure world of medicine, where emotions run high and passion, comfort and love are the best medicine.

True Love

Celebrate true love with tender stories of heartfelt romance, from the rush of falling in love to the joy a new baby can bring, and a focus on the emotional heart of a relationship.

Desire

Indulge in secrets and scandal, intense drama and sizzling hot action with heroes who have it all: wealth, status, good looks…everything but the right woman.

HEROES

The excitement of a gripping thriller, with intense romance at its heart. Resourceful, true-to-life women and strong, fearless men face danger and desire - a killer combination!

To see which titles are coming soon, please visit

millsandboon.co.uk/nextmonth